COLD, COLD HEART

The fat man's screams were high and pure and operatic, but no one heard them. He flailed his arms and shuddered helplessly, trying to heave himself out of his chair.

Shakespeare emptied the clip into the fat man's chest, seven shots.

The fat man sank into his chair like fallen bread dough. His hair remained perfect.

Shakespeare turned the Hank Williams tape down a notch or two, opened the back door and walked into the fresh air, whistling the chorus to "Cold, Cold Heart." Feeling pretty good.

Feeling real cheerful as a matter of fact.

Other Avon Books by
Walter Sorrells

POWER OF ATTORNEY
WILL TO MURDER

WALTER SORRELLS

CRY FOR JUSTICE

AVON BOOKS ▲ NEW YORK

CRY FOR JUSTICE is an original publication of Avon Books. This work has never before appeared in book form. This work is a novel. Any similarity to actual persons or events is purely coincidental.

AVON BOOKS
A division of
The Hearst Corporation
1350 Avenue of the Americas
New York, New York 10019

Copyright © 1996 by Walter Sorrells
Published by arrangement with the author
Library of Congress Catalog Card Number: 95-96209
ISBN: 0-380-78021-6

First Avon Books Printing: July 1996

Acknowledgments

Thanks to those who helped me with great patience during the writing of *Cry for Justice*: Jeff Davis, assistant counsel with the State Bar of Georgia who guided me through the arcane procedures of legal disciplinary actions; Gwinnett County Superior Court Judge Michael Clark; Gwinnett County District Attorney Danny Porter; Cobb County Assistant District Attorney Van Pearlberg; Julie McGhee, law clerk, Cobb County Superior Court; Rockdale County Assistant District Attorney Jim Miskell; Matt Roane of Lawson and Davis; former Douglas County Public Defender Jeff Lacy; Fulton County Assistant District Attorney Vivian Hoard; Fulton County Public Defender's Office Trial Assistant Cynthia Price. Thanks also to Private Investigator Mike Finn. Special thanks goes to my friend Craig Jones.

As always, I don't have enough words of gratitude for my wife, Patti, whose efforts and sacrifices have made my writing career possible.

All errors of fact or law contained in this book—and I don't doubt for a minute that there are a host of them—are my own damn fault.

THE
ANNOUNCEMENT

●

Here's the good news: A busload of lawyers ran off a cliff. The bad news? There were three empty seats.

• Prologue

A labrador, yes. Or an Irish setter. Even a mastiff or a Doberman—something *manly* for godsake! But these yappy, snippy, yippy, prissy, furry, faggy little creatures? No way. Other than the occasional glimpse of some rheumy stains under all that floating white hair, you couldn't tell one end from the other. No, ma'am! No, thank you.

Shakespeare had been following the lawyer for a couple of days, getting a feel for the guy's schedule. Sure of it now: had to take the lawyer while he was walking his hateful little dogs. What an annoyance. All that awful fluffy hair. God. Probably set off the old allergies again.

The lawyer's name was Raymond Lata—a partner in the firm of Clay, Brock, Vinyard & Cain. Big firm: nine floors in one of the tallest skyscrapers on Peachtree Street smack in the middle of downtown Atlanta.

Shakespeare wore a shiny blue jogging suit bought just for the occasion at the K-Mart out on Jimmy Carter Boulevard. Running shoes from Foot Locker in the Northlake Mall. Underneath the jogging outfit: blue jeans, T-shirt from Penny's, underthings from Sears. Everything anonymous, disposable, available anywhere. Afterward the clothes would all be burned. Shakespeare carried a reversible gym bag—red on one side, green on the other. Inside: a pair of surgical gloves, a two-foot piece of steel reinforcement bar, and a very sharp boning knife.

Shakespeare smiled pleasantly at a couple of yuppie runners. Ivy League sweatshirts—he, Princeton; she, Dartmouth. The running yuppies ignored him.

A block ahead, Raymond Lata stopped to let his dogs wheedle on somebody's azaleas. A tall, thin man; very dark, very short razor-cut hair; anxious tightness at the corners of his mouth. Peering across the street through small tortoise-shell glasses, pretending to be interested in something in another yard while his two little dogs did their best to poison the bushes.

Shakespeare bent over. Bogus shoe-tying. Didn't want to catch up to Raymond Lata just yet.

The dogs minced, dribbled, kicked some leaves, yipped once or twice. Raymond Lata started walking.

Shakespeare followed. Almost there. Wait. Wait.

Dark trees rising above them, above Raymond Lata, above his awful dogs. Getting closer and closer to the park. To the place where Shakespeare would do the job.

Wait . . . Wait . . .

Now.

On Tuesday, May 7, at a few minutes past seven o'clock in the morning, Shakespeare had driven down to a residential neighborhood in Buckhead. Very desirable area. Old money, new money, you name it: lots of money, period. Shakespeare had parked over on Peachtree Battle, several blocks from the side street where Raymond Lata lived.

Now. Shakespeare was ready.

Heading down the street toward the park, a small triangle of flood plain: the creek on one side, the road on the other, houses all around. Far side of the park: a wooden cupola— weather-beaten, dry-rotted at the foundations. Usually deserted this early in the morning. Dew still on the ground. When Raymond Lata reached the edge of the park, Shakespeare jogged quickly through a patch of knee-high weeds, across the park and toward the cupola. Timing was crucial.

At the cupola Shakespeare yelled: "Oh my God! Help!"

Raymond Lata kept walking. Acting like he hadn't heard anything.

Shakespeare again: "Hey! Little help over here, man!"

Raymond Lata turned tentatively. Not the kind of guy to stick his neck out.

"Something wrong?" The lawyer's brow furrowed

slightly. Looking down into the park from the elevated stretch of sidewalk.

"Over here!" Shakespeare waved, pointed at the ground behind the cupola.

The lawyer studied the situation for a minute then finally led the dogs gingerly through the wet weeds. When he'd gotten close to the cupola, Raymond Lata said: "Oh. It's *you*."

Shakespeare smiled. "Yes. It's me." Out of sight, both of them, from any stray commuters heading off to work. Unzipping the blue tracksuit, taking out the heavy piece of steel re-bar.

Now.

Shakespeare smiled and whacked Raymond Lata upside the head with the steel bar.

Priceless! They always had that look on their face: Who *me?* The idiots didn't have the first clue what was going on.

"What are you doing?" The lawyer shrieked, holding his head. "What do you want?"

"Down boy!" Talking to Raymond Lata like he was a dog.

Raymond Lata stumbled backwards a couple steps, falling to his knees, the two leashes still clutched in his left hand. The dogs were yipping, leaping, running around.

"What do you want?" Blood coming down the side of his face.

"Stay!" Shakespeare, being funny. "Stay, Raymond." This was a fairly new thing for Shakespeare, killing people. Surprisingly amusing, though, if you looked at it from the right angle. Shakespeare hit Raymond again—this time in the shoulder. Crunching noise. Raymond Lata squealed in pain, clutched at his hurt arm, tried to shuffle away on his knees. Face going white from the pain.

"Roll over, boy! Roll over!"

Shakespeare laughed as the lawyer started making high, squeaky noises. Blood ran into his eyes.

"Roll over, boy!"

Raymond Lata crouched on the ground, still making the squeaky noise. The cotton ball dogs yipped, jumped up and down.

The lawyer: "What do you want with me?"

Giving the lawyer a long stare. "Justice, that's all."

Then Shakespeare lifted the piece of re-bar, brought it down with an awful crack on Raymond Lata's head. Raymond Lata's body jerked spasmodically, then pitched over, facedown.

Shakespeare smiled a little. "Play dead, counselor."

The dogs were licking at their dead master's face.

Shakespeare rolled the body over, sighed, then put on the surgical gloves, took the knife out of the gym bag, unzipped the lawyer's pants, grabbed hold of his shrivelled little thing, looked away. Had to saw back and forth a couple times before the thing came free. Blood everywhere. Shakespeare stuffed the limp, bloody thing in Raymond Lata's mouth. Very unpleasant, but it couldn't be helped.

The dogs—yipping and yipping and yipping and yipping, brown eyes rolling under the floating white fur.

Then the final part. Shakespeare took a small cream-colored envelope—about four by five inches—out of the gym bag and tucked it in the pocket of the dead man's jacket. The name RAYMOND LATA, ESQ. was typed on the outside of the envelope.

Shakespeare took off the bloody gloves, put them in a zip-lock bag. Stripped off the jogging suit, reversing the color of the gym bag, and stuffing the clothes and the zip-lock inside. Started to walk away. Flash of color on the ground.

A second card had fallen out of the bag. Cream colored, 4 x 5. Typed on the envelope, a name: GARRETT C. BROCK III, ESQ. Name number five.

That was a mistake: hadn't meant to bring that one. Shakespeare put it back in the bag, walked away. Slowly, calmly, without attracting attention. Smiling pleasantly.

Halfway down the block Shakespeare started to sneeze. The dogs. The damn dog hair was setting off the allergies again.

Hell, maybe I should have killed the dogs, too.

When Detective Lieutenant Janelle Moncrief arrived at the crime scene in her white Crown Victoria, she found a knot of cops milling around, one of the evidence techs getting ready to take pictures. Moncrief was a tall, solid, black woman wearing a large white hat, a white dress with a big blue-piped collar and flat-soled white shoes that pinched her feet.

The park was up in one of the rich Buckhead neighborhoods—all shade trees and azaleas and BMWs. It was just a little park, an acre or two sandwiched between a creek and a couple of roads. No jungle gym, no fitness trail, no softball field. Just grass and some trees and a wooden cupola covered with flaking gray paint.

A homicide detective, Dave Bean, was waiting for her. Bean had gotten the first call, but once he'd seen the body, he'd summoned Moncrief. She was heading up the task force investigating the Shakespeare killer—and this one had Shakespeare written all over it.

"Another one?" Moncrief said.

"Must be," Bean said. He was a white guy, balding, wearing a dark suit. A couple years from retirement, not a big fan of blacks or women or lieutenants. "Soon as I saw the guy's got his pecker stuffed in his mouth, I paged you. I haven't touched anything."

"Then how you know what the vic's got in his mouth?"

Bean rolled his eyes. "So can I go now?"

"You want to *go?*"

"It's not my case, is it?"

"We have not determined that as of yet. Stick around." Janelle Moncrief wouldn't let this boy off the hook, not yet. Best she could tell, he mainly spent his time trying to avoid doing police work. No point holding with that.

She walked over to the crumpled form in the middle of the yellow tape, bent over the body. Male white, six-foot or so, brown eyes, brown hair. Multiple contusions on the head and face. Lots of blood around the mouth. She took a small plastic spatula out of her purse, pried open the vic's teeth. Joints in the jaw still moved freely: no rigor mortis yet. Inside the mouth was a clot of bloody, hairy tissue. Still wet. If she hadn't seen it before, she probably wouldn't have known what it was.

"Get a picture of this," she told the photographer.

"Hold it like that," the tech said. "Yeah, good."

Moncrief put on surgical gloves, patted the front of the vic's windbreaker. Inside was the envelope: cream-colored, four by five inches. She held it up, smiled faintly. "Uh-huh. It's Shakespeare alright."

Dave Bean said, "Can I go?"

"I want you knocking on doors," she said. "Every residence on this street. Up to Peachtree and down to Northside."

"Hey, whoa," Bean said. "I got my own caseload. I'm not on this task force of yours."

Janelle looked the white cop in the eye. "You are till I say you aren't."

"Hey now . . ."

"Chief said I get all available manpower. Right at this moment, that means you."

"You can't do that!" Sounding like a hurt little boy. "I got cases to clear."

"Oh indeed I can."

Bean stared at her resentfully, then trudged back to his car.

Janelle sighed. This thing was making her crazy. Picking fights with a loser like Bean? Have to watch herself. Wasn't no percentage in acting that way.

But a case like this, it had a way of getting you stirred up. This was the fourth murder by this Shakespeare creature. Shakespeare was what the jerks on TV were calling him, taken from that quote, *Henry IV*, part two, "First thing we do, let's kill all the lawyers." She'd looked it up in her college Shakespeare book one time to make sure whether it was *Henry IV* or *Henry VI*. Two months, four dead lawyers, all of them had the same MO. Blunt instrument trauma was the COD; then you had a perimortum sexual mutilation; then placement of the envelope in the pocket.

Lieutenant Moncrief noticed she was still holding the envelope in her hand. She opened it carefully, pulled out the cream-colored card inside. Neatly typed on one side of the card: *What's the difference between a dead snake in the road and a dead lawyer in the road?*

She flipped the card over. Punch line: *Skid marks.*

• 1

Grace Brock, four years old, was sorting the mail in piles, playing mail lady in her room by herself. Well, not by herself, exactly. Actually, she was playing with Funny. Funny was her friend. Her Mommy and Daddy called Funny her *maginary* friend. Grace was not completely sure what "maginary" meant.

Grace liked Funny. Funny was always nice and fun and happy. Not like Mommy and Daddy. Lately Mommy and Daddy had been yelling a lot. Sometimes they yelled at Grace. Mostly they yelled at each other, though. Then they walked around the house with their eyes scrunched up, ignoring each other. Ignoring Grace, too.

Grace had three piles of mail, the mail her Mommy gave to her. One pile for the letters with little windows in them. One pile for regular envelopes. One pile for cat-a-logs. Grace's Mommy let her go out to the mail box every day. Then, whatever mail Mommy didn't open, she'd give it to Grace to play with.

Funny and Grace played together secretly, quietly. It was part of their game, not making any noise and not letting anybody see Funny. If anyone else came in the room, Funny would hide in the closet or roll under Grace's bed, the new *big* bed that Mommy had given her for her fourth birthday.

"Why's it called a cat-a-log?" Grace said, flipping through a cat-a-log full of ladies with skinny arms and big mouths. "There's no cats and there's no logs in it."

But Funny didn't answer. Funny just said, "It's time for me to go. But first I have something special for you!"

9

Funny reached into a jacket pocket, came out with an envelope. A very pretty envelope. Grace decided maybe she would make a separate pile for pretty envelopes.

Funny handed her the pretty envelope, whispered something to her, then kissed her on the cheek.

"Don't go *yet!*" Grace said.

But Funny just smiled, a sad kind of smile, then climbed out the window.

• 2

"I don't see it, Dru," Garrett Brock said to his wife. "It's not like he's drooling on his shirt or exposing himself in public. The old guy's always been a little eccentric."

"Well, I'm getting fed up with it," Dru said. "Yesterday I went over there and he was letting Grace play with that huge gun of his. I asked him what they were doing, you know what he said? Killing Indians!"

"I'm sure it wasn't loaded."

Dru's voice was scathing. "That's not the point. It's bad enough that he's putting these terrible things in her head— killing *Indians,* my God!—but Brock, letting a four-year-old girl play with a real gun?" Dru shook her head. "Huh-uh. Not while I'm still breathing. We've got to find a place for him."

Brock sighed. What a morning. His coffee was cold, his neck was killing him, he was an hour and a half away from what could easily be the most critical event of his professional life, and now—for the umpteenth time—they were arguing about Brock's grandfather. Brock had installed the old man in the carriage house at the back of their property a couple of years earlier; he had been like fingernails on a chalkboard to Dru ever since.

"He's not ready for a nursing home," Brock said. "Even if he is eighty-nine years old."

"Not a nursing home. A retirement center. We've been through this before. It's a totally different thing. It's not like he can't afford it."

11

"Money's not the issue. He just doesn't like being around old people."

Dru made a face. "He *is* old people."

"Well I just don't see the necessity."

"That's because you're working ninety-nine hours a day and you don't have to be around him." Dru pursed her lips. "Do you know Grace said the *f*-word in front Christine Hanson the other day?"

Brock didn't say anything. He was getting tired of this incessant arguing. Was it his fault? Hers? He couldn't figure it out. Hell, blame wasn't something you could portion up like pie anyway—*this is yours, this is mine*. Didn't work that way. All he could tell is that he'd been feeling resentful and bored and bottled up lately. Only he didn't know what it was exactly that he was resentful or bored of, much less what to do about it. And it wasn't getting any better. Recently he'd felt something swelling inside, as though all that resentment and boredom had started to make a phase change into something more volatile, into an awful desperation. He buried his head in the folder of notes and didn't reply. Best thing he could do for right now was buckle down, try to keep a lid on things.

But Dru wouldn't let it rest: "The *f*-word, Brock. And who do you think she got that from? From your grandfather, that's who."

"Look, Dru. I'll *talk* to him. Okay?" Brock felt a painful tightness pulling at his neck as he tried to rein himself in, to keep from standing up and shouting something stupid. "But right now I really need to go over my testimony. Okay? Okay? This is a very important hearing."

Dru stood in the doorway of the kitchen, fists on her hips, glaring at him.

"Well it *is!*" Brock said. "If I crash and burn at this hearing, I will very likely get disbarred."

"Why does work always always always seem to win out over your responsibility to your family?"

Brock felt the resentment and desperation bubbling up, his face getting hot. No. No, god*damn* it, now was not the time. Trying to keep his voice calm, reasonable: "Look, we agreed when we had Grace that you were going to quit working, and that meant I was going to have to take up the slack financially." He slammed his folder of trial notes shut. "I mean what the hell am I supposed to do? Quit work so we all starve?"

Dru's face went white and then she disappeared into the kitchen. Brock closed his eyes for a moment, took a couple of deep breaths. *Good move, you jerk.* Why had he let himself pop off like that?

"Look, Dru, I'm sorry. This hearing today, it's just got me edgy." Brock dropped his folder on the couch and went into the kitchen. Dru was sitting at the kitchen table resting her forehead on the tips of her fingers like some nineteen-forties movie star with a headache. He put his hand softly on the nape of her neck, but she shrugged him off.

"I'm sorry," he whispered. "I didn't mean to say that. It's just that I'm scared."

"Why don't you just go," she said. "We'll talk about it later."

Brock closed his eyes for a moment. "I'm sorry," he said. "But I mean there *is* a legitimate possibility I could be disbarred. I can't ignore it."

Dru, still with her forehead resting on her fingertips: "The charges against you are lies, right?"

"Yes."

"Then I don't see what you're so worried about."

"I wish it were that simple," he said. Then he went back into the living room, picked up his folder and tried to go over his testimony for the hearing. It was no good. He could feel Dru's anger smoldering in the other room.

What was going on these days? It seemed like ever since she'd quit working—ever since Grace was born four years ago—she'd had a chip on her shoulder about something. Brock was one of the top trial lawyers in Atlanta, and long hours came with the territory. She *knew* that. He ran a solo practice, and if he let things go, the whole operation went down the tubes. Taking with it, needless to say, the nice house they lived in and the nice clothes Dru wore and the nice day-care center Grace went to three days a week and the nice BMW and the nice Acura and the nice vacations to Italy and all the rest of the nice nice nice shit that seemed so damned important to Dru these days.

Brock was sick to death of *nice.*

And on top of everything else, he was stuck in the middle of the case from hell, this Jimmy Dale Evans thing. When he'd filed the suit, it had seemed like a lark. But it wasn't a lark anymore. Not since one of the defendants in the case had charged Brock with trying to bribe him into perjury. Not since the State Bar had come raging after his license.

Well, he just had to get this hearing behind him. Dru was right. He'd done nothing wrong. Everything would get straightened out at the hearing.

"Grace!" Dru was standing in the doorway to the kitchen again, a bowl of neon-colored cereal in her hand. "Grace, your breakfast's ready!"

Brock took a sip of his tepid coffee, made a face, set the cup on the arm of his chair.

"Daddeeeeee!"

It was Grace, tumbling out of the hallway, trying to get his attention. Thank God for Grace. Grace could always cut through the frigid atmosphere in the house.

"Daddy's trying to work," Dru said coldly.

"It's okay, honey," Brock said.

"Funny came to see me again," Grace said. Her eyes were full of excitement and childish glee. She was blond, black-eyed, tall for a four-year-old, with two small front teeth that protruded endearingly over her lower lip. "Funny gave me something for you," she said.

Her imaginary friend. It was so sweet, the way she was always talking about this person Funny. Funny, who didn't like grown-ups and who hid under the bed when anyone came in the room. "So what did Funny give you?"

"Not *me*. It's for *you!*" she said. Grace took her hand out from behind her back. She was holding a cream-colored envelope, the size of a wedding card or a law firm announcement. Probably one of the envelopes Dru gave her to play mail lady with.

"Isn't that nice?" Brock took the envelope and sat it in his lap. He noticed Dru standing in the doorway, looking at him with an unreadable expression on her face.

"I know this disciplinary hearing is a scary thing," Dru said tentatively.

"Daddy!" Grace, bouncing up and down, clapping her hands.

"In a minute, Grace," Brock said softly. "I'm talking to your mother."

"Open it, Daddy!"

"In a *minute,* sweetheart." Brock turned back to Dru. "Georgia's the only state in the country where they have to prove a disciplinary case beyond a reasonable doubt. Most states have a different standard—clear and convincing evidence or else preponderance of the . . ." Brock was about to give a dissertation on the differing legal standards for disbarment in various states, but he realized that wasn't what Dru was interested in.

"Daddy!"

"What I'm saying," Brock said, taking another sip of his cold coffee, "is the state bar has a tough case to make against me. And they're not going to do it. I've got a persuasive witness to back me up. Everything's going to be okay. I promise."

Grace jumped up and down, grabbed his arm, knocking his elbow into the coffee cup. The brown liquid sloshed into Brock's lap.

"Grace, dammit!" he yelled.

His daughter's face balled up, went tomato red, and she started to cry. He cradled her head in his hand. "Oh, look honey, come on, it's okay, it was just an accident."

"Can you *please* watch the language," Dru said. "It's bad enough with your grandfather around."

Brock went back to their bedroom, muttering. His best suit—a single-breasted twelve-hundred-dollar handmade job that practically shouted humility, prudence, horse sense, prosperity—all the things his suit needed to say at the hearing today—looked like it belonged to a man with no bladder control.

While he was changing into his backup suit, a gray sack from Brooks Brothers, he kept imagining the questions he was going to be asked at the hearing, the answers he'd give, the way he'd modulate his voice, the expressions on his face. As a good trial attorney, he was hyperaware of every detail. He had to seem relaxed, had to smile. Relaxed but a little indignant at this challenge to his integrity. He had to strike the right tone. Tone is everything. His father, who was also a lawyer, had told him that once.

He put on the Brooks Brothers suit, went into the bath-room, looked in the mirror. He was a tall man, gaunt-faced, with dark wavy hair and black eyes. He felt the nervous thrum of his heart, a sour feeling of apprehension climbing up his throat. "Of course it's ridiculous," he said to the mirror. "I did not at that time nor at any other time approach Mr. Giddens, nor did I discuss with him . . ." Too many *nors?* Too pompous, too shystery? He tried again: "I didn't ap-proach Mr. Giddens, I didn't talk to Mr. Giddens, and I certainly didn't suggest that he perjure himself."

Better. Now smile.

He stretched his tight, sore neck then smiled at the mirror. It was a nice smile: self-effacing, shy almost. But the effect only made him weary. No matter what Aristotle had to say on the subject, self-awareness was mostly a pain in the ass.

When he got back to the den he found the cream-colored envelope lying on his chair, splashed with coffee. He smeared the brown liquid off the envelope with the ham of his hand, turned it over. His name was typed on the front in capital letters: GARRETT C. BROCK, III, ESQ. But no stamp, no mailing address. Odd. He wondered where it had come from.

Brock checked his watch. Time to run. He tossed the uno-pened envelope on the coffee table and headed for the door.

"Daddy! You didn't read Funny's message."

"When Daddy gets home," he said gently.

Dru came out and kissed him. "Good luck. You'll do fine." She wore a strained smile on her face. "And Brock? Tonight? We need to talk about some things."

Brock fled, briefcase thumping against his leg.

• 3

Brock first heard the song in his car. An accident, really. He was hitting the scan button, hoping to find an old Stones tune or any country song not by Garth Brooks—and there it was.

He later found out it was called "Scream!" that it was by a California heavy metal band called One Eighty-Seven, playing heavy rotation even on the alternative rock stations. But at that moment it was just noise. The song came roaring out of the radio, lots of shrieking guitars and this kid yelling at the top of his phlegmy young lungs: "Scream! Scream! Scream!"

Brock was about to change the station, but his hand just hung there in front of the scan button, didn't move. The band shouted the words *scream! scream!* behind a jackhammer guitar hook. There was something about the moronic song that stirred his juices. Something gloriously primal and careless and nasty.

As he drove, listening to the song, the dull pain he'd been feeling in his neck for the past few weeks let up a little. Brock grinned and pounded out the beat, his wedding ring clacking against the steering wheel.

By the time he'd gotten up to the sixth floor of the Cobb County Courthouse, the song was still worming around in his head—*Scream! Scream! Scream! Scream!*—full of raging guitars.

• 4

Mic Giddens shifted heavily in the witness box. He was a big Australian, handsome in a brutal sort of way, with a thick jaw and a shiny Italian suit that was a little too snug through the arm and shoulder. His jet-black hair was swept straight back from his brow and hung down to his collar. His nostrils were red-rimmed, and he had the straining-at-the-bit look of a speed freak.

The general counsel of the State Bar of Georgia took a moment with his notes, drew himself up to his full five feet six inches and said, "Mr. Giddens, are you acquainted with a Mr. Jimmy Dale Evans?"

Mic Giddens flexed his big shoulders. "Yis, I am."

Someone who came into the courtroom by accident might have thought they'd stumbled onto a legal trial. In fact, it was not. It was a hearing convened on behalf of the investigative panel of the state's legal disciplinary board. There was no judge: the presiding official was a Special Master, appointed by the Georgia Supreme Court, who acted as both judge and jury. The State Bar's general counsel—a short, toothy guy named Frank Reed—was, in effect, the prosecutor. Brock and his lawyer, Press Cain, sat at the defense table.

"And how did you come to know Mr. Evans?" the general counsel asked.

"He was bookkeeper for Laughing Dolls, the nightclub I manage. Not a regular employee. He just came in a couple times a week, entered everything into the computer, kept track of deposits and withdrawals, that sort of thing."

"A contract worker."

"Right. He called himself a consultant. I called him a bean counter. Same bleddy difference, right?" Giddens flashed a smile at the Special Master.

The Special Master was a former federal judge, who had been known facetiously as "The Angel of Mercy" because of his fondness for the death penalty. He was a crumpled little man who wore a crooked bow tie and a very sober three-piece suit with the kind of extravagant lapels that hadn't been fashionable for several decades. He had something wrong with one of his tear ducts, causing a milky fluid to well out of his left eye periodically and run down the side of his nose. He liked to smile. It was said that the more he smiled, the worse it was for the defendant. Right now he was beaming paternally at Mic Giddens.

"I'm getting nauseated," Brock whispered.

"Don't worry," Cain whispered back. "The old boy's always like this."

Brock didn't find this reassuring.

Frank Reed allowed his large, beaverlike front teeth to protrude over his lip for a moment. "And when did he stop working for you?"

"Right after he filed the lawsuit," Giddens said.

"The lawsuit. Would you be talking about *Jimmy Dale Evans versus Laughing Dolls?*"

"That's right. He got hurt in the club one day, filed suit a couple months later."

"And how did his injury occur?"

"Bit of a freak accident. One of the dancers fell off a table right on top of him. Broke his back, paralyzed his legs. Tragic, really."

Giddens and Reed shared a moment of stagey mopeyness intended to convince the Special Master how aggrieved they were about Jimmy Dale's tragedy.

"And what's the status of that lawsuit at this time?"

"The trial's next week."

Frank Reed riffled through his file. "Now, Mr. Giddens, are you acquainted with a Mr. Garrett Brock?"

"Yis. That man there." Giddens pointed an accusatory finger at Brock. "He's Jimmy Dale Evans's lawyer."

"Could you tell me what the circumstances were when you first met Mr. Brock?"

"It was, I believe, the tenth of September, last year. I remember because it was the day before the deposition where he was going to ask me questions about how Jimmy Dale got injured. A day or two before the deposition, there was a couple of documents that I needed to review for the deposition. At the last minute I realized I'd misplaced them. My lawyer happened to be out of town, so I called up Mr. Brock, asked if he had copies. He says sure, why don't I come over and pick them up at his office.

"So I drive over with an employee of mine named Kit Fulghram. When we get there, I check the envelope he's left at the front disk and one of the papers is missing. Mr. Brock pops out of his office and says why don't I come back, he'll have his secretary make a copy. Real pleasant, real apologetic about the delay. He has his secretary make me a cup of joe, we sit down in his office, chitchat a bit. That was when he done it."

Frank Reed leaned forward portentously and, in case the Special Master wasn't paying attention, rapped his knuckles sharply on the podium. "That's when he did *what*, Mr. Giddens?"

Giddens, full of bogus dismay: "Tried to suborn me!"

Brock leaned over to Press Cain, whispered, "I bet this yahoo can't even spell *suborn*."

Frank Reed, struggling manfully to keep his teeth concealed under his lips, said, "Please explain, Mr. Giddens."

"Well, he hints around a bit, you know, how lucrative this case could be for all concerned. Back injury, paralysis, all this rubbish, he says juries'll pay through the nose for that type of thing. All of a sudden I'm getting a bit uncomfortable. But the secretary's not back with the papers yet, so what am I gonna do? Well, I wasn't sure for a moment what he's going on about, but then he spells it out for me. He says to me, 'Look, you're insured, right?' He goes, 'This case could be worth half a million bucks. Maybe more.' He goes, 'The money's all coming from the insurance company.' So I say, 'Hold on, mate. Before the insurance company pays the first nickel, I got a ten thousand dollar deductible to meet.'"

"And how did he respond?"

"He just smiles. Then he goes, 'Ten thousand? But let's suppose someone was to give you a spot of assistance, cover your deductible?' I say, 'Like how much assistance?' He says, 'How's twenty thousand sound?' Now, I'm not a legal genius, right, so I go, 'Excuse me but, like, how would that work, mate?' He says, 'All you got to do is give the right testimony. You set it up so that you basically admit Jimmy Dale's injury is all your fault. Then we give you twenty grand. Ten goes to the deductible, that leaves you ten grand to play with. For a couple hours work.'"

"And did you agree to this, Mr Giddens?"

Giddens raised his eyebrows in mock surprise. "Christ, no! But then he says, 'Okay, what if I was to make it thirty?' Well, thirty grand, that's a lot of money. I have to admit, that for a second I'm a bit tempted. But then I think, No! This is dirty pool!" Giddens's big face was full of bogus outrage.

"I mean, it's this type of thing that raises the insurance rates for everyone. Got me a bit bleddy steamed, I confess. At which point I got it into my head to make sure he didn't get away with this. So I said, 'You want to put that in writing?' He says, 'Are you kidding?' And I says, 'Hey, look, if I go and perjure myself and then you stiff me—don't bother to pay me my thirty grand—what happens then? Right? I'm up a creek, because I can't hardly go to the cops.' So he shrugs, gives me this little smile, punches a button on his computer. Had the offer typed up already. I mean he had the whole bleddy thing planned."

Brock whispered, "This is bullshit, Press. There's no letter and he knows it."

Frank Reed riffled around in an accordion file and came out with a piece of paper, which he handed to Mic Giddens. "Do you recognize this, Mr. Giddens?"

Cain looked over at Brock questioningly. Brock shrugged. There was no letter, so there was nothing to worry about.

Giddens nodded at the general counsel. "That's the letter Mr. Brock gave me."

Press Cain popped out of his chair, face flushed. "Objection! We've been through close to a year of discovery in this action, and there's never been any mention by the complainant of this alleged letter."

"Your honor," Frank Reed said, "apparently it just

slipped Mr. Giddens's mind. He was reviewing his files yesterday evening in preparation for this hearing and at that point in time, lo and behold, he discovered this letter. Which he'd forgotten about.''

"Lo and behold," Giddens said.

The Angel of Mercy smiled. Giddens smiled. Frank Reed smiled, teeth poking out at all angles.

"This is outrageous," Cain said. "Move to exclude this *so-called* evidence."

The Special Master wiped his infected eye, from which a tear had leaked and fallen onto one of his large lapels, leaving a small heart-shaped stain. "If this were a normal state case," he said, "I might be inclined to agree. But in a disciplinary hearing like this, a little latitude is in order."

"Then we'd like a ten-minute recess to examine the document," Cain said.

The Angel of Mercy's smile widened. "Denied."

"This is crazy," Brock whispered. "What kind of asshole would put something like this in writing? It doesn't make sense." He felt a muscle in his neck seizing up, the pain shooting down into his back.

The general counsel handed Cain a copy of the letter. Brock studied it over his shoulder. Definitely his letterhead. Sure as hell looked like his signature at the bottom, too. And now they had no time to hire a graphologist to testify that the signature was a forgery. No time, even, to put together a half decent cross-examination.

"Would you read me the contents of this letter, Mr. Giddens?" Frank Reed said.

"Says, 'Dear Mr. Giddens: This letter is to express our offer to you regarding your testimony in Evans versus Laughing Dolls. If the following conditions are met, to wit: A) that you testify in such a way as to portray the plaintiff's claims in a favorable light; and B) a verdict is returned for the plaintiff with damages awarded in excess of three hundred thousand dollars, the plaintiff is prepared to offer you payment of thirty thousand dollars, payable in two lump sums. One nonrefundable payment of ten thousand dollars shall be made upon completion of Mr. Giddens's deposition testimony, with the balance of twenty thousand dollars to be made upon final disbursement of the settlement in *Jimmy Dale*

Evans versus Laughing Dolls.' Then it's signed down here, 'Sincerely yours, Garrett C. Brock the third.'''

"And what happened then, Mr. Giddens?"

"I said okay, I'd do it."

"And did your conversation continue?"

"Mr. Brock then told me what I should say in the deposition the next day. He said he'd give me the letter after I testified. I said, 'Forget it. No letter, no deal.'''

"And then?"

"We wrangled a bit. Finally he gave me the letter."

"And did you, at that time, intend to lie in your deposition the following day?"

Giddens, looking pious and wide-eyed: "No, sir, I did not."

"So did you follow Mr. Brock's instructions the next day in the deposition?"

"No, sir, I did not. I told the truth."

"Did anyone else witness this conversation?"

"Yis. Like I said, this girl Kit Fulghram came over with me. She was standing outside the door of Mr. Brock's office, so she heard the whole conversation."

Frank Reed let his teeth escape in a large horsey grin. "No further questions."

The Angel of Mercy closed his infected eye, pressed on it briefly with the ham of his hand, and then said, "Let's take a break, folks."

Brock had been having neck problems since he'd gotten out of law school.

A few years back he'd gone to a doctor complaining of intermittent pain. *What kind of pain?* the doctor had asked. Well, sometimes it was like a knitting needle was being wormed up the inside of his neck. Sometimes it just hurt when he turned his head, a sort of pulling in the muscles that radiated down into his back. And sometimes, on long car trips, for instance, it would start throbbing and there would be a dull ache through his left shoulder and then he'd get a headache that made him feel a little sick to his stomach. *And how did he feel today?* Well, today it felt just fine, actually.

"Mm-hmm. Mm-hmm," the doctor had said. He'd poked

and prodded a little. "Doesn't sound like you're a candidate for surgery. You want to go see a chiropractor?"

"A chiropractor? All those degrees on the wall and you want to send me to a chiropractor?"

The doctor smiled tolerantly. "Necks, you've got three choices. First, surgery—which can be relatively effective for various severe problems that you don't have. Second, chiropractors. Modestly effective for some conditions. Third, you got meditation, Tai Chi, Feldenkrais, accupressure, Rolfing, aromatherapy, voodoo . . ." The doctor had shrugged. "I'm told these things work wonders occasionally."

Brock had looked at him dumbly.

"I had a patient who signed over her entire week's paycheck to one of those TV evangelist guys. That one that always wears a white suit? Apparently it gave her a great deal of relief." The doctor had scribbled something on his Rx pad, tore it off, handed it to Brock.

It said ASPIRIN in large, clear letters.

"Many of my patients find a two-dollar bottle of analgesics to be about as effective as eight grand worth of surgery."

So Brock had gone to a second doctor.

"You've got what I like to call a gremlin in your neck," the neck-and-back specialist had said.

"A gremlin. That's a cute word for . . . what?"

"For your neck hurts."

"But surely, Doctor—"

"Oh, yeah, there's a medical reason. Your third cervical vertebrae is infinitesimally out of line, and you have a slight deterioration of the disk. But it might as well be a gremlin for all I can do about it. Have you thought about a chiropractor?"

So finally he had gone to a chiropractor. The chiropractor wanted him to come in for manipulations every Monday at four-ten and every Thursday at two-forty-five.

"For how long?"

"I expect we can make some real good progress in, oh, six months or a year."

So Brock had given up on the professionals and bought three huge bottles of Tylenol. He stowed one in the glove compartment of his car, one in his medicine cabinet at home, and one in the top drawer of his desk.

And if it gets really bad, he'd figured, *hell, maybe I'll try voodoo.*

"Where is she?" Brock asked, rubbing his sore neck. He was talking about their witness, the dancer Caitlin Cobranchy, the one person who could rebut Giddens's testimony.

Press Cain shook his head. He was one of those people who carries a kind of pale imitation of a smile on his face at all times—a smile that suggests he remains hopeful in the face of overwhelming evidence that all is lost. "Miss Cobranchy will be here, Brock," he said. "I spoke to her yesterday."

Brock's neck was moving from the knitting-needle-up-the-spine stage to the railroad-spike-driven-into-the-base-of-the-skull stage. "What about today? You talk to her today?"

Press Cain pursed his lips, patted the pocket of his pants pretending to look for a quarter. He was small and neatly tailored, the kind of man who didn't carry change in his pockets so as not to throw off the drape of his suit. "If it would make you feel better . . ."

"It *would* make me feel better."

Press Cain threw Brock a brilliantly disconsolate smile. Though Cain was one of the senior partners in the big downtown law firm run by Brock's father and had a great reputation as a litigator, he wasn't fighting the case with quite the vigor Brock had hoped for. Which made him a little nervous.

Scream! Scream! Scream! Scream! Somewhere inside the silence of the courthouse corridor Brock heard the nasty grinding of electric guitars.

• 5

After the ME's people took the body, Janelle Moncrief stood on the bank of the creek and stared at the crime scene, trying to relax her mind. Even after you'd been working homicide as long as she had, something like this gave you the creeps. Couldn't let it show around all those men, but it did. Sometimes she wondered if the men felt it less than she did. Or maybe they were just like her, faking how tough and hardass they were, all of them feeling cold and rotten inside most of the time.

Shakespeare's first vic was two months ago: Mel Prochaska. Real estate lawyer, solo practice. A male stripper had found him in a dumpster behind a gay lingerie modeling shop. The location, the sexual mutilation angle: they had figured it was a fag beef, a lover's quarrel, that kind of thing. They couldn't make sense of the card, though: the four-by-five-inch card, neatly tucked inside a cream-colored envelope, with the joke printed on it. *What do you call four lawyers buried up to their necks in sand?* Flip the card over: *Not enough sand.*

But then two weeks later they found the next guy, Lee Darden, a trial lawyer from up in Cobb County. Found him in a park downtown, same as today's vic. Same MO: blunt instrument, private parts in the mouth, the card with the joke on it stuffed in the-pocket of his suit. Punch line: *Because there are some things even rats won't do.*

Two weeks after that, Boyd Michaels. Criminal defense lawyer. Punch line: *One's a scum-sucking bottom feeder. And the other one's a fish.* After Boyd Michaels, the media had figured out there was a serial killer in town—killing *lawyers*, no less—and the whole business went nuts. The press still didn't know the forensic details: the sexual mutilation, the joke cards. But the fact that they were all lawyers—there was no way to hide that. So it had gotten to where you were hearing that damn quote from *Henry IV* on the TV fifteen times a day.

The Bar had started screaming at the mayor, and the mayor had screamed at the chief, and the chief had put together the Joint Task Force, appointed Janelle as investigator-in-charge. Then the Chief screamed at Janelle, just for good measure.

One month since they'd found Boyd Michaels and they still had zero to go on: no witnesses, no physical evidence that was worth a damn. Nothing but a bunch of cream-colored cards.

And now this guy, Raymond Lata. He was carrying a pocket calendar with his business cards in it. Partner in a big firm downtown—Clay, Brock, Vinyard & Cain.

Janelle Moncrief watched the uniforms picking things up off the ground, putting them in bags. Judging by the success of their previous ventures, there wouldn't be anything there. Bunch of junk was all they'd turn up. Candy wrappers, cigarette butts, condoms. But real evidence? No, this bastard was too smart.

The only interesting forensic evidence they'd found was on the second body—Darden. The ME had found some little flakes of a white material in the knife wound, sent them over to the crime lab. The report had come back that the flakes were Ivory soap. Like Shakespeare had used his knife to cut up a bar of soap. Very strange.

Something bugging her about this thing. Something bugging her, big time. Couldn't sleep nights, thinking about it. Something about the connection between all these lawyers. That and the way they were killed. The mutilation thing— that made the killer out to be a perv, a deviant. But the fact that they were all lawyers, that pointed somewhere else. But where?

Across the park one of the uniforms yelled, waved. "Lieutenant!"

The uniform had found a short piece of metal bar—looked

like that stuff they used to reinforce concrete. She hunkered down, peered at it. Something stuck to the end: a dark stain and a couple of hairs.

"What you think?" the uniform said.

She stood, took a deep breath, chills running up and down her body. Hoping the uniform didn't notice.

• 6

Cain finished his uneventful cross-examination of Giddens, and then the next witness took the stand. Her name was Kit Fulghram. She had bleached-blond hair, bad skin, and a very deep but peculiarly orange-looking tan. Her arms were more muscular than most men's.

She explained that she was a professional body-builder and a part-time bouncer at Laughing Dolls. The Angel of Mercy tried unsuccessfully to stifle a smile, and was force to daub at his eye with a large handkerchief to hide his mouth.

Kit Fulghram proceeded to confirm Giddens's story in every detail.

After Press Cain finished his cross-examination, Brock said, "You didn't lay a glove on her."

Cain said, "Yes, but just *look* at them. They're freaks. We put you and Caitlin on the stand—normal, credible-looking people?—we'll demolish them."

"Call your next witness," the Special Master said. His left eye was tearing in an almost constant stream now.

Reed let his teeth out for some air and said, "The State Bar of Georgia rests."

Brock's neck was still laced with hot pain when Press Cain called him to the stand. Cain asked Brock to tell his side of the incidents that had taken place on September 10.

Brock explained that Mic Giddens had come to his office to get copies of an insurance binder and some other papers he'd misplaced. Giddens had claimed that one of the pages

29

was missing. They'd had a brief conversation unrelated to
the case while Brock's secretary made another copy, and then
Giddens had left.

"Was Mr. Giddens accompanied by anyone?"

Brock hesitated. "Yes. He was with Kit Fulghram."

"So let me understand." Cain smiled reassuringly at
Brock. "It's your testimony, Mr. Brock, that other than this
document you alluded to, you had no discussion of *Jimmy
Dale Evans versus Laughing Dolls?*"

"That's right."

"And the only papers you gave him were those that were
to be used as deposition exhibits the following day?"

"Correct."

Cain took the letter Giddens had produced that morning,
walked slowly to the witness stand, handed it to Brock. "So
I trust you would claim that you did not give this to him?"

Brock studied the letter. It was an excellent forgery of his
own signature. "Absolutely not," Brock said finally. "I mean
come on, what kind of moron would put something like this
in writing? Giddens must have stolen some stationery off my
desk and forged the letter."

Frank Reed popped out of his chair. "Objection!"

The Angel of Mercy smiled. "Sustained. You know better
than that, Mr. Brock. No wild speculations, please."

Brock thought back to the day Giddens had come to his
office. The fact was, he didn't remember it too well. Had
Giddens somehow palmed the stationery while he was in
the office?

"So this is your stationery?" Cain said.

"It appears to be."

"And does that appear to be your signature?"

Brock grimaced as a sliver of pain shot down his neck.
Suddenly the strain of the whole business made him boil
over. "Appear? Sure, it *looks* like it! But the fact remains
that I did not write or generate or produce this document. I
did not dictate it, I did not cause it to be written or generated
or produced, nor did I suggest to anyone on my staff that
they should write or generate or produce it. And I *sure* as
hell didn't sign it! It's a goddamn forgery!"

"It would help, Mr. Brock, if we could keep this as calm
as possible." The Angel of Mercy smiled down at him from

the judge's bench, a tear gleaming on the side of his nose. "We're trying to be collegial here, Mr. Brock."

"Fine," Brock said, rising out of the witness box. "Let's be collegial as hell! Fine. But the fact remains I did not write this damn letter!" Brock found himself pounding the flat of his hand on the railing of the box. "Even if I were such a jerk as to suborn perjury, I'm not an idiot. Only a lunatic or a fool would put something like this in writing—and believe you me, your honor, I am neither. That man is a fucking liar!" Brock pointed at Mic Giddens, shaking his finger.

The Angel of Mercy starting banging his gavel, and as he did so his old smile started spreading across his face. It was the smile of a hunter with his prey in the cross hairs. "Siddown, boy," he hissed.

Brock looked around the courtroom blankly, feeling as though his mind had jumped out of his body for a moment. He sat down, shaking his head. Stupid, stupid, stupid. What a strange feeling, though: the anger completely seizing control of him. In his entire adult life he couldn't remember just flat out losing it that way. Usually the more pressure he was under, the cooler and more restrained he got. But not today. Odd.

"I'm sorry, your honor," he mumbled. "I guess I've been under a lot of strain."

"Proceed with your examination, Mr. Cain," the Special Master said dryly.

"Was there anyone else present during your conversation?"

"Yes, there was." Suddenly Brock felt calm and cool again. What a jerk. How could he have lost control like that?

"And who is that?"

"Her name is Caitlin Cobranchy. I was preparing her for deposition. She's the dancer who fell on Mr. Evans, causing his back injuries."

Cain said, "I believe this concludes my examination."

"I assume the respondent has another witness?" the Special Master said after he'd excused Brock from the stand.

Brock looked over at Press Cain.

"If you'd indulge us for just *one* moment," Cain said,

holding up one small manicured finger and showing the Angel of Mercy his dubious smile.

He buttoned his nice suitcoat, walked briskly out into the hallway and was gone for a long time. Brock had the uncomfortable feeling that someone was bleeding all the oxygen out of the room. There was a thrumming in the back of his neck that seemed to be extending around to his windpipe, tightening like a noose. He tried to put a confident, pleased look on his face, but his knees were trembling under the table.

When he reentered the conference room, Press Cain still had the same half-smile on his face. Before he sat down, he said, "Your honor, the respondent has one additional witness. Unfortunately she has been held up. With the court's permission, the respondent requests a continuance until tomorrow morning."

The Angel of Mercy took a handkerchief out of his breast pocket, dabbed at his eye for a moment, and said, "Oh, goodness! I apologize for being such a persnickety old goat, but it just annoys the fool out of me when folks fail to appear in my courtroom." Then he smiled, his old blue eyes twinkling under sagging folds of skin. "Respondent request denied. Call your next witness."

Cain stood frozen in a sort of half crouch. "The respondent . . . ah . . . the respondent rests," he said finally.

The Angel of Mercy leaned close to the microphone, beaming serenely. "I guess we'll hear closing arguments now."

Brock started hearing that song in his head again—*Scream! Scream! Scream! Scream!*—and a jackhammer pain shot up into the roof of his head. Without giving it any particular thought, Brock pushed his chair back and headed for the door.

"Mr. Brock!" the Special Master called out. "Mr. Brock, where in the samhill are you going?"

Brock didn't stop until he was out in the corridor. The only people there were two middle-aged men leaning against the wall, big round buttons stuck to their chests that read JURY in red letters.

Press Cain burst through the door. "What's gotten into you, Brock? You're acting like a four-year-old."

"It's over," Brock said. Pitiless guitars racing through his throbbing head. *Scream! Scream!* "Don't you see, Press? It's over."

When Brock got home, he heard a loud bang, a sound like the report of a gun. Dru was sticking her head out the door, pointing.

"The backyard!" she yelled. "He's in the backyard!"

What was she talking about? Brock felt a sudden rush of fear. Heart pounding, he slammed the door and raced around the garage into the backyard. It was the old man. He was standing there with a shotgun, reloading.

"I've had enough of this," Dru said, trotting up behind Brock. "For godsake why do we have to put up with this?"

"Go back inside," Brock said. "I'll talk to him."

Brock's grandfather stood in the middle of the backyard, about ten yards from a bank of twelve or fifteen black-and-white TV sets stacked up against the azaleas that flanked the carriage house where he lived. He'd stretched a couple of extension cords across the lawn and tuned all the TVs to different channels. The old man had an ancient 10-gauge Marlin duck gun cradled in his arms. Several of the televisions had gaping holes where the screens should have been, and the yard was littered with transistors, capacitors, resistors, glinting bits of vacuum tube.

The sun was tangled in the trees, dusk settling over the yard.

"What's going on, Judge?" Brock said. His grandfather had been a circuit court judge in Arkansas a long time ago, and everybody called him Judge, even his family.

The old man seemed very intent on the televisions. Eventually he fired the duck gun and Big Bird disappeared in a shower of sparks. The recoil of the gun nearly knocked him off his feet. He had not been a large man even when he was young, but now that he was eighty-nine, most of the flesh stripped away, there was little left but bones and rococo swags of spotted skin.

"I'll tell you the thing about *Sesame Street,*" the old man told Brock. "It's designed to manufacture little idiots, little mass-produced cretins, compliant little shrink-wrapped mental zeros who can't follow an argument or a thought or even a sentence that lasts more than five seconds. The sumbitches are just softening up our youngins so they won't understand anything but advertisements and that shit on MTV."

"You could be right, Judge," Brock said.

Without turning from the televisions, Brock's grandfather said, "Well, spit it out, boy. How'd it go?"

"Not good," Brock said. "My witness was a no-show. The special master's not handing down his recommendation for two weeks, but right now, it doesn't look too good."

"Damn!" the old man said. Brock wasn't sure if he was talking to him or the televisions. "You know, this happened to me a couple times, too. Nothing to worry about."

"They tried to disbar you?"

"Sure, sure. Numerous occasions."

"How'd you get out of it?"

"Hired a widow woman, put a mojo on the bastards."

"And that worked?"

The Judge shot another TV. Bill Cosby and his cigar imploded. Transistors and bits of glass zinged through the air. "I also slipped a King Biscuit flour bag full of ten-dollar bills into the backseat of a Cadillac owned by a certain chief justice of the Arkansas Supreme Court." Bam. There went a pretty good episode of *Cops.* The Judge reloaded. "So I can't, with any degree of certainty, say whether it was the King Biscuit flour bag or the widow woman."

"You're saying you actually paid off a member of the state Supreme Court?"

"Well, sure. Back then it was SOP."

"So were you, I mean—"

"You mean, was I guilty as charged?"

"Right."

"Of course I was! Back then lawyers were *men,* not these

prancing little fairies you got today. Jesus God, in my day if you knew you were in the right, you bent the rules a little, didn't think twice about it.''

"Yeah, but how'd you know you were in the right?"

The Judge's eyes narrowed. "I was *always* in the right, boy. *Always*.'' BAM! Three or four TVs fell over all at once. There was a lot of electronic popping and belching, then one of the sets blew up of its own accord, a nice white flash of light in the darkening yard. "Guess I was just lucky that way."

The Judge took a few more desultory shots until finally there was only one TV left. It was playing the local news. He lifted his duck gun.

"Hold on,'' Brock said. On the TV a chubby black reporter was talking about how the police had found another dead lawyer that morning.

The old man lowered his gun. "What's that now? Four?''

"Yeah. Four dead lawyers.'' They watched in silence as the chubby guy interviewed a woman detective in a big white hat. Then a tape of two EMTs and a cop loading the corpse into an ambulance while a couple more cops held up a sheet so the camera couldn't get a view of the dead guy. The upshot of the story was the cops still didn't seem to have the first clue what was going on. They hadn't released the name of the victim. Brock wondered if he knew the guy.

The yard was starting to get dark, the one television leaving a patch of greasy blue light in the middle of the grass. Watching the story about the dead guy, Brock felt a sense of foreboding. Everything seemed to be falling apart. He massaged his sore neck, but it didn't feel any better.

After the story was over, the Judge said, "I talked to an old buddy of mine, his son's an Atlanta cop, he said there's a very peculiar angle to this."

"What's that?''

"This psycho's leaving little notes on the bodies after he kills them.''

"Notes?''

"Dead lawyer jokes. You've heard 'em. A lawyer's visiting the aquarium. He falls in the shark pond. Ten minutes later he climbs out unscathed. *How come the sharks didn't eat him? Professional courtesy.* That kind of thing.''

A commercial came on the surviving television. "What is it exactly you enjoy about shooting these things, Judge?" Brock said.

"The vanquishing of wickedness," he said. Then he shot the last TV. By then the sun had gone down completely.

The Judge lifted the gun again, like he was going to blast the television carcasses a couple more times, but Brock reached over and pushed the muzzle gently toward the ground. "You're scaring the hell out of Dru, you know that?"

The old man scowled, looked at the dark patch in the yard where the dead TVs lay. "What do you want me to do?" he said finally. "Go over there tomorrow and kiss her ass?"

"It wouldn't hurt," Brock said. "Also, you better give me the gun."

The Judge grunted sullenly. Brock put out his hand, wrapped it around the stock of the 10-gauge. The old man struggled feebly for a moment, then let go.

"I'm sorry, Judge," Brock said. Then he started walking across the lawn toward the house, a hollow feeling in his gut.

"For chrissake," the old man said. "Sure got you by the short and curlies, doesn't she?" Brock kept walking.

• 8

"Unmitigated disaster," Brock told Dru. "Total carnage. First—out of the blue—they produce a forged document. And then my witness no-shows on me."

Dru was looking sourly at her watch. "What in hell was he doing out there?"

"He was shooting televisions."

A muscle twitched in Dru's jaw. "We have a little girl here, Brock! For godsake. Did you tell him that?"

"Look, he's not going to do it again. I took the gun away."

"We've got to do something about him. We've just got to. He's getting weirder every day."

"Weird is not a crime. He's doing okay."

Dru whirled, waved a large spoon at his face. "What if he'd shot our daughter? Don't you have any concern for *her* safety?"

"I *said* he won't do it again."

Dru glared. "I'd like to think you cared about your own daughter as much as you do about that old man."

"Can we talk about this another time? I'm on the verge of getting disbarred and so, okay, I admit, I'm a little distracted. I'm sorry."

Dru rolled her eyes. "Oh, come on. You're not going to get disbarred, Brock,"

"Dru, listen to me." Brock took her by the arms and looked into her face. "It's no joke. Okay? It *could* happen. And if it does? Bye-bye law practice, bye-bye paycheck, bye-

bye nice house. This is the real thing. I could be selling shoes at the mall.''

Dru looked back at him, studying his face skeptically. He could see back inside her eyes, the doubt. It made him wonder if maybe he'd cried wolf about his career that many times before. Had he really told her so many versions of this same do-or-die story that, when it was finally and utterly true, she was incapable of believing him?

After a long moment Dru put her arms around him, held onto him for a while. ''It's going to be okay,'' she whispered in his ear. ''But let me tell you this, Brock—*we* are getting near the edge.''

''The edge?'' he said.

Still whispering: a soft, breathy voice that could hardly have carried across the room. ''I mean our marriage. You're going to have to ask yourself some hard questions. I've said before that you need to think about getting some junior partners or joining a bigger firm or . . . something. Anything to lighten your load a little.''

''I know, I know.''

Brock felt the hard bite of Dru's nails in his back. ''No. You *don't* know. You keep saying that you know, that you understand. But you don't. It's time to make changes. Time to ask whether your relationship with me and with Grace is more important than your relationship with Jimmy Dale Evans and your grandfather and all that macho trial lawyer bullshit.''

''Well, I've been thinking . . .''

''No.'' The nails in his back again, the hot breath in his ear. ''You've been giving me a song and dance for, what, three or four years? No more. No more quips, no more talking or thinking or stalling or stonewalling or intellectual jujitsu. When this goddamn Jimmy Dale Evans thing is over with, you come to me with a plan. Names, dates, timetables: first, about your grandfather, and second, about your sane new professional life. Period. Or I file the papers.''

Dru slid her hands to the back of his neck, kissed him gently on the cheek, then walked into the kitchen.

Brock felt a dull pounding in his neck. It wasn't as bad as it had been during the hearing, but his ears were ringing from swallowing so much Tylenol.

"You want your dinner?" Dru called from the kitchen. Her voice was light, like nothing was going on. "It's still warm."

"Yeah, that sounds good." Brock slumped down in his chair, turned on the television with the remote control. How many times had he done this—come home, sat down in front of the TV, ignoring his family as he ate warmed-over supper off a tray table? Brock felt numb and vaguely embarrassed. How had it come to this?

He turned off the TV. Grace was playing on the floor, face intent, making a little house out of her Lego blocks. Humming to herself. She picked up a naked ratty-haired doll, pranced it around in the different rooms of her Lego house.

"Hey, honey," Brock said. "What did you do today?"

Grace said nothing, kept humming to herself.

"Daddy's talking to you," Brock said. "Did Funny come see you today?"

Grace looked up from her blocks resentfully. "You didn't open the message," she said quietly.

"The what?"

"Funny's message. I gave you Funny's message this morning and you didn't open it."

Brock remembered: the cream-colored envelope with his name typed on it. "You're right sweetheart. I didn't. Daddy was in a rush this morning because of work."

"Mommy says—"

"I know," Brock said. "Mommy says I worry too much, I work too much. Mommy's probably right."

"Funny was here a few minutes ago. Funny wanted to know if you read it. Funny got mad."

Brock smiled halfheartedly. He wasn't much in the mood for playing with Grace, but he hated to disappoint her. "Okay," he said. "Where is it?"

Grace jumped up, ran across the room, picked up the envelope from the floor, handed it to him.

Brock took the cream-colored envelope, stained and puckered from the coffee she'd knocked over on him this morning. He slid his finger under the flap.

"You should be more nicer to Funny," Grace said.

"I promise." Brock grinned. "I'll be more nicer."

Grace did not appear to be appeased.

For a moment he forgot what he was doing, and his finger

stayed there, buried under the flap of the envelope. The fiasco at the disciplinary hearing played across his brain. The bang of the Special Master's gavel started mixing in his mind with the report of his grandfather's gun. One depressing thought running into the next: his stupid outburst on the stand, his grandfather getting old and loopy before his eyes, Dru's flat whisper in his ear. *You come to me with a plan or I file the papers.*

It was like some kind of bad joke. Question: How much shit can you pile on a desperate lawyer?

Only, Brock couldn't think of a punch line.

Was there something wrong with him? Why wasn't he in the kitchen, screaming at Dru, telling her she was wrong about him, that their marriage was still sound? Or begging her forgiveness, or telling her she was full of shit? Christ, *something!* He felt numb, cleaned out. Bored, almost. Where was his passion? *I should be afraid. I should really be afraid.*

Brock breathed out a long slow stream of air.

"Daddy!" Grace's small, moist hand, pressing against his arm. "Open it!"

Brock ripped open the flap, pulled out a card of the same cream coloring as the envelope that contained it.

Before he could read the card, Dru came into the room carrying a plate of food. She looked completely calm. "I hope it's warm enough," she said, setting the plate on a tray table. Some kind of stir-fried stuff, full of bright red peppers, chicken, broccoli.

"Daddy. Daddy. What's it say?" Grace was pulling on the card.

"Grace, Daddy's got to eat," Dru said.

The phone rang.

"Can you get that?" Brock said. The plate of stir-fried vegetables and rice steamed, its moisture clinging in tiny beads to the hairs on the back of his hand.

"Daddy!"

The phone rang again. Dru answered it.

"Daddy!"

"I'm reading it," Brock said. "I'm reading it."

"It's for you," Dru said, handing him the receiver.

"Hello," he said, reading one side of the card, then flipping it over, reading the other.

What the message said alarmed him so much that he leapt to his feet, knocking over the tray table and sending his dinner cascading to the floor. Red peppers and rice slithered across the floor in a steaming mass.

"Brock?" Dru said. "What—"

On the phone he heard a voice talking to him. "Such a sweet kid," the voice said. "Intelligent? Imaginative? Her friend Funny has *such* a nice time playing with her."

"Who is this?"

"You got my message?" the voice said.

It took Brock a moment, a terrible moment, to assemble all the pieces. "Who *is* this? What do you want?"

"The Jimmy Dale Evans case?" the voice said. "It's time to back off."

"You were in my house!" Brock screamed. "You were in my goddamn house!"

"And it could happen again." A soft mocking voice followed by a brief crack of laughter. Then the dial tone.

Brock sprinted down the hallway into Grace's room. Her gauzy curtains stirred languidly in a soft breeze from the open window. Wide open. Too wide for a four-year-old girl to have opened it.

His hand still held the message. WHAT DO YOU CALL A NOSY LAWYER? it read on one side, the question neatly typed in capital letters.

"Brock!" came Dru's voice from the other room. "What's wrong with you?"

On the other side of the card was the punch line.

DEAD.

• 9

"No way, Brock. This is not about you." Five minutes later
and Dru was in cold fury. "This is not about *your* case or
your reputation as a lawyer or *your* job or *your* anything."

Dru was stuffing clothes into an overnight bag. It had taken
her a few minutes to understand his story—about the call,
about Funny, about the card, about Shakespeare. But as soon
as he pulled the whole story together, she had gone into a
cold rage. He didn't blame her—he was still shaking a little
from the call himself—but that didn't mean they had to flee
town on five minutes' notice.

"Dru," Brock said. "Come on, we'll be okay."

"That's not the right answer, dammit, Brock!" Dru waved
a finger in his face. "The right answer is to put your family
first. The right answer is that when some wacko threatens
your family, you make your family safe."

"Dru. Look, this could be a prank for all I know. Besides,
I've got trial in three days. I can't just pull up the tent stakes
and herd the camels out of town."

"Camels?" Dru looked up from her bag of clothes with a
face blanched with disbelief. "We're not talking about camels. We're talking about someone who's been sneaking into
our house, lurking in our daughter's room, doing God only
knows what—"

"I know, I know. But I've got Jimmy Dale's trial coming
up and I—"

"No no no no no no . . . don't explain. Okay? Do me that
favor. You have your reasons, fine. All I'm telling you is
that Grace and I are packing our toothpaste and our under-

42

wear, and we are driving up to Mother and Dad's, where we will stay until this gets resolved. That's what *we* are doing. What *you* do is *your* decision."

Brock looked at the floor. He'd made a commitment to Jimmy Dale Evans; he had to prepare for trial. Three days, no, he couldn't waste even one day up in Tennessee at Dru's parents' house. There was too much to do for Jimmy Dale's trial.

"Dru, I can't go."

Dru hoisted the bag off the bed, dropped it with a thump on the floor, went into the bathroom and starting rummaging around in the medicine cabinet. Brock sat down on the side of the bed, feeling weak and paralyzed.

Banging noises came out of the bathroom. "Where's the toothpaste?" Dru said. Then in a louder voice: "Where's the toothpaste, where's the fucking toothpaste?" Then the sobbing started.

He went in and put his arms around her. "We're going to get through this," he said. "I promise, sweetheart."

In the mirror he could see her eyes, and they were still full of rage, and he couldn't tell if all that anger was directed at him or at whoever had sent the note or at herself. He hugged her hard. For a moment she squeezed back, but then she went limp.

"Let go of me," she quietly. "Please. I have to pack."

Forty-five minutes later the house was empty. Brock sat numbly on the couch drinking a second Scotch. Strangely, the pain in his neck had abated. Maybe it was the booze.

What happened? he kept thinking. *What just happened here?* Ice clattered in his glass.

For the third or fourth time he stood and walked around the house looking in closets, pulling back shower curtains, checking door handles. He had already nailed the window shut in Grace's room.

The idea that somebody had been creeping into his daughter's room for the past couple of months made him queasy with anger. Had they touched her? Had they molested her? Jesus Christ. There hadn't been any signs of it in her behavior. Or had there? Maybe he just hadn't noticed.

The house seemed excessively quiet. He went into the master bathroom, turned on the light, went into the walk-in closet, pulled the chain hanging from the bare bulb on the ceiling, then went through the house flipping switches until every single bulb in the place was lit. But still a shadow moved behind a curtain in the den; still the ticking hotwater heater obscured the corner of the mud room; still three burned-out bulbs in the ugly dining room chandelier threw variegated shadows around the room. Darkness seeped in everywhere.

Noises outside: A whistling tree branch. Car tires shrieking on some distant road. A thump. A dull, repetitive clack. Brock's blood swished and thudded in his ears. The sounds faded toward the limits of hearing and identifiability until they had all mixed into a gumbo that was part sound, part memory, part imagination, part bowel-loosening fear.

Brock went upstairs, got his grandfather's duck gun out of the study, took it downstairs and leaned it against the couch. Once he'd sat down again, he realized the gun wasn't loaded. Should he give the Judge a call, tell him what happened, get some shells, circle the wagons? No. No, this was silly. Everybody was overreacting.

Brock sat on the couch again, turned on the TV, turned it off, turned it on again. Patterns moving on glass, sounds that did not signify. Brock flipped through the channels, stopped on MTV. That song again, "Scream!" It was played by a bunch of loutish kids with elaborate tatoos. The lead singer had a long pointy beard with orange and red and blue rubber bands wrapped around it.

Scream! Scream! The darkness was crawling from under the furniture, scratching at the flowered curtains, leaking from the corners of the room. Brock looked around the room, seeing it as though for the first time. Dru's touch was everywhere. Brock had had no part in decorating this place with its inlaid Damascus coffee table or its matching, Bargello-patterned chairs or the framed pen-and-ink architectural renderings Dru had drawn when she was in college. For a moment he felt as though it was *he* who was the stranger sneaking into someone else's home. All familiarity dropped away.

The loutish boys on TV were writhing and yelling, faces contorted with ritual adolescent anger. A quick montage: skulls, graveyards, mushroom clouds. A woman's ass in a tight black skirt. Brock felt an indistinct, childish emotion stirring in the back of his mind. Something strong but not quite identifiable: rising, rising.

Scream! Scream! Scream!

Even alone in the room Brock felt silly admitting to himself that he liked the song. It was as though Dru's skeptical presence clung to the furniture. He stared at the TV with a kind of fearful, distant reverence.

Brock had always had a fear of hollowness—a dim fear that his own inner life was flat and barren and dull; and that the further he got from his youth, the flatter and duller it was becoming. It wasn't something he had ever talked about, not even to Dru. Maybe he'd hinted at it on the occasional late-night drunken ramble with some old high school buddy, but his fear had gone no further toward articulation than that. Where was all the grand passion? Where were the night sweats and the dark turgid fears and the blinding sexual appetites that had dogged and excited him when he was young? They seemed to have been replaced by a cheerful, dull, monotonous routine—one that grew more monotonous and less cheerful with each passing year. Breakfast of dry toast and decaf with skim milk; tedious depositions and briefs and amended consolidated requests for production of documents; two glasses of white wine at the Young Trial Lawyers Section mixers on the third Thursday evening of the month; baby-sitter and dinner for two on Friday night.

And only the manic adrenal buzz of trial relieved the boredom. Well, no, that wasn't right. There was Grace. Even though she could be moody or mean or thoughtless or uninterested just when he needed her most, still there were those elusive moments that happened when he held her or read to her or watched her playing intently on the floor, when everything suddenly seemed complete and unimprovable.

But other than that, nothing seemed to move him powerfully anymore. His world had become so cram-full of obligations and duties and habits and routines that all the life seemed to have been squeezed out of it.

So it was with some astonishment that Brock felt the terror rising in himself that night. The integuments that joined him to the rest of the human race had suddenly ripped free, leaving him utterly alone. He hadn't been alone—not for more than a night or two—in, what, eight or ten years? Jesus God, how had that happened?

Colors moving on the TV screen, colors shot through with darkness. Brock got up and walked around the house again, checking the closets, then, heart pounding, down into the humid basement, then up again to the bedrooms. No Shakespeare, no crouching demons. Lights everywhere. Lights shining, but the darkness creeping in, creeping in, creeping in.

Outside a motor revved, a car door slammed. Someone's brief, hysterical laughter. He looked out the window. Nothing there.

He set his empty Scotch glass on the coffee table. Thinking, *What now? What now? What's supposed to happen now?*

In the kitchen, the sound of dripping, water dripping in a pan, the tone changing slightly as the pan slowly filled, filled, overflowed.

Suddenly, rising out of the pool of his own terror, Brock felt something unexpected: a small flash of joy.

Joy? Where was that coming from? You weren't supposed to feel this way when terrible things were happening.

My god! Wait! What's wrong with me?

And in his mind, that song: *Scream! Scream! Scream!* Inexplicably Brock felt his lips spreading, molding themselves into a harsh and ugly smirk.

He opened the front door, looked out at the yard, feeling not only the terrible fear but an expansive, almost sexual sense of possibility. He stretched his neck from side to side and, for a brief moment, there was no pain at all.

The darkness was rising up out of the pine trees and the katydids were sawing at the heavy, resinous air.

• 10

Around two o'clock that morning, Shakespeare drove by Brock's house in a faded green pickup truck.

Big house, nice without being ostentatious. Brick, two brass lanterns by the dark green front door. Good-sized piece of property, a stand of pine trees flanking it on two sides, probably cost way up in the three hundreds. The house was all lit up, looked like Brock was burning every single bulb in the place.

The BMW was still in the driveway, but the Acura, the car Brock's wife drove, was gone. So Brock had stayed. He had done the macho thing, sent his women away and stayed there alone—alone in the house with all the lights burning.

Soul searching: that's what he was doing. Asking himself if he had the balls to see this thing through, to stare down the fear and see Jimmy Dale's case through.

Shakespeare downshifted to first. Taking a moment to savor Brock's fear. Up the street: a pair of headlights materializing around a corner. A neighbor? No, a cop car. Brock had probably called them, asked them to swing by every few minutes, splash their spotlights around the big lawn. Shakespeare laughed briefly, goosed the accelerator, sped off down the street.

Good. So far everything had gone like clockwork.

Now it was time to unfold the second phase of the plan.

THE CONCORDANCE

●

Q: How do you get an attorney out of a tree?

A: Cut the rope.

• 11

"Sorry about yesterday," Brock's grandfather said. "The thing with the TVs."

"What was that all about?" Brock said.

Brock had slept in a chair in front of the television, gotten up early the next morning, stiff and groggy. After taking a shower, he had looked out the back window and there was his grandfather: watering the lawn, six-thirty in the morning. Brock had put on his bathrobe and stepped out onto the patio.

"Just something I always wanted to do," the old man said.

"You scared the hell out of Dru."

"I *told* you I was sorry."

Brock stood there with his hands shoved down in the pockets of his terry cloth bathrobe, feeling the lint with his fingertips and watching the Judge shuffle around the yard, the yellow sprinkler nozzle clutched in his arthritic hand. It was a lovely cool morning.

"Dru left last night," Brock said. "With Grace."

The Judge looked at him for a moment, went back to watering the lawn. His pants were too big for his shrunken frame now, slipping down off his belly, the folds piling up around his ankles. "Not because of me, I hope," he said finally.

Brock explained about Funny, the threatening card, the anonymous phone call. The Judge started dragging the hose over toward a little plot of flowers in the far corner of the yard—zinnia, impatiens, some other plants Brock didn't know the names of. Dru planted them, but the old man did most

of the tending. It was a line of truce between Dru and the
Judge. As Brock followed the old man toward his plot of
flowers, his bare feet got pleasantly wet with dew and covered
with grass clippings.

"What the hell should I do?" Brock said.

When the old man reached the flowers, he turned a little
petcock on the yellow nozzle, stanched the flow until only a
small dribble was coming out, bleeding into the mulch around
his flowers. He looked over his shoulder at Brock.

"I'm not Dru's biggest fan," he said finally. "But that
woman loves you."

"That's not what I'm—"

"Shut up, boy. You come out here for sage advice, you
got to humor the sage." He turned the petcock back on,
directed the glistening arcs of water across the flowers. After
a while he said, "Me, I never loved your grandmother. You
never knew her, so I guess I can tell you that."

"Judge—"

"Listen!" The sun was just coming up over the trees, the
light slashing through the bright needles of water. "No
human being gets through life without regrets, but my deepest
regret is that I didn't marry a woman I could have grieved
over deeply and profoundly when she died. As you know,
my wife died when your daddy was a little boy, so this is
ancient history to you. Point I'm making is I got too wrapped
up in other things to pay any goddam attention to my life."

"Okay."

"I was chasing after all kind of things. Advancement, pres-
tige, all that shit. Hell, I can remember my first Packard, the
smell of the leather, the sound of that straight-8 engine. I can
remember every suit I ever owned, the feel, the cut. I can
remember women I catted around with, the color of their
eyes, the way their underclothes caught the light in the Pea-
body Hotel. My God! It was all a bunch of foolishness—
chasing after wind. And it bored me. It bored me silly 'cause
I wasn't clear on what it was I wanted out of life. You get
to be my age, by God, the scales come off your eyes.

"I watch you, boy. I read your mind. You ain't happy
with things right now, I can see it a mile away. But the
answer lies in the bosom of your family. It's a cliché, but
it's true. You get to be eighty-nine years old, you start to

find out how much of the world's piously phrased horseshit turns out to be the unalloyed truth."

"What—are you saying I should drop Jimmy Dale's case?"

The Judge shook his head sadly, like Brock was too much of a damn fool to catch on to a fairly obvious point.

"Three things happening," the Judge said. "One. Some crazy bastard's sneaking around your house, leaving notes, making terroristic threats at you because of this Jimmy Dale Evans case of yours. Two. This fellow Giddens is trying to get you disbarred for something you didn't do. Three. Your wife just left you. Temporarily, one assumes."

The Judge bent over and picked a beetle off one of his plants, dropped it on the ground, smashed it under the toe of his white leather shoe. "Here's what I think. All your problems are hooked together. Solve one of them, you solve them all. What it looks like to me, you just stumbled into something in the Jimmy Dale Evans case that's making somebody real nervous. Could be Shakespeare, could be this fellow Giddens, could be somebody one of them knows. Hell, Giddens might *be* Shakespeare. I don't know. But if you want to fix this thing, you got to get out there, find out what's going on in this strip club." The old man grimaced as he turned off his sprinkler. "The oracle has spoken, boy. Now you can go back inside, eat your bran flakes."

He started shuffling away, dragging the hose behind him, his pants sagging off his hips.

"Wait a minute, wait a minute," Brock said. "Dru's pissed because I'm sticking with the case. How is this supposed to make her happy?"

"Happy!" The old man whirled around, eyes wide and disparaging. "Who said any goddamn thing about *happy?* Dru's a woman. She doesn't know what the hell she wants. It's your job to show it to her. But to find what she needs, you got to go out to the edge, boy. Out to the edge!"

"What does that have to do with Dru?"

"Out to the edge," the old man said again.

Brock had no idea what the Judge was talking about. Maybe Dru was right. Maybe it was time to start looking for a place for the old man. A soft gust of wind hit the yard, ran cold across Brock's wet feet.

• 12

At 6:05 in the morning, Judge Reggie B. Vinyard slid a pair of very tight iridescent green running shorts over his large hips, a Knicks T-shirt over his large belly, and a green sweatband over his large head, and then told his wife Florence he was going running. She gave him a funny look; her husband had never gone running in all the years she'd known him.

What he did not tell her was that lately he had been experiencing an unusual level of nervousness about some things, and that nervousness had moved him to take some commensurately unusual precautions.

Judge Vinyard ran down the street, turned right, ran a couple more blocks and then trudged, gasping, into Hardees, where he ordered three jelly biscuits, eggs, coffee, and a large OJ.

Judge Reggie B. Vinyard was not, in fact, a judge; he hadn't been for some years. He had served on the federal bench for about six months back during the Carter administration and made sure no one forgot it. Once a judge, always a judge. Presently, he was one of the top three partners in Clay, Brock, Vinyard & Cain—a firm composed mostly of smooth-talking white boys, graduates of places like Sewanee and Princeton and Vanderbilt. Judge Reggie B. Vinyard, however, was neither smooth-spoken, nor white, nor was he a graduate of any high-tone white school. He was Morris Brown College, Class of '54, Howard U. Law, '57, an Omega Psi Phi man, damn proud of it. Still had the horseshoe-shaped scar on his shoulder to prove it.

"Believe I'm gonna throw up," he said to the man who

54

was waiting for him in a booth down near the toilets.
"Brother, I haven't run that far since college."

"What, six blocks?" the man waiting in the booth said.

Reggie B. Vinyard showed his teeth. He believed in giving
people a little rope. They wanted to joke about the man who
was paying their bills, that was fine—as far as it went. "What
you come up with?" Reggie Vinyard said through a wad of
jelly biscuit.

The man in the booth was named Cleland Davis, and he
was a private investigator. Davis was a very dark-skinned
black man with a close-cropped goatee and one yellow eye.
The other eye was permanently shut: a knife wound from his
police days had left nothing in the socket but a shiny gob of
scar tissue. It should have given him a sinister look—but
somehow didn't, quite. He wore black shoes, a pin-striped
suit and a white shirt, open at the collar, no necktie. He had
set a pack of Newports and a Bic lighter on the table but he
wasn't smoking.

The detective slid a thin stack of paper across the table.
"It's all in my report," he said.

Reggie B. Vinyard blinked, set down his biscuit. "I'm sure
you got a real fine prose style and everything, brother, but I
thought I told you not to put anything in writing."

The investigator looked at Vinyard with his yellow eye,
then pulled the report back across the table. "You'd of said
that, Judge, I'd of remembered." He slid the report in his
lap. "I understand where you're coming from, however."

"Just give me the five-cent version, I'll ask you questions." Vinyard shoveled some eggs in his mouth.

"Five-cent version." Cleland Davis ran his tongue dubiously around the inside of his cheek. "Five-cent version
would be that I spent your entire two thousand dollars, didn't
learn a damn thing."

Vinyard stopped chewing his eggs, raised his eyebrows,
lowered his eyelids, then went back to chewing again. He'd
been afraid this would happen. This whole situation was de-
veloping very badly. Very badly, indeed. "Can you rule anybody out?"

The investigator nodded. "Only person I can rule out
is—"

Judge Reggie B. Vinyard raised a wide finger and shook

it. "Hold on," he said. Then he took a napkin off his tray. "Give me a inkpen, Mr. Davis."

Cleland Davis handed him a gold Cross pen. Vinyard wrote down a series of names, each with a number next to it. Then he shoved the napkin across the table. "While we taking precautions," Vinyard said, "just refer to them by number, off chance somebody around here got big ears."

The investigator glanced at the napkin. "What I was gonna say, we can rule out, ah, Subject Number One. He was under surveillance by my most trusted operative at the time of the latest murder."

"Your most trusted operative. Who would that be?"

Cleland Davis smiled lazily. "Me."

"Uh-*huh*," Judge Vinyard said.

"Subject Number Six, we can also rule out, due to the obvious fact he was also Victim Number Four."

Vinyard grunted.

"Other than that, Judge, I could give you a lot of detail, probably add up to nothing."

"So where you go from here?"

"That's your call. You really want to get serious? I'd say the only alternative, we put all your subjects under twenty-four-hour surveillance until something surfaces."

The Judge felt all them jelly biscuits balling up inside his stomach. "Which would cost . . . what?"

Cleland Davis smiled, fiddled with his cigarette lighter. "Bare bones, eight grand a week. Do it right, maybe twenty grand a week."

Reggie Vinyard's eyes opened wide. "You expect me to shell out twenty grand a week for god knows how long?"

"Depends on how crazy, how desperate, how rich you are."

"None of the above, brother. None of the above."

Cleland Davis blinked his one yellow eye and nodded. "There you go then."

Reggie Vinyard stripped the foil top off his orange juice, took a long belt. "Anyway, I got something else for you."

"Okay."

"You remember I showed you a folder in my office? Had documentation on all the arrangements we've made, the ones I spoke about. Leases, incorporations, straw man companies, all that crap. It's about yay thick." Judge Vinyard held his fingers about two inches apart.

"Uh-huh."

"Well, that file's come up missing."

"Oh dear."

"Yeah, but that's not the worst part of it. In order to understand how all that stuff fits together, what name goes where, you got to have a key. You know, Subject Number One has lease-back arrangement with Entity Number Four, which thereby channels funds to Offshore Bank Account Number One, so on, so forth. Now, it use to be the key was right here." The Judge tapped his temple. "But when I handed over some of the administrative element to, uh, Subject Number Six, I had to make out a sort of list or index—being the sort of guy who never used a fifty-cent word when a five-dollar word would do, he called it a *concordance*—so he could keep all our arrangements clear in his mind."

"Oh dear," the investigator said again.

"You just said that. Now all the incorporation documents, all that jazz, it wouldn't make sense to nobody who didn't know exactly what they was looking for. But the concordance, that's different. Whoever got that concordance, they gonna look at it and among those names, they gonna see, ah, Victims Number One through Four and they gonna say, 'My my my, something very peculiar going on here.' "

"If they stole it, they probably know something peculiar going on anyway."

"That may well be. But maybe it just got mislaid."

Cleland Davis reached into the breast pocket of his jacket, took out a small silver toothpick holder, stuck a toothpick in his mouth, rolled it around on his lower lip for a while. "So what you want, Judge?" he said finally.

"That concordance could flat sink my ship."

"Yeah, but what you want me to *do?*"

Reggie Vinyard reached across the table, picked up the investigator's cigarette lighter, set fire to the napkin with the names on it. After the napkin had burned completely to ash, the Judge stood up. "I want you to find that goddamn concordance."

Cleland Davis said, "Anybody ever tell you how foxy you look in a green headband?"

"Foxy! I ain't heard that word in *years!*" Judge Reggie B. Vinyard showed his teeth, then walked away, leaving his tray on the table.

• 13

"In here!"

It was Jimmy Dale's voice coming from deep inside the house. Brock's heart jumped. Something about Jimmy Dale's voice didn't sound right.

Brock had been scheduled to drop by Jimmy Dale Evans's place first thing in the morning for some trial preparation, and now he was standing on the peeling concrete front porch of Jimmy Dale's house. Jimmy Dale lived in a small subdivision out near Stone Mountain—*subdivision* being the euphemism used to describe a cul-de-sac full of pink brick ranch houses with weedy yards and carports held up by fake wrought-iron posts of the sort designed to suggest ivy trellises. The cars were slack-springed Buicks, chrome-wheeled Suzuki Samurais, Camaros with primer on the doors.

Brock had parked his car on the cracked and weedy driveway, banged on the front door. The neighborhood was deserted, eight oh-five in the morning, everybody headed off to work by now.

"In here, Brock! For godsake help me!"

Brock pushed the door open. "Jimmy Dale? Jimmy Dale!"

"Help!" The voice coming from deep inside the house.

Brock rushed into the house, down the hallway.

"In here!" A muffled voice behind the bathroom door. Brock threw open the door, and there was his client lying on the floor.

"Help me, Brock," Jimmy Dale said. "Get me the damn chair." Jimmy Dale was sprawled across the worn vinyl floor, his head leaned against the toilet bowl, his useless legs flung

59

out at odd angles. His wheelchair sat next to the door, over-turned, one wheel spinning slowly.

"What happened?" Brock said, righting the wheelchair. Jimmy Dale just lay there looking up at Brock, his face twisted with anger. Brock leaned over to pick him up.

"Don't touch me," Jimmy Dale said harshly, but Brock kept moving toward him. "Goddammit *don't!*" He slapped feebly at Brock's arm with a wet hand. "Just get me the chair."

Brock pushed the wheelchair over to the side of the bath-room where Jimmy Dale lay, then stood back as his client hoisted himself painfully into the chair. It wasn't pleasant to watch. Under ordinary circumstances Jimmy Dale was not a good-looking man; his lips were a little too large, his ginger hair badly cut, his blue eyes hyperthyroidal and accusatory, his skin pale and mottled. But now, wringing wet, his hair matted, his skin rouged with humiliation and anger, he looked even worse. His eyes jumped around the room.

"How'd you fall?" Brock said.

Jimmy Dale didn't say anything till he was back in the chair. "Give me the blanket, Brock," he said.

The plaid blanket he covered his legs with hung halfway in the toilet.

"You sure? It's soaked."

"Goddammit!" Jimmy Dale stretched out his hand. Brock shrugged, picked it up, handed it to his client. It was wet, too, but Jimmy Dale didn't seem to care. He just folded it up and set it on his lap.

Brock was puzzled by Jimmy Dale's anger. Sure, it was probably embarrassing to fall out of the chair, but why take it out on Brock? "What happened?" Brock said again.

Jimmy Dale didn't answer or even look at Brock, just rolled over to the bath and turned on the water. "Damn it!" he said, glaring at the water flowing into the tub. "God-*damn* it!"

"You need some help?" Brock said.

Jimmy Dale kept looking at the water. "Just leave me alone, okay?" He leaned over, let the water flow over his hands. "I got to get cleaned up."

Brock raised his arms in surrender. "Whatever," he said, heading for the door.

When Brock was halfway out of the room, he heard Jimmy Dale's voice, softer now. "Wait. Brock."

Jimmy Dale had turned his chair around now and was staring at himself in the mirror. "He pissed on me," he said finally. "That bastard threw me out of the chair and he pissed on me. How you think it feels? Huh? How you think that feels?"

"Who did?" Brock said quietly.

"He kept saying something about a cordinance."

"Cordinance?"

"Yeah. He made it out like it was some kind of list or index or something."

"A concordance."

"That's it. Concordance. *'Where's the concordance? Where's the list?'* " Jimmy Dale's lips twisted. "The son of a bitch."

"Who, Jimmy Dale? Who?" Brock was feeling impatient.

"Then he goes around tearing up the house, snorting coke and acting crazy and there's nothing I can do. *Where's the concordance? Where's the concordance?* Making jokes about me, taunting me. Then finally he takes me in here ..." Jimmy Dale Evans stared at himself in the mirror some more, then turned around and looked at Brock for the first time since he'd come into the room. His eyes were full of a cold blue anger.

"Who?"

"Who you think, Brock? It was Mic Giddens. Him and that freak of his, Kit Fulghram, that girl bouncer."

Brock went in the kitchen. Cereal boxes and glasses and TV dinners had spilled across the floor. Giddens had obviously torn the place up looking for something. Brock picked up the mess on the floor, swept up the broken glass, then sat down at the kitchen table and massaged his neck.

A chromed paper napkin dispenser, the kind they had in the lunchroom back when Brock was in elementary school, sat dead in the center of the cheap table. No salt, no pepper, not even a sugar bowl. It was as though Jimmy Dale Evans had stripped every comfort out of his life. The house was bleakly furnished: sofas and chairs of an ugly green plaid upholstery and darkly stained pine; a coffee table made of varnished two-by-fours full of weeping knots; a nineteen-inch black-and-white television. No stereo; no musical instruments; no books. Brock wondered what lay underneath the surface of Jimmy Dale's cheerless life.

The case had been a pain in the ass from the get-go. Brock had taken it mostly because paraplegia was a big-money injury, a good jury issue. But also it had appealed to him because it seemed to promise some amusement. A guy who'd gotten his back broken by a falling stripper? *Hardy-har-har.* Good for a couple war stories at the Young Lawyers Section mixer, right? Well, that's what he got for indulging his goddamn sense of humor: the case from hell.

After a while Jimmy Dale rolled his wheelchair up to the table in the dining room, all cleaned up, his hair slicked to his head with water. Which reminded Brock of the other problem with the case: Jimmy Dale himself. Putting aside all the other things there were to dislike about him—he was irascible and thin-skinned and he droned endlessly about one conspiracy theory after another—there was what Brock supposed you'd call a *tic*: Jimmy Dale liked sticking needles into his legs. He'd be sitting there talking, and then Brock would notice he had a needle or a safety pin in his hand, and after a while spent toying with the needle, Jimmy Dale would suddenly jam it down into his dead leg. It was nauseating to watch.

And once Brock had noticed the habit—even if Jimmy Dale just had the needle in his fingers, not doing anything with it—he kept waiting, gritting his teeth, wondering when Jimmy Dale was finally going to sink the thing in his leg.

At the end of the day, Jimmy Dale Evans would have a little collection of brown dots all over the thighs of his polyester pants. Red pants with brown dots. Green pants with brown dots. Awful, awful pants, speckled with little brown dots.

"You've got to call the police," Brock said.

Jimmy Dale shook his head. "What, bring a bunch of big buff cops in here, let them tromp around acting all sorry for the poor cripple and then going back outside, making jokes about me in their squad cars? No thanks."

"He's just going to do something worse next time."

"Beside, the cops out here are in tight with this big burglary ring. That's common knowledge. You invite the cops in the house, they scope it out, two days later all your valuables are in the backseat of some scumbag's Pinto.''

Brock sighed. *What* valuables?

"Common knowledge, man. Common knowledge. Not to mention, that steroid freak girl was with him. Kit. She'll tell the cops a bunch of lies, just like she did at your disciplinary hearing.''

Brock didn't say anything. He couldn't help watching the needle going around and around in Jimmy Dale's fingers.

"You know I'm right," Jimmy Dale said. "It'll just make things worse.''

Brock nodded. "Jimmy Dale," he said hesitantly. It was time to change the subject. "Somebody came out to my house last night. Left a threatening note. My grandfather tells me it's the same kind of note as this Shakespeare guy has been leaving, the one that's been killing all the lawyers.''

"What kind of note?"

"It was like a dead lawyer joke. Then I got a phone call telling me to drop your case.''

Jimmy Dale's protuberant eyes narrowed. "You know who's behind this don't you? It's Giddens. It's got to be.'' The needle hung poised above his thigh.

"I don't know," Brock said. He didn't say it, but it was the thing he'd been thinking all along: Giddens didn't have the kind of qualities it would take to ingratiate himself to a four-year-old. A guy who pissed on a paraplegic was unlikely to think of something that subtle.

"He came to my house," Brock said. "He played with my kid. I mean, my wife is very scared.''

The needle, hanging there above his thigh. Jimmy Dale's eyes suddenly locked on Brock's face. "Wait a sec. You telling me you're gonna drop my case? Just because of some lame threat?''

"I didn't say that.''

"I *need* you, man." Jimmy Dale's voice had a note of pleading in it, a vulnerability Brock hadn't heard from him before. "Look at me, for godsake! I can't even stop a man from ripping up my house, pissing on my head. Brock, man, you can't do this to me!''

"I've got my family to think about.''

"Oh, for goshsake." Jimmy Dale looked away, his eyes bleary with a sudden desperation. "After all we been through together?"

"All I said is I have to think about it."

"Yeah. Well, please . . . *please* don't think for long." The needle still hanging above the rust-colored polyester surface of his thigh. "I'm begging you, man."

And then the needle fell. Once, twice, three times into Jimmy Dale Evans's useless leg.

• 14

Detective Lieutenant Janelle Moncrief was a dark-skinned black woman with a low, thrilling voice. She was tall, solid-looking, very neatly put together, with lots of gold jewelry.

"Now explain to me again, Mr. Brock, how you knew Shakespeare was putting cards like this on the bodies." She was dangling a plastic evidence bag by the corner, swinging it back and forth, the cream-colored card Brock's daughter had given him looking innocuous inside the bag.

Brock had come in to tell the police about his experience from the night before. As soon as the uniformed cop at the front desk had seen the card in Brock's hand, he had gotten a funny look on his face and gone back to find somebody. That somebody turned out to be Janelle Moncrief, who identified herself as the head of the task force investigating the Shakespeare murders.

Brock explained about his grandfather, about how he knew a lot of lawyers and law enforcement types and that he had nothing better to do than call them up and con them into telling him things. It was from his grandfather, he explained, that he'd heard about the killer leaving cards like this on the victim's bodies. When he was done with his neat explanation, he smiled. The detective did not smile back.

"Well," she said finally, dropping the evidence bag on her desk. "That's not a piece of information that should be public knowledge. I'd appreciate your not spreading that fact around. TV people get hold of it, we gonna have umpteen million fools coming in here with dead lawyer jokes wrote down on napkins, toilet paper, wedding announcements . . ." Janelle

Moncrief sat down behind her perfectly clean desk, slid her feet out of her shoes, pulled a notebook out of her desk drawer.

"Mr. Brock," she said. "Do you have any acquaintance with Mel Prochaska?"

"He's the first guy that got killed, right?"

She nodded.

"No. Never met him."

"How about Lee Darden? Or Boyd Michaels?"

Shakespeare's second and third victims. "Michaels, no. Darden . . . I think I litigated a case against him once. Maybe six, eight years ago."

"Who won?"

"Hard to say. As I recall it was one of those cases that kind of withered up and blew away." Brock smiled. Again, the detective didn't smile back.

"Raymond Lata?"

Brock frowned. "L-A-T-A?"

"That's right."

"Rings a bell, but I can't remember exactly why." He paused. "Was he the one they found yesterday?"

"I'm afraid that's something I can't comment on right now." The detective tapped the desktop with her plastic fingernails. "Any reason to think this might be a hoax? Anybody that would want to scare you right now?"

"The only thing that comes to mind . . ." Brock hesitated. "I'm involved in a fairly tendentious case right now. One of the defendants, a guy named Mic Giddens, has falsely accused me of trying to bribe him. He's also assaulted my client. But, I don't know—this guy Giddens, he's not Mr. Subtlety. Sneaking around with kids doesn't seem like his way of doing things."

The detective kept tapping her fingernails on her desk.

"I'm saying, somebody has been breaking into my house, playing with my child, ingratiating himself with my daughter while we were literally standing in the next room, First, Giddens isn't the type. More importantly—I mean, all that trouble just to leave me a note? Doesn't make sense."

"I'm sorry, I'm not sure I follow."

"Come on!" Brock said. "If he wanted to leave me a

note, he'd have stuck it in the mailbox. Why go to all this trouble? He's got to have something else in mind.''

The detective glanced at him for a moment, then sat for a long time, staring over his shoulder. Finally she stood up, put out her hand. ''Well, thanks for coming forward with this information.''

Brock looked at her hand. ''Wait a minute,'' he said. ''Wait, wait, wait. I come in here with what looks like evidence that this Shakespeare guy is breaking into my house, sneaking around with my child, threatening my life, and that's *it?* Thanks for your help?''

The detective crossed her arms, her long shellacked fingernails sticking out from her sleeve. ''That's correct, sir.''

''Don't I get any protection? Isn't somebody going to talk to my daughter, get a physical description?'' Brock pounded his hand on the desk. ''Isn't somebody going to *do* something?''

The detective stood there for a while. ''We through now?'' she said finally.

Brock glared at her.

''Answer to your question, sir,'' she said. ''Yes, we will want to speak to your daughter. But I thought you said she was in Tennessee.''

''She is. But not forever.''

''Fine. We'll talk to her when she gets back. Other than that, sure, we can send a patrol car by your house periodically. In the meantime, we got to trot this card to forensics, find out if it matches the others. One thing at a time, Mr. Brock. One thing at a time.''

• 15

Lieutenant Moncrief picked up one of her shoes with her big toe, jounced it up and down under her desk. Nope, this Brock fellow's card didn't add up to being from Shakespeare. Far as they knew, none of the victims in the case were given prior warning. Had to be some kind of copycat trying to throw a scare into this guy.

She picked up the plastic bag with the card in it, stared at it for a while. It sure *looked* like the other cards, though— at least to the naked eye. Typewritten name on the front, joke inside. Well, not exactly a joke, but it was the same idea.

She picked up the evidence bag again. They were going to have to send the card over to the state crime lab, see if it was a match.

She called out the door, "Mitchell, you out there?"

A uniformed officer stuck his head in the door, a dumbass-acting white boy who was supposed to be doing footwork for the task force—although mostly he sat around shooting the breeze with the girl at the front desk. Might as well put him to some use. "Here. Want you to run this evidence over to the crime lab, tell them to put a rush on it, see if we got a match here."

The idiot white boy licked his lips, studied at the bag.

"What you waiting on, son? Hitch up the wagons and go!"

• 16

The song was everywhere. Brock had decided to duck into the record store at Underground Atlanta, and when he came into the store, the song was blasting over the stereo system. *Scream! Scream! Scream! Scream!* A sullen kid with long hair, baggy pants, and an incipient goatee stood behind the checkout counter, grooving to the song, jerking his head forward violently on the downbeat.

"I'd like a copy of that," Brock said, pointing at the CD cover behind the desk on a little stand that said: NOW FEATURED ON OUR CD PLAYER! He tried grooving his head a couple times, like the kid. Seeing how it felt. It felt like someone was sticking a fork in his neck, so he quit.

The kid looked at Brock's suit and short hair, scowled. "Back there," the kid said. "New releases section. Band's called One Eighty-Seven."

Brock considered upbraiding the kid for his poor attitude toward customer service, but then decided, hell, that wasn't the kind of thing a One Eighty-Seven fan would do. He walked back to the display, found a copy of the CD. On the cover was a parental advisory label and a picture of a skull with a drill bit sticking out of one eye socket.

Brock looked up, noticed a man coming in the front door—a tubercular face, hollowed-out cheeks, sallow skin, black eyes set back in bruised caverns of bone. His lips were pursed, going in and out like a toilet plunger. With him was a short gray-haired man with an empty face, oily graying hair, a red polyester shirt, red polyester shorts, and white tube socks pulled up to the knee.

The man's eyes met Brock's all the way across the store, then he looked quickly away.

Brock looked at the names of the bands. Metallica. Pantera. Alice in Chains. Ugly Kid Joe. Thinking, maybe he'd buy a whole stack of this shit, play it really loud on the stereo while he still had the house to himself. Wouldn't that be fun? But then the thought of the empty house made him feel vaguely depressed, and he put all the records except for "Scream!" back on the shelf.

As Brock walked toward the counter, the guy with the tubercular face was making himself busy in the Country section. Brock noticed his reflection in the front window of the store. The thin guy seemed to be ignoring the Hank Junior disc in his hand. Instead, he was staring at Brock—staring at him all the way to the front of the store. Black eyes in the window. It gave Brock a creepy feeling.

After Brock had bought the CD, he walked out of the store, down past a long stretch of storefronts, turned and looked back. No thin-faced man; no guy in red polyester shorts and white knee socks. Hell, maybe the guy wasn't looking at him, after all. Probably just feeling paranoid because of the phone call the day before.

Brock went down to the food court, had a bite to eat, then on impulse, went back to the CD store and bought a portable disc player. He left the store again, plugged in the earphones, listened to his new CD. The first song was terrible: really fast, really loud, and you couldn't even understand what the singer was yelling. He managed to make out the word *fuck,* though, which seemed to play an important part in the band's lyrical pantheon. Fuck the police. Fuck the diesels. Or was it, Fuck the dead girls? Fuck the death knells? Brock couldn't tell.

He walked out of Underground from the exit near the courthouse and headed up the hill, flipping to the next song. It was "Scream!" Much better. It was still loud, still full of ear-blistering guitars and screaming, phlegmy vocals, but the guitar hook was funkier, more intricate, and the tempo was a little slower than the first song on the disk. Not to mention which the singer seemed to have discovered some semblance of a tune in the song.

Scream! Scream!
Show you what I mean!
Scream! Scream!
Things aren't what they seem!

Things hadn't changed that much since Black Sabbath did the *Paranoid* album back in, what was it, seventy-three? Same old, same old. Brock smiled a little. *Damn,* he missed being a kid sometimes!

As he was walking along up Marietta Street he noticed a reflection in a shop window—a guy wearing a clown mask. At first Brock assumed the clown was probably a street performer who was doing his act down in Underground. But as he kept walking by window after window, and the clown began getting closer and closer, Brock started wondering why a street performer would be wearing a loose, oversized track suit and Reeboks. Besides, it was a Bozo mask, the orange hair sticking out from each side of the head. No self-respecting clown would pretend to be Bozo.

Brock began to feel faintly nervous, and a rope of pain began tugging at the side of his neck. He flipped off his CD player, walked a few paces further, listening for footsteps. Were they getting closer or not? Were they there at all? Brock turned around. The clown was gone.

Brock suddenly felt sheepish. Probably just feeling paranoid after what had happened to Grace.

He flipped the CD back on and continued up the street, turning when he came to the deserted pedestrian mall that led over toward the MARTA station on Peachtree.

Suddenly he saw a flash of orange out of the corner of his eye. Before he could react a firm hand grabbed him just above one shoulder blade and propelled him face-first into the window of an unoccupied shop. He was about to swing wildly at his assailant when he felt a cold piece of metal against his neck.

In the window Brock could see a reflection of the attacker's face. A clown mask. Orange hair sticking out on both sides of his head.

A hand came up and ripped the earphones off his head.

A whispered voice: "Don't yell, don't move, don't even think an unpleasant thought or I'll cut your throat."

"My wallet's in my back pocket," Brock said. "Take it. Take the CD player, too." He could smell the plastic mask—an odor that reminded him of childhood, of the smell of Halloween.

The sharp metal bit into his neck. A muffled whisper, barely audible from the mask: "Shut your goddamn lip."

Brock nodded. There was something odd about the voice. Like the guy was disguising his voice. Making his voice higher or lower or changing the accent or something. Brock couldn't quite make out what it was that felt wrong about the voice.

"Did she give you the concordance?" the clown whispered.

Concordance? Brock's mind went blank. What the hell was going on? That was the same thing Giddens had wanted from Jimmy Dale.

"Did she give you the concordance, counselor?"

"What concordance? I don't know what you're talking about."

"Don't fuck with me, you—"

Before the clown could finish his sentence, Brock heard a squeal of tires and the slamming clank of a car bottoming out against a curb.

The clown whirled, and Brock shook himself free of the clown's grasp. Behind them a big red car, a Cadillac, had swung off the street and up onto the deserted pedestrian mall.

"Shit," the clown hissed.

The heavily tinted driver's side window came down and a fist clenching a small snub-nosed revolver appeared. The gun flashed twice and two sharp cracks rang through the air.

"Get in!" came a voice from the Cadillac, and the passenger's side door swung open.

The clown tried to make a grab for Brock, but Brock was too quick. He dove for the door, jumped in, pulled the door shut, found himself sitting next to two men.

The Cadillac's tires howled and the big car leapt backward, fish-tailing into the street. The clown hurled himself toward the car, slammed into the hood, lost his footing, spun away.

"Go!" Brock screamed. "Now!"

The driver stomped the gas and the car surged away from the curb.

• 17

Shakespeare ambled over toward the entrance to the MARTA station watching the red Cadillac roar away. Smiling as the glare of polished chrome disappeared over the lip of the hill.

Perfect. Bye-bye, Mr. Brock. Say bye-bye.

Leaning against the wall, letting the lungs recover.

After a while, taking out a pocketknife and a bar of Ivory soap, 99 and $^{44}/_{100}$ percent pure. Starting in on a soap carving. It was Shakespeare's only hobby. Pretty soon a nice little sculpture took shape. A cute girl in a billowing dress and a bonnet. Little Bo Peep, something like that. An unspoiled child. 99.44 percent pure.

"Hey, lookee here." A voice at Shakespeare's elbow. A lady cop, grinning, motioning to her partner. "Where'd you learn to do that?"

"You got kids, officer? A cute little girl, maybe? Tickles a little girl to death, taking a bath with a soap carving like this." Shakespeare smiled. "Hold on, let me give her a name, you can take it home with you." Starting in with the knife, cutting some letters in the base of the carving, then handing it over.

The lady cop turned the soap statue over so she could read what Shakespeare had carved, then nudged her partner. "Grace. Ain't that the cutest name?"

• 18

"Close shave," the driver said.

"Thanks," Brock said. It was only then that he noticed what the two men looked like. Next to Brock sat a blank-faced man wearing red shorts, a red shirt, and white socks pulled up to the knees. The driver was lean and hollow-cheeked, with deep-set black eyes and sallow skin. Jesus Christ—it was the guy who'd been staring at him in the record store.

"Name's Gene Meales," the tubercular-faced man said with one of those thick hill-country accents that sounded like he was swallowing boiled eggs while he was talking. His lips went in and out a couple of times, sucking on something. "Want a Life Saver?"

"Thanks, no," Brock said. His heart was still pounding. Now that he was inside the car, he wondered if maybe he hadn't made a big mistake blithely hopping into a Cadillac with a couple of blank strangers. It all seemed a little too convenient.

"Peppermint," Gene Meales said. "My favorite."

"You were following me, weren't you?"

"Lucky thing, huh?" The driver's voice was flat and expressionless.

"Okay," Brock said, "what do you want? Talk to me."

"Grateful, ain't he?" The driver said to the man in the red shorts. He took out a roll of Life Savers, popped one into his mouth. "I got something to tell you about this Laughing Dolls thing. Something might help you out, bo."

"Oh?"

Brock looked at the driver, then at his companion. Where the driver had a look of ferrety intelligence, the passenger's face was slack, open, vacant. His graying hair was slicked down and appeared not to have been washed in a few days.

"Georgie's my older brother," Gene Meales said, indicating the slack-faced man. "He's what they call intellectually challenged. Meaning, he's a moron." Meales said this dispassionately, without apparent malice.

"Talk," Brock said.

The car slid effortlessly through the Peachtree traffic. The driver sucked on his Life Saver some more before answering. "Here's the thing," he said finally. "I happen to be a competitor of Mic Giddens and his people. Wouldn't mind seeing you and that Jimmy Dale character put a hurt on them fools."

"A competitor?"

"I own a place called Legs. Maybe you been there?" When Brock didn't respond, Meales said: "Also a joint down on Stewart Avenue called the Gold Mine."

Brock said, "Look, everybody seems to be under the misapprehension that this case is a big deal. It's not. Laughing Dolls holds a perfectly good property and casualty policy. They lose the case, the P&C carrier pays. No harm done. I don't see what the fuss is all about."

"I'm sure. I'm sure." Gene Meales took a right. "You aware the folks that own Laughing Dolls also own a bunch more clubs in town?"

"Who are you talking about? You mean, Mic Giddens?"

"They own, let's see ... Brassy, uh, Kandy Kane, also T&T Lounge, which is for our friends of the Affican-American persuasion. Plus Peggy Sue's, up on Howell Mill."

"Who's this *they* you're talking about? Laughing Dolls is owned by Mic Giddens."

Meales's lips worked doggedly at the Life Saver. "I read in the paper about your little situation, this disbarment deal they got going. You ever asked yourself why that coked-up, pumped-up Australian sumbitch is lying about you?"

"Sure."

"Figured it out?"

"Nope."

"Here's the reason, bo. See, Mic Giddens don't own Laughing Dolls, not really. He's like a front man. My guess, he's afraid you gonna poke around a little too much, maybe find out who *really* owns his place. That's why you got him and these other folks all worked up and anxious.''

The retarded brother, Georgie, reached surreptitiously inside his pants, started playing with himself.

"Georgie!" Meales said. "Cut that out. We got a guest in the car.''

Georgie put on an innocent face and took his hand out of his pants.

"So you gonna tell me who owns Laughing Dolls, Gene?"

"Would if I could," Meales said. "But I don't really know myself. Reason I'm telling you, I think you're the type of guy who could figure it out.'' He pulled up at the curb in front of a convenience store, took a big flash roll out of his pocket, thumbed off a twenty-dollar bill, handed it to his brother. "You mind letting Georgie out? He wants to get hisself a Slurpee.''

Brock got out of the car, let Gene Meales's brother out, then sat back down again.

"Why do you think *I* can figure out who these people are?" Brock said.

"You a lawyer, bo. The way they got everything hidden, who owns what, where the money goes, so on, it's a legal maze. Shell companies, lease-backs, all kind of inneresting stuff.''

"And you don't have any idea who these people are? I mean, why would they care if I found out who they were?"

"Could be some IRS exposure, could be, hell, anything. Point is, obviously they don't want you sticking your nose under their tent.''

"So where am I supposed to start?"

"That girl? Caitlin Cobranchy? I'm told she got her hands on some information.''

"Like what kind of information?"

"A list.''

"A list.'' Brock had a sudden bad feeling.

"A list, bo. *The* list. They call it a concordance. Complete index, who owns what. Once you know that, you can dig up the right pieces of paper, figure out how everything fits together.''

Brock didn't like the way this felt. How exactly had he

ended up in this car? Had there been a chase at all? Had Gene Meales been sitting there waiting for him? If so, how had he known when Brock would be there? Finally he said: "I'm still not clear what your angle is."

"My angle, Mr. Brock, is these sumbitches are taking over the town. You realize how much it costs running a nude dancing establishment nowadays? Use to be easy as falling off a log. But all a sudden everybody's raising the stakes. Can't compete if you ain't hiring girls off the Playboy channel, doing radio ads, print ads, billboards, all that crazy shit. After a while it starts crimping your cash flow. These sumbitches, the ones that own Laughing Dolls, they built three new places in the past year and a half. And these boys got deep, deep pockets. So now I got spend all this money on advertising just to keep my head above water. This keeps up, I'm gonna go under."

"Wouldn't that be sad," Brock said dryly.

Georgie came running out of the store with a half-eaten microwaved hot dog and a giant orange Slurpee. His legs flopped as he ran, like his knees were connected to his thighs by a pair of loose springs. Brock let Georgie back in the car. They drove in silence back to Brock's office. The Caddy nosed over to the curb and Brock got out.

"This concordance," Brock said, leaning in the window. "Where am I supposed to find it? I can't even find Caitlin."

Meales reached into his pocket, handed something to his brother. "Give this to the man, Georgie."

"Here," Georgie said, smiling as he put his hand out the window. In his fingers was a small, bright object. A key.

Brock narrowed his eyes, looked at the outstretched key. "What's that for?"

"Caitlin Cobranchy's house."

"Get real," Brock said. "I can't do that." Georgie kept holding out the key, an expectant look on his face. Finally Brock took it. The key was sticky with orange Slurpee and hot dog grease.

"After you get the concordance, a old buddy of mine gonna give you a call. Name's Fat Man. I advise you listen to him."

Meales reached across his brother, pulled the door shut. It slammed with the dull crack of a breaking femur.

• 19

After an hour of so of trial preparation in his office, Brock took a break from his work and called the number for his in-laws.

"Well?" Dru said. Her voice had a snowy edge.

"Well what?"

"Are you going to drop the case?"

Brock hesitated. He didn't look forward to breaking the news to her. "Look, I've got ethical obligations. Client abandonment is a disbarrable—"

"Don't give me that, Brock. You know as well as I do it wouldn't take you ten minutes to find some fairly respectable schmuck out there who'd happily take over the case and split the fee with you."

Brock looked at the stack of deposition transcripts and pleadings sitting on the conference room table. A blizzard of paper. "How's Grace?" he said finally.

"Give me a break, Brock."

"Look, Dru, please. I have to think about this. Okay? I can't decide something like this at the drop of a hat."

After a brief pause, Dru said, "Yeah, well maybe that answers my question."

"Dru—"

"I've got to go, Brock." Grace's voice crowed about something in the background. "Your daughter needs her lunch."

Brock sat at his desk for a while, looking at the key in his hand. Was there really a killer out there that had his name on some death list? He felt a stubborn anger welling up, a refusal to bow to somebody else's will. But whose: Dru's or the killer's?

The key, a winking conspirator in his hand.

The hell with it. Why not?

Caitlin Cobranchy lived over in Little Five Points, a sort of art freak neighborhood over on the east side of Atlanta—the kind of place where lots of kids with nipple rings and silly haircuts lounged on the curb drinking beer out of paper bags, hiding the bottles under their coats when the cops cruised by.

No-show witnesses. Brock started to fume thinking about it. And Caitlin Cobranchy, well, she'd been a problem in the case from day one.

Brock had only spoken to her once. In a case like this, sometimes it was best not to put things in writing until as late in the game as possible; instead of making a key witness sign an affidavit or do a deposition—and thereby giving up strategic information to the other side—sometimes you just interviewed the witnesses. That was what Brock had done with Caitlin: asking questions, taking no notes, storing the information away in his head.

She had surprised Brock a little. He wasn't sure if there was such a thing as an average stripper—but if there was, surely Caitlin Cobranchy wasn't it. He'd expected a hard-bitten country girl, maybe a bleached blond with skin already turning to bread crust from the sunlamps and the cigarettes. Instead, he found a bright, pale, well-spoken young woman, achingly beautiful, with loopy, crazy auburn hair and long legs. But the most striking thing about Caitlin was that every delicate line of her face seemed smudged with melancholy. She was the kind of woman that men wanted to take care of, to buy cars and furs for, to hold and whisper "everything's going to be all right" to in a dark bed at three o'clock in the morning.

So when Caitlin had said that sometimes she got a little claustrophobic in dark offices and wondered if maybe they could go sit up on the roof and look at the view while they talked, Brock had said, Sure, why not?

And she had stood up there on top of his tall building for

a long time, just staring at the sky, her eyes wide and sad as a lost child's.

After she'd talked about the incident—her account of which matched Jimmy Dale's on all important points—they had sat over near the edge of the roof, just talking. Brock had had things he needed to do, but she was beautiful and sad and her loopy red hair danced in the wind; and so if furs and cars and three o'clock in the morning were out of the question, a little conversation didn't seem so unreasonable. They talked about this and that, and finally it had just popped out: "I guess this is a jackass question, but . . . why stripping? Why you? You don't seem like the type."

She'd put her arms around her knees and stared out at the smoggy distance, and then she'd told him that it was a good way of making a living and that her body didn't mean much to her anyway. A body, she'd said, was no different from dirt or trees or river water; it didn't amount to much of anything, not to her, anyway. Brock had asked her what she meant by that, but she just looked into the wind, her hair coiling and leaping around her face, and said nothing more.

After that Brock had shown her a picture of Grace. *Do you treat her right?* Caitlin had said. *I don't see her as much as I'd like,* he'd responded. Caitlin had repeated herself: *No, but do you treat her right?*

Sure, he'd said. *Sure I do.*

After they finished talking Caitlin climbed over the fence that surrounded the roof of the building and stood only inches from the edge. "How high are we?" she'd said.

"Fifty-two stories. Please. Please be careful."

But the height obviously didn't bother her. Her face had glowed with excitement. "How do you get any work done?" she'd asked. "If I were you, I'd just come up here and stare at the sky all day."

But when she'd said it, she hadn't been staring at the sky: she been looking over the edge, smiling fondly down at the long, long fall.

As he drove to her apartment, Brock thought back on that odd, indeterminate conversation. It didn't offer up many clues to why she'd skipped out on him.

He pulled up in front of her house, set the brake on his

car. The apartment was in the bottom floor of a big house
on Colquitt. The wide front porch sagged a couple of inches
on one end, and the white clapboards had scaled here and
there. Someone had tried to cheer the place up by painting
the sashes a pale blue a few years back, but that flash of
optimism was now peeling and water-stained. Brock sat for
a while, looking at the blank windows of the house. Was this
prudent? Was it smart? No. But the whole situation was so
screwed up, it was beyond prudence or common sense.

While he was mulling the thing over, still considering
whether or not to go in, he took out his new CD, stuck it in
the car stereo and listened to "Scream!" for about the fifth
time of the morning. Suddenly his blood was rushing anar-
chically through his veins and he wasn't thinking about Grace
and Dru anymore, wasn't thinking about prudence or smart-
ness or his career. All he was thinking about was that taunting voice on the phone and the awful succubus of fear that had
stirred in him at that moment. It made him feel vaguely
ashamed—that moment of fear—and now he wanted to make
things right, turn the tables. *Fuck* the son of a bitch! He
clenched the key in his hand until it bit into his fingers.

And suddenly Brock had the heady sensation that something was blossoming inside him, some aspect of his character that he'd never recognized or at least never paid attention
to before, something inside him that was illicit and just a
little twisted.

So the hell with it. He was going in. If it meant tearing
this place apart, so be it: he was going to find the bastard
that had invaded his home, that had messed with his daughter,
that had frightened him so badly. Going to find his ass, going
to take Shakespeare down.

The song was moving and throbbing in his head as he
walked into the dark foyer, the front door clattering shut
behind him. He knocked several times on the door of Caitlin's apartment. No answer. The key was in his hand, but for
some reason, he didn't want to put it in. He felt as though
he were on the edge of some kind of betrayal. Of himself?
Of Dru? Of Caitlin? He wasn't sure.

The key in the lock. He turned it, heart thumping, and
called through the door: "Hello? Hello!"

Quiet inside. He slipped inside.

The apartment was hot, stuffy, dark. There was a faint smell of rot on the air, like someone had forgotten to wash the dishes. For a moment Brock felt slightly nauseated. Trap, he kept thinking. Maybe this was all part of Mic Giddens's game to add to his disbarment troubles. He pulled the shade aside, peered out the front window to see if anyone was coming. The street was empty, quiet.

Brock walked around the apartment. It was furnished with hand-me-down chairs and tables, drunken-legged, scarred, the varnish flaked away leaving patches of bare wood. Cheap reprints on the wall—big breasted Chagall nudes, Matisse cutouts, and similar signposts of the Bohemian youth aesthetic. Lots of books. Brock ran his finger down one shelf: Dickens, Hume, Danielle Steel, Genet, Proust, Stephen King—all literary bases covered. The apartment was reasonably neat and well kept-up.

A desk in the corner of the living room. Address book. Coffee can full of bright colored markers, Bic pens, yellow pencils. Three-hole punch. File folder that said ODI, WENTWORTH on the tab. A small stack of envelopes, unaddressed, unsealed, no letters inside. Nothing that jumped up and shouted *index of bad guys*. He rooted through the desk drawers, found some old W-2 forms, a stack of ring-bound notebooks from college, rubber bands, tooth-marked pencils. Nothing interesting to speak of.

Brock felt peculiar poking around in a stranger's house. There was something uncomfortably pleasurable about opening drawers, picking up photographs, running his finger across a piece of underwear. On the wall in the bedroom hung four cheaply framed, antique erotic photographs, black and white—the kind they used to call French postcards. The first was a picture of a blowzy nude woman reclining on a fringed couch, eyes closed, breasts lolling. She could almost have been dead. Probably late-nineteenth century. Two more nude women in various states of undress.

Brock stopped to study the fourth picture. At first he'd thought it was a boy, staring fixedly at the camera. But then he realized it was a hermaphrodite: the genitals of a man, the breasts of a woman. She or he, or whatever you called it, was holding the leash of a small ghostlike dog that appeared to have dematerialized as it moved during the slow exposure of the plate. The hermaphrodite's face looked neither happy nor sad. Odd. Wasn't the kind of thing Brock would want hanging over *his* bed.

Nothing in the apartment suggested that Caitlin had left town. Her closet was full of funky black dresses; the top drawers of her bureau were stuffed with bras and panties; in the kitchen unwashed dishes lay in the sink.

Next to Caitlin's bed Brock found a stack of snapshots. He picked them up, leafed through them. Vacation shots; Florida, maybe. Caitlin in a tiny bathing suit, doing a campy supermodel pose on a beach. Caitlin, pretending to light the fuse on a huge cannon at some oceanside fortification. Caitlin, arm-in-arm with a thin guy, dark-haired and dark-skinned. Brock had the feeling he recognized the guy from someplace but he wasn't sure where.

The next picture showed the dark-haired guy standing by himself on a jetty. He wore a white baseball cap, a pink polo shirt, boat shoes, no socks, and he was squinting against the sun. Without knowing quite why he did it, Brock slid the picture into the pocket of his coat.

Brock checked the small notepad by the phone to see if she'd left any numbers on it. Nothing there.

As he was about to leave he had a thought. He'd seen on TV shows people taking a pencil and rubbing it against pieces of paper to find the impression of things written on an earlier page. Why not give it a shot? He took the pencil sitting next to the phone, rubbed it gently against the pad of paper until something began to resolve.

A phone number: 787-2819.

Brock picked up the phone, dialed. On the other end an answering machine picked up. "You've reached Maid Rite," the recording said; "Atlanta's premier in-home maid service. If you wish to leave a message . . ."

Oh well. Nice try.

As he put the pencil down Brock glanced at the floor. A piece of paper lay face down, halfway under the bookshelf that the phone was lying on.

He picked up the paper. At the top, written in blue ink, it said, GIDDENS. Ah-ha. Then underneath that, in the same hand, two words: ODI, WENTWORTH.

That rang a bell, didn't it? Wait, that's right. He'd seen

the same words on the file folder that lay on the desk in the corner of the living room.

Brock walked over to the desk, picked up the manila folder. Inside was a stack of photocopies two inches high. On top was a lease agreement of some sort. The address, 2629 Piedmont Road. That was the address of Laughing Dolls. Listed on the line that said LESSOR was a name. But it wasn't Mic Giddens: it read: Wentworth, Ltd.

Brock smiled. Now maybe he was getting somewhere. Only ... what the hell was Wentworth, Ltd.? He'd been litigating Jimmy Dale's case against Laughing Dolls for two years and he'd never heard that name before.

Underneath the Wentworth lease was another rental agreement, this one for a property with an address Brock didn't recognize. He flipped through the stack. A bunch of leases. Also a couple of boilerplate partnership agreements. ODI, Ltd. Wentworth, Ltd. Then came articles of incorporation for something called Brassy, Inc. He kept flipping. More contracts, leases, partnership agreements.

At the bottom of the stack he found it. A typewritten sheet, a list of names. Yes! This was it. *This* was the concordance everybody was so desperate to get their hands on. At first he didn't really notice the names, just the fact that there were several names followed by a series of code letters. The first name had the letters BP-P following it, then a slash, then W-L, then some more letters.

It was only after puzzling over the codes for a moment that Brock actually read the first name on the list: Mel Prochaska.

And the next name: Lee Darden. Then Michaels, then Raymond Lata.

Before he had a chance to scan all the names on the list, Brock was interrupted by a loud noise, someone banging on the front door. Brock's pulse fluttered, adrenaline foaming through his veins. Brock grabbed the folder. Time to get out of there. He headed for the kitchen where he'd noticed a door into the back yard.

More banging. A voice, a man calling: "Anybody home?" A grating voice. Flat Australian vowels. More banging. "Caitlin? Hey, Caitlin?"

Brock yanked on the back door of the apartment, but it wouldn't give.

In the living room he heard the sound of a key going in the lock, metal on metal. Brock set the manila folder down on the stove, heaved harder on the door, but it wouldn't open. The sill was caked with heavy green paint, freezing the door closed. Probably hadn't been used in years.

No time. He'd have to hide while Giddens did whatever he was going to do, then he'd hit the road with the concordance.

In the other room, the lock clicked.

Brock tiptoed across the kitchen toward the pantry. He heard the squeak of metal on metal, the knob turning: the front door opening as he slid into the pantry, pulled the door closed. The smell of flour, brown sugar, nameless rotted foods.

In the other room, the crowing hinges of the front door. Footsteps creaking inside the house.

Sweat beaded up on Brock's face. He stood without moving for a long time. Could Giddens hear him breathing? Sonofabitch. *Scream! Scream! Scream! Scream!* The song beating its way through his mind.

The sound of drawers being pulled open, something thudding on the floor.

Footsteps getting closer. Through the crack between the door and the frame, Brock saw a shape appear in the doorway of the kitchen. He leaned forward, put an eye to the crack. It was Giddens all right, standing in the doorway, his broad back to the kitchen.

That was when Brock noticed the folder. He'd set it down on the stove trying to get the back door open; and in his hurry to hide in the pantry, he'd forgotten to bring the folder with him, the one with the concordance in it.

Brock leaned a little closer to the crack, trying to see better. The pantry was full of cans. As he was leaning toward the door, his sleeve caught one of the cans and it fell off the shelf with a bang. Giddens whirled, and suddenly there was a gun in his hand, a big nickel-plated revolver. His eyes were bloodshot, nose red-rimmed, cheeks flushed. He pointed his gun at the pantry, eyes narrowed. For a long moment Brock thought Giddens might fire. But then he lowered his gun, mumbled something, turned away.

As he was about to leave the kitchen, the Australian did a

double take. Staring at the stove. *Damn it!* He'd seen the folder.

For a moment Giddens looked puzzled. The big man looked slowly around the kitchen, then chuckled softly, tucked the folder under his arm and walked out of the room. The sound of his footsteps receded, and then the front door slammed.

Brock slumped into the wall. Jesus Christ! He'd been so close. Giddens must have come here for the same reason he had: to get the concordance. Brock could have kicked himself. What an asshole, leaving the folder on the stove.

Still, cowering there in the dark closet, he felt an odd sense of triumph, a feeling that he had passed unscathed through some forbidden place.

Scream! Scream! In his head, the angry howl of guitars.

• 20

After the two men had left Caitlin's apartment, Cleland Davis had sat for a while in the front seat of his Ford and smiled. Judge Vinyard was going to find this very interesting.

Just went to show you what a smart investigator could do with an inspired hunch. First the tall thin white guy goes into Caitlin's house, then a few minutes later Mic Giddens goes in. Ten minutes later, out comes Giddens, carrying a big fat manila folder. Had to be it. Had to be this concordance thing, this list. After Giddens drives off, out comes the tall thin guy. Cleland Davis had written down his license plate number, figured he'd run the tag through the DMV, find out who this cat was.

Next stop, figure out how to get that concordance from Mic Giddens. Davis slipped the Ford into gear and headed back toward his office.

• 21

Shakespeare walked into Meales Steaks, a chophouse in a black neighborhood on the south side of town, threaded his way through the labyrinth of dark rooms until he found Gene Meales, sitting at his usual table. He had a couple of hard-looking girls with him—too much suntan, too much silicon filling out their shirts. Plus his brother, the retard, of course. Shakespeare had never seen Gene Meales without his brother.

Meales was talking on the phone, the candle in the middle of his table doing nothing to soften the harsh lines of his face. When he saw Shakespeare coming, he said, "Hold on, I'll call you back," and hung up.

"Siddown," Gene Meales said. He waved the back of his hand at the bimbos. "Girls . . ."

The bimbos left and Shakespeare sat down.

"Here's a new one," Shakespeare said. "What do you get when you send the Godfather to law school?"

"I don't know. What do you get if—" Gene Meales stopped, grimaced. "Look, you want to know how it went or not?"

Shakespeare winked. "Tell me."

"No problem," Gene Meales said. "Picked him up, told him what you wanted, gave him the key, dropped him off."

"No hitches?"

"We have any hitches, Georgie?" Gene Meales said.

"I spilled my Slurpee and Gene got mad," the retarded brother said.

"See?" Gene said. "There you go. No hitches."

Shakespeare slid an envelope across the table, three hundred and fifty bucks inside, got up to leave.

"Wait a minute," Meales said. "That joke. What *do* you get when you send the Godfather to law school?"

"An offer you can't understand."

Gene Meales looked at him for a minute, his lips going in and out, in and out, sucking the hell out of his Life Saver. Didn't even crack a smile.

Shakespeare turned around and left. What a moron. Made you want to puke sometimes, the people you had to deal with just to get a little justice.

• 22

Jimmy Dale Evans was rolling his wheelchair around and around in his tenant's living room. The tenant was a pale, mopey-looking guy with a small, hairless beer gut, no shirt, and a pair of light-blue polyester shorts.

Jimmy Dale had no particular profession. He did bookkeeping for a couple of marginal liquor stores and dry-cleaning shops, and he owned some marginal rental property. It was in the service of extracting some overdue rent from this loser tenant that he had dragged Brock along to one of his slummy duplexes.

"Roaches?" Jimmy Dale was saying. "You complain about *roaches?* Just look at this place!" He gestured contemptuously at the crushed Pabst Blue Ribbon cans, the plate of half-eaten macaroni and cheese, the stained fried-chicken bucket lying on its side under a cigarette-scarred coffee table.

The tenant had a truculent look on his unshaven face. "Yeah, well, man, I ast you to send out a extermilator three weeks ago. And here it is, you still ain't done it." He licked his lips. "'Ass why I ain't paid the rent yet."

Jimmy Dale's eyes were looking unusually blue, unusually protuberant. "No, what you gonna do is give me . . ." Jimmy Dale stopped his wheelchair suddenly. "How much money you got on you?"

The deadbeat tenant folded his arms across the bag of spindly ribs that was his chest. "I don't see that's your bidness."

"You think I brought my lawyer along just so I could jaw with you?" Jimmy Dale said, nodding at Brock. His eyes

90

had gotten wider, his face a shade redder, and his jaw was sticking out in a threatening manner.

"You can't thow me out," the tenant said finally. "I know my rights. You got to send the extermilator."

"Give me a hundred bucks," Jimmy Dale said. "A hundred now, I'll send the exterminator tomorrow. Then you give me the rest on payday."

Brock sighed. He wasn't getting paid for this kind of bullshit. He'd come to talk trial prep with Jimmy Dale and here he was getting dragged into this ridiculous dispute.

The tenant said, "I ain't got no hunnerd bucks."

"Well, how much you got?"

The tenant hesitated, pulled a moist-looking wad of bills from his pocket, started fumbling around with it. With surprising speed, Jimmy Dale's wheelchair leapt forward. The tenant tried to pull his hand back, but he was too late—Jimmy Dale had already snatched his money away.

"Hey!" the tenant said. "Hey, goddammit!"

"Get me out of here, Brock," Jimmy Dale said, holding tight to the wad of money.

"Sorry I had to put you through that," Jimmy Dale said as Brock rolled his wheelchair down to the car. "But these people, they make you mean. You take these people living in Section VIII housing, they're paying seventy dollars a month out of their own pocket, guess who's picking up the tab—the other four hundred dollars?" Jimmy Dale Evans glared up at Brock from his wheelchair. "You and me, that's who!"

"Uh-huh," Brock said, helping Jimmy Dale out of the wheelchair and into the front seat of the car. Brock had heard all of this, one version or another, at least a dozen times before. Deadbeats, welfare cheats, blacks, Jews, the federal government, the Japanese, the Department of Housing and Urban Development—to hear him tell it, all of these groups had conspired at one time or another to gang up *personally* on Jimmy Dale Evans.

"And guess what? They don't cut the grass, they don't clean the windows, they don't fix the roof. Seventy dollars a month, see, they got no investment. Result being, they're dirty, they're lazy—"

"Look," Brock said, starting the car. "Hate to interrupt, but trial is in three days and there's a lot of ground to cover."

Jimmy Dale blinked. "Oh," he said. "Yeah."

"I've recently learned that Mic Giddens is not the main guy behind Laughing Dolls," Brock said. "Apparently there's a group of investors behind him. Now obviously something connected with this case must have the potential to hurt them badly. If we can figure out what that is—who's behind Giddens, what their angle is—then maybe we can exploit that weakness in trial, or else force a fat settlement before the jury comes out. So what I need you to do is tell me everything you know about Laughing Dolls, anything you can think of that might shed any light on these investors."

Brock swung around a turn, heading out of the neighborhood where Jimmy Dale's rental units were. It was a mostly black neighborhood, scattered with working-class whites who couldn't afford to bail out as the property values fell. Another five, ten years, the white people would die off, drift away; it would be all black. Ten-year-old Cougars and Monte Carlos and Coupe de Villes parked outside the four-room white-frame houses.

"I was just a part-time bookkeeper, so I don't know that much," Jimmy Dale said finally. "Day to day, Giddens runs the show. It was my understanding that there's some kind of limited partnership behind the business. I always figured that was mostly Giddens's money. But maybe he only has a little piece of the action and somebody else was the big player."

Brock nodded. "So you don't know who the money men were?"

Jimmy Dale shook his head. "Like I say, I was only in there once or twice a week. Giddens did the cash receipts, the deposits, that kind of thing. He also made payments to the investors. The registers are computerized, so my job was pretty cut-and-dried: set up a little accounting package, make sure everything goes in the right general ledger accounts, tidy things up, reconciliation, print out the reports."

"But the money must have flowed from the club to the investors, right?" Brock asked. "Didn't you see who the money went to?"

"It's not that simple. There was a limited partnership that owned the business. Then another partnership owned the property. There was some kind of freaky leaseback arrangement. I think the whole thing was designed so that the real profits went to the partnership that owned the property. Laughing Dolls itself, it didn't even break even most of the time." He tapped on the dashboard a couple of times. "My guess, it was being run to generate tax losses."

Brock was stumped. What was at stake here? Less than a week from trial and Brock had the sinking feeling that there was still a big piece missing from the case. It obviously had something to do with the names on the concordance. But how was it all connected? He mulled it over until they reached Jimmy Dale's house.

"Tell me more about the financial end of the business," Brock said once they were sitting in Jimmy Dale's living room.

"You *really* want to know?" Jimmy Dale rolled his wheelchair over to a closet door, pulled it open. Inside was a stack of four banker's boxes. "These boxes, they're full of account records—deposits, check receipts, account transfers. Four years' worth."

Brock's eyes widened. "You're kidding me. You saved all this crap?"

"Sure. Made copies of everything I touched." His protuberant blue eyes narrowed. "You never know when someone's gonna try and *screw* you."

"How come you never told me about this stuff before?" Jimmy Dale blinked. "You never asked."

Brock lugged two of Jimmy Dale's boxes back to his office, set them in the middle of his conference table, and hauled out the stacks of paper. It took a while to make sense of the information, but once he did, he figured out that all the daily receipts were deposited into a bank account that was held under the name of Laughing Dolls.

From there it looked like most of the money went back into the operation of the club—liquor suppliers, payroll, and so on. But whatever was left at the end of the month was then moved to another account, which was listed as GCB, Ltd.

That money, in turn, was immediately funneled to an account held by something called Wentworth Properties. Brock

searched for records in the box that might explain what Wentworth Management was, what it did, who owned it. Same
name that showed up in the folder he'd found—and lost—in
Caitlin Cobranchy's house.

But there was no indication in Jimmy Dale's bank records
of who was behind the name.

Dead end. Brock felt like kicking himself for letting Giddens get away with that damn folder. And especially the
concordance.

• 23

"**Y**ou heard about Raymond Lata?" Brock's father said.

"He's the guy that got killed yesterday," Brock said. "I keep thinking I recognize his name, but I can't remember where I know him from."

Brock and his father were having lunch together, as they did every Wednesday, in the restaurant at the Piedmont Driving Club—a club in which Brock was emphatically not a member. The Piedmont Driving Club, bastion of hokey, snotty Old South bullshit. Brock hated the place. And yet every Wednesday at 12:55 P.M., there he was, having lunch with his father, Garrett C. Brock, Jr.: bastion, keystone, buttress—choose your favorite metaphor—of the old privileged classes of Atlanta.

"Raymond is—or was—a member of the firm," his father said.

"*Your* firm?" Brock's father was managing partner of the third largest law firm in Atlanta, one that had been around in some form or other since the nineteenth century.

"Yes. Civil litigation." Brock's father wiped his mouth, then scrutinized the white linen napkin for a moment. Brock's father, like Brock himself, was tall and thin. But instead of Brock's taut, harried look, his father appeared calm, reserved, almost scholarly. He wore gold-rimmed glasses with small round lenses over soft, courtly eyes that camouflaged a very shrewd and very tough mind.

"Awful thing," he added. With that, Brock's father moved on: "Forgot to mention. Thursday night. Reggie's having his portrait unveiling. Sent you tickets, didn't I?"

Reggie being Judge Reggie Vinyard, one of his father's law partners, the sly head of the firm's municipal bond department.

Brock said, "Do I *have* to go?" The idea of another portrait unveiling didn't excite Brock much. Sitting around making conversation with a raft of social-climbing lawyers, wading through all that chicken cordon-bleu and gummy sauce, and listening to the boring speeches about Reggie Vinyard's selfless and noble spirit? What a pain in the ass.

"Make some good contacts. Plus, Reggie likes you. Ought to be there."

A thought popped into Brock's mind: that band, One Eighty-Seven—the ones that did "Scream!"—storming into the restaurant of the Piedmont Driving Club with their weird tattoos and their four-hundred-watt Marshall stacks. *Scream! Scream!* All the rich old farts looking up from their well-done chops, startled and indignant.

"Yeehah," Brock mumbled.

"Pardon?" Brock's father raised his eyebrows slightly.

"Nothing."

His father looked at him for a moment, ate a small bite of fish, then said: "This Jimmy Dale Evans mess. The phone call, the note, the disciplinary hearings? What's your game plan, son?"

Brock looked up from his steak. Momentarily Brock wondered how had his father heard about the threatening phone call or the note Grace had given him? But of course he knew: his father's business was not just law. It was information. Anything of importance that happened in Atlanta, his father managed to find out before the papers, before the TV people, before almost anyone.

"I don't know," Brock said. "I had a little setback yesterday at the hearing. My main witness no-showed."

"Press Cain told me. Not good. Something going on under the surface, don't you think?"

"You mean, is the disciplinary action against me connected to this threat and the dead lawyer joke card?"

"Right."

"I have to assume so. I don't know what to do about it, though. Any thoughts?"

"Me?" Brock's father acted surprised.

"Sure. What would you do?"

"I'd drop the case."

"Why?"

"Is it high profile? No. Anybody watching? No. Thus, no downside. Walk away now, your professional reputation suffers not one whit. Hand it off to someone else. I'm all for professional responsibility. But not at the expense of your life. Or of those you love."

Brock felt a stab of pain in his neck. "I don't know, Dad. Ethically, I don't feel too comfortable with that."

"Recuse yourself. Find a stand-in. Wouldn't take ten minutes. Your client? He's still adequately represented."

Brock nodded slowly.

"Set up a meeting. Press Cain and this Giddens character. Horse-trade. You drop the case; he goes back to the disciplinary board, says: 'Sorry, fellows, big mistake.' "

"And you think that'll be enough to get me off with the disciplinary board? They'll smell some kind of deal a mile away."

"Doesn't matter. If their complainant comes back and says he lied, they have to believe him."

Brock nodded glumly. But it didn't matter. He'd pretty much made up his mind to gut the thing out.

After the meal Brock reached into his coat pocket to get out his wallet and his fingers struck the edge of a photograph, the one he'd taken from Caitlin's bedside table. A thin, dark-haired man in a pink shirt.

He pulled out the photograph and held it for his father to see.

"You recognize this guy, Dad?"

His father squinted at the picture. "Where did you get that?"

"You know who it is?"

His father's puzzled eyes looked up from the picture. "Son? That's Raymond Lata."

• 24

Brock's secretary called to him through the door of the wood-paneled conference room where he'd spread his trial prep material. "Merlee Pentecost? You know her?" she said. "Should I take a message?"

"Who is she?"

"Says she's a lawyer. Calling about Caitlin Cobranchy."

Brock's pulse quickened. So maybe somebody knew what the hell had happened to Caitlin. "Send me the call."

The phone twittered and Brock picked up the receiver.

"Brock?" a woman's voice said. "I don't know if you remember me. We went to law school together? My last name used to be Dawson."

"Oh, sure," Brock said, remembering. Merlee Dawson. She'd been a kind of oddball: there had been a whiff of trailer park about her, a kind of naïve hick gaucheness that Brock had found appealing among all the law school yupsters. "My secretary says you have some information about Caitlin Cobranchy."

"I'd like to meet with you in person if I could. It's kind of a long story. Unfortunately I've got something going until pretty late this evening."

"Where? I could meet you there."

She named a church out in Stone Mountain, a place called the Temple of the Living Water.

"You're going to church on a Wednesday night?" Brock said.

"Not exactly," Merlee said.

*   *   *

A few minutes later Brock got a call from the detective, Janelle Moncrief. "Something came up," she said. "Mind if I drop by, chat with you a little further?"

"Why not?" Brock said, looking around the conference room at the litter of deposition transcripts and filings from the Evans case. "I'm only trying to prepare for my biggest trial of the year."

"Is that supposed to be sarcasm?" The cop's voice flat, unaccented.

Half an hour later Lieutenant Moncrief was in his office, sitting in a big green leather chair. Her face was oddly unreadable, her eyes hooded. The detective picked up a picture of Grace off the desk, looked at it solemnly.

"This your child?" she said.

Brock nodded.

"Cute little thing. Her hair just so pretty." She set the picture down. Something about the look on her face was making him nervous.

Moncrief turned her head away from him slightly. "This case been bothering the fool out of me," she said finally. "Something doesn't add up."

"How so?"

"Most murders aren't too complicated. They're solved before the case jacket gets any thicker than a matchbook. But this Shakespeare thing? You ought to see my filing cabinet. Not just medical examiner's reports, forensics, crime-scene photographs. Nah, last I checked we had a hundred and sixty-seven supplementary witness reports—friends, relatives, neighbors, business associates, potential witnesses, possible suspects, cranks, confession nuts. Hundreds of pieces of crime-scene evidence. All kinds of strange and unusual forensic test reports. I mean, we got seventeen inches of files . . ." Her voice trailed off. "And you know what? So far we got nothing. Not a damn thing to go on."

The detective picked up the picture of Grace again, squinted at it, staring for an uncomfortably long time. When her deep voice came out again, it was slow and quiet—like she was talking more to herself than to Brock.

"See, classically you got two types of what we call multiple murderers," she said. "You got your spree killers and you got your serial killers. For all the stuff you read about serial killers, all the publicity they get, spree killers are actually more common. *Way* more. Spree killer, I'm talking about some fool who cracks one day, caps a bunch of people with whatever weapon's handy, keeps killing till he gets caught or killed or maybe even kills himself. You're looking at marginal characters: low self-esteem, drug or alcohol problems, irascibility; lots of them got a long history of mental problems and criminality. Hard people to get along with.

"Spree killers, what happens is they get in a position where a bunch of things go wrong—the marriage fails, they lose a job, they drinking too much, whatever—and finally, it's like somebody just throws a switch. Click. Time to kill. They grab a gun, an apple corer, a baseball bat, *pow, pow, pow,* that's all she wrote. What marks these guys is the kills are clumped together. All the crimes happen within a matter of hours, at most a couple days. Then it's over. Out like a lamp."

Janelle Moncrief scratched the side of her face with her bright yellow fingernails, making a dry rasping noise that set Brock's teeth on edge.

"But a serial killer, ooh, they a whole different breed of cat," the detective went on. She turned and looked out the window. "These are cold people, ice people. A serial killer kills somebody, waits a while, kills somebody else, waits a while. We talking patient, careful, I mean real *obsessive* people.

"But that coldness, that iciness, it's just a facade. 'Cause somewhere underneath, baby, these people got a lot of rage. Rage so strong that it warps the mind, till the person's whole brain gets focused on one thing—killing, killing, killing, killing, killing, killing—playing over and over in they mind. And what that leads to, eventually they get into a pattern. You know, like biters, stranglers, slashers—maybe they cut the victim up, stick them in the freezer like that Daumer freak up in Wisconsin. Point is, once they find a pattern that makes them feel good, they gonna do it again and again. There's a rhythm to it. Like sex, Mr. Brock, I'm talking about a biological rise and fall, hunger and satiation. Hunger and satiation."

The detective looked up suddenly as though surprised to find herself in Brock's office.

"But the killing, Mr. Brock, even the killing starts to lose its edge. So they got to speed up the rhythm. Feeling cold, got to have more. Feeling cold, got to do it again. Usually the first kill is separated by months, even years, from the second kill. But as time goes on—if they aren't caught quick—they start to get bolder, more obsessed, crazier . . . and the killings get closer and closer together."

"Okay," Brock said.

"Another thing. Most serial killers have some kind of sex thing going. Not all, but an awful lot of them. They rape before they kill, maybe. Or there's sexual mutilation, or, you know, they masturbate on the corpse. Excuse me, I know this is kind of nasty stuff, but you see what I'm saying? Some kind of sex thing."

Janelle Moncrief paused for a moment, fixed her eyes on Brock's face. "You understand why I'm telling you these things?"

"No," Brock said. "I guess I don't."

"What I'm saying is, this guy Shakespeare just doesn't feel right. First three times, I'm like, okay it's hard to tell. But by this last guy, Lata, all of a sudden I'm sure of it. Something awful strange going on here."

"How so?"

"Let's tick these things off." She held up her large hands, counted off the words on her fingers. "Ritual. Planning. Rage. Rhythm. Sex. Increasing frequency. That's the score-card. So how does Shakespeare's scorecard look? Well, we got ritual, right? Because we got the card with the joke on it, sexual mutilation, various other things that happen every time. Check that off. Planning? Check. Obviously we got that, because we got the card all typed up and everything. Rage? Check. This freak's killing people and cutting their johnnies off, he sure enough got to be mad about something."

She paused. "Rhythm." Raising her eyebrows slightly, looking off in the distance. "Rhythm. This guy just comes out of nowhere on March ninth, and then it's like every two weeks, somebody else goes down. Like a metronome. So we got rhythm, right?"

Brock nodded.

Moncrief shook her head. "No. No, see Mr. Brock, it's all wrong. We got *too much* rhythm. You know how in a piece of music there'll be a part that speeds up a little, a part that slows down? That's what gives it feel, humanity. That's how you know it's a human being and not a computer that's making the music. But this, no, huh-uh! It's like a metronome, Brock. Every two weeks, like a gotdamn metronome! Got no human feel to it.''

Janelle Moncrief's dark eyes stared into Brock's face, unwavering.

"See? See? *See?* It's like this guy read in a book how to be a serial killer, now he's trying to hit all the marks. But the rhythm's wrong. It's lockstep. The first two kills are too close. He should have waited a month, a year, working up his courage thinking about it, stewing over it, worrying, planning. But not this boy. Mel Prochaska goes down. Two weeks later, boom, there goes Lee Darden. And then what happens? They don't accelerate. Like he's taking his time. I don't feel no biology here. It's like our boy marked it down on his daily planner, you know, every two weeks, big red X mark. Time to kill.''

Moncrief was staring at him with haunted, bewildered eyes. "There should be this . . . *dance!* You see? There's a dance between the killer's rage, his obsession—see? see?—and his fear of being caught on the other! The rhythm picks up as the killer grows more bold.'' The cop was pumping her fists slowly in the air, up and down, like she was milking a giant cow.

"You're saying—''

"Let's drop back and look at the ritual again. Okay, we got the card, the dead lawyer jokes, and then we've also got the mutilation. But here's the problem. These kills are all done in public spaces. Public spaces?'' The detective shook her head slowly. "Huh-uh. A serial killer wants to *enjoy* the kill, savor it. See? He wants to find a safe place—indoors—maybe even in his own house. Or else in a real isolated place—a cabin in the woods, something like that. He wants to control the body, violate it, overpower it, enjoy it in its death throes.

"I'm giving out information I trust you will keep to yourself, but other than the first vic, Mel Prochaska, these bodies have not been moved. Forensics proves it. No drag marks, no dirt under the heels, no evidence of restraint either pre- or postmortem. This guy's popping them and dropping them. Most serial killers, they got a Crime Scene A and a Crime Scene B. They make the abduction one place, then they move the person. Might only be down to the basement or up to the attic, but they move them. The really bad stuff? It always happens at Crime Scene B. The rape, the mutilation, the torture?'' She tapped Brock's desk with a bright yellow fingernail. ''Crime Scene B.''

Brock said, ''And all we've got here is Crime Scene A.''

Moncrief nodded. ''With this joker, Crime Scene A is the whole ball of wax.''

They sat for a while.

''You got a match on the card I gave you,'' Brock said finally. ''Is that what this is about?''

Janelle Moncrief looked up with hooded eyes. ''Couriered it over this morning, told the GBI lab folks to put a rush on it. I don't know why I told them that. It stood to reason the thing was a copycat, a fake, had nothing to do with our boy.''

''But it matched.''

Janelle Moncrief smiled thinly. ''Oh, yeah. Perfect match. Shouldn't have, but it did.''

''Why shouldn't it?''

'' 'Cause if our boy's the real thing, a real serial killer, then he's breaking stride, changing his habits.''

''Why would he do that?''

''That's my point. I don't think he would.''

''Then . . .''

A smile blossomed on Moncrief's face. ''This bastard's a fake. He's no more a serial killer than you or me.''

''You're losing me. You're saying he killed four people but he's not a serial killer?'' Brock looked at her for a minute. Then something struck him. ''Wait a minute. You're saying there's something else going on here? Something besides the killings?''

The corners of Moncrief's mouth tightened. ''Look, I shouldn't be telling you all this, but I will because . . . well, look, here's the point. See, I believe there's a connection between these four lawyers. I mean, obviously they're all lawyers. But there's something deeper.''

The muscles in Brock's neck started to tighten, threatening to snap like overstretched rubber bands. The concordance.

All four victims' names were on the list. Should he tell her about the concordance, about how he'd broken into somebody's house trying to find it? No. No, he couldn't take that chance—not with the disciplinary action still up in the air.

"Like what?" he said.

"There's the rub, Mr. Brock. We can't figure out what that connection is. They crossed paths now and then. But nothing that connects all four of them." She waved a long finger at him. He noticed her yellow nail polish was cracked along the tip of one nail. "But there *is* a connection. I can smell it."

Laughing Dolls. That was the connection. But right now Brock couldn't tell her. Not quite yet. Besides, he didn't have anything tangible to show her. No concordance, no documentation, no nothing. The pain in his neck started snaking up into the back of his skull.

Suddenly Janelle Moncrief's face tightened. "You play chess, Mr. Brock?"

"When I was a kid. Not anymore."

"You remember that guy Bobby Fischer? They said he could plan, I forget, eight moves in advance, something like that—every single permutation and combination."

Brock just looked at her.

"I think we got a chess player here." Moncrief raised her eyebrows slightly. "And right now, all he's doing is pushing pawns around."

Brock nodded.

"The reason I'm telling you all of this is that I think our boy is about to shift gears. He sent you that card for a reason, and soon maybe we'll find out what that reason is."

"You think he's going to try to kill me?"

Janelle Moncrief squinted out the window. "My guess, you're just another pawn in his game. He gets a mind to sacrifice you, he'll do it without two seconds' thought." She turned and looked Brock in the eye. "So if you think of something, some kind of connection between these victims, you better call me and call me quick." The detective slipped her feet back in her yellow shoes and stood up. "God help us when he starts moving his queen."

Brock watched her leave, the muscles knotting and writhing in his neck.

*   *   *

Back at the office, another phone call.

"Brock." A man's voice: the high, clear tone of a counter-tenor. "You find the concordance?"

"Who is this?"

"Names aren't necessary. You can call me the fat man."

Brock felt a prickling sensation on his arms, running up through his shoulders. "I didn't get the concordance," Brock said.

Long pause.

"Well what in the holy heck happened?" Before Brock could answer, the fat man said, "No, wait. Don't answer that now. You and me need to talk."

"I'll be in my office until—"

"That's no good. Meet me at the Painted Lady down on Stewart Avenue."

The Painted Lady. Another strip joint. "How's nine sound?"

"I'll be there." The phone went dead.

• 25

The gun store was in a run-down strip mall on Buford High-way, sandwiched inbetween a Precision Tune and a Ray's Rent-2-Own. Brock sat in his car for a long time, his palms sweating, thinking: *Why am I here? This is crazy.*

But he knew why. Shakespeare was out there somewhere, out there playing out his game, and he was closing in on Brock, and Brock had to do something, had to be ready. Four men ended up lying dead in parks and dumpsters and dry creekbeds because they hadn't been ready. Had they all met a guy in a clown mask when those awful last moments came? Maybe so. Well, that shit was not going to happen to Garrett Brock.

He played the song by One Eighty-Seven one last time before going into the store.

The man in the gun shop wore a nylon holster in a desert camo pattern strapped to his leg, a large automatic pistol nestled beneath its Velcro flap. His face was mild and deeply lined, and his hair had the same hard, oily sheen as his merchandise.

"What kind of a piece we looking for?" he said.

"I have to admit," Brock said, looking at the rows and rows of guns inside the glass counter, "that I've never fired a handgun before in my life."

"Lucky you," the man said. "Lucky you."

"How's that?"

"First time with a girl, first time in a airplane, first time riding bareback on a horse—there's only so many first times.

After that, you spend the rest of your life looking back at them, wishing it could feel that way again." The clerk smiled in fond, crooked remembrance.

"I see," Brock said.

"You thinking, what, automatic or revolver?"

Brock looked up and down the row of neat, hard little machines, glistening with gun oil. His heart was beating and he felt hot, sweaty with embarrassment.

"I wouldn't know, really."

"Personal protection, am I right?"

Brock nodded.

The gun salesman still had that fond look on his face, like he was thinking of his first girl's delicate thighs—when he came up from behind the counter with two weapons. One was a black automatic, the other a stubby silver revolver. He laid them reverently on a red velour cloth.

Looking at the guns, Brock had an odd feeling in the pit of his stomach, and—unaccountably—the pain in his neck seemed to lessen for a moment. A little wisp of excitement was worming its way out of some hidden recess in his brain.

It struck Brock, as he stood there looking at the two guns, that sometimes he felt like an old-fashioned watch that was starting to run down: He would meet with his father and come away feeling as though he'd eaten something poisonous; he would lie in the dark, sleepless, after making love to Dru, unable to summon up a sense of wonder at the thing that had passed between them; he would lose or win a case and be unable to find a good reason for the verdict, much less any particular satisfaction in the victory. Maybe everyone started to feel this way at his age, started to feel the keenness of life leaching away.

Yet here—*here* in front of these small and intricate killing machines—he felt the stirrings of a youthful excitement. So maybe the man with the oiled hair and the camo holster was right. There were a few things left, a few things that he had yet to do.

"Glock Model Seventeen," the man said, pointing at the automatic with his middle finger. "Constructed of your basic space-age polymer. Carries ten rounds, nine-millimeter parabellum load; gives you a good combination of control and stopping power. Ten in the clip, one in the pipe. Manufactured right up the road by the fine folks at Glock up in Marietta. Fine, fine piece for personal protection.''

"Can I pick it up?" Brock said.

The man smiled his secret smile. "Indeed you may."

Brock picked up the gun, hefted it in his hand. His heart was beating hard against his ribs. The gun had a lively, primeval weight to it, like a club or a sharp rock, and he felt inside himself a sudden and profoundly joyous yearning to destroy.

"Pull back the receiver, then flip that lever with your thumb," the man said, pointing again with his middle finger. "That's it. Just like in the movies. Cocks your hammer, chambers your round."

Brock pulled back the slide, flipped the lever and the weapon stirred sleepily in his hand. Brock squinted over the rear sight, aimed it at an advertising on the wall: a woman with a Remington carbine at port arms. He sighted on her coy smile. It gave him a light, sick feeling.

"See?" The gun salesman said. "Ain't that lovely?"

"Do you give lessons?" Brock said.

After they'd cleaned up the paperwork, the salesman took him back to the gun range, a dim hot room with the feeling of a stretched-out toolshed. The salesman pointed the gun at a target shaped like a man's torso down at the end of the long room. "Like so. See? Weight evenly distributed, sight on the thug with your right eye. Then you pull the trigger, real gentle—like you'd squeeze a baby girl's wrist.''

He handed Brock the gun. Brock worked the slide, aimed, tightened his finger slowly.

"Gentle, gentle." The man's whisper: rapt, tender.

The gun cracked, jumped in Brock's hand and he felt a sudden whirling inside him—a whirling, mad rage. He gasped.

"See?" the gun man said. "What I tell you?"

When Brock had emptied the clip, he stared at the black outline for a moment. A shadow of someone, unknown. There was a wonderful sharp smell in the air, and the skin on his hand felt extraordinarily sensitive. A cloud of impossibly pale smoke caught a shaft of sunlight, drifted and dissipated in the languid air.

When he got back to the office Brock called Dru, and in the conversation it slipped out that he'd bought the gun. After a long silence, Dru said, "What's going on with you, Brock? I don't understand you lately."

"What am I supposed to say?"

"You're supposed to say, 'Okay, Dru, I experienced a moment of insanity. Now I'm going back to the store to tell the guy I made a mistake. I'm going to drop the case. I'm going to make life normal again.' *That's* what you're supposed to say." Her voice was full of a dead, threatening calm.

Brock didn't say anything. He felt angry—angry at Dru—and was not sure why.

"Guns are for killing people," Dru said.

"Yes. That's exactly right."

A moment of silence. "Are you getting ready to *kill* somebody? Is that what you're thinking?"

It was only then that Brock realized that, yes, that was more or less what he had in mind. He wanted to find Shakespeare and kill the son of a bitch. He couldn't think of any good reason why that was what he wanted, but that's the way it was. Again, he said nothing.

"This is not some macho fantasy, Brock. This is not a fucking Schwarzenegger movie."

"I am not a child, Dru."

"Well, you're behaving like one."

"I'm not so sure," Brock said. "I don't have any frame of reference for what I'm going through right now. I've never felt this way before, and I don't know if it's childish or not."

"It *is,* Brock!" Dru said. And there was, for the first time since she'd left the house, a thin hysterical edge creeping into her voice. Was it fear for Grace? Fear that he'd do something stupid and get hurt? Or maybe it was just that she'd lost control of him, that for the time being he had wobbled out of her comfortable domestic orbit.

After a moment Dru sucked in her breath sharply.

"I can't talk to you," she said. The note of hysteria had

grown in her voice. "I can't . . . I can't—" There was a long moment of silence. Then the line went dead.

Brock noticed that he'd been holding the Glock in his lap through the whole conversation, messing with it, caressing it. He threw the gun on the bed in horror, stared at it for a long time. A black thing in the middle of jade-green sheets.

And then he picked it up again. It felt good—*right*—in his hand.

• 26

Brock was standing at the rear of the huge sanctuary of the Temple of the Living Water listening to Merlee Pentecost tell him things about his neck. "I could tell you had neck problems the minute I saw you," she said. "There are dark spots in your aura."

"My aura," Brock said. "Of course. My aura."

"Yeah. You've got blocked meridians. The *chi* isn't flowing properly, and so it makes your neck hurt."

"*Chi?*"

"You know, your bio-energy. Your life force. It's from the Taoist medicinal systems of China."

Brock nodded. Great. Evidently Merlee had turned into a New Age fruitcake in the past ten years. He scanned the huge, semicircular sanctuary, listening to the pumping sound of a hard rock band. Cramming the pews in front of them was a vast mob of kids, mostly boys, their eyes riveted to the stage. "So what am I supposed to be looking for?"

"There." Merlee pointed toward the stage. There was some sort of show going on: big weightlifter-types in red, white, and blue singlets talking about the bible, doing various circus strongman tricks—breaking handcuffs, deadlifting railroad ties, that kind of thing—while Christian heavy metal blared away from the speakers above the stage.

"Where?"

"The top of the pyramid. See?" Merlee hadn't changed much. She was still a bottle-blond, petite, with bright green eyes and one side of her mouth pulled down a little as though she were trying to stifle a derisive laugh. Her lips and fingernails were painted a bright red, and a pendant of smoky quartz hung between the marvelous curve of her breasts on a silver chain.

Brock squinted. On the stage or the altar or whatever it was, the group of weightlifters were forming themselves into a human pyramid.

"I don't get it," Brock said. "What's going on here?"

"Evangelical bodybuilders," Merlee said. "The act is called 'His Strength.' I represent them."

"You do entertainment law?"

"That's right."

"So how do you know Caitlin?"

"She has neck and back problems, just like you. I do bodywork on her."

"Bodywork?"

"Massage therapy, kinesiology—you know, unblocking the meridians. I do it as a sort of hobby. Of course, ultimately, physical problems come from some sort of disjunction in one's emotional life. Caitlin's a very disturbed young woman. Speaking of which, have you considered some sort of holistic therapy, Brock?"

"Would you consider voodoo to be holistic therapy?"

Merlee made a face, pointed at the stage again. "Look."

"I'm sorry," Brock said, "but I'm still trying to figure out why you brought me here."

In front of them the crowd of boys pumped their arms in time to the beat while a guy with a microphone whipped them into a frenzy talking about how Jesus could move mountains and—by implication, Brock presumed—beef up one's pectorals.

"You don't recognize that one?" Merlee was still pointing at the short weightlifter who was bench pressing a great deal of weight while lying on top of the human pyramid. The crowd roared encouragement.

Brock shrugged.

Merlee said, "The show's almost over. Follow me back-stage and we'll talk to her."

"*Her?*"

"You still don't get it? That's Kit Fulghram."

*   *   *

Fifteen minutes later the show or service was wound up, and they were in a long green-carpeted hallway. Brock followed Merlee as she turned into the first door on the left. Inside were a bunch of sweating, pumped-up young men down on their knees in a circle around a square-jawed, sincere-looking guy with huge biceps and a limp bible draped over his hand.

"Scuse me, y'all," Merlee said. "You know where Kit is?"

The guy with the bible looked annoyed at the interruption. "Two doors down."

They started back out the door. Merlee stopped, turned, and said, "Y'all were fabulous. I mean it, fabulous."

After they were back in the hall, she said, "All those good Christian bozos—take a guess how many of them *haven't* tried to jump my bones?"

"Uh . . ."

She held up one long finger, tipped with a bright red nail. "One. You believe that? Only one. I never met as big a bunch of jackasses as bodybuilders."

She knocked on the second door, opened it a crack. "You decent, Kit?"

"Why?" the voice said.

"It's Merlee. I've got a guy with me. We want to talk to you."

"Okay."

Merlee turned and whispered, "Let me talk, okay? You have to handle her in a certain way."

They went in. The room was small, some sort of office that didn't appear to be used much, with a bare desk and a cabinet along the wall. A gym bag lay on the floor by the door. Kit Fulghram sat in a chair, staring belligerently at a small bible in her lap, as though trying to scare it into revealing the secrets of God, fate, destiny.

Merlee smiled. "Are those pressure point exercises I showed you helping your shoulder?"

Kit rotated her arm, the muscles dancing under her skin. "Yeah, thanks. Still a little stiff, but it's getting better." Then she looked down at the bible again.

"Well, well," Brock said. "You get to the part yet about bearing false witness?"

"Hold on, Brock," Merlee said sharply, grabbing Brock by the arm.

Kit Fulghram looked up, took a moment to recognize him. The light came on in her eyes, and then she looked accusingly at Merlee. "What *is* this?"

"We just came to ask you a couple questions," Merlee said.

The bodybuilder glared at Brock, then Merlee, then back at Brock again. Her weirdly tanned thighs and shoulders were bunched with muscle. Brock couldn't tell for sure, but it looked like maybe there was some razor stubble on her chin, too.

"Well I got nothing to say," Kit said.

"Look, let's just forget about Brock's situation here," Merlee said. "Let's just forget about what you told those guys at Brock's disciplinary hearing. Okay?"

Kit looked back down at her bible for a moment, her lips moving silently.

"Maybe we shouldn't forget that just yet," Brock said.

Merlee's green eyes flashed at him, then she turned back to the bodybuilder. Brock frowned. He was not happy with all of this. Hell, he probably shouldn't even be here, not with his disciplinary action still pending. His gaze rested on the gym bag. It had a Reebok logo on the side and the zipper was undone. Inside were some clothes, a roll of Ace bandages, a couple of small brown pill bottles.

"The reason I'm here," Merlee said, "is that Caitlin Cobranchy is a friend of mine. She was supposed to come over for some bodywork and she never showed. Nobody knows where she is."

"I don't know nothing about that," the girl said sullenly. A muscle twitched in her cheek.

"Look, Kit. Caitlin's a friend of mine. Okay? I want to make sure she's alright." Merlee had an intent look on her face.

Kit's face showed no expression.

"Come on. Is she okay? Did Mic send her off to Florida for a couple weeks or something?"

"You just want the money," the bodybuilder hissed. "She's a whore and you want her whore's money. 'You have polluted the land with your vile harlotry. Therefore the showers have been withheld and the spring rain has not come.'"

"Don't be quoting scripture at me, little sister." Merlee's voice came out like a whip crack. "You can't win that game. 'And you, O desolate one, what do you mean that you dress in scarlet, that you enlarge your eyes with paint?'" Merlee walked over and fingered Kit's red singlet. "'In vain you beautify yourself. Your lovers despise you.'"

Kit's burly orange legs squeezed shut, closing the bible between them. A muscle danced in her thigh. "You can't talk that way to me," she said.

Merlee's voice dropped back to a soothing contralto. "I'm just trying to help a friend, okay?"

Brock leaned over and pulled out a bottle full of round white pills from the gym bag. "Anadrol-50," he read off the side of the bottle. Steroids. He threw it back in the bag, pulled out another one. "Halotestin. Didn't I read this stuff turns little girls into little boys?"

Kit glared at him.

Brock shook the bottle, the pills rattling inside. He was starting to get mad now, thinking of the way it felt to sit in front of those self-satisfied jerks from the bar association, leering at him while Mic Giddens lied about him. "You better talk to us, Kit. You better damn well start talking right now."

Kit said nothing, her face a furious mask.

"Is this why you're growing a damn beard?" Brock said, thrusting the bottle of hormones at her. As soon as it came out, he realized he'd said the wrong thing. But he couldn't help it; all the anger he'd been feeling lately was rising up again, flooding his head. "Is this why you aren't a woman anymore?"

Kit suddenly sprang from her chair, knocking him to the floor, her hands around his throat. A scream—eerie because it was not just angry but anguished—exploded from her lungs as she grabbed him. The pill bottle flew from his hands and he stumbled backwards, tripped, fell to the floor. His skull banged against the tile, and for a moment he felt only the sick numbness of the concussion, and his vision went gray.

"Kit!" It was Merlee's cigarettes-and-whiskey voice, snapping through the grayness. "Kit! Get off him right now!"

After a moment Brock felt the hands release their hold around his neck.

"Sit down, Kit!" Like she was giving commands to a dog. Kit stared down into Brock's eyes, her orange face a mixture of hatred and fear. She gave him a last squeeze, shoved him slightly, then got up and sat back down in the chair.

"I'm sorry about that, Kit," Merlee said. "I'm sorry about the way Brock's behaving. But you've got to understand that your testimony has the potential to destroy his life. You can't blame him for being pissed off at you." She kneeled down in front of the hulking woman, held her hand. "Come on, Kit, you've got to talk to me. What's going on?"

Suddenly the bodybuilder's shoulders were quaking and tears were leaking out of her eyes. "I don't know," she said, her voice warbly and indistinct. "I just—Mic's been acting so weird lately. It's like he's paranoid or something."

Merlee stroked her hand gently. "I know. I know."

"He's been real scared. He's been doing too much speed, too much coke. And he keeps going on about how somebody's been stalking him."

"Stalking him? Who? Why?"

Kit looked up, her skin streaked with black makeup under her eyes. "I don't know. Something that might come out in Jimmy Dale's trial—it might make him look bad."

Merlee looked questioningly at Brock, who was sitting against the wall, his head throbbing. Brock shook his head slightly, causing a cord of pain to shoot down his spine.

"I don't understand."

"I don't either. But he just keeps saying if they have the trial, the cops are gonna arrest him."

"For what?"

Kit picked up her bible, rubbed an orange thumb across the cover.

Merlee's voice was gentle, insistent. "For *what*, Kit? What are the cops going to arrest him for?"

Kit slumped over until her forehead was resting against the bible. "For killing those dudes," she whispered.

Merlee looked at Brock, then back to Kit. "Are you saying he's Shakespeare?"

Kit's shoulder's shrugged slightly. She didn't answer.

Merlee narrowed her eyes. "Did he kill those lawyers?"

Kit shook her head. "I don't know nothing about that."

"What about Caitlin?" Brock said. "Where is she?"

"I don't nothing about that either."

"You're sure?" Brock said.

Kit looked at him for a moment. There was something hopeless in her eyes. "Yeah," she said finally. "I don't think Mic did nothing to her, though. He likes her."

Out in the parking lot, Brock said, "Sorry, Merlee. I didn't mean to fly off the handle that way."

"I understand," Merlee said. "You kind of touched a raw nerve. I get the feeling she has some gender identification issues to work out, you know what I mean?"

They stopped at Brock's car, and he looked at her for a minute. Why had Merlee brought him out here? If she wanted to find Caitlin, she could have done this herself. So why the interest in his case? "I don't buy it," he said finally.

"Really? I believe her," Merlee said. "If Mic did anything with Caitlin, I don't think Kit knows anything about it."

"That's not what I mean." Brock looked Merlee in the eye. "I don't think you went to all this trouble just because Caitlin didn't show up for her weekly back rub."

Merlee flushed, pursed her bright red lips, looked away for a moment. She didn't say anything.

"I'm right, aren't I, Merlee?"

A headlight from a car far across the lot caught her face and for a moment Brock could see the lines around her eyes, age starting to trench its way into her skin.

"Back in law school," she said after a moment. "What did you think about me?" Looking out across the dark parking lot.

Brock had a funny feeling he'd better be careful how he phrased his answer. "How do you mean?"

Still looking away from him. "Like, maybe I was kind of a redneck? A hick? An amusing rube?"

There was an edge to her voice, but Brock wasn't sure whether it was some kind of vague self-loathing or whether she was just making fun of him. In law school she'd always been on some kind of crusade or other, raising money or organizing protests or passing around petitions. Battered women, tort reform, multicultural curriculum—it had always been something. She always had the enthusiasm level cranked up to ten.

"Most people in law school were too cool, too temperate to care about anything but bagging a lucrative job," Brock said. "The thing about you, you always seemed to be finding something *new* in the world."

What he didn't say was that back in law school he'd always kind of despised Merlee—for her peroxide hair, for the cigarette she'd always been smoking, for the way she didn't seem to discriminate much about where her enthusiasms wandered. It had seemed to him that she'd been chasing the rush instead of looking for a cause that made sense.

But that sparkle, that naïve enthusiasm, had worn well. It was like a physical presence—and an alluring one at that.

Merlee raised her eyebrows slightly, and the corner of her mouth twitched. "I had the biggest crush on you," she said.

Brock stifled an urge to smile. So that's what this was about.

"Of course I was too chickenshit to do anything about it." She ran her hand through her hair, looked up at Atlanta's blank, starless sky. "I wanted like hell to be like those rich girls, you know, with the casual hair and the Saab 9000 and the stockbroker boyfriend. But I just didn't have the confidence." She cackled suddenly. "So maybe that's why I called you up. Just thought I'd try to get a look at you after all these years, see what I'd missed."

Merlee turned her back on him then, folded her arms against her small ribcage.

"Well, that's sweet as hell," Brock said.

"Oh please! I'm worse than that steroid freak in there. I mean, I know you're married." When she turned back around, Merlee had a look of disgust on her face. "Normally I'm not this pathetic, I promise."

Brock didn't say anything.

"So, look, now the cat's out of the bag, can I buy you a beer or something?" she said. "Sometimes I play a little pool down at the Austin Avenue Grill."

Brock smiled gently, touched her arm with his fingers. "I'm sorry, but I've got to be somewhere. Really."

Suddenly she reached toward him, pulled his face down

and kissed him lightly on the lips. Then she turned and jogged away.

As he drove toward the last bruised scrap of sun on the horizon, he kept seeing her in his mind, her skinny shoulders catching the light, the barely visible wrinkles beneath her liquid green eyes, and he found a strong, scary, chaotic desire stirring inside. The raw taste of lipstick lingered in his mouth.

I shouldn't be here, Brock was thinking as he watched the girl on the platform.

What was it about naked female flesh that made him feel so strange, so desperate? She was looking back at him, violet-eyed, spreading her legs, thrusting her pelvis at him. Buck naked except for a pair of high silver pumps. She started walking down the bar toward him, turning once, looking over her shoulder at him, turning again, coming toward him.

I should just get in the car and go home.

He was in the Painted Lady, the club where he was supposed to meet the fat man. It was a working man's beer-and-a-chaser kind of place. Most of the dancers looked okay when they were fifteen or twenty feet away, but up close you started to see the hard lines on the face, the blurred tattoos, the nascent fat erupting like cauliflower beneath the skin of their thighs.

This one was different, though. The closer she got, the better she looked. Ever since he'd left Merlee an hour earlier, he'd felt a lingering and shamefaced hunger for female companionship. And this wasn't helping. *I shouldn't be here. The fat man hasn't showed, so I should get out of here right now.*

She leaned over, let her fine young breasts sway near his face. He could see her heart beating, the pulse throbbing in her neck. Her hair was short, spiked, dyed an unnatural velvety red. She moved slowly, her upper body gyrating, her nipples drawing slow, insistent circles in the air. Her lips were parted in false passion.

"Can I dance for you?" she said. "*Just* for you?"

120

Her pubic hair was aggressively waxed to accommodate the G-string that had come off a few minutes earlier. God, he wanted to reach up and grab her, upend her, spread her legs, bang her right there on the bar. Ridiculous!

A moment or two passed. Her eyes studying him, calculating.

"Yes," he said. "You can dance for me."

She smiled, revealing straight, shockingly white teeth. It took Brock a moment to realize that they were dentures. Christ, what had happened to her teeth? For a moment he felt queasy.

But as she came down off the platform and walked toward the back of the bar, his eyes rested on her smooth buttocks, and he felt the dumb stirrings of desire again. To watch her flesh bounce under him. Oh, shit. He wondered vaguely if he was being taken back here just so she could dance for him— or for something more. Would she grind herself against him? Sit in his lap and nuzzle him with her secret lips? He'd heard they did that in some of the clubs. Lap dancing—wasn't that what it was called? The beers were running around in his head, muddying his thoughts.

Or maybe she'd offer him a blow job. Take her teeth out and do him with her gums.

Shit. Shit. Shouldn't have had all those beers. Not thinking clear enough.

And then in a flash he saw an imagined tableau: Dru and Grace holding hands, staring at him with flat gazes as they shared a moment of feminine disgust at the weakness and duplicity of men.

He should never *never* have had that first drink, that was the problem. If he'd just sat there and drunk soda water, then he wouldn't have had the urge for the second beer or the third. And if he hadn't had the third beer, he'd still be sitting at the bar waiting—waiting for this alleged fat guy.

The girl went through a doorway in the back, past a bathtub-sized bouncer with a stupid, malevolent face. They entered a small room.

Brock felt for a moment as though he had walked forty years into the past. It wasn't just the dingy fifties decor, or Hank Williams's high nasal whine as he sang "Take These

Chains From My Heart'' from a boom box over by the bricked-up window. It was something else, a scent of perversion, of the rich, baroque ugliness that used to lie so comfortably beneath the soft, plain surface of the Old South. It was a South that now lay buried beneath a tidal wave of concrete and migrants and franchise restaurants, beneath the insufferable and soulless *spiffiness* that had conquered the South a generation or so ago. But in that room Brock felt the old atavistic terrors and lusts lying close to the surface: he could almost smell the days of axe handles and lynchings and camp meetings and county line juke joints.

Or maybe it was just the smell of the fat man.

The fat man was seated in a large troughlike piece of furniture, a strange contraption which was not quite a bed, not quite a chair, not quite a hammock. Rolls of fat heaped up here, sagged there, so that the man contained within the chair or bed or hammock resembled a giant glob of soft-serve ice cream with a man's head lolling on top. His features seemed tiny because his head was so large, his cheeks cascading down into his vast trunk. His longish blond hair—elaborately styled in the manner of, say, Jerry Lee Lewis—glowed in the blue light of the bare circular fluorescent bulb suspended from the ceiling.

"Thank you, Petunia," the fat man said, smiling at the naked girl.

"Oh," Brock said. "I get it." There was an odor in the air of unwashed flesh. The fat man, he supposed. You got that huge, you just couldn't quite clean all that moist, infolding skin.

Brock felt a pang of fear, a speeding of the heart, and something clenched up in his neck. What if Shakespeare knew he was here, had maybe even followed him? In a place like this anything could happen. What if it was a trap?

"That's her real name, you know," the fat man said. "Petunia. Isn't that delicious?"

"You're the guy I was supposed to meet?" Brock said.

"How's my hair, Petunia?" the fat man said. "Is it alright?"

The naked girl walked over and touched the fat man's coif with practiced hands. It shimmered with beads of hair spray. "There," she said. "That's better."

"Thank you, my dear." The fat man waved a hand covered with gold rings at the girl. He even had a ring on his thumb. "I'm very particular about my hair, you see, Brock."

"What's this all about?" Brock said.

The fat man studied him for a while. "Your hair," he said finally. "It needs something. It's just not right."

"My hair's fine."

"Petunia, get your things, give Mr. Brock a haircut."

"I don't want a goddam haircut."

"Oh, nonsense. Sit down." One ringed hand levitated from the mass of his body and made a dainty gesture at a barber's chair bolted to the floor on the other side of the room. "Isn't a haircut part of the drill before you go to trial?"

"Usually," Brock said.

"Then what's to lose?" A simpering smile. "Besides, Petunia's haircuts are not like anything you've ever had before. They're more . . . exotic."

Over on the other side of the room, the naked girl got busy with a pair of clippers, cleaning them out with a toothbrush. Her breasts were marvelous.

Brock stood for a beery moment, wondering what to do.

"Come on, come on," the fat man said. "Sit. I'll explain everything."

"Everything?"

The fat man looked at him with beady, humorless eyes. "I know what Shakespeare wants. Now sit down."

Brock sat in the barber's chair. Petunia came over with a barber's apron, put it around his neck, fastened the clasp gently around his neck, smoothed the fabric over his shoulders. Her hands were cool, professional, silky against his skin. She ran her fingers through his hair, letting them linger for a moment around his ears. The sensation flooded through him.

"Isn't she splendid?" the fat man said.

Petunia put her mouth next to his ear, clicked her false teeth, breathed against him. *Oh, man!*

"Yes," Brock said, in spite of himself. He closed his eyes. A click, and then the clippers started buzzing.

"Give him a shampoo first, for pity's sake, you asinine girl!" the fat man said.

"Who are you?" Brock said, eyes still closed.

"It's not really that important," the fat man said. "A for-

mer lawyer, as they say. I had a little gambling problem at
one time and was forced to borrow funds from an escrow
account. Which I was later unable to repay. Fortunately I
have since been cured of my gambling addiction.''

"He's too fat to go to Vegas is what he means,'' Petunia
said dryly, her hands running through Brock's hair. "Lean
back.''

Brock leaned back over a basin and Petunia ran scalding
water over his hair. Brock grimaced.

"Don't worry,'' the fat man said. "It's just to make your
scalp a little more sensitive. For what comes next.''

Brock opened his eyes, looked up at Petunia's face. She
was smiling at him, just barely, and her eyes were full of a
calculating light. Her breasts hung at the level of his head.
She worked some shampoo into his hair, gently, slowly—the
odd, false smile still clinging to her face.

"This guy Shakespeare,'' the fat man said. "We been
looking for him for a while.''

The girl moved closer to Brock, leaning in toward him.
Closer, closer, until her left breast touched his head. Then,
as though she had touched him by mistake, she pulled away.
A small white fleck of suds clung to her hard nipple.

"We? Who's we?'' Brock was feeling distracted now as
Petunia began massaging his neck.

"Heard a psychiatrist the other day on the TV,'' the fat
man said. "This guy said our boy's attempting, through trans-
ference, to make himself immortal. By killing lawyers—who
represent all that is small and crabbed and provisional and
finite and mortal—he's attempting to destroy his own death.''
He held up three fat fingers, Scout's honor. "Isn't that a
hoot? I kid you not, Brock, it was right there on *Noonday
Atlanta,* channel five.''

Brock closed his eyes, felt the girl's nipple brush his ear.
"You said 'we.' Who are you talking about?''

The fat man sighed. "Let's put that aside for a moment.
What's more important is that we stop him before anything
else happens. You said you saw the concordance?''

"I saw a list. I assume it was this concordance you're
looking for. Unfortunately I got interrupted by Mic Giddens
before I had a chance to read all the names. Why do you
need this thing?''

"We believe it would be helpful in, shall we say, thinning out the competition a bit. Right now, though, we don't even know who these people are. Can't know the players if you don't have a scorecard, that type of thing."

The girl was methodically rubbing her breasts against him now. It had nothing to do with washing hair anymore—it was just an exercise in seduction. Brock felt himself growing hard underneath the barber's apron.

"You're going to have to do better," Brock said. "If you want my help, you better tell me who wants the concordance."

"Truth is," the fat man said, "I'm only a go-between. The folks I work for, well, honestly, I don't even know who they are."

"Bullshit." Brock was having trouble concentrating on the conversation. The girl was breathing into his ear again, making little moaning noises.

"Enough of that, Petunia," the fat man said. "Rinse it and start cutting."

"What if I were to tell you we had a signed affidavit from Caitlin Cobranchy exonerating you of any wrongdoing in the Jimmy Dale Evans case?"

Brock opened his eyes, looked up, startled. "Are you serious?"

The fat man waved a document in the air. "Right here."

"Let me see it."

The fat man laughed, his chest heaving up and down for a moment in the chair contraption. Afterward his face went wine red and he seemed to have trouble catching his breath. "Not that easy. First you have to get us the concordance."

"Look, Mic Giddens has it. You want it, go ask him for it."

The fat man smiled. "We'd prefer that you did."

"Let me see the affidavit."

"Lean back," Petunia said. She rinsed out his hair in the sink behind his chair, then dried her hands and went over to get the affidavit from the fat man. She held it up in front of Brock, let him read it without putting his hands on it.

It was a statement by Caitlin saying that she had been sitting outside of Brock's office when Mic Giddens visited and that there had been no discussion of Jimmy Dale's case, no discussion of Mic's deposition testimony.

"That's her signature?" Brock said.

"Sure. Properly executed, notarized, the whole bit."

"How'd you get this?" he said. "Is Caitlin okay?"

"Simple deal," the fat man said. "You get us the concordance, we give you the affidavit."

"Is she *okay?*"

"I don't know anything about that. All I know is if you want the affidavit, you better get us the concordance."

Brock closed his eyes. How the hell was he supposed to get the concordance from Mic Giddens? Well, it hardly mattered. He'd have to try. "Okay," he said. "I'll see what I can do."

The girl came toward him with a pair of scissors. All of a sudden Brock had to get out of there. Maybe it was the smell of the fat man, or maybe it was his fear of what he might do if the girl kept rubbing her tits in his face.

"I'm serious," he said, taking off the apron. "No haircut."

• 28

After Brock left, Shakespeare dusted off the soap parings, came out of the utility closet. Been sitting there listening to the conversation with Brock, carving a little girl out of Ivory soap, 99 and $^{44}/_{100}$ percent pure. The dancer Petunia had already gone back into the club. Alone with the fat man. Shakespeare's nose wrinkled at the smell of him. Disgusting, letting yourself go like that.

"How'd we do?" the fat man said.

"You're not bad," Shakespeare said, smiling. "That business with the hair? Really inspired. Really funny stuff."

The fat man made a peevish face. "Well, it happens to be true. I *am* particular about my hair."

Shakespeare walked across the room, turned up the Hank Williams tape as loud as it would go. To cover any noise that might happen in the next few moments. Shakespeare set the little carved soap girl next to the boom box. A dancing nymphet in a tutu, her eyes looking heavenward.

Shakespeare said: "Then I guess I better not shoot you in the head, huh?"

At first the fat man smiled dutifully, assuming it was just more of Shakespeare's morbid joking. But then when the little pistol came out, the .380 auto, the fat man started to get the picture. His screams were high and pure and operatic, but no one heard them. He flailed his arms and shuddered helplessly, trying to heave himself out of his chair.

Shakespeare emptied the clip into the fat man's chest, seven shots. The blanched soap nymphet—99 and $^{44}/_{100}$

percent pure—was dancing in her tutu to Hank Williams, averting her eyes from all the unpleasantness.

The fat man sank into his chair like fallen bread dough, and a thin stream of urine leaked onto the floor. His hair remained perfect.

Shakespeare turned the Hank Williams tape down a notch or two, opened the back door and walked out into the fresh air whistling the chorus to "Cold Cold Heart." Feeling pretty good. Feeling real cheerful, as a matter of fact.

THE FILINGS

●

Q: What's black and brown and looks good on a lawyer?

A: A Doberman pinscher.

• 29

"Now explain it to me again," Brock said.

"Simple," Jimmy Dale said, his protuberant blue eyes fixed on Brock's face. "Back when I did the books for the club, I always came in first thing in the morning, when nobody else was there. So Giddens gave me a key."

"No, not that part. I mean, about the alarm."

It was the morning following Brock's visit to the Painted Lady, and they were sitting in his law office speculating about how Brock could get his hands on the concordance again.

"Oh, that." Jimmy Dale had a needle in his fingers, though he hadn't stuck it in his leg yet. "The alarm? Nothing to it. There's a code number that you have to punch in when you enter the club. Naturally they change it periodically. Way it used to happen, they'd fire the assistant manager or something, so they'd change the code. And then Giddens would forget the new number and he'd set off the alarm, and the cops would show up, and then he'd get all pissed off. So finally he talked to the alarm people, and they tell him there's a way of programming a master code. He gives out one code to the employees, and then he keeps the master for himself."

"So how come you know the master code?"

Jimmy Dale smiled faintly. Turning the needle over and over between his thumb and finger. "Call me an observant guy."

"I wonder . . ." Brock said.

"What?"

"I wonder if Mic would have left that list at the club?"

"Why not? He's got file cabinets and a safe there."

They sat in silence for a while. Finally Jimmy Dale spoke. "Look, if you're gonna do it, you better go now. Mic usually comes to the club like ten, ten-thirty."

Brock looked at his watch. Nine-fifteen. That didn't give him much time. The club was only over on Piedmont, but it would take a good half an hour to swing by Jimmy Dale's house to pick up his old key to Laughing Dolls.

He stood up, grabbed his coat.

"Punch the star key, then one-one-seven-five, then the star again," Jimmy Dale said. Then he jammed the needle into his leg.

"Do you *really* have to do that?" Brock said.

Brock pulled into a parking lot across the street from Laughing Dolls, scanned the area. At night, with all the neon and the flashing lights slathered all over it, the place probably looked half decent in a tacky, strip-joint sort of way. But during the day it just looked sad and down-at-the-heels: a drab, one-story building of faded pink stucco, brown water stains trailing from the downspouts.

Brock hiked across Spring Street to the front entrance of the club, tried the key. He was a little surprised when it worked. He pushed open the door, entered a small anteroom with a battered wooden stool in the corner. The keypad for the alarm was right where Jimmy Dale said it would be. A small red light winked slowly at the bottom of the keypad. He pressed the buttons: #-1-1-7-5-#. Now the green light was supposed to come on.

The red light was still flashing lazily.

What had Jimmy Dale said? If the green light didn't come on, hit the "clear" button and start over.

CLR-#-1-1-7-5-#.

The red light: blip, blip, blip. Damn it. How much time had passed? Maybe Giddens had changed the master code. Maybe Jimmy Dale had just forgotten it.

Again. CLR-#-1-1-7-5-#.

No good, the red light was still flashing.

Brock was starting to panic. Then the air was filled with a shrill howling noise and the emergency lights above the door began flashing. Somewhere else in the bar a bell was clanging.

Just as Brock was about to bolt for the door, it hit him: what an idiot. Not the *pound* key. Star! He'd been hitting the damn pound key the whole time.

He jabbed desperately at the keypad. CLR-*-1-1-7-5-*.

And just as quickly as it had begun, the howling ceased, the light stopped flashing and a small green light winked on.

Brock closed his eyes for a moment and slumped against the wall. His body was suddenly drenched in sweat. Man, that had been way, *way* too close.

Through the next door, he entered the main room of the club. It was full of round tables surrounded by chairs upholstered in an awful synthetic leopard skin fabric. The room was completely dark except for the dim, eerie red glow from a couple of EXIT signs. A smell of beer and drain cleaner floated on the motionless air.

His heart was pounding, but at the same time he felt an odd lift, a feeling of—what? Satisfaction? He didn't have time to cogitate on it, to track it down, but there it was. And there was something sexy about it, too. Not the idea of naked women dancing on top of tables, but the feeling of sneaking unchallenged into a place where he didn't belong.

Then he stopped and thought, *What the hell am I doing here?* Standing in the middle of a strip joint with a Glock pistol shoved down his pants like some kind of macho fool in a movie. Hell, maybe he'd been fighting his real nature all these years. Living out somebody else's idea of a pleasant bourgeois existence when what he should have been was a criminal scumbag. Brock laughed loudly.

Stupid. Stupid to even think that sort of thing. He tried to put all the thinking out of his mind. Time to concentrate on the job at hand. He threaded his way through the bar until he reached a hallway that extended toward a pair of rest rooms. Once his eyes had adjusted to the dark, he checked for office doors. Nothing marked *Private* or *Employees Only*—just the bathrooms. He wondered why the place needed a ladies' room. Maybe for the dancers. On a whim, he walked into the women's bathroom, turned on the light. The fluorescents buzzed and popped. The walls were fake marble, and everything was very clean.

He turned off the light and walked out. Time to find the office. That's where the concordance would be.

• 30

Mic Giddens's Corvette screeched into the parking lot of Laughing Dolls, the engine muttering to a stop. Mic grabbed a bindle of crank out of the glove compartment, getting ready to snag a little toot so as to get the morning started right, when he noticed the blue Ford Taurus parked over by the dumpster.

Probably just some drunk wanker left his car there last night. Don't get paranoid. Giddens snorted some crank in his left nostril, pinched his nose shut. Much better. He'd been feeling so jittery lately. Spooky as a bloody cat.

He hauled himself up out of the car and was stuffing the bindle in his pocket when he noticed the step ladder propped up on top of the dumpster. That wasn't right. A wave of paranoia rolled over him, and he felt his heart going like a drumroll. Who was it? Somebody bloody spying on him? Waiting inside to set some kind of trap, blow his fucking head off?

He undid the retainer strap on his shoulder holster, just in case, and trotted over to the building. He climbed up on the dumpster, surveyed the roof. Nothing. Bastard had probably been trying to break in through the roof. Might already be inside.

He'd been feeling bloody frightened lately. Like somebody'd been watching him all the time, sneaking around on him, peeking at him through windows and out of parked cars.

He jumped off the dumpster and headed for the front door. Before he opened the door, he pulled out his pistol, held it down against his leg. Couldn't be too bloody careful.

Brock hadn't had much trouble finding the office or getting into it. It had been locked, but a little paring knife borrowed from behind the bar worked just fine for jimmying the bolt.

He went into the office, closed the door, turned on the light. Other than the fact that it didn't have a window, it wasn't a bad office. A nice mahogany veneered desk; an Oriental rug on the floor. Also a couple of large pictures on the wall, pen-and-ink nudes. Not bad ones, either. Must have gotten there by mistake.

Brock started by opening the drawers of the desk, hunting for the file. Plenty of bar receipts rolled up in rubber bands and the usual collection of dull pencils and leaky pens. But no file. The Glock kept sliding down into his pants. How did those guys in the movies do it? He tightened his belt a notch.

Brock tried the filing cabinet, which was locked. There were no keys, and the paring knife was too weak to jimmy the thing. He went back out to the bar to find a stronger implement. The dark cavernous room had begun to take on an ominous quality, and Brock had an urge to turn on the lights. When he got back into the office with the can opener he'd retrieved from the bar, he thought he heard a noise. A soft, shuffling noise. Adrenaline squirted into his veins. It sounded like the noise was coming out of the ceiling.

He turned off the light, opened the door of the office, peered out into the dark club. Nothing.

But there it was again: a soft sliding noise and then a very brief scrape, like nails on a blackboard. Was it out in the bar? No, it sounded like it was coming from over his head.

Strange. Brock stopped breathing, listened. Dark shapes moved and danced in the shadows of the club. A trick of the eyes.

The noise again.

The ceiling. The sound had definitely come from the ceiling. Brock laughed out loud. Hell, it was probably just squirrels on the roof. Or maybe even rats, prospecting for half-full beer bottles thrown up on the roof by drunk customers. Brock snapped on the light switch and the noise stopped.

He closed the office door and began prying open the top drawer of the flimsy filing cabinet with the paring knife. He began to sweat. Finally the small bolt snapped and the drawer slid open. Inside were invoices and computer-printed reports. No manila folder. No concordance. The next three drawers turned out to have nothing interesting, either. He noticed a safe recessed in the back wall of the room. If it was in there, then he was out of luck. He tried the handle. Locked. So if not there, then where? Brock sat down in the desk chair, looked around the room, his heart thumping noisily. He rifled the desk drawers, turned up nothing, then ducked under the desk to see if anything interesting was taped underneath it. Nada.

"You bleddy shit!" a voice behind him said.

Brock jumped, his heart pounding madly, banged his shoulder on the desk drawer as he straightened suddenly. It was Mic Giddens, his big shoulders filling the doorway, pointing a huge silver revolver at Brock's chest. Giddens's face was hot with anger.

"And a fine good morning to you too," Brock said. Thinking: *Stay calm, stay calm, stay calm.* His heart hammered in his throat.

Brock tried to smile, didn't get much of anywhere with it. He let his right hand slide toward the Glock in his waistband.

"How'd you know I was here?" Try to get Giddens talking, maybe he'd forget about doing anything with that silver revolver.

"I can see through walls, mate. I got eyes in the palms of my hands." Giddens's pupils were small as pencil points.

The way Brock was sitting behind the desk, the Glock was hidden from Giddens. He slid his hand slowly toward the gun. There. He had his hand around the grip. His heart was pounding and he had a sick feeling in his gut. Now what?

The Australian kept pointing the revolver at Brock, but his eyes were moving around the room, restless, agitated. Next move, Brock supposed, would be to dial 911. Then a quick call to the State Bar; after which there'd be a Petition for Emergency Suspension of License, and bye-bye legal career.

Then again, maybe Giddens would just shoot him.

"The concordance," Brock said. "I guess it's in the safe, huh?"

"Everybody's hung up on the concordance." Giddens scrabbled in his pocket with his free hand, took out a small folded piece of paper, unfolded it, revealing some clumpy white powder. "I wish you could stand in my shoes, Brock. See what it feels like, all the hassles, all the shit you got to put up with. Stupid customers, lazy bartenders, asshole investors, bitchy dancers."

"I just want to see the concordance," Brock said. "Just give it to me and I'll never bother you again in my life."

"Too much bleddy pressure on me, that's what it is. Too much bleddy pressure."

"I know how you feel." Keep talking. Keep talking.

There was a noise in the ceiling again. Both men looked up.

"Who's out there? Who's bleddy out there?" The Australian put his head out the door for a moment.

"Squirrels," Brock said. "Just squirrels."

Giddens came back in the room muttering: "They're coming after me. This whole thing, it's all a sick plot. A bleddy conspiracy. They're all coming after Mic Giddens. Well, they're gonna learn their bleddy lesson." His face was red with anger.

Brock nodded. Keep playing along, maybe he'd have a chance to make a break. There was the noise above them, again: a soft shuffling. Giddens jerked his gun at the ceiling. The noise stopped.

Now.

Brock pulled out the Glock, leveled it at Giddens. Damn it. A sudden awful feeling: he'd misjudged. By the time he had the Glock pointed at Giddens, the Australian's revolver was pointed at Brock again.

For a moment neither of them moved. Staring at each other, gun against gun.

"You stupid bugger!" Giddens hissed.

"We're five feet apart," Brock said. "You squeeze the trigger, I'll have time to blast you, what, three or four times before I'm dead." Feeling light-headed. For a moment Brock had to stifle an inappropriate urge to giggle. The whole thing was just too ridiculous. "It's not worth it."

The two men stared at each other, the guns pointing both directions, unwavering. Giddens got on his knees on the other side of the desk, the gun still pointed at Brock's chest, crushed some of the powder with his fingernail, then snorted it directly off the paper. He jumped up, smiled.

"Well," Giddens said. "Lookee here. Mexican standoff."

"The concordance," Brock said. "I want the concordance."

After a moment Giddens started to laugh. "You don't understand anything, do you?"

Brock said nothing.

Giddens thumped himself in the chest. "*I,* on the other hand, understand everything. Everything."

It took Brock a moment to understand. "What? Are you saying you know who Shakespeare is? That's what you're saying, isn't it?"

Giddens's eyes roamed the room suspiciously. Suddenly a sly smile spread across his big red face. "Yes, as a matter of fact, that's exactly what I'm saying."

The smile made a cold sensation creep across Brock's skin. "Is it you?"

Giddens kept smiling. "Hypothetically," he said. "Let's just say, hypothetically, it was me."

"Hypothetically."

"Let's just say it was me, maybe I got my reasons."

"Cutting people's dicks off, stuffing them in their mouths?"

"Like I say, *if* it was me—hypothetically—then maybe I got my reasons for what I'm doing."

Brock said, "Well, that's very nice. Let me see the list."

The two men stood still, the guns pointing, pointing. Hands wavering from the strain. Brock's mouth was so dry his lips were sticking together and he could hardly swallow.

"Let me ask you a question, sport," Gidden said. "Why do you want the concordance?"

"Among other things, I'd like to find out why Shakespeare seems to want to kill me."

After a moment Giddens raised his eyebrows slightly. "Maybe I should give you that concordance. Might be instructive."

He went over to the other side of the room, dialed the combination of the safe, his gun still pointed in Brock's direction. He took out a thick manila folder, tossed it on the desk. "Something you might notice, your name's not on the list."

"Yeah. So?"

"So maybe Shakespeare's not really after you."

"I don't follow you."

Giddens stared angrily at Brock, then his face softened. "See, maybe if you get off the Jimmy Dale case, then you won't have to worry about me. I mean about Shakespeare. You see what I'm saying?"

"I'm not sure."

"Maybe Shakespeare's got something else in mind. Something that's got nothing to do with you."

"Let's say that's true. Then why did he send me the card? Why did he mess with my daughter? What does all this have to do with Jimmy Dale's case?"

"Do you have any idea who's on this concordance?"

"Prochaska, Michaels, Darden, Lata . . ."

"So, *think!* Look at all these bleddy interrogatories you've been sending us for Jimmy Dale's case, all those stupid questions about who owns Laughing Dolls, who the investors are. We answer them correctly, guess what? It's all gonna come out, every name on this list. And then, guess what? Somebody says, 'Oh, my goodness, here's Mel Prochaska's name on this incorporation document! Here's Raymond Lata! How strange.' All of a sudden they'd realize that Shakespeare is killing my investors."

"And then . . ."

"And then they start background checking every single employee of Laughing Dolls. And if they check with Interpol, they'll find I've got an outstanding warrant in Australia."

"For . . ."

Giddens's eyes flicked around the room. "Look, a guy

back in Australia got beat over the head. He died. So if the cops find the connection between Shakespeare and the investors in my club, then I end up hip-deep in shit. That's why I don't want Jimmy Dale's case going forward. Too much chance of the wrong things coming out."

Brock leaned across the desk, started to open the file with the list inside. Giddens pulled it away. "Not yet, mate. First, let's try and extricate ourselves from our little Mexican standoff. What I'd like you to do is sit down at that computer and sketch out a settlement offer. Say, twenty-five thousand dollars in cash? Plus another twenty-five in attorney's fees?"

"Or else what—you'll shoot me?"

Giddens laughed. "Or else I call the cops and tell them I just found this overzealous attorney breaking into my office."

"What if *I* call the police? What if I tell them you just admitted to me that you were Shakespeare?"

Giddens turned the phone around, shoved it across the desk. "Go ahead. Make the call. But I warn you, there's no physical evidence here to connect me to those murders. Shakespeare's a careful boy. *You* on the other hand, mate, are in hot water. Think about your next hearing with the disciplinary board when three or four cops testify they found you in my place of business waving a gun around, making crazy accusations about Shakespeare."

A feeling of defeat settled over Brock like a blanket of mud. His gun was still pointing at Giddens. Giddens's big revolver pointed back. Brock's shoulder had started cramping from holding the gun, the pain running up into his neck. Giddens was right. If he called the cops now, it would be just one more nail in his coffin.

"Tell you what, Giddens," Brock said finally. "I'll make some kind of settlement offer that the insurance guys will go for." Anything to convince Giddens to let him get out of the room. Then Brock had a thought. "But only on condition that you write a notarized statement to the Disciplinary Board of the bar saying that your testimony before them was bogus."

Giddens shrugged. "Why not?" Above them the scratching of squirrels again. Giddens twitched, looked at the ceiling again, eyes narrowed. "What the *fuck* is that noise?" he said.

Before Brock could answer, a section of black ductwork

separated itself from the ceiling and crashed to the floor. Brock looked at the big black pipe, then at Giddens, then at the pipe. For a moment he wasn't quite sure what had happened. But then he saw a man's arm emerging from the pipe.

"You set me up!" Giddens screamed. "You bleddy set me up!" He was jumping up and down now, waving the gun wildly, pointing it at the man who was slowly emerging from the duct, then jerking it back at Brock, then back at the man in the duct. A black figure was emerging slowly from the pipe, a nightmarish figure with a knot of white tissue where his eye should have been.

"Easy!" Brock said. "Take it easy!"

"I'm gonna fucking kill you both!" Giddens screamed, trembling with rage. He pointed the gun at the pipe and fired.

"Hey, yo, wait a minute!" the one-eyed man in the pipe yelled. Giddens fired again at the pipe, then swung the gun toward Brock. He was still jumping up and down, wired from whatever he'd been snorting.

It was not until Brock was in the parking lot, the manila folder with the concordance in it clutched under his arm, that he figured out quite what had happened next. Pulling the trigger, the Glock jumping in his hand—once, twice, a third time.

Giddens's gun going off again. Banging, all sort of banging noises racketing around in Brock's ears.

Then the side of Giddens's face had disappeared, replaced by a wash of red. As Giddens's knees buckled and he heaved over onto the desk, Brock had frozen for a moment, then run out of the room, stumbling through the bar, knocking over chairs as he ran.

Giddens must have reset the alarm, because as soon as Brock opened the front door, the air was filled with the screaming of sirens and the clanging of bells.

• 32

Two hours later the cops were still questioning Brock down at the homicide station on Somerset Terrace. The interview room was fairly clean and well-painted, but it had a bad smell, like the pipes had burst a long time ago and all that rotten water had never been quite squeezed out of the floor, the ceiling, the walls.

Brock felt like someone had jammed a crowbar down his spine.

"Tell me again," the white guy with the crew cut was saying. Sergeant Nichols or Nicholas or something; Brock hadn't paid attention. He had large, hunched shoulders and wore a green spotted tie and a white dress shirt with short sleeves. "Go over it again one more time, how it happened."

The first time they'd asked him the question, Brock had figured it was time for a little creativity if he wanted to hold onto his license to practice law. Since then, he'd been repeating the same story: "I was coming over to pick up these documents. The door to the club was open, so I just walked in. I didn't see Giddens so I just walked into his office to see if maybe he'd left this folder on his desk. I guess he thought I was a thief, because he walked in on me with his gun drawn. Next thing you know this guy falls out of the ceiling and Giddens freaks out, starts shooting. He was on coke or speed or something and was acting paranoid. It was obvious he was going to shoot me next, so I pulled my gun and fired back."

"But the part in the middle there. You left out the part where he told you he was Shakespeare."

"Well, like I said, he and I have not had the most cordial relations up to this point. He's been trying to get me and my client to drop this lawsuit for a long time. Anyway, he went through this elaborate hypothetical thing—you know, like *if* he was Shakespeare, then blah blah blah. But it was pretty obvious what he meant."

"Spell it out for me."

"Well, finally, he basically says, if you don't settle this lawsuit cheap, then I'll kill you like I killed those other guys."

The cop made some notes, looked up and said, "When you pulled the trigger, you're standing . . . where?"

"Sitting. Behind the desk."

Nichols or Nicholas took out a piece of paper and a newly sharpened pencil, drew a large rectangle. "Here's the room," he said. "Where were you?"

Brock took the pencil from him and drew a rectangle to represent the desk, then drew an *X* and put his name next to it.

"And Mr. Giddens?"

Brock erased a hole in the wall on the other side of the office, drew a line representing an opened door. "About ten, twelve feet away. Next to the door." He drew another *X*, wrote Giddens's name next to it.

"And the guy who fell out of the duct in the ceiling?"

Brock drew a third *X*.

"And you fired at Giddens how many times?"

"Three. I think three." Brock closed his eyes. He felt like someone was hammering rock climbing pitons in between the vertebrae in his neck. "How many times do I have to say this?"

"And your gun, did you keep a round in the chamber?"

"No. I guess I cocked it and then fired."

"So you've got a ten-round clip, you fire three times, Giddens goes down."

"Right."

"And the guy in the pipe—did he get hit?"

"I don't know."

"Did he have a gun?"

"He had something in his hand. Something black. I think it was a flashlight."

"Did he fire a gun?"

"I don't think so."

"And Giddens—when you're shooting at him—which direction is he facing?"

"I told you. He was facing me."

"You're sure?"

"Yeah, because I saw . . ." The scene played itself back in his mind again, the side of Giddens's face suddenly peeling back, exposing white bone, bloody flesh. "I saw the side of his face disappear when I shot him. If he'd been facing the other way, I couldn't have seen that, could I?"

"And you only had one gun? This gun." The detective held up his Glock in a plastic bag. Brock nodded. He could see the telltale signs of powder where the evidence people had dusted it for prints. "Just for the record, exactly why did you go there?"

Brock hesitated. He couldn't exactly say he'd broken into the place. "To get some documents for the case," he said finally.

"And did you get them?"

"Yes, I did." Brock handed him the folder.

Nichols or Nicholas leafed through the folder. It was obvious from the glazed expression in his eyes that he wasn't making anything of it. Legal mumbo jumbo. He'd never notice the concordance. Best just to forget about it for now.

The big detective lumbered over to the door, opened it, spoke to someone outside the door. "How 'bout you go grab the lieutenant now."

Brock was rubbing his neck when Lieutenant Janelle Moncrief arrived. Her suit was a sort of red-sky-at-morning-sailors-take-warning shade, with very large black lapels. "How you feeling?" She smiled in a way that seemed just a little too ingratiating.

He felt like shit, what did she think? "Okay," he said.

Moncrief sat down, took off her crimson pumps, wiggled her toes inside her hose. "Everybody treating you okay?"

"You ever think about wearing flat shoes?" Brock said. "I understand they're a lot more comfortable."

The detective looked at him for a few moments, no expression in her dark eyes.

"Look," Brock said. "I appreciate the concern and all. But I shot this guy, and I think we're getting to the point where I need to know if you're going to charge me with something."

The detective put her tongue between her lips for a while and frowned. Then she said, "Shakespeare. Scourge of the legal community. So you think you shot him, huh?"

"I guess he's Shakespeare. He pretty much admitted it."

Moncrief shook her head. "We been busting our humps on this one. Funny how it ends up an amateur gets the guy by accident."

Brock shrugged. "Didn't seem that funny to me."

"I bet not. In any case, we're running some physical evidence down to the state crime lab right now. In fact, Mr. Giddens himself, as we speak, is sleeping on a metal bed with drains down the side getting chopped up by the medical examiner. We gonna have answers real soon, find out if this is really our boy."

"What do you think?"

"Motive." Her eyes were dark and curious. "I want to understand his motive."

"He's a paranoiac coke-head."

"Mmmmm," she said, not sounding like she bought his explanation. Brock didn't blame her. He didn't buy it either.

"You suppose I could take a few minutes to call my wife?" Brock said. It had occurred to him that he hadn't talked to Dru yet, hadn't told her what he'd done. She'd want to know that Grace was safe, that Shakespeare was dead.

Moncrief looked at her watch and said, "Take five or ten minutes. I got something I need to check on anyway."

"I'm down at the police station," Brock said.

"What for?" Dru said.

"They found Shakespeare. It was Mic Giddens. It was him all along."

"What?" Dru's voice sounded lighter.

"It's all over. He's dead."

"My God . . . How did they . . ."

Brock groped for the words. But there was no way to sugarcoat it, no way to say it that would take the edge off what he had to tell her. "Dru, I killed him. I shot Giddens."

There was no sound on the line, no signal of approval, of disapproval, of anything at all. Brock plunged on, told her everything that had happened that morning. When he was through, there was still silence.

"Dru," Brock said. "It's over now. You can come home."

"You," Dru said finally. "*You* killed a man."

Suddenly all of Brock's impulses to escape his dull, predictable life evaporated. He wanted his wife and his child. He wanted things to be normal again, to be dull and predictable. No more guns; no more strip joints; no more obese perverts; no more men in clown masks. "Come home, Dru. Get Grace and come home."

There was a long silence, and then Dru said, "I don't think that's such a great idea."

"Wait a minute," Brock said. Feeling something cold seeping through him. "What are you saying?"

So that was it. She wasn't coming back, not just yet, anyway. She didn't say anything about filing papers, nothing like that—just that she "needed some time to process everything."

When he had imprudently said, "What the hell does that mean?" she had gotten her hackles up, and then the conversation fell apart. "I'm sorry, baby. I'm sorry, I'm sorry, I'm *sorry!*"

She hung up on him.

Brock was sitting in the interview room again with Janelle Moncrief. "Everything okay?" Moncrief said.

"Fine," Brock said morosely. *I just killed a man and my wife despises me. Everything's great.*

The detective laced her fingers together, looked over them at Brock's face. Today her long nails were painted a sort of orangey red that matched her outfit. Her eyelids hung low and heavy over her black eyes. After a long moment she spoke.

"Richard Dean Settles," she said, distinctly pronouncing each syllable.

Brock squinted. "Excuse me?"

Janelle glanced over at the two-way mirror, like she was saying *I told you so* to somebody who was watching from the other side.

"Richard Dean Settles," she said again. Then she opened her eyes wide. "You're going to *deny* that you know him?"

Brock shrugged. "I guess so."

The detective sat down on the other side of the table, clasped her hands, and put a new look on her face—softer, more understanding. Brock didn't buy it.

"And if I told you that Richard Dean Settles had been murdered last night?"

"I'm sorry. I'm lost."

The detective leaned her chin on her fingers for a while, looked into Brock's eyes. "And if I told you that your fingerprints were all over the room?"

Brock shrugged.

"And if I told you that we've got two eyewitnesses putting you at the scene of the crime?"

"Look—" Brock was starting to get mad.

"And that those eyewitnesses indicate you to be the last person to have seen the victim?"

Brock looked at the mirror, wondering who was watching. "Am I under arrest or something?"

"Where were you last night?" Janelle Moncrief barked.

"Last night? Various places."

"Pin it down for me." The detective's voice had gotten low and hard. "Times, places, faces, names."

"Well, around eight I went out to this church out in Cobb County to talk to a . . . uh . . . client. After that I drove over to this place called the Painted Lady." Brock paused when he saw a light go on in Lieutenant Moncrief's eyes. "I was supposed to meet a guy there."

"A guy."

"Yeah. So I had a couple beers and then I was shown into this back room by a dancer named Petunia. I don't know, she *said* it was her name, but you kind of wonder. So anyway I met with this guy, then I left."

"And what did this meeting concern?"

"He told me that if I could get hold of a certain folder full of documents, the one I told you that I was coming over to get from Giddens this morning, this guy said he would give me an affidavit that would be helpful in another case I'm involved in."

"What was this fellow's name?"

Brock shrugged. "He didn't say."

"You mean to tell me you're giving confidential documents to a guy, didn't even tell you his *name?*"

"Look, basically he was blackmailing me. He had an affidavit that would have saved my bacon in a very important case. That affidavit was a lot more important to me than his name."

"I don't suppose you noticed what he looked like?"

"He was so fat he had to be rolled around in this hammock kind of thing." Brock smiled humorlessly. "Also, he had very neat hair."

"You recognize this?" the detective said, handing him a document enclosed in a plastic evidence bag.

At the top of the typed document were the words *Affidavit of Caitlin Louise Cobranchy.* The document was splashed with dried brown liquid. Brock had a bad feeling he knew where this was leading. He nodded, set the bag back on the table. "That's the affidavit I just told you about."

"Why did he want these documents?"

Brock shrugged, trying to act nonchalant. "Don't know."

"And these are the documents you got from Mr. Giddens?"

"Yeah." Brock pushed it across the table. "Take a look. It's just a bunch of contracts and leases and stuff."

Moncrief looked at the folder a little more carefully than the first detective had—but not much. After a moment she got up, walked out of the room. Brock was sweating heavily and his neck was hurting like hell. He considered taking off his coat, but decided it was better to pretend he felt comfortable.

The door opened and the detective came back into the room carrying an 8 X 10 photograph. "Richard Dean Settles," she said, pushing the photo across the table. It was a picture of a corpse. The dead man's face had a bluish tint, his lips and eyes were open as though in a state of mild surprise, and his blond hair lay perfectly around his face. The tentlike shirt covering his corpulent body was soaked in blood.

"Jesus," Brock said. "He never told me his name."

The room was silent for a long time.

Finally the detective said, "I don't believe in coincidences."

"Neither do I," Brock said. He waited for a beat or two. "So are you planning on arresting me for something or can I go?"

Moncrief raised her eyebrows, looked skeptically into Brock's face. "I'm not prepared to charge you with anything—at this point in time."

"Look. Giddens was perjuring himself to the Disciplinary Board in an attempt to get me disbarred. This affidavit might well have gotten me off the hook. If I'd killed this guy Settles, surely I would have taken the affidavit with me!"

The lieutenant ran a crimson fingernail across the table top, thinking. Brock decided to stand up, see if she asked him to sit down again.

She didn't, so he picked up the folder with the concordance in it and headed for the door. As he put his hand on the knob, something occurred to him. "Hold on," he said. "Can I take that affidavit out of the bag, get a closer look at it?"

She hesitated, then handed him the bag. "I guess so. It's already been checked for fingerprints."

He turned to the back page of the document, the part where it said, *This affidavit has been duly witnessed and sworn to by and before me, a notary public in the County of Fulton, State of Georgia.* Underneath was a foppish signature, full of big loops and squiggles. But the name was clear enough: *Reggie B. Vinyard, Esq.*

"Huh," Brock said, slipping the bloody papers back into the evidence bag.

Outside Brock stood in the bright sunshine, watched a couple of gleaming cop cars ease by, wash water streaming off of their windshields and beading up on the hoods. A sick headache was working its way up out of his neck. Should he have told them what was in the folder? Should he have showed them the concordance?

No. The more innocuous that folder seemed, the less likely the police were to suspect that he might have been breaking into Laughing Dolls to get it. No way he was going to hand over more ammunition to the Disciplinary Board. Things were already hairy enough on that front.

33

"I'm a pro," Cleland Davis told Reggie Vinyard. "I mean, what kind of guy you think I am?"

Davis was lying on his stomach in a bed down at Grady Hospital, his butt up in the air, dressed like a Christmas turkey. Man, oh, *man*, it hurt! Something fierce.

"I'm relieved to hear that," Judge Vinyard said.

"I told the police I was there conducting surveillance on a confidential matter for a confidential client and that without a subpoena I was not willing to reveal any further information as to what I was doing."

"To which they responded . . ."

"Oh, you know. How they was gonna charge my ass, breaking and entering, ADW, accessory to homicide before and after, various other bullshit."

"And you still didn't tell them."

"I kind of fibbed a little, said the only person who can testify one way or the other as to whether I was up in that gotdamn duct by invitation or not was lying on the floor with half his head blown off. Therefore they was in no position to charge me with diddley shit. I told them I used to be a detective myself, I knew my rules of evidence, brother, they could go stuff they threats up they motherfucking ass." Normally Cleland Davis was not a profane man, but the combination of little blue pills and extreme pain had put some snap in his tongue.

The Judge sat for a while. The evening news was playing silently on the television. "So you didn't get the concordance?"

"Nope. Brock's got it."

"He show it to the cops?"

"They didn't mention it to me."

Judge Vinyard smiled, looked at the pale green food tray: gray lumps of uneaten bread pudding and chicken-fried steak and reconstituted potatoes. "What, you don't want your dinner?"

"Don't seem real hungry right now," Davis said.

Reggie B. Vinyard reached into his pocket, came out with a roll of money. He peeled off ten bills, hundreds, set them next to the green tray. "Little something extra for you," he said, "case you want throw a couple steaks on the grill when your appetite comes back."

34

After the police finally finished with him, Brock tried to call Dru again, but his mother-in-law said she was down at the grocery store. He wasn't sure he believed her—but it wasn't worth pressing the point.

When Brock got home after working all afternoon on Jimmy Dale's opening statement, he opened the kitchen cabinet, took out a bag of barbecue potato chips, two Dixie cups, and a bottle of Jim Beam, then walked over to the carriage house. "Judge?" he said, putting his head inside the door. "Hey, Judge?"

"Over here," his grandfather said. Brock came in and sat down at the table where his grandfather was poring over a biography of John C. Calhoun. The Judge closed the book and said, "You look whipped, boy."

Brock sank into a chair. "It would be fair to say it wasn't a great day. First, I killed a guy, and then Dru told me she doesn't want to come home." He poured some bourbon into one of the Dixie cups. "Join me?"

"Don't mind if I do."

Brock poured a couple of fingers in the second Dixie cup.

"Saw on the news," the old man said, "that some heroic lawyer just killed Shakespeare."

Brock said, "Apparently so." The anesthetic whiskey started numbing his throat, moving slowly through his body. The pain in his neck eased back a notch or two. "What is it about women, Judge? Dru just doesn't understand what I'm going through.''

"Aw, hell, you got to stop seeing yourself through that woman's eyes," the Judge said.

"Oh, it's not like that." Brock felt a burst of annoyance.

"Look, boy, it's an irremediable part of the human condition that men and women don't understand a goddamn thing about each other.''

Brock sipped his drink, savoring the fine, familiar burn of the bourbon in his stomach. He still felt jittery and half-sick, though, like he was on the verge of coming down with a fever.

"All these *feminists!*" the old man said. "Hah! They think that women have been taken advantage of all these years. Well, I got news for them. Modern history is nothing but the story of men throwing themselves on the grenade for the sake of women. Sure there's rape and murder and harassment and all kind of bad things done to women. Why? Because men are so goddam angry about scraping off their shoes to keep the rug clean, about having to know which is the fish fork and which is the salad fork, about having to put out the trash, about sleeping in the same bed with the same woman every day—hell, every man in the world is walking around pissed off *all the time.*''

The old man stared down into his Dixie cup.

"Men want to please women," he continued. "That's our curse. We want to *please* women! It's all we want—other than wanting to get in fights and fart in public and let the house fall to rack and ruin and bed down with eighteen-year-old girls. Women are different. They don't want to please men, they want to *own* them. What a woman wants is a clean nest and a large, docile man. The kind of guy she can keep busy rearranging the furniture and fixing that busted handle on the toilet.''

Brock's cup had gone empty, so he decided to have another whiskey. He went in the kitchen, cut the second drink with some tap water.

"I gather you're not trying to make me feel better, Judge.''

"Hell, no. I never been any damn comfort to anybody in my life. Why start now?" The old man grinned savagely. "Besides, you're gonna feel terrible about killing that guy, because you're a decent man. Nothing gonna make you feel better.''

"Ah."

The Judge lifted his twisted old index finger, a crafty tilt to his eyebrows. "However! It is my personal belief that decent men—men such as yourself—permit themselves to get beat down, spending all their time serving women. They *think* they're self-aggrandizing because they work so hard. Truth is, boy, they're just doing what the boss says."

"The boss?"

"Haven't you been listening? The woman's the boss! But then—here's the perversity of human nature—soon as the woman breaks her man, she gets uneasy. She begins to sense that her man has no spirit. She doesn't like to admit it, but she knows deep down in her moist womanhood that her man has to reclaim his ugly soul. It threatens her, makes her mad—but she knows it's true. A man with no spirit, hell, he's no better than a lap dog."

"Is this some kind of advice, Judge?"

"You killed this scumbag. That's a fine, manly thing. Now it's time to go out and get drunk, talk reckless words, get laid." The Judge stared at him with fierce, wet eyes, then leaned in close. "Women are the source of all ancient human wisdom. Reason Dru's not coming home yet, she's giving you space to reclaim your soul. She may not even know it exactly, but that's what she's doing—giving you room to perform the sacraments of manhood."

Brock looked at the old man for a minute. The Judge glared back. Brock said, "You sound like an Indian medicine man out of some bad movie."

"As it happens, my mama's great-great-grandfather *was* an Indian medicine man," the old man said. "A Creek, as I recall. Took a knobbed stick on the Trail of Tears, killed one of Jackson's cavalry officers, and escaped by floating down the Tennessee River for more than thirty-five miles. Underwater! Breathing through a reed!"

"You're full of shit, old man."

The Judge giggled.

Seeing his grandfather's empty Dixie cup, Brock lifted the bottle. "More?"

"I'm a thousand years old, for chrissake. That stuff ruins

my bowels.'' The Judge looked down at his book, waved the back of his spotted hand at Brock's face. ''Now get the hell out of here. I'm trying to relive the glories of our shameful past.''

• 35

As soon as Brock got back inside his house, the phone rang. It was his father's secretary. "You're not forgetting, are you?" she said.

"Forgetting," Brock said.

"Judge Vinyard's portrait unveiling. At the Ritz-Carlton."

"Oops," Brock said.

"I'll inform Mr. Brock you're running a few minutes late," she said pleasantly.

One of the little crosses Brock had to bear as the son of an *éminence grise* of the Atlanta legal community was that periodically he got roped into showing up at social functions of the sequined-gown-and-tuxedo variety. This particular event was the unveiling of a portrait of one of Brock's father's partners, Judge Reggie Vinyard. Some charitable organization had been strong-armed by Vinyard's cronies into commissioning a portrait of Vinyard, and now the Atlanta bar would roast him a little. This was how you got initiated into the grand-old-man club. Most times they waited until you retired, but if you were enough of a big shot and enough people wanted to kiss your ass, they might do it while you were still relatively young and vigorous.

Brock arrived late. Judge Vinyard and his father and the mayor and Martin Luther King III and a couple of other solemn and well-dressed worthies were sitting at the head table. An old black guy, bald, with large serpentine veins in his temples was talking about what a profound honor it was for him to be able to pay tribute to such an eminent jurist, blah blah blah.

Brock lost the thread of the speech, tried to catch up on the meal. Behind the old bald man, a former president of Morris Brown College, was The Portrait, still covered in a white sheet. Assorted grandees and wannabe grandees and sucker-uppers and political hacks and riders of the great gravy train which was the City of Atlanta were seated at large round tables set with heavy silver and heavy plates and lots of little ramekins and trivets and servers filled with sweating pats of butter and congealed sauces. Most of the people in the room were black, very well-groomed, very serious-looking.

After the speech came a performance by the very intent young singers from the Sword of the Naked Flame Youth Ministries, and then an honor guard of Junior ROTC kids from Ralph Bunche Middle School marched woozily around the room. More speeches followed, including one of singular passionlessness offered by Brock's father. Reggie Vinyard sat regally and never cracked a smile at any of the foolishness.

Finally they pulled the white sheet off the awful portrait and everyone applauded and Reggie Vinyard surprised everyone by telling a story about the courage of a young girl he'd known in Selma during the early days in the civil rights movement—a story that left Brock's eyelashes full of tears.

That's what Brock liked about Vinyard. The sly old son of a bitch could sure blindside you.

Brock had been about to hightail it for the door when he saw Reggie Vinyard bearing toward him from across the room. "Hey there, boy!" Vinyard called to him. He had that aggressive twinkle in his eye that made people both love and fear him.

Brock laughed, shook the Judge's hand. "Congratulations. Good thing you don't look anything like that picture they gave you."

"That's mighty white of you." The Judge bared his teeth, clamped his large hand around Brock's wrist. "I understand you've had a rough week."

Brock raised his eyebrows. "Word travels fast."

"Everybody okay? Dru, Grace?"

Brock probably hadn't talked to the Judge in three or four years, but still Vinyard remembered all the pertinent details—

names, dates, family relationships. It was this kind of memory
for personal detail, this social intellect, that had made the
Judge such a powerful man. "We'd had some threats from
this Shakespeare guy," Brock said. "So they went up to stay
with Dru's folks for a while."

Vinyard nodded approvingly. "Your daddy told me. Very
wise," he growled. He took out a large cigar, studied it for
a moment. "Now that Shakespeare's out of the picture, I
guess that would free you up to join me and Press Cain and
your daddy downstairs for some brandy and smokes."

"Love to, but I've got a trial coming up," Brock said.

The Judge put a match to his cigar. The flame leapt and
danced in front of his face. He drew on the cigar, smiled,
then fixed his gaze on Brock's face. There was something
hard in his voice when he said: "Don't refuse me."

Two hours later they were still sitting in a suite of over-
stuffed chairs in a wood-paneled private lounge near the hotel
bar. Many six-dollar cognacs had come and gone. Brock felt
an odd giddiness that came not just from the alcohol but also
from the company. Unlike his father and Reggie Vinyard and
Press Cain—men who made up the ruling class of the city—
Brock had made a point of living a very private life. He had
set out to be a good litigator and nothing more; he had never
had an interest in playing the ruling game.

But sitting there in that knot of leather armchairs tucked
away in that woody corner of the hotel, the talk of familiar
encounters with senators and CEOs and financiers and civil
rights leaders washing over him, Brock began to feel an odd
sense, not of envy exactly, but perhaps of lost possibility, a
sense that if he'd lived a slightly different life he might have
been in that room and that place not just as someone's son
but as an equal.

Reggie Vinyard had just finished growling out a story
about his one and only encounter with Malcolm X, and the
group had lapsed into silence. Somewhere in another part
of the hotel a maudlin jazz trio played a song that Brock
didn't recognize.

In that moment of silence, it occurred to Brock to wonder
why these men had chosen this moment to be together. It
was as though they had decided to include Brock in two

hours of superficial, undirected conversation for no particular reason at all. But Brock knew these men didn't operate that way. That wasn't how the ruling game was played.

Brock studied the three other men. They were an odd combination: his father, grave and reserved; Cain, quick and dandified; Vinyard, brash and scrappy and black. An odd combination of men. Sometimes Brock had wondered how they ever came to be partners. Brock had asked his father a few times, but only gotten vague answers. They seemed such an unlikely combination. His father and Press Cain had gone to Duke together. But Vinyard? Brock had never gotten the story on their connection to Reggie Vinyard.

Brock had seen the pictures of him from the sixties, in marches and sit-ins and standing before the Supreme Court. He had been thin, elegant, almost beautiful then. But now he was massive, a fat cat, a good old boy. Prime rib and cigars.

He'd been a federal judge briefly during the Carter administration, then resurfaced—rather suddenly it had seemed at the time—as a partner in Clay, Brock & Cain.

At exactly ten-thirty Brock's father stood, smiled his courtly Southern smile. "I'd better run along," he said, "I've got an early morning tomorrow."

Cain jumped up too, checking his watch. "Good God!" he said. "How'd it get so late?"

Brock made noises about leaving, too, but Vinyard had already motioned to the waiter, instructing him to bring two more cognacs. "Look," Brock said, "I've got a trial coming up in two days. I really need to run."

"Stay," his father said as he turned to leave. "By all means, son, don't leave on my account."

Again Brock had the unsettling feeling that this whole evening—the invitation to the portrait unveiling, the studied idleness of this closeted conversation, the brandy and cigars, the entire mood of the evening—had been stage-managed. But why? And by whom? Whatever was going on, Brock decided he'd better stay and see it through. He waved at his father, who fixed him with a momentary stare before disappearing through the door at the far side of the room.

After his partners had gone, Vinyard heaved his bulk up out of the chair where he'd been sitting, then lowered himself onto the couch next to Brock. The Morocco leather let out a satisfied groan. "Join me in a cigar before you go," he demanded, his voice falling to a rasping whisper.

"Thanks, no," Brock said. "I don't smoke."

The big man let out a soft, almost sexual growl. He was very close—so close that Brock could smell his rich, heavy odor: tobacco smoke, cologne, brandy. The drinks arrived. The Judge lit his cigar, then clinked his glass against Brock's. Brock felt uncomfortable at this sudden invasion of his space—and yet there was something warm about it, something flattering.

He waited as Vinyard sloshed his brandy, sipped, pulled on the cigar, crunched manfully on some oyster crackers. Brock suspected this symphony of appetites was all just part of the Judge's shtick. But where was the performance leading?

"We're in a bind, son," Vinyard said finally. Brock had thought maybe Vinyard was a little drunk, but then the Judge swung his dark gaze around, and Brock realized that, however many drinks he may have had in him, Judge Reggie Vinyard was stone cold sober.

"We?"

"The firm. Clay, Brock, Vinyard & Cain. Raymond Lata's death has caused us a problem. We'd already lost two of our top litigation partners last year—jumped ship on us, the backstabbing sumbitches. Other than Press Cain, that leaves our litigation section picked clean. Result being, we in trouble."

"How so?"

"See, our biggest client, a multinational corporation that you doubtless know the name of, has got a major, *major* civil trial coming up. One month from today. A four-hundred-million-dollar case. Now, we can't afford for this company to get weak in the knees, go running off to some other firm just because we're temporarily light on litigation talent. It's out of the question. You understand me, son?"

Brock wasn't sure.

"You sure you don't want a cigar?" The Judge was so close that Brock could see every pore and fold of flesh in the big man's dark face. His breath was heavy with smoke and ancient grapes.

"Thanks, no."

The Judge looked away for a moment, then slid his arm

around Brock's neck, wrapped his large fingers around
Brock's shoulder, squeezed. Brock felt the heat of the man
through his coat.

"Imagine this, boy," he said. "A whole new class of client. No more slip-and-falls on aisle seven, no more neck
braces, no more hit-and-runs, no more third-rate bookkeepers
getting knocked down in titty bars."

"Now wait a sec," Brock said, feeling a brief flame of
indignation. "I happen to have one of the top personal injury
practices in the city. Thriving, interesting, beholden to no
one."

"Listen!" Vinyard was still squeezing Brock's shoulder,
his big fingers digging into the flesh.

"What?"

"Listen!" And then after a brief pause. "Hear that? It's
the Big Time! I hear the Big Time calling you, boy."

"Whoa. Slow down. How about spelling this out?"

"Full partnership," Reggie Vinyard said. "Full partnership
in the firm of Clay, Brock, Vinyard & Cain. This is just
between you and me, but Press Cain is looking to slow down
and smell the roses a little, cut back on his commitment to the
firm. This would leave you *de facto* head and heir apparent of
the litigation section. You'll have five associates and two
junior partners as direct reports. Salary starting at four hundred and ten grand a year. Plus profit share."

Brock opened his mouth, but nothing come out. Four hundred and ten thousand a year. Jesus Christ! But then something else struck him, a bitter memory.

He said, "You know, Judge, when I got out of UGA
Law—where I admit I graduated by the skin of my teeth—I
had some trouble finding a job." Vinyard was looking at him
through lowered eyelids. "So much trouble, in fact, that I
finally dragged myself over to Dad's office and begged him
for a chance to work at the firm. But Dad said no. Out of
the question. He said, *It wouldn't be a good match,* or something equally tactful, equally insulting. I badgered him and
badgered him but he wouldn't budge. Finally, in his gentle
way, he went point by point through this list of reasons why
I wasn't suited to be a member of his hallowed firm: It wasn't
fair to others with better academic records; I wasn't prepared
for the extraordinary demands against my time or energy; I

didn't like neckties; my hair was too long; it wasn't a social atmosphere I was likely to be comfortable in. On and on!''

Brock hesitated. He had gotten kind of worked up, remembering how angry he'd been at his father fifteen years ago. It had been, in some ways, the defining moment of their relationship: Brock, once again, falling short of his father's expectations. Finally, though, his father had said in an almost proud voice: *You don't have the temperament for this place. I don't hold that against you. It's not a positive or negative aspect of your character. But this place would be a straightjacket to you. Go your own way, son. Go your own way.*

"Of course he was right," Brock said. "His law firm was not the place for me."

Vinyard nodded. "It's a different place now, you know. I'm testimony to that.''

"Yeah, but why the turnaround? All these years go by, and suddenly, out of the blue, Dad wants me on the A-Team? Sure, I've proved myself. Sure, I'm a damn good litigator. But so what? There are other guys around town who've won million-dollar cases. And plenty that have more experience in these big civil cases you guys handle. I don't know dick about shareholder derivative suits or any of that stuff.'' Brock felt an edge creeping into his voice, one that betrayed the old resentments against his father.

Vinyard released his hold on Brock's shoulder. "I understand,'' he said softly. "But we need somebody *now*. Not tomorrow, not the next day. Now. It's vital to the firm. Absolutely vital. We've seen you fight tough battles and win. We know you and we trust you, and frankly, right now, we ain't got time to fuck around with search committees and compensation consultants and headhunters who are just gonna find us some prima donna shithead that's gonna beat us to death about how many windows gotta be in his office and how big his desk gotta be and where his name gotta sit on the gotdamn letterhead.'' Vinyard's voice had gone low and jivey all of a sudden, like a preacher in the AME church. He squeezed Brock's shoulder again, digging for the bone with his thumb.

"We need *you*, boy,'' he said. "*You!*''

"But I don't have experience in this kind of litigation.''

"Ah! But you know juries and you know courtrooms. That's all that matters.'' His meaty face heaping up into a big smile. "The law? Why you think why we hire all them pencilhead Ivy League kids? The law ain't shit. Our pencilheads'll *teach* you the law."

Brock hesitated. He could feel the seductive tug of a new life. Moving closer in to where the wheels of power lay. Maybe he was ready for that now, ready in a way he hadn't been when he was a younger man.

"There's a hitch," Brock said. "I'm going to trial in two days."

The Judge dismissed this with a wave of his cigar. "Aw, get a continuance. If Judge Wellborn gives you trouble, I might could help her to understand all the strain you been under with this Shakespeare business, threats to your family, everything. Me and Wellborn go back a ways. Then we'll sic one of your shiny new junior partners on the case, you can just put the whole business out your mind."

It was an attractive thought. Forget about Jimmy Dale, get his wife and daughter back from Tennessee. And Dru, this was just what she wanted: she'd been pressing him to join a bigger firm for years, to take on some partners, to spread the killing workload of a one-man practice. Wouldn't it be nice to be able to push the boring depositions and tedious legal research onto a flock of eager-beaver kids just out of law school? Hell yes, it would.

"You got to ask yourself right now, to*day*: am I happy with my life? Am I completely satisfied? And if the answer's no, then maybe it's time for a change. A new challenge."

Brock nodded.

"But you got to understand, boy, sometimes a moment comes—maybe only once in a life," the Judge said. "You're standing at the crossroad, time flying by, you hesitate, boom, it's gone. Gone forever."

A sudden intrusion on the pleasant thoughts: "What about my disbarment proceedings?"

Vinyard raised his eyelids slightly. "That obstacle is eminently surmountable."

"What the hell's that mean?" Something flashed in Brock's mind: Reggie Vinyard's signature on the last page of Caitlin's affidavit—the one the fat man had offered to trade him for the concordance. There were some odd connections going on here, but Brock couldn't quite make them out. Not yet.

Reggie Vinyard smiled thinly. "Simple. You make the right move, I have a hundred and ten percent confidence that the Disciplinary Board will see the light on this issue."

"I don't see how you're in any position to say that."

Vinyard's dark eyes looked at him coolly. "Trust me," he said. "I am."

Brock thought about it. How could the Judge know whether the Disciplinary Board would clear him? It didn't make sense. But Vinyard didn't say that sort of thing lightly. "This sounds a lot like blackmail," he said finally.

Brock thought he saw a flash of anger in the judge's black eyes, but then they went warm and avuncular. "Don't be silly. Here. Take a cigar. Think about it."

Brock took the cigar, rolled it between his palms, smelled the bitter, nutty, seductive odor. It would be a relief to cut himself off from the Jimmy Dale Evans mess, get back to a normal life. And a guaranteed four hundred grand a year wouldn't hurt much either.

Still, something here didn't scan quite right. But he didn't have the slightest idea what it was.

Judge Reggie B. Vinyard stood, stabbed out his cigar in the ashtray. "Tomorrow, boy," he growled. "I need your answer tomorrow by five."

Brock put the cigar in his mouth but didn't light it.

• 36

Brock knew he should go home, put in another hour on a brief for one of the pretrial motions, but the cognac was swirling around in his head and he just didn't feel like it.

He called Jimmy Dale from the lobby of the Ritz-Carlton, but there was no answer. He considered calling Dru again, but couldn't dredge up the emotional energy, so he went down to the parking garage and got in the BMW. Instead of heading home he drove aimlessly around the city, the unlit cigar clamped in his teeth. First he cut through Buckhead on Peachtree, looking out the windows at the young girls. Bouncing breasts, squeals of seductive laughter, short skirts. The bars were full of people, swirling in and out. He considered stopping, going in, seeing if his grandfather was right.

Then felt revolted. Christ, three days away from his wife and he was thinking about picking up women in bars. Besides, all these young girls, they'd probably snicker at him, take him for some pathetic divorcee, good for nothing but a couple of free drinks until somebody better came along.

He slid the One Eighty-Seven CD into his stereo, surrounding himself with the crunching of brutal, sexy, adolescent guitars.

He left Buckhead, drifted on down Peachtree, cut over to Northside, drove until he reached the tumbledown neighborhoods just west of the city center. It was then that he realized why he'd come out here. What was that place Merlee had mentioned at the church last night? It had been in the back of his mind, but he just hadn't wanted to fess up to what he was doing. The Austin Avenue Grill—that was it. All the way on the other side of town.

He headed past Georgia Tech, past Techwood Homes, through the empty caverns of the city center—the huge and lifeless monoliths of commerce rising around him—then through another desolate section of town where hookers and black kids in baggy pants hung around on the street corners cracking jokes and making hard eyes at each other. Finally he reached Little Five Points, parked his car on Euclid, walked into the bar.

It was a weird place—a mix of hip yuppies, burnt-out alcoholic rednecks, and the black-boots-and-nipple-ring set. A blues band was thrashing away in the one room—three white boys backing up an old black guy in a leather baseball cap who played a slightly out-of-tune pedal steel, and sang in a high voice. Brock stopped by the bar, picked up a Miller, and lit his cigar.

It didn't take long to find her. She was in the back, chalking a pool cue, her dyed hair glistening in the smoky blue haze, while a very large guy in a Gold's Gym shirt with the sleeves ripped off racked up the balls. Merlee looked more lithe and delicate and sexy than the last time he'd seen her. She wore a knit tank top of a revealing nature and a blue jean skirt, sufficiently short to put most of her legs in view. Nice legs: pale, blue-veined, well-proportioned.

"Well," Brock said. "What a surprise."

Merlee looked at him out of the corner of her eye, then set her chalk on the edge of the table. "Want to play the winner?"

"If it's you," he said.

She turned back to him, looked at him frankly, searching his face. "I do believe you're drunk," she said, then she lined up the cue ball, her smoky quartz pendant dangling between her lovely breasts, smacked it with a good smooth stroke. Her break sank four balls. "How 'bout you go get me a double Jack Black, maybe I'll catch up with you."

When Brock came back with Merlee's drink, the guy in the Gold's Gym shirt looked at him, let his head rock back on his big neck, resting his tongue in his cheek. The nitwit Alpha Male challenge. The guy slammed the two ball into the corner pocket, then muffed the next shot.

"You're stroking too hard," Brock said. The guy in the Gold's Gym shirt flexed his triceps, gave him a nasty look.

Merlee ran the table.

"Nice," Brock said, picking up a cue. "I hope you weren't expecting any friendly wagers out of me."

"We're playing two out of three, bud," Gold's Gym said.

"Since when?" Merlee said.

The weight lifter glared at her, then at Brock. His neck seemed to be filling with blood and a vein the size of Brock's pinky twitched in one of his biceps.

"Been hitting the steroids a little hard, my man?" The voice of five brandies speaking through Brock's lips.

"Hoooo-hooooo!" said a redneck burn-out propped up against the bar. "You gone take that from this boy, Randy?"

Randy set his cue down gently across the table and said, "Two out of three, sweetheart."

"At what point did she become your sweetheart?" Brock said.

"It's okay," Merlee said quietly. "Two out of three."

"It's not okay," Brock said. A little voice inside his head going *shut up, shut up!* but not quite getting heard.

"Hoooooo yeah!" the burn-out at the bar said, beside himself with the prospect of a good bar fight. "Yeah! It's *not* okay!"

"Shut up," Gold's Gym told the burn-out, before turning to Brock and unleashing: "You got a problem, pal?"

"Let me guess," Brock said to Merlee. "This jerk isn't one of your born-again friends."

At which point Gold's Gym picked up his pool cue off the table and broke it over Brock's head. The cigar Reggie Vinyard had given him flew out of Brock's mouth, showering sparks across his shirt. In the other room, the blues band had taken a break. Somebody cranked up the jukebox and Brock's song came on.

Scream! Scream! The phlegmy voice and the howling guitars. Brock felt an angry smile welling up on his face. Then an idiot voice came from his lips: "You want to try that again, dickhead?"

When he regained consciousness, Brock found himself staring up at the distant, stained ceiling of the bar. Merlee's face floated above him. Brock could hear the pool balls snicking into each other.

"Nicely executed," Merlee said.

"Hmmm," Brock said. "Kinda stupid, huh?" The pain ran in two bands down from his head and into his neck and back.

"Let me take a look at your head," she said.

He didn't object. Her cool hands probed his scalp. It felt kind of nice actually, and he found himself very close to the quartz pendant which hung between her breasts. Which was not so bad either.

"No cuts. Just a couple big lumps." The fingers explored a little further. "Your aura has a big dent in it."

Brock stood up, and then his stomach flipped and he went down on his knees. "I think it must have put a kink in my *chi*, too," he said.

Merlee nodded seriously. "Why don't I just drive you home?"

"My home or yours?" Brock said. And back inside the bone cavern of his mind a calm and reasonable voice was telling him something but he couldn't make out what it was saying.

Merlee looked at him with her large green eyes, studied his face for a moment. She seemed to be mulling something over.

"God help me," she said. And then she took his hand. "My place is right down the street."

Merlee lived in a yellow one-story house on a side street off Moreland. When they got inside Brock said, "Where'd he hit me the second time? I feel like somebody jammed a fork in my spine."

"Right smack across the back of your neck."

"Oh great. You got any aspirin?"

"No, but I could make you some ginseng tea."

"What will that do for me?"

"It's a general anodyne. Then maybe I could do some bodywork on you, open up your meridians to speed up the healing process." She put her hands on his shoulders. "Lie down."

"So I guess this is kind of like going to a chiropractor?"

"It's not chiropractic. Chiropractic is just another mechanistic Western idea,'' Merlee said dismissively. ''This is more of an Eastern approach. You're trying to unblock the channels in your body so the *chi* can circulate better.''

''What channels?''

''The *chi* channels. The meridians. See, your kidney meridian and your pericardial meridians are flowing badly. And—ooh!—God, your triple-burner meridian is completely blocked. No wonder your neck hurts. You should be dead by now.''

''My triple what?''

''Triple burner. It's considered to be the organ responsible for water metabolism.''

Merlee ran her hands gently across his back, massaging his muscles with her palms, grunting softly once or twice. Suddenly she dug her thumbs into his neck. Pain shot up his left arm, burst into his skull with an explosion of white light. Brock screamed. ''Ow! That *hurt!*''

''Of course it did. Unblocking the Tianyou cavity is always pretty painful. Feels better already, huh?''

And she was right—it did.

''Now Brock, I can't fix everything. Your yin and yang vessels are out of whack, and the only way to fix that is to do exercises designed to regulate them. I'd recommend you take up a daily regimen of Chi Gung or Tai Chi.''

''Oh, sure.'' Brock relaxed, closed his eyes, pictured Merlee leaning over him, rubbing her soothing hands across his body. After a few moments Brock felt himself getting hard.

Her hands ran down his flanks, brushed across his buttock, stroked the edge of his face. ''You sure this is part of the therapy?'' Brock said.

Merlee let out a soft, choking gasp, then folded her soft body against him.

And then they were kissing. Mouths open, hungry, wet, all over each other. Merlee rolled over on top of him, and Brock's hand moved up under her skirt, cradled her remarkably firm buttocks.

His ears were roaring, the feel of the beer and the cognacs and the pool cue and the lustful abandon filled his head with a pounding pressure. Merlee's tongue explored his lips. He pulled her hips to him, and she shuddered, moaned.

Various articles of clothing drifted floorward. Brock was standing in his underwear and a pair of black socks. Merlee was down to nothing but a very flimsy, lacy pair of panties and the crystal pendant that hung between her fine bare breasts.

"Come on," she demanded. "Come *on!*"

Then they were down on the floor, sprawled on her soft carpet, and she was wrestling his underpants off, running her tongue down his hardness. Brock's lips were tingling. Merlee was busy with her mouth, her tongue, her hand. The tingling in his lips deepened and turned to numbness. Christ, how long had it been since his lips had gone numb when he was having sex? Not since before he and Dru were married.

She crawled up next to him and he saw that she was stark naked, and he turned over, ready to enter her.

"Uh ..." she said, putting the flat of her hand against his arm.

"Yes?" Brock said. The word didn't want to come out quite right because of the tingling of his lips.

"I don't have—I mean, have you got a rubber on you?"

Brock slumped back onto the carpet, put his hands over his face. "Oh, shit. The old rubber setback."

Merlee ran her fingers down his chest. "Well, look," she said. "It's not that big a deal. Maybe we could ..."

"No, no," Brock said. "It's not that." And suddenly his lips were in perfect working order. His conscience had suddenly appeared too. He felt hangdog, foolish, wicked, ridiculous. "It's just—we both know it, this is a bad idea."

Merlee sighed, stared up at the ceiling. Brock leaned his back against her couch. "Man, I feel like a jerk," she said.

"Don't say that," he said. "It's all my fault. It's just ... I've been going through all this crazy shit and I'm kind of confused right now."

"I believe that's number three," Merlee said dryly.

"Number three what?"

"All romantic misunderstandings are reducible to seven one-line excuses: I'm real confused right now; I'm pregnant; I'm just not ready to commit; I'm married; I'm gay." She smiled in a way that had nothing to do with humor. "I forget the others."

"I see," Brock said. They lay next to each other for a

while, staring up at the ceiling. "So does that mean it would be really tacky if I put my clothes back on now?"

Merlee laughed. "Why don't you stay and have a cup of good strong coffee?" Then she got up and walked into the kitchen. Her skin was translucent, her buttocks as smooth and firm as an eighteen-year-old's. "God *damn*," Brock said.

"What?" Merlee said from the kitchen. "I can't hear you."

On the way home he stopped at a payphone outside a twenty-four-hour gas station. The night had gone foggy and the lights of the gas signs filled the air with a red haze. He dialed the number for Dru's parents.

"Please," Brock said. "Please come home, Dru."

"It's like two o'clock in the morning, for godsake. My folks are in a panic."

"Dru," he said. "Dru, I'm going crazy here by myself."

"Are you drunk?"

"They offered me a partnership," Brock said. "Dad, Press, and Reggie. Drop Jimmy Dale, sign on the line, take over a big civil case—voilá, everything changes."

A rust-rotted Oldsmobile limped slowly by in the red night, its muffler clanking on the pavement, throwing up sparks. Inside a pale face stared at him through the window. The words of his song taunting him from the car's open window: *Scream! Scream! Living in a nightmare dream!* Fading down the street.

"What do you think, hon?" he said.

"What do *you* think?"

Brock stood for a while, mulling the thing over. Good question. What *did* he really think? It took him a minute to get it straight—but as soon as he did, he was sure.

"I think I ought to tell them to stuff it up their asses."

Way to go, Mr. Tactful. Brock listened to the recriminating hum of the dial tone. *Way. To. Go.*

Shakespeare was building the cage.

Building the cage and singing along with Willie Nelson, tears running down the face. Shakespeare didn't show a lot of emotion to the world, but alone in a safe place, you could let go, experience the passion. A lot of people thought country music was maudlin crap, but Shakespeare knew better. When country music got it right, it was like drilling straight down to the rawest, barest emotions. It was too raw, maybe, for some people. Some folks just couldn't stand being that close to the flame.

Even Shakespeare could only let loose that way in a safe place. Like the room. Call it a prison or a cage if you must—but it was safe. You could let the inner turmoil loose—all the years of hurt and despair and put-downs—let them free.

Shakespeare, getting busy with a hammer, tears running down the face as Willie sang about a boy leaving home, innocent and optimistic, then coming back to his Mama later with skin like iron and his breath as hard as kerosene. Shakespeare understood that. It was a hell of a thing, life in this awful world.

Shakespeare wanted everything set up properly. That's why the cage had to be built. Just in case.

A U-Haul truck had been rented in North Carolina a few weeks back, fake name. There, Shakespeare had bought a used bed frame and a used Sealy Posturpedic mattress set and a chest of drawers and some bright-blue print curtains in a sort of nautical theme of little compasses and boats. There wasn't a window in the room—not anymore—but Shakespeare thought maybe curtains would be a nice touch anyway. Make the place feel a little more homey.

Shakespeare had constructed the cage inside the back bedroom of a small rented house in a bedraggled neighborhood down in East Point. Started by putting plywood over the window, then built a whole new superstructure inside the room by nailing two-by-sixes to the floor and walls. After that came the blown foam. Took this machine that was made to put packing material into shipping boxes and covered the walls and floor with a six-inch thick coating of polyethylene foam. Finally came the plywood, nailed over the two-by-sixes.

And there it was: a new room inside the old room, a room that was a foot smaller in all dimensions. A cage. Smaller but quieter. Had a kind of Alice in Wonderland feel, like when Alice swallowed the growing tonic and got too huge to fit in the room.

The test: a boom box in the cage, cranked up as far as it would go—Willie playing "Whiskey River," his band loose and sloppy and loud. Shakespeare went out in the dark yard and pretended to look for something under the scraggly boxwood hedge. Perfect. You couldn't hear a thing.

Someone could scream and yell and bitch all they wanted inside that cage, and no one would ever hear them.

Shakespeare wasn't sure the cage would ever be used. It was sort of a Plan B thing. But if Brock didn't do what he was supposed to, then the cage would have to be used. It was that simple.

Shakespeare went back inside and finished laying the carpet—some remnants pulled from a dumpster behind a carpet store, untraceable. 1:30 in the morning. Time to knock off. Big day tomorrow, needed some sleep. Tomorrow, plenty of time to finish the room.

Shakespeare, feeling the tears again, a swelling bittersweet moment as old Willie sang about how it was never quite possible to really know another person, to ever make your love come into synch with another person's mind.

Shakespeare, singing along, arms clutching at the plywood sky in the safe and quiet cage.

THE CITATION

●

An attorney was waiting for court to begin one morning when Satan suddenly appeared in front of him. The devil said to the lawyer, "I have a proposition for you, counselor. You can win every case you try for the rest of your natural life. Your clients will love you; your associates and colleagues will worship you; and you'll make outlandish sums of money. All I want in exchange is your soul, your wife's soul, plus the souls of your children, your parents, your grandparents, your friends, and your partners."

The lawyer studied Satan carefully, narrowed his eyes, and said, "Okay, pal. What's the catch?"

• 38

When Brock shuffled groggily downstairs from bed the next morning, he found his grandfather sitting in the kitchen with a stack of photocopies spread across the table. It was the concordance, along with all the rest of the papers that had been in the folder. He'd left it on the table the night before.

"What the hell happened to you?" the Judge said.

"All kind of manliness. You'd have been proud of me. I got drunk, then got hit over the head with a pool cue. Among other things." He went into the downstairs bathroom, took five Tylenols, walked back to the kitchen.

"So, did you look at this stuff?" the Judge said.

"Not carefully," Brock said.

The Judge raised one eyebrow slightly. "Well, I believe it would reward a little study."

"Oh? What did you find?"

Before the Judge could tell Brock anything, the phone rang. It was Dru, calling from Tennessee.

"Look, I'm sorry about last night," she said. "It was late and, well, I overreacted."

"Okay," Brock said.

"I was being stupid. It's—what I'm saying is, I'd like to come home."

Brock felt an odd combination of relief and anger. "Just like that?"

"Please, Brock. Please don't make this hard."

"I'm sorry. I don't mean to. I want to see you. I want to see you both." Brock had done some thinking the night before—albeit in a foolish, ass-backwards way. And the conclu-

177

sion he'd come to was that he needed his family. He wanted to be *here* with them, not out getting drunk and trying to get laid and getting thumped with pool cues. That was no way for a grown man to act. No matter what his grandfather might think.

"We've both been under a lot of stress, Brock. And I guess we reacted differently to this whole thing. I can see that now. And that's okay." Dru's voice broke a little. "I just want to come home, Brock."

"No conditions, no ultimatums?"

The sound of a slow exhalation of breath. "I think maybe you've had kind of a blind spot about our marriage. You've let things slide. You've taken things for granted. But I can't put it all on you. I haven't been as sympathetic as I might have been. It's something we're going to have to work on together."

"You have any thoughts about this job with Dad's firm?"

"I think you know my feelings. But it's your choice. You have to do what makes you happy."

Three days in Tennessee and it was like a whole new Dru. Amazing. Or maybe three days by himself and he just heard her differently. "So when were you thinking of coming home?"

"Probably late this morning. We should be back, I don't know, mid-afternoon or something."

"See you then."

"Love you."

"Yeah," Brock said. "I love you, too."

"Here's somebody that wants to say hi."

Grace's voice came on the phone. "Hi, Daddy!"

"Hey, sweetheart."

"Guess what? I sat in a ant nest and they bited me."

"Bit. They *bit* you."

"Yes! They *bited* me! Now we're coming home."

"I know. I love you, Grace." Brock felt an upwelling of love and need for this marvelous child.

After Brock hung up the phone, he poured himself a bowl of cardboard-flavored bran flakes and skim milk, and a very large cup of coffee.

"They coming back?" the Judge said.

"Yeah," Brock said. "What were we talking about?"

"We were talking about these papers I found on the table this morning. I just started going through them, trying to figure out what was going on."

"Did you find the concordance?" Brock said.

"I'll get to that in a minute. First, let me show you the rest of the stuff in here."

"Incorporation papers, mostly. I assumed it was documentation that shows who owns Laughing Dolls."

"Yup. Your standard maze of front companies. Five different strip joints. Two holding companies. Three different operating front companies, plus one property manager, three more-or-less bogus real estate ventures. And one property owner." The Judge slid a piece of paper across the table. "Here. Took me two and a half hours to put the pieces together."

Brock picked up the diagram drawn in the Judge's neat hand. "So what's all this?" he said.

The Judge smiled. "See, I take all the names of the lawyers who filed this crap," the Judge said, "and guess what? Turns out they're all on this list in the back of the folder."

"The concordance. Let me see."

The old man put a gnarled hand on the folder. "Hold on. The fun's only just beginning. See, there's a little code next to each of these names. After Darden here, there's BP, that stands for Brassy Partners, with a P after that I'm guessing means he's a partner. Each one of the guys on this list either filed some of the paperwork or were officers or partners for all the companies on the chart. The codes spell out what they did."

Brock studied the chart. "Hm. But what's it all mean?"

"My guess, they're funneling the profits offshore."

"Tax dodge?"

The old man nodded. "I bet these places produce nice fat tax losses that get funneled up to these limited partnerships—see? LDI, TTL, Peggy Partners, Brassy Partners? Those losses in turn flow up to two master partnerships, ODI and Wentworth. The partners in those two write the 'losses' off on their taxes."

Brock nodded. "And the real profit flows out through these dummy companies right here—Wentworth Properties, ODI-

II, and Lynx.'' He tapped his finger on the box at the bottom of the chart.

"Exactly,'' the old man said. "The general partner of which is a company called Wentworth, Ltd. Which is incorporated—get this—in a country called Vanuatu.''

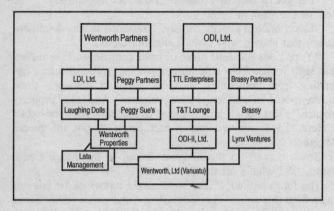

"Vanuatu?'' Brock said. "You're making this up.''

"Haven't been confabbing much with your financial planners, have you, son? In the good old days, you used to incorporate in Switzerland if you wanted to set up an offshore corporation to shelter money. Then the smart money started going to Panama and the Caymans and the Netherlands Antilles. Now they're going to this dinky little island in the South Pacific—Vanuatu. Real strict secrecy laws, I understand.''

Brock stared at the chart, then at the list of names, then at the chart again. He thought back to the stack of deposit slips he'd gotten from Jimmy Dale's closet two days earlier. "Anything in there about something called GCB, Ltd.?'' he said.

"GCB?'' His grandfather looked at the chart. "No. No GCB.''

"Huh. Because as I recall, that's how the money got moved from Laughing Dolls to Wentworth—through GCB.'' Brock stared at the chart for a moment. "This is pretty interesting, but I still don't see why all these people were so hot to get hold of these documents.''

The Judge cackled, flipped open the folder, turned to the last page. "That's because you haven't read it yet."

Brock looked at the concordance.

"*These* are the people that own Laughing Dolls?"

The old man nodded.

"My God."

Brock stared at the concordance for a while.

MEL PROCHASKA
LEE DARDEN
BOYD MICHAELS
RAYMOND LATA

Those were the names he'd seen the first time he looked at the list. But there was one more name, a name he hadn't had time to read when he'd glanced inside the folder at Caitlin's house. The name of a man who wasn't dead yet.

"Jesus Christ," Brock said.

"You in a nest of snakes, boy."

Brock slumped back in his chair.

"Good news," the old man said, "is this here could do some interesting things for that Jimmy Dale Evans case."

While Brock was thinking, the phone rang. It was Janelle Moncrief, the detective. "Mr. Brock," she said. "Would it be convenient for you to come down to my office?"

"Not especially," Brock said. "Why?"

The interview room in the homicide section down on Somerset still smelled like broken pipes. A uniformed cop had led Brock into the room, where he sat smelling the bad air for five or ten minutes. Janelle Moncrief finally came in. She was wearing bright green, like she was going to the Catholic church on St. Patrick's day, and she looked annoyed about something.

She stood for a moment looking down at him. "Goddammit, Brock," she said. "I got a bone to pick with you."

"What now?" Brock said.

"Time to stop playing games! Who's the other shooter?"

Brock was feeling a little confused, his head still aching from the night before. "I'm sorry? The other what?"

The lieutenant crossed her arms, glared at him, showing the whites of her eyes. "You heard me. I want a straight story. Who's the other shooter?"

Brock touched the welt on his head. "I don't understand."

"You didn't shoot Mic Giddens," she said finally.

Brock frowned. "You're telling me that I had a conversation with a guy, that he pulled a gun on me and stuck it in my face, that I then *shot* the guy . . . and yet somehow I didn't really notice who he was? Does this seem vaguely plausible to you?"

She shook her head slowly. "That's not what I'm saying. It was Giddens that got shot. I'm just saying it wasn't *you* that shot him."

Brock didn't say anything. It didn't make sense. He'd *seen* it happen. He'd pulled the trigger. He'd seen the side of Giddens's face go red.

Janelle Moncrief sat down across the table. "Look here, Brock. I don't know who you're covering for, but I just got some reports back from the forensics folks and from the medical examiner. The ME says Giddens was shot twice from behind—once in the head, once in the upper back. Crime lab says it was a .380. Your piece is a nine. You told us you fired three times. Evidence techs dug three nine-millimeter slugs out of the wall."

Brock stared at her.

"How long you been shooting, Brock?"

"Uh . . ." Brock flushed. "A day. I bought the gun the day before yesterday."

"Well, brother, you need to spend a little more time on the pistol range. You missed your mark, all three shots."

"Then who . . ."

"That's what I'm saying, child! Who *did* shoot him?"

"The guy in the pipe?"

"The guy in the pipe, I might as well tell you, is a private investigator name of Cleland Davis. He's in the hospital now. Giddens shot him in the bee-hind. Based on the evidence we got, he wasn't the shooter either." She studied Brock's face. "According to the ME, the wound trajectories in Giddens's body point to a shooter firing from a level position, that is, roughly from chest or head height. According to both of you, Davis was lying on the ground."

"But that's impossible. There was no one else there."

Janelle Moncrief took a piece of paper out of a folder, spread it out on the table. It was the diagram of Giddens's office that Brock had drawn for the other detective the day before. Somebody had added dotted lines, which Brock presumed represented the trajectories of the bullets in the shooting. Moncrief tapped the diagram with a long white fingernail. "You told Sergeant Nichols, did you not, that this door was open?"

Brock nodded.

"And that Mr. Giddens's back was to that door?"

Again, Brock nodded.

"And furthermore that the barroom was dark, hard to see out into it?"

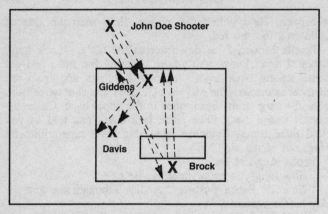

This time Brock just sat there. Moncrief took a Bic pen out of her purse, the end gnarled with tooth marks, and drew a fourth *X* on the diagram. After a moment she wrote *John Doe Shooter* next to it. From the shooter she drew the trajectories of three bullets. Two of the arrows hit Giddens. The John Doe Shooter's third bullet ended up in the wall very close to the mark representing Brock.

"There was somebody else in that bar, Mr. Brock. There *was*. Look at the trajectories."

Brock studied at the picture. After a while a question started jostling around in his mind and it made him feel a little queasy, like something sick and hurtful had lodged in his neck, started working its way down to his stomach.

"Question," the lieutenant said. "Could Giddens have jumped in front of the door just as John Doe started firing?"

Brock shook his head. He didn't like what she was implying.

Moncrief blinked. "See! Was John Doe aiming at Giddens? Or was he aiming at you?"

Brock stared at the diagram, feeling like someone had taken an eraser and blotted all thought from his mind. There was a certain relief to be found in knowing that he hadn't shot and killed a man. The problem was that if somebody else had been in the bar, then you had to ask ... But he couldn't even ask the question, much less face the answer.

Janelle Moncrief took her chewed-up pen, wrote something on the diagram, pushed it across the table. "Here's what I'm thinking."

She'd drawn a circle around "John Doe Shooter" and then written one word underneath it: Shakespeare.

"No," Brock said. "Oh, no, no, no."

• 40

The phone rang as soon as Brock got to his office. He sat down, put his feet up on the desk.

"Hi." A distant-sounding woman's voice. "It's Merlee."

In his mind he could still see Merlee carrying her coffee pot around the living room, her naked body shining slightly in the soft light. It gave him a strange feeling, excited and appalled at the same time.

"Merlee. Yeah. Look, I'm sorry about—"

"I think we got the perfunctory apologies out of the way last night, Brock." There was a pause. "The reason I'm calling is that I got a message from Caitlin Cobranchy this morning."

"No kidding."

"She sounded a little incoherent, but I gather she's in some kind of trouble."

"What kind of trouble?"

"Wouldn't say." Merlee hesitated. "But she mentioned something called Wentworth. You ever heard of that?"

Wentworth. That was the company that his grandfather figured was being used to funnel money from the strip joints out of the country. Brock took his feet off the desk. "It's the company that indirectly controls Laughing Dolls."

"She said something about Jimmy Dale Evans. Something about getting a copy of their corporate filings from the secretary of state's office. Do you know what this is about?"

"Not exactly." Brock thought about it for a moment. Suddenly something occurred to him. "What are you up to this morning?"

"One thing and another. Why?"

"I've got motions and *voir dire* in the Jimmy Dale Evans trial tomorrow. So I don't have time to do this." He paused. "Have you got time to run down to the secretary of state's office, pick up a copy of everything that's been filed for Wentworth, Ltd.?"

"What's it worth to you?"

"You want me to *pay* you?" Brock laughed. "She's your client."

Merlee laughed mercilessly. "Yeah, but it seems to be your ass in the sling right now."

Brock hesitated. "How's fifty bucks an hour sound?"

"Hah. Seventy-five."

"Next thing you know, you'll be wanting a place on my letterhead."

"You wish."

"Oh, and check out something called ODI, Limited, too."

After Merlee hung up, Brock tried to put in a call to his father to discuss the partnership offer, but the secretary said he was in a meeting.

After an hour's work getting together some citations for one of the pretrial motions, he put on his jacket and headed for the elevator. Might as well go talk to Reggie Vinyard.

Brock rode up to the twenty-first floor, got off in the lobby of Clay, Brock, Vinyard & Cain. Somehow the architects had managed to sculpt, from the interior of a skyscraper, a space three stories high, with natural light at its crown, supplied through skylights on all four faces of the building. A fountain of red-veined marble burbled and spit in the middle of the room, throwing an occasional dash of water onto the shoes of the nervous supplicants waiting on leather couches scattered across the lobby. It was the kind of arrogant squandering of very dear square footage that demonstrated to the client that they were patronizing a law firm of unparalleled might, discipline, wealth, and taste—the kind of display intended to allay any fears that those bills for two hundred and ninety dollars an hour might not be worth every last red cent.

Though only one story high, Vinyard's corner office had the same kind of palatial sweep as the lobby and appeared to have shared the same designer. Vinyard didn't have a desk—nothing so mundane as to imply that ordinary *work* was done here—only a large conference table, cut from the same iron-veined marble as the fountain in the lobby. A knot of uncomfortable-looking modern furniture was pushed together in a sort of salon arrangement in the corner next to the windows. Vinyard invited Brock to sit in the chair with the best view.

Judge Reggie B. Vinyard smiled pleasantly, crossed his large, hamlike legs, arranged the creases of his Saville Row suit and said, "Should I be pouring us some single malt, Brock?"

Brock didn't answer immediately. "Quite a place you've got," he said finally.

Vinyard languidly retrieved a large cigar from the handy humidor, snipped off the end with a pair of small gold scissors, and put the rolled tobacco in his mouth. He struck a match, held it up, but then didn't light his cigar. "Well, boy, what's it gonna be?"

The match flickered, burned out, sent up a curl of smoke.

"First, answer me this." Brock put his feet up on the leather hassock in front of him. "Just precisely what the fuck is going on here, Reggie?"

Vinyard winked, struck another match, lit his cigar. "I like you, boy," he said, then he laughed, a sound like rocks thumping around in an oil drum. A heavy cloud of smoke came out of his mouth and surrounded his big face. "I like the hell out of you."

"Notwithstanding which . . ."

"Notwithstanding which, what do you want to know?"

"This partnership offer. Why now? Why all of a sudden?"

"Like I said yesterday." Vinyard shrugged. "Lata's gone, we got to have somebody. Fast."

"Don't insult my intelligence. Talk to me."

Vinyard took his cigar out of his mouth, held it over his paunch as he looked at Brock with sleepy eyes. "I keep forgetting," he said. "You were to the manor born. Me, I wouldn't have to be asked but once, I'd be scrambling up the ladder. But you, Brock, you weren't born a poor nigger dirt farmer like I was, staring at the ass-end of a mule every day back when a white man in most little jerkwater towns in this state could walk right down the street in white sheets and a pointy hat, not even get a second look.''

Brock crossed his feet. He knew for a fact Reggie Vinyard had never seen the ass-end of a mule or probably any other farm animal. Best he recalled, Vinyard's old man had been a dentist.

"But not you. No, sir! You, Brock—you got to ask all kind of questions.'' Vinyard put an avuncular smile on his lips. "Don't get me wrong. I respect that. No! Not respect. I *envy* that. I wish I had the comfort being inside my own skin that you do.''

"That doesn't sound like an answer to me.''

Reggie laughed. "It's not. But let's be honest here. When your daddy joined this firm back in the sixties, it was the most hidebound, traditional, lily-white firm in town. Lily-white!'' Vinyard grinned. "I knew your Daddy back then, and ooh, I wanted to be just like him! Ain't that ironic?

"Anyway, point is, past twenty years, this firm's gotten all watered down—Jews, Yankees, women, black folks, couple Latino brothers, even got us a Chinese girl doing intellectual property up on twenty-seven. Now, you may laugh at this, but people still respect a firm where the top boys are white men with Anglo-Saxon names. Between you and me, I think it'd be a hell of a thing, bring you on board here, groom you to be managing partner.''

"You're shitting me,'' Brock said.

"Do I look like I'm cracking jokes?'' Vinyard hoisted himself out of his chair, walked over and looked out one of his large windows. "Believe you me, boy, if anybody in this world understands about appearances versus reality, what's up versus what's down, it's Brother Reggie Vinyard. Here's how it is. Your Dad, he's getting on. Coupla years he gonna be ready to slow down, buy him a boat, cruise the Mediterranean or something. Cain, too. Then who's it gonna be? A major law firm run by a spear-chucking jigaboo integrationist rabble-rouser? No, sir! Will not fly, my friend, in the boardrooms of Georgia. Our blue-chip clients, brother, they be fighting like cats in a bag to see who can haul ass away from this firm the fastest.''

Brock shook his head. This was too ridiculous for words. So ridiculous it almost made sense.

"You want me to be a figurehead."

Vinyard took a long drag on his cigar. "I want you to join us, in a very pleasant and lucrative and well-connected law practice. After that, it's up to you. You a bright boy. You want to make things happen, they gonna happen. All I'm telling you—a man of your particular pedigree and talents got a lot of options."

Brock started to laugh. He hammed it up a little, pretending he was about to fall out the chair. Reggie was the kind of man who appreciated theater.

Finally Reggie took the hook. "What's so funny, Brock?"

"You, Reggie." Brock wiped his eyes. "Man, I almost believed you for a minute."

"That right?" Reggie didn't have the big sleepy smile on anymore and he seemed to have forgotten about the Partegas smoking faintly in his hand.

Brock stood and joined Vinyard in looking out the window. He could see Peachtree winding its way through midtown and up toward Buckhead. The sky was a little hazy, but the sun still sparked and snapped against the skyscrapers. From here the town seemed manageable, trouble free. One could imagine steering the whole thing from this window—as though at the bridge of some great and ponderous ship.

Brock felt suddenly woozy standing only inches from the edge, looking down hundreds of feet to the ground. Why was Vinyard lying about something so simple, so obvious?

"I can't," Brock said finally. "I can't take the job."

When he turned around, Vinyard's face had gone furious, like a round kettle bubbling with poison. All of the bonhomie and theater and fatherly indulgence had gone out the window, exposing the naked man. His voice came out in a low, feral growl. "I think you need to reconsider."

"I've made my decision," Brock said quietly. Then he took out a photocopy he'd made of the concordance and read it off. " 'Mel Prochaska. Lee Darden. Boyd Michaels. Raymond Lata.' "

"What is *that?*" Vinyard said.

"Let me finish. I've got one more name on the list." Brock looked Vinyard in the eye, read the last name: " 'Reggie B. Vinyard.' "

Vinyard leapt suddenly across the six feet of carpet that

separated them, pouncing with a catlike agility that Brock
wouldn't have expected in a man of his bulk. He grabbed
Brock by the lapels and slammed him into the floor-to-ceiling
window. Brock could feel the big pane of glass bending with
their combined weight. Beneath him the ground, hundreds of
feet below, seemed to rear up toward him.

"Listen here, you skinny pipsqueak motherfucker," Vinyard whispered, his voice rough as emery paper. The pane
of glass groaned ominously. Brock clutched at a sideboard
table, knocking it over, unable to regain balance. "If you
think I'm gonna stand around, let you introduce all that shit
about my connection to Wentworth and ODI and Laughing
Dolls and a bunch of serial murders in open court, you *sadly*
gotdamn mistaken."

Brock felt the window give a little more, and he imagined
the two of them falling out the window, hurtling toward the
ground, Vinyard cursing him all the way. To keep from falling Brock put his arms around Vinyard, squeezed him like a
lover as the big man's small hazel eyes burned into his own.
They stood in silent embrace for a long time.

Finally the Judge stepped backward and Brock lost his
balance. He dropped to the floor, gasping. As he lay there
trying to catch his breath, all he could see of Vinyard was
the soft break of his lovely chalk stripe pants against his
shining benchmade shoes.

"Who killed them, Judge?"

"You still got that matter before the Disciplinary Board,
boy. I have a way of making myself felt in this town. I could
help you or hurt you either one."

"Who is Shakespeare? It damn sure wasn't Mic Giddens."

Vinyard's shining shoes spun around, started walking
across the carpet. "You remember what I said. I can help
you or I can hurt you. Your choice."

• 41

As Brock was leaving Reggie Vinyard's office, he saw his father down at the end of the hall. Brock approached him, found him scrutinizing the apples in a basket of fruit. His father picked up a winesap, set it down, picked up a golden delicious, polished it on his suit, took a big bite. He was wearing a bow tie and a dark blue suit.

"Dad," Brock said.

His father turned around, chewed the apple, and swallowed. "Well," he said. "Judging from the look on your face I'm guessing you turned us down."

Brock looked up and down the hall to see if Reggie Vinyard was anywhere nearby. "You got a minute?"

"A couple. Come on."

Brock followed his father back to his office. If anything, it was larger than Judge Vinyard's. But somehow, the way it was put together, it seemed quiet and unostentatious—like a public library or a hospital waiting room. It was furnished with antiques, some of them a little the worse for wear, and there were law bibles and prospectuses and papers stacked up in various places around his father's rather small Empire desk. Of course Brock knew the apparent humility of this room was in some ways as theatrical as the extravagance of Reggie's office.

They sat in silence until Brock's father had finished the apple, wiped his hands on a disposable towel.

"How do you feel about Reggie?" Brock said finally.

"Feel?" His father looked puzzled, a deep furrow tracing itself between the two planes of his long face.

"Feel," Brock said. "Not as a lawyer. As a man."

His father nodded suddenly. "You know, son, finding law partners is a peculiar thing. It's not about friendship, exactly. But it is about choosing people whom you understand on some level. That's where trust comes from. Understanding. If you can trust a person, they'll make a good partner."

"So you trust Reggie Vinyard?"

His father nodded slowly. "Oh yes! Implicitly."

Brock looked out the window. Whereas Vinyard's view was of the white north side of Atlanta, with its glass towers and tree-lined streets—his father's windows faced the old warehouses, the freight yards, the Federal penitentiary, the weather-worn neighborhoods west of the city.

He took the photocopy of the concordance out of his pocket and tossed it on the desk.

"What is this?" his father said.

"You know he's an investor in Laughing Dolls? And in a bunch of other strip joints? He and Raymond Lata both."

His father looked out the window for a moment. "Yes," he said finally. "I know that."

"And you know that's why he wanted to hire me. He's afraid that this whole bag of worms will come out when I take Jimmy Dale's case to trial. Shakespeare, strip joints, murder, offshore accounts—it doesn't look good."

Brock's father wouldn't meet his eye. He perched his fingertips on the edge of his desk, studied them for a while. Finally his father nodded gravely. "Yes. I knew all this."

"And yet you still trust him?"

His father smiled sadly. "Oh, yes. We have our differences. But we're closer than it might seem at first glance."

"I just don't see it," Brock said. "I don't understand. This goes against everything you've ever tried to teach me."

"I know. You think he's shifty. Too slick for his own good." His father made a cage of his fingers, studied his thumbs. "But you see, I understand him. Even when he's being shifty, I understand him. Difficult to explain, son. It comes of certain shared experiences. We're like two fellows that fought the same campaign in a war. The two of us, we both love this city. We've both stuck with it for a lot of years. When we started practicing law—he with the NAACP, I with the prosecutor's office—this was not much of a city.

No national sports franchises. No skyscrapers. Population not even half a million. A little no-account, jerkwater provincial capital. But the two of us, we've both put our backs to the wheel, we've seen a lot of things come and go . . .''

His face looked wistful and proud and sad all at once. Brock was not used to seeing emotion this close to the surface of his father's face.

"And that makes it okay for him to go thundering around trying to keep me from bringing a little justice for my client?'' Even in his own ears, Brock's voice sounded grating and a little too loud. "You guys are up here on the hill, pulling the strings of our little nation-state, and God forbid anything be disturbed? That's what it is?''

"It's not that simple, son.'' Brock's father ran his hand through his shock of white hair. Then his face composed itself suddenly, and he leaned forward in his chair, all business. "Are you sure you won't reconsider?''

Brock shook his head.

"Might I ask your reasons?''

Brock wasn't sure; he hadn't articulated them yet. It was a gut decision. All he could say for certain was that just thinking about the offer had set off a sort of ticking in his chest, like the pressure valve on a steam boiler, *click click click,* getting ready to blow. But it was only as he sat there looking at his father that the anger that had been building for days began to resolve out of the steam and take on a definite form.

Ever since Mic Giddens had filed his bogus charge with the State Bar, it had seemed like the whole world was asking him to sell out his client. The worst sin a lawyer can commit. There were lines you didn't cross.

"Maybe it sounds naive, Dad, but I have a client to represent. I told him I'd do a good job for him and that's what I'm going to do. Period.''

His father smiled sadly. "If you were one of my clients, I suppose I'd be full of high sentence and sage advice. But with you . . .'' His father's eyes flicked to his face, then flicked away again. "With you, son, I've never known quite what to say.''

Me either, Dad. Brock thought it, but couldn't bring the words out. And maybe the truth had nothing to do with ethics or some commitment he'd made to Jimmy Dale or any of that abstract bullshit. *Maybe I'm just too ornery to do what other people tell me. Maybe I just don't have the common sense to let myself be manipulated every now and then.*

"You can't tell me this doesn't have anything to do with the Shakespeare murders," Brock said. "You know it does."

His father sat silently, jaw clenched. Holding something in. Whatever it was, though, he wasn't saying.

Brock stood. "Guess I better run. Got a lot to do for Jimmy Dale's trial."

"Help yourself to an apple on the way out," his father said. "They're quite tasty."

Brock stood, and they shook hands, awkward as strangers.

• 42

Merlee was sitting in the waiting room when Brock got back to his office. "How's your neck?" she said.

Brock stretched it from side to side. It didn't feel too bad, all in all. "A little better," he said.

"I knew it," she said. "It was the Tianyou cavity."

"Yeah, well . . ." Brock said, "what did you find down at the secretary of state?"

"I ought to get a bonus," she said, following him into the conference room, "for fast and efficient work." She set the papers on the table.

"It's probably all that great *chi* you've got. All that circulation in the what-you-ma-callems." Brock picked up the paper. It said *Wentworth, Ltd. Amended Articles of Incorporation* at the top.

He flipped through it. Standard boilerplate legalese. The partnership was listed as being formed for the purpose of real estate investment. The general partner was Wentworth (Vanuatu), PLC, with an address on the island nation of Vanuatu.

He kept flipping through the pages of the document until he came to the last page, read the names of the two lawyers who had filed the partnership papers. It took him a while to make sense of it.

"You okay?" Merlee said.

"Fine," Brock said.

"'Cause you look a little funny."

"I said I'm *fine*," Brock snapped.

*   *   *

After Merlee was gone, Brock went into the bathroom and splashed water across his face. He was feeling a little faint. When he had gotten hold of himself, he went back into the office and stared at the document again.

No wonder his father had been so reticent. No wonder he didn't see any need to stop what Reggie Vinyard was doing.

Brock looked at the signatures of the filing attorneys, two of them, each name typed under the line in bold black print. He sat in the still space of his office, suddenly conscious of every sound—the buzz of a fluorescent bulb, the whirring of the fan inside his computer. A swath of light fell from the window onto the floor, warming his right foot.

It didn't make sense. The first name was Press Cain. Jesus Christ. His own goddamn lawyer. And the other was Garrett Brock, Jr. His father.

• 43

Brock pulled into Press Cain's drive over on The Byway near Emory, got out and knocked on the door. Press Cain lived in a large yellow brick house with fan-shaped windows peering like astonished eyes from the roof. There was no answer. Brock knocked again, harder, but Cain still didn't come to the door.

Brock tried the knob, and the door opened easily. He stepped tentatively into the silent house. It was a beautiful place, sparely decorated, with simple arrangements of fresh flowers here and there, Japanese wood-block prints on the walls, modern furniture in black and white. The room was peaceful, contemplative, dispassionate. In the next room large Japanese paintings of hairy naked wrestlers hung on the walls, their faces knotted with fury as they clenched each other's bodies.

"Press? Hey, Press!"

The house remained ominously silent. Where the hell was he?

Brock looked out the back door, saw a dark figure huddled in the brightly lit backyard.

"Press?" Brock said, pushing open the back door.

It was Cain. He was seated on a cardboard banker's box, a small fire burning on the grass in front of him. A second box sat open next to him with the top off.

"Press, what the hell's going on?"

Press shifted around, and his lips smiled their usual hope-less smile. He didn't answer Brock, just took some papers out of the box next to him and put them on the fire. Then he picked up a bottle of Cutty Sark, took a long pull.

"I hope that's not evidence," Brock said.

"Evidence of what?"

"You know damn well what I'm talking about." He could smell the alcohol from Cain's breath. "You want to explain, Mr. Trusted Attorney and Confidante, why you never bothered to tell me you had a conflict of interest when you represented me in the disciplinary hearing?"

Now that he'd gotten closer, Brock realized that Cain was not burning documents, he was burning photographs and what appeared to be old letters. Cain picked a photograph out of the second box, shoved it at Brock. "What does this look like to you, Brock? Evidence of what?"

Brock took the photo. It was an eight-by-ten black-and-white, brittle with age. It looked like two young men at a fraternity party, circa 1960. They had their arms around each other's shoulders, gazing fondly at each other. Brock didn't recognize them. "Who are these people?"

"You wouldn't know them." Cain took the picture out of Brock's hands, threw it on the fire.

Brock walked toward Cain, dropped the incorporation papers on the ground next to the banker's box. "Here. Explain this."

Cain picked up the incorporation papers for Wentworth, the ones that listed him and Brock's father as general partners. For a moment he looked puzzled, but then he began to laugh. It occurred to Brock that he'd never heard his lawyer laugh before. The laugh was high and uncontrolled, as though Cain were threatening to lapse into hysteria.

"What, this is funny?" Brock demanded.

"Our friend's been a busy little bee," Cain said. Then he tossed the articles of incorporation on the little fire. Brock started to make a grab for it.

That was when he saw the gun. Cain was pointing a small silver revolver at him—a .32 maybe. Brock took a step backwards. The articles of incorporation rolled up in the fire, the edges went black, and then it disappeared in a small burst of orange flame.

"You realize that was a forgery don't you, Brock?"

"Oh, come on."

Cain shrugged wearily. "Not that it matters. It's all over now but the shouting."

Brock stood silently as Cain emptied the last photographs from the box into the fire.

After that Cain took another pull on the Cutty Sark, then took off his suitcoat, dropped it on the fire, doused it with lighter fluid. The flames leapt up as Cain pulled off his suspenders, then his pants, then his shirt, slipping them one by one into the blaze until finally he stood naked in the yard. Brock was surprised to see that he was powerfully built, in marvelous shape for a sixty-year-old man.

"Give me the gun and the bottle," Brock said quietly. "It's time for you to go sleep it off."

"Nonsense. I'm just getting back to the essentials."

"That may be. But you're drunk enough already."

"*Il faut être toujours ivre.* That's Baudelaire, Brock: one should be drunk all the time. Now just leave me alone. I've got one more minor matter to tend to, and I'd just as soon do it with a little private dignity."

Cain sat back down on the box, then lifted the gun slowly to his own temple.

"Stop that!" Brock shouted. "Now, why are you doing this?"

Cain looked at him for a moment, then lowered the gun. "Oh, don't be so obtuse, Brock." A drop of whiskey dripped off his chin, left a wet trail across his pale, hairless chest.

Brock felt confused, sick. "Give me the gun, Press."

He started to move toward his lawyer, but as he did, Cain lifted the pistol, pointed it straight at Brock's chest. "I may be a tired old fruit, but I come from eight generations of mean Southern white men. Don't think I don't know how to use this."

Brock slid forward another step.

"Goddammit, Brock, I'll cut you right down." The gun didn't tremble or hesitate.

Brock lifted his arms, stopped. "Alright, Press. Alright. Just tell me what's going on."

"Don't you get it?" Cain said. "Giddens isn't the one. He was never the one."

Brock nodded. "Is it okay if I sit down?"

Cain shrugged.

"You'll stop pointing that gun at me?"

Cain lowered the gun, and Brock sat down. What was going on here? It was as though there had been some sort of flaw hidden inside Press Cain's life, like a bad weld in an airplane strut: completely invisible until one day, without warning, the wing shears off and the whole thing crashes to earth. But what was Cain so worked up about? All Brock was sure of was that Cain was on the raw edge about something, and right now every move counted.

The two men sat in silence, watching the clothes burn slowly down to a feathery white ash.

"You're too close," Cain said finally.

"Okay," Brock said, getting to his knees. "I'll move."

"I don't mean *that,* you idiot," Cain said.

Brock sat back down. Too close? Too close to what?

"This has nothing to do with Laughing Dolls," Cain said finally. "Don't you understand that?"

"No," Brock said. "From the very beginning, if there's one thing I understand clearly, this has everything to do with Laughing Dolls."

Cain laughed again, a high, whinnying laugh.

"You really want to know what this is about?"

"I guess it would help, wouldn't it?"

"No," Cain said. "It wouldn't. It might be a lot better at this point if you *didn't* know."

"Tell me," Brock said sharply.

"Our friend wants revenge. And he's going to get it. It's all over."

"What friend?"

"I forget. I forget, he doesn't know shit, the kid, he doesn't know anything ..." Cain leaned forward slightly, mumbled something that Brock couldn't hear.

Brock watched him out of the corner of his eye. After a moment Cain took another swig of his whiskey, then lifted the gun toward his temple.

"Press! Cut that out!"

Cain looked mildly over at Brock, his eyes glittering. Brock rose slowly to a half-crouch. Press pulled back the hammer of his bright little gun.

"Don't bother, Brock," Press said.

Brock inched forward. "It's gonna be okay, Press," he said softly. "It's gonna be fine."

Cain's lips curled nastily. "Do you want to know, Brock?"

Brock took another slow step toward Cain.

A cunning, ugly smile on Cain's face. "If you want to know, you'd better not move another step."

Brock stopped. For a moment the two men didn't even breathe. Brock's heart was pounding. Unidentifiable emotions were running across Cain's face. A muscle in his forearm twitched.

"Press . . ."

Cain didn't move.

"Press, wait. You said, 'Our friend wants revenge.' Who are you talking about?"

Cain's shoulders slumped wearily. "It happened a long time ago. Let it lie."

Brock had had enough. "Press, goddammit . . ."

"You really want to know?" Cain said slowly. "*Eugene Norman Bailiford versus State.* One Oh Seven Gee Ay App, six twenty-three, habeas corpus appeal, cert. denied."

Brock's forehead tightened. "107 GA App, 623—that's a case citation. What are you getting at?"

Cain shook his head, closed his eyes. "Too late," he mumbled. "Too damn late." Brock lunged, but it was no good: The gun jumped, a sharp crack split the air, and Press Cain slumped forward, one hand twitching spasmodically in his lap.

"Wait!" Brock heard his voice, high and anguished. "Wait! Wait! Wait!"

A single drop of blood gathered at the tip of Press Bain's nose and dripped onto the delicate white ash. For a moment the tiny crimson bead shimmered and sparkled in the sun. Then it was engulfed in a soft red flood.

• 44

Putting the finishing touches to the room. The cage.

On the ceiling Shakespeare had mounted a bare lightbulb, then bolted a wire cage to the plywood so that no one could get to the bulb, do anything tricky with the electric wires. The switch was outside the room.

All that was left was to hang the door. Shakespeare shimmed the heavy frame and then hung a solid core metal door of the sort used for the exteriors of houses in bad neighborhoods. Like everything else about it, the way he hung it was unusual: the hinges were on the outside, so the door opened out rather than in. That way a person inside the room couldn't escape by jimmying the hinge pins and taking down the door. After that he installed a dual-bolt lock, the kind that anchors the bolts in both sides of the frame, making it nearly impossible to kick the door down.

Once you got in that room, you'd never get out. Not unless Shakespeare said it was okay to leave.

Last job was the alarm.

Shakespeare wired the entire room using a conventional home alarm. Had to string wire all around the room. Wire to the contacts in the door. Pressure sensors in the walls and the ceiling and the floor. Couldn't have the cops cutting through the walls or tunneling up through the floor. Certainly not.

It took a fair amount of time communing with the instruction manual to get the connections wired correctly, but Shakespeare finally got the alarm straightened out, everything functioning properly.

Only it wasn't really an alarm. Not anymore.

Instead of connecting the alarm circuits to the loudspeaker, the one that made all that awful hooting and screaming, Shakespeare did something more interesting. The wires leading to the speaker were disconnected, rerouted to an amplifier circuit that increased the current, and then sent it to a pair of detonators that Shakespeare had affixed to the inside of a large plastic container under the house. When the time came there would be forty gallons of gasoline and a good-sized plug of Semtex plastic explosive in the container. If somebody opened the door to the cage at the wrong time—*bang*— the room would be blown to bits and the whole house goes up in flames. And everybody dies.

So sad, so sad!

In the other room Keith Whitley was singing "Tell Laurie, I Love Her," a song he had written for his wife before his life was cut so tragically short by his excessive drinking. A very touching song, one that always made Shakespeare feel a little weepy.

When the Keith Whitley tape was finished, Shakespeare turned off the boom box, went out onto the front porch and locked the door. Shakespeare stood in the bright sun and stretched, smiling broadly.

Now—everything was ready.

• 45

Brock went out and sat in the car outside of Cain's house. His hands were trembling and he couldn't seem to get his breath to come slowly. Should he call the cops? No, he didn't have time to wait for the cops anymore. Whatever was happening, was happening too fast.

Could the 911 people trace a call from a car phone? He thought probably they could. Best thing to do was make an anonymous call from a phone booth at one of the gas stations up on Clairmont.

Brock started the engine. Damn it! This whole thing was crazy. He kept seeing the blood coming out of Cain's nose. There'd been no exit wound, no horrible gout of brains and bone, just the blood coming out of . . .

Brock tried to put it out of his mind. Too fast. He had to get moving before everything fell apart, before Shakespeare surfaced up again.

What next? Concentrate, concentrate! There had to be a way to find out Shakespeare's identity. He was close, he had to be. And once he found Shakespeare, that would solve all the rest of his problems, he was sure of it.

107 GA App, 623. That was it. Brock dialed Merlee. "Hey Merlee, you got another hour you could do something for me?"

"Are you okay, Brock? I'm sensing something's not right with you."

"I'm fine. I'm cool." Brock didn't feel fine. But there wasn't time for that, wasn't time to think about Press Cain, about the terrible flood of red liquid on the soft white rocks. "I need you to run down to the courthouse and dig up the transcripts of a criminal case from 1963. *Georgia versus Eugene Bailiford*. I don't have a docket number, but it was appealed. You can find the docket number in the GA App, volume 107. They keep them in storage somewhere. Or on microfilm. I don't care if you have to bribe somebody to dig it out of a warehouse, we need the transcript and we need it now.''

"What's this about? What am I looking for?"

"I don't know yet."

"Okee-dokey, boss." Her voice ironic, dubious.

"Look, if I knew I'd tell you." His voice was harsher than he meant it to be.

"I know that," she said softly.

The car phone rang as Brock reached the gas station where he was going to call 911. It was Janelle Moncrief.

"I was right, Brock. It's not Giddens."

"*What* wasn't Giddens?"

"Shakespeare. If he really told you he was Shakespeare, he was lying. GBI crime lab did a triangulation of the gunshots that hit Giddens, and they figured the shooter was sitting in a chair in the club. A particular chair. So we went over that chair with a fine-tooth comb—and guess what?"

"I don't know."

"We got a piece of fiber and a hair from the chair. Turns out they match something we found at one of the earlier crime scenes."

"You're saying—"

"I'm saying it's a match. Whoever shot Giddens was definitely Shakespeare."

Brock didn't say anything.

"So, the point I'm making, be careful Brock." She hesitated. "You sent your wife and kid out of town, didn't you?"

"Yeah."

"I was you, I'd make sure they stayed there a while."

Brock hung up the phone. He'd been so distracted with Cain's suicide he hadn't even thought about Dru and Grace. They were almost bound to have started driving back from Tennessee by now. A cold feeling was building behind his eyes as he dialed the number for Dru's parents in Chattanooga.

Dru's mother answered.

"Hey," Brock said. "Dru hasn't left yet, has she?"

"They just went out the door ten minutes ago."

Brock hung up and tried Dru's car phone but he couldn't get through. She'd sure be pissed when she got here and he had to tell her to turn around and drive right back to Tennessee. Just to be contrary she might even refuse.

He got out of his car, walked over to the pay phone, dialed 911 to report Press Cain's suicide.

Back in his office, Brock sat at the conference table and stared. Nothing added up. Cain had implied that Shakespeare had nothing to do with Laughing Dolls or the other strip joints or Jimmy Dale's case or Brock's disciplinary board hearing. What did he mean by that? It didn't make any sense. Brock tried calling his father again—what the *hell* was going on?— but he wasn't in the office. Neither was Reggie Vinyard.

Cain, Dad, Vinyard. What was the connection?

He pulled out Caitlin's file folder, set it next to the box of bank documents he'd gotten from Jimmy Dale and the chart his grandfather had made. There was something he'd meant to follow up on: the chart that his grandfather made from the information in Caitlin's file had jibed with Jimmy Dale's bank records on all counts but one. The disconnect was in something called GCB, Ltd. According to the bank records, money had flowed from Laughing Dolls, then to the property management company, then out through this GCB, Ltd. outfit—an entity that didn't show up on the chart—on its way to the offshore tax shelter in Vanuatu.

Brock suddenly had an uncomfortable thought. Could it be? No, surely not . . .

Well, there was only one way to find out. He picked up the phone, put in a call to a company down in Texas that had computer connections to most of the banks in America; for about a hundred bucks they could find every bank account in America listed under a particular name. Account numbers, current balance, the whole nine yards.

Brock gave the company a name, told them to look up his accounts, and hung up the phone.

He sat for a while wishing his neck would stop hurting. And maybe that his hands would stop shaking, too.

*   *   *

Half an hour later Merlee came in the room, plopped down on the couch. "Found the case, Brock. You owe me a hundred bucks extra, though. I had to make a charitable contribution to an undermotivated civil servant's favorite charity to get her to dig around in the warehouse and come up with the transcripts."

"You do good work," Brock said.

Merlee smiled. "I think you'll find they make for pretty fascinating reading."

"Save me the time, give me a quick rundown."

"Okay. May 12, 1963, a young black college student named Jacqueline Canty is working for a caterer at a function hosted by this charity downtown. That night she goes to the police, claims she's been raped while working at the charity ball. According to the initial police report, guess who she charges did the deed?"

Brock shook his head.

"A certain hotshot young attorney named Press Cain."

"Jesus Christ."

"It gets better." Merlee leaned forward. "Two weeks later, she recants the charge, says she made a mistake. She claims the real rapist was a white kid named Eugene Bailiford who worked in the kitchen at this hotel where the charity ball was being held. Bailiford, as it turns out, had a criminal record, had already served a couple years down at Reidsville."

"Okay."

"Now the fun begins. A hard-driving young assistant DA takes the case. You want to take a wild flying guess?"

Brock hesitated. "Dad."

"That's right. Garrett C. Brock, Jr., attorney at law. Now, as it happens, as of 1963 a white man had not been convicted of raping a black woman in the state of Georgia since Reconstruction. So what we've got is a slim, attractive young college girl and some whitetrash dishwasher. This, as you might expect, provokes a certain interest from the civil rights community who think they can set some nice legal precedents. The NAACP puts their legal team on the case, files amicus briefs, does some interesting work on the jury selection issue and so on."

"Let me guess. Their point man is Reggie Vinyard."

"You're such a clever boy."

"The upshot?"

"Bailiford gets nine to twelve at Reidsville. The NAACP wins a big case. Garrett Brock makes the front page."

"And Press Cain?"

Merlee looked at him with the smallest hint of a smile on her face. "His name never even comes up. Never even formally charged. Here's the weird part. The original police report—the one where she said Cain was the rapist?—it never made it into the trial. In fact, Press Cain's name was never even mentioned in Bailiford's trial."

Brock thought about the news, tried to fit the pieces together with everything that had been going on lately: Jimmy Dale's case, the disciplinary hearings, Shakespeare. And it just didn't add up. He felt like his brain was churning through mud, unable to get any purchase.

"Well, there's an unsettling coda to your story," Brock said softly. "Press Cain just shot himself."

"My God. Are they sure it was suicide?"

"*I'm* sure. I saw him do it." Replaying in his mind like a loop of video tape: that first drop of blood dripping from Press Cain's nose. Brock's neck was knotting up again.

Merlee touched his shoulder, gently, as though afraid he might shy away. "Are you doing okay?"

Brock put his head in his hands for a while, then looked up. "Well, my neck hurts like a son of a bitch."

Merlee looked slightly hurt. "I'm *serious,* Brock."

"I don't have time to figure out whether I'm okay or not."

Their eyes met for a moment, a fleeting sense of something passing between them and then gone. Merlee took her hand away.

Brock got up and located the Atlanta white pages by the phone, flipped through the B section. No Eugene Bailiford. Then to the Cs. Brock smiled. "Well, look here," he said. "Jacqueline Canty. Four forty-one East Palisades Place. Still alive, still living in Atlanta."

"You want me to call her?"

"Tell you what," Brock said. "How about you run downtown, see what you can dig up on this guy Bailiford. What's he done since he got out of jail? Does he live around here? Married? Pay taxes? I'll see if I can find this Canty woman."

"**G**arrett *Brock?*" the woman said, eyes narrowed slightly. Jacqueline Canty was a fine-boned woman with skin the color of old masking tape and a face that was still very beautiful. She wore a bright drape of yellow kinte cloth; a matching hat covered a shock of pure white hair.

"You're thinking of my father," Brock said. He was standing in front of 441 E. Palisades Place, trying to look pleasant.

"Ah. You do favor." She smiled an odd, distant smile with not much warmth in it. "And what can I do for you?"

Brock was sweating slightly. He wiped his face with the back of his hand. "Eugene Bailiford," he pronounced the name slowly. "I don't know how else to say it."

Jacqueline Canty looked at him for a long moment, eyes flashing, then she closed the door. The lock clicked shut.

"Ms. Canty! Ms. Canty!" Brock knocked on the door. "Please Ms. Canty, someone's life is at stake." He kept knocking on the door until his knuckles started hurting. After he stopped, he turned, looked up and down the street. Nothing moved. It was a group of graceful old homes, the heart of a district that had once housed the black elite of Atlanta—the talented tenth, as they used to call them.

"I'm just going to stand here until you open up," Brock yelled.

He must have stood for ten minutes, just waiting, before the door opened and Jacqueline Canty gestured him to come inside. Her eyes were hard, suspicious.

"I guess," she said, "you can't let well enough alone . . ."

They sat down in a room that was decorated with large oil paintings of shotgun shacks and sharecroppers.

"So, it's still Jacqueline *Canty?* You never married."

"I was married for twenty-three years. Roy was a vice president with Atlanta Life. We divorced after the kids left the house and I went back to my maiden name." She pressed her lips together tightly, suddenly impatient. "What you want to know?"

"It was really Press Cain, wasn't it?"

Jacqueline Canty clenched her jaw. "Kids today, black kids, I hear them say things like, 'Nothing's changed! Everything's the same!' Huh! What a load of foolishness. It was a whole different world back then."

"It *was* Press Cain."

Jacqueline Canty's eyes got distant.

"Why are you doing this? Why you want to go dredging up bad things?"

"It's very important. Lives are at stake."

She looked at him skeptically, then took a sip of tea, sucked meditatively on a piece of ice for a while. Finally she said, "See, I was working as a clean-up girl, putting myself through Spelman. That night I was working for the caterer at this party—the Piedmont Hospital Spring Ball down at the Georgian Terrace Hotel—you know, carrying a tray around, picking up drinks, bringing them back to the kitchen. Now, at that time I have to say I was kind of a wild girl—oh, I was *innocent,* don't get me wrong, but I was wild in a damn-fool girlish way—and so on that particular evening I was fed up with waiting on white folks and listening to this fat white man riding me about getting the empties back too slow and all that, and so I started sneaking a sip of champagne here, sip there, mouthful of whiskey here or there. Just for kicks, right. By the middle of the evening, I was kind of high. Not crazy high, but, you know . . . Made me enjoy my thankless job a little better.

"Anyway, the main part of the event was in the big ballroom, but there were a couple of rooms off to the side, one of which was being used as the men's smoker. Well, one of the boys in the smoker starts bantering with me, and since I'm young and flirty and wild and innocent—oh, man, I was *stupid* innocent!—I played along and then the next thing you know, me and this white boy slip out the back door and he gives me a cigarette and he says, *Would I like to go for a ride in his car?* It was one of those little foreign jobs, a sports car, bright red. So I said yes—knowing this was a damnfool thing to do and doing it anyway—and we drove around the block a couple times smoking cigarettes, feeling liberal and free, him asking me about Negro music—you know, *Negro*—that was the word back then. Asking what the *Negro* kids were listening to. He was a bad boy, see—wanting to be with a Negro girl. And I was a bad girl, fixing to lose my job if I wasn't careful.''

Jacqueline Canty was looking at the floor now, her eyes half closed, a sad, reproachful look set in the corners of her mouth.

"So we went back to the party, and this white boy and a friend of his, we all snuck into this room next to the men's smoker—this room that wasn't supposed to be open for the party. Only when we walk in there, turns out we're not alone. It's two more white fellows in there and these two fellows— well, something funny's going on. I mean, they're standing too close together. And they're doing something funny with their hands. Touching each other, right? Got their faces real close together.

"Bang! The two white men, they see us standing there and they jerk apart like somebody'd kicked them! I *mean!* Then everybody starts laughing. This is nineteen sixty-three, we still innocent, right? We don't understand what it is we just seen. The two white boys that were touching each other, one of them makes a joke, and then the boys I'm with, they make a joke, and pretty soon everybody's laughing, acting like nothing happened.

"Now, you got to realize, the white boys all knew each other. The top society in town, the big folks in Atlanta, it's only a handful of people, so they all know each other. The other thing you got to bear in mind, back then being gay was hell of thing. No way you could have a big deal career as a lawyer, not if folks were going on about how you were some queerbait light-stepping little faggot, right? Now, you better believe I'm feeling real uncomfortable all of a sudden, so I get to picking up empty glasses, putting them on trays, taking them back to the kitchen.

"Well, I get back to the kitchen, that fat-faced SOB, the catering fellow, his face gets all red, he starts using words like tramp and hussy and nigger, and so I say, 'Am I being fired, sir?' and he says, 'You damn right.' So I take off my apron, throw it on the floor, hightail it out of there."

Jacqueline Canty lifted her glass of iced tea, but didn't drink. Instead she just sat there shaking her head, her eyes looking back into the past. "Foolish child! Instead of hightailing it out of the building—oh, *Lord,* foolish child!—I sneak back into that room next to the men's smoker. See, I was gonna *show* that red-faced son of a bitch! I was gonna be *free!* Three of the white fellows were still there: the boy I went driving with, and his friend, and one of the two fellows that were touching each other in this strange way. He's a little short fellow, real sharp dresser, with pearl studs and pearl cuff links and some kind of French cigarettes in a little gold case. And the other two fellows were making fun of him, making jokes about how they'd caught him in a 'compromising position' and so on."

She looked up suddenly, raised her eyelids as though caught by surprise. "You see, Brock? It never crossed those two fellows' minds that they *really* saw what they saw. This boy was their friend, you see? You see? Known him since he was knee-high to a grasshopper. It couldn't *be* that he was a disgusting, repulsive, swishy little fairy. No sir! Couldn't be. So they kept making jokes, and the short guy, he's sweating and he's nervous and he's drinking Old Crow from a half-pint bottle.

"Conversation moves on now that I'm there. They ask me about the Negro Question—see because they're young men, and they're liberal and forward thinking and sympathetic, at least as much as rich young Southern men could be in 1963. And then we move onto interracial marriage and dating and miscegenation, and—oh! I'm so innocent! I am so divorced from the reality of life in 1963! And I let one of them hold the bottle while I drink, and I am so divorced from sanity that I'm feeling like, *Free at last, free at last, thank God, I'm free at last!* Oh yeah! Thinking I'm gonna build me a beautiful little world of racial harmony right there in that room. And so I allow one of these young gentlemen to kiss my fingertips. Then one of the young men winks at the short fellow, the neat dresser, says to him, 'Of course she doesn't interest *you,* am I right?' ''

"Well, the short fellow, I can see he's getting mad. Crazy mad. He's mad and scared and the sweat's popping up on his forehead, and he starts fooling with me, got this awful look in his eye. He says, 'Boys, I'm interested. Believe me.' And why I didn't leave that place right then and there, I do not know, because the hand was dealt and the cards were on the table and only one thing that could happen if I stayed in that room.''

She stopped talking then and rested her cheeks in her hands and stared for a long time at the rug.

"Go on," Brock said.

"A man of your generation, you can't even begin to imagine what an impossible situation this was. Because these white fellows—I mean, it was *inconceivable* to them that some lowly little colored girl might just want to sit in the room and talk innocently with a couple of white men. That such a thing might be a reward in and of itself! No, I had to have some other motive. And yes sir, they were sure they knew what it was.''

Jacqueline Canty pushed up her lower lip in a dismissive frown. "The thing makes me angriest is I knew better. Nineteen sixty-three? Every black girl in America knew better. But I let them do it.''

"Do what?"

"What you think, boy?" Canty's eyes flashed. She spit the words out, full of anger and disgust. "I let that little white boy brush his lips against my ear. I let him touch my *chin.*" She said the word like she was spitting out a piece of rotten meat. Then she shook her head angrily, shrugged. "And that was all it took. Next thing I know, he was tearing my clothes off and dragging me behind the couch and the other fellows were trying to get him off me and he was crying and yelling: 'Tell me I'm a fairy now! Tell me I'm a fairy now, you bastards!' ''

She looked up suddenly with a clear face. "I'm sorry I didn't offer you any tea, Mr. Brock.''

"That's all right, thanks," Brock said. He waited as Jacqueline Canty disappeared into another room.

When she came back, her tea glass refilled, she continued:

"I suppose you've figured out the cast of characters. It was Press Cain that raped me. Trying to prove he was a man, you see. That's how bad it was back then, that a man would have to do something that terrible to prove that he should not be despised for what he was. The fellow I went driving with, he doesn't matter. But the third man, the friend that came in the room later, that was your father."

Brock nodded.

"Well. To finish the story—like I say, I'm a young, innocent fool. A little wild, but I've got big ideas, you know, because of the people I've been around, the things that were in the air. Rosa Parks, Dr. King, the marches and the sit-ins. So I just made up my head not to let it rest, and I walked right down the street, holding my torn dress shut and I went into the police station and I told them I'd been raped. Innocent! Oh, was I such a fool! Of course as soon as I got to the part about who'd raped me, a white man in a tuxedo—" Jacqueline Canty laughed harshly. "Well, they just stopped writing then and there. These cops, you should have seen their faces! They were dumbstruck I even had the audacity to bother telling them my story. Just balled up the report, dropped it in the trash."

"So I said, 'We'll just see, won't we?' Two hours later I came back. And guess what—I had Reggie Vinyard with me, the NAACP's top lawyer in Atlanta. Plus two reporters, one from the *Pittsburgh Sentinel,* and one a white reporter from *Time* magazine who was down here doing a piece on The Movement. Well the cops called the zone captain out of bed and he drove down, pulled up at the curb in his wrinkled-up clothes, took one look at Reggie Vinyard and the man from *Time* magazine, and he said, 'Take the nigger's statement.' And, brother, he didn't even get out of that green Buick, just revved her up and drove away."

Brock shook the ice in his tea glass. The story made him feel thin and soft, a person who'd never faced real adversity. His face was warm with embarrassment and shame, not because of anything *he* had done, but because he could not shake the feeling that he was implicated in his blood for all the crimes thrown up against all the Jacqueline Cantys of the world.

"Okay, but why did you change your story? Why'd you say it was Bailiford?"

Jacqueline Canty looked momentarily startled. "What I keep telling you, young man? I was an innocent. A holy fool!"

"I don't understand."

"I did it because Reggie asked me to."

A distant smile came and went. "He told me that he'd worked a deal with your Daddy, that the thing they'd worked out, it was for the good of The Movement."

"A blank stranger. He just asked and you did it, sent the wrong man to jail for nine years."

"Blank stranger? Reggie was no stranger. He's my brother." Jacqueline Canty tilted her head to the side. "You didn't know that? Half-brother, actually. That's why we've got different last names. Yeah, he was my big brother. I'd looked up to him all my life. So when he asked me to lie, I just did it."

Something was missing here. But what? It didn't make sense. "My father must have offered him some kind of deal. What did he give your brother?"

She shrugged. "I don't know. Reggie's always been a hungry boy. He must have offered him something too sweet to pass up."

Brock sat for a while in silence. It was incomprehensible. His father? His father, the tower of integrity and all of that crap—*he* had cooked up a plan that included perjury and the false conviction of an innocent man? It was unfathomable.

Brock set his tea on the sideboard. "Do you know where Eugene Bailiford is today?"

"Now, look here," she said sharply. "That man was no saint. Reggie showed me his police record. He was a bad, bad man. I wouldn't have done it otherwise. Wasn't such a terrible thing, getting that lowlife creature off the street."

"But you don't know where he is."

She looked away. "Don't know, don't care to."

Brock drove away from the small enclave of nice houses in which Jacqueline Canty lived and was soon surrounded by the ugliness of Atlanta's West End. And as he drove the noise of the wind around his BMW sounded like a sad and wordless lament rising from the warp-roofed houses and the boarded-up gas stations and the hand-painted signs of the twenty-four-hour check cashing stores around him. Rising, rising into the blue and unsolicitous sky.

• 47

As Brock pulled onto the downtown connector, going north, he had a sudden thought. He picked up his car phone, put in a call to Merlee's beeper. She called back as he was taking the Piedmont exit.

"Find anything?"

"This gets stranger by the minute. Best I can tell he ceased to exist about three months after he got out of Reidsville. No credit bureau, no UCC filings, bank accounts, no nothing."

"Is he dead?"

"I checked. No death certificate in the state records. But there are forty-nine other states he could have died in."

"What if he changed his name?"

"Of course!" she said. "If he made a legal name change, it'll be in the state records. I'll call you back."

Jimmy Dale was waiting for Brock in the office. They needed to start going over his testimony, start getting him prepped for trial. "Sorry I'm a little late," Brock said. "Had to check out something on this Shakespeare thing."

Jimmy Dale looked at Brock peevishly. "Is it possible we could put that guy out of our minds long enough to concentrate on this case for maybe a whole minute at a time?"

Wasn't it marvelous, Brock reflected, to be so beloved by one's clients? "I don't know Jimmy Dale. I'm starting to think Shakespeare *is* this case."

Jimmy Dale just blinked his protuberant eyes and looked at him.

* * *

They had been working for about an hour when the phone rang. It was Dru.

"You'll never guess," she said.

"What?"

"The car just quit on me. The engine was going fine and then, click, nothing."

Brock exhaled slowly, trying to contain his exasperation. Did every goddamn thing in the world have to go wrong at once? "Sounds like the timing belt went out. Where are you?"

"About ten miles north of the perimeter. Just north of the mall. Can you come get me?"

"Hon, this really isn't a good time."

"Brock."

"I know, I know." Besides, if Shakespeare was still out there, getting ready to do God-only-knew what, he'd better get her to a safe place as quickly as possible. Brock could hear trucks thundering by in the background.

"I'll be right there," he said. "Just hang on."

Brock hung up the phone. "Look, Jimmy Dale, that was Dru. Her car just broke down and I need to go pick her up."

Jimmy Dale made a face. "What ever happened to Triple-A?"

"For chrissake, Jimmy Dale. With Shakespeare running around loose? I've got to go."

"Well, where is she?"

"I-75, north of the perimeter. It'll just take me half an hour, okay?"

Jimmy Dale shrugged. "Look, you been running around all worried about this Shakespeare character and I'm, like, hey man, don't you have a case to try tomorrow?"

"So come with me. We'll work on your testimony in the car."

Jimmy Dale shrugged. "Okay. Fair enough."

Brock got up and started wheeling Jimmy Dale across the office. Just as he reached the door, the phone rang. He hurried back across the room, reached across the desk and hit the speakerphone button. "Yes?" he said.

Merlee's voice boomed into the room. "You want to talk about your classic revenge drama," she said.

"Look, I'm about to run out of the office."

Jimmy Dale's insistent voice: "Can we *go?*"

"Pardon the bad pun, but this is like something out of Shakespeare."

"What do you mean?"

"I got it all figured out. Bailiford gets out of prison. Bailiford changes his name. Bailiford sets up the three guys who screwed him, who framed him for a crime he didn't commit. Meticulous planning, obsessive in the details, masterful in the execution—"

"Merlee, look I've got a minor emergency. You want to cut to the chase?"

Jimmy Dale again, from the other room: "Let's *go*. Talk to her later."

"I'm saying he framed your dad, Brock. This whole thing, it's a frame-up."

"Who? For godsake *who?*"

"That's what I'm saying, Brock. Bailiford is Shakespeare."

"But—"

"You were right. He changed his name."

"What did he change it to?"

"This is too funny, Brock. Bailiford changed his name—"

"Merlee—"

Merlee's slow drawl: ". . . to Jimmy Dale Evans."

Brock froze momentarily. When he turned around, there was Jimmy Dale. But a Jimmy Dale Evans who had changed somehow. For a moment Brock couldn't quite pinpoint what the difference was.

But of course it was obvious: what was different was that Jimmy Dale Evans was walking. Rising up from the wheelchair. *Jimmy Dale could walk? All this time he'd been faking it? Jesus Christ!* Jimmy Dale Evans walked purposefully toward him. Brock saw it, but still it didn't quite compute and so he wasn't able to react. On Jimmy Dale's face, an ugly sneer. In his hand, a marble trophy Brock had won in moot court back during law school. The trophy: floating upward, then falling.

No time to raise his arms or even duck.

"Merlee. Call the—"

The trophy came down on Brock's head—once, twice—and Jimmy Dale Evans's sneer was gray and far away and then everything was vanishing into a consuming darkness.

• 48

Dru saw the van coming. It pulled off the side of the inter-
state, nosed in close to the rear bumper of her dead Acura.
A red-haired head emerged from the window. It was a man,
yelling something. From inside the car Dru couldn't make
out what he was saying. She opened the door a crack, peered
out carefully. Help was on the way, so Dru figured she might
as well take the better-safe-than-sorry route with the guy.

"Mrs. Brock?" the man yelled.

That was when she recognized him. Brock's client, the
creepy paraplegic.

"Mr. Evans?" she said.

"Hey." He waved desultorily. "Your husband sent me to
pick you up. He forgot that he had to drop something off
at court."

Grace was playing on the front seat. "Is that man going
to take us for a ride?"

"I guess so, honey."

Dru got out, locked the Acura, then shepherded Grace into
the van. Jimmy Dale's hand rested on a set of knobs that
allowed him to operate the pedals of the van with his hands.

Dru put Grace in the seat, buckled her in. When she looked
up, she saw the gun in Jimmy Dale's hand and for a moment
she was puzzled, angry. "I'd appreciate it if you'd put that
gun away, Mr. Evans," she said. "We've got a four-year-
old *child* here." Then it occurred to her to wonder why he
had the gun in his hand in the first place.

"Okay," Evans said. "Here's what happens next. You get
out of the car, Mrs. Brock. Then I drive away."

Dru stared. Something was terrifyingly wrong, but she still wasn't quite clear what it was. There had to be an explanation.

"What are you *doing?*"

"If you call the cops, I kill the girl. If you follow me, I kill the girl. However, if you and your husband do everything I say, then little Grace here will live to see—how old are you, sweetheart?"

Grace looked away shyly.

Dru grabbed Grace's arm. "Tell him how old you are!"

Grace's eyes widened. She held up four stiff fingers.

"Four!" Jimmy Dale said cheerfully. "You want to live to be five, sweetheart?"

Grace looked fearfully at Jimmy Dale, then at Dru. There was a look of incomprehension in her eyes, a recognition that somehow she was about to be horribly betrayed.

"Out." Jimmy Dale motioned at the door with his gun. Dru hesitated. "Out. What you do is you hike down there, call a cab, take the cab straight to your husband's office. Then you wait for further instructions."

"But—"

"Out." Smiling genially, the gun pointed right at her face. "Do what I tell you, everything's cool with the girl."

"I'm four," Grace said, looking slightly bewildered. "I'm *four!*"

Dru stroked Grace's head, leaned her cheek against the hard vinyl. Her breath was sticking in her chest. She felt paralyzed, as though this were just the unfurling of some drug-induced dream, something that was taking place not in a real Chevy van on a real highway under a real sky, but on an operating table, perhaps, or in a dentist's chair.

"Close the door behind you!" Jimmy Dale had stopped smiling.

Dru couldn't move.

She saw him lean toward her, felt him hammer the butt of his gun against her cheek. The glancing blow stunned her, and for the first time her confusion was replaced with a vacuous and total fear. She tried to hold onto Grace's seat, but Jimmy Dale banged her twice more with the side of the gun, and she fell out of the van onto the pavement.

"The door!"

She hesitated for a moment, her cheek throbbing, then climbed slowly to her feet and slammed the door of the van. Grace's eyes, wide with terror, watched Dru as the van pulled away. Her hands thrashed wildly at the window. It wasn't until the van had disappeared into the rush-hour traffic that Dru put her face in her hands and began to sob.

THE TRIAL

●

An attorney died and went to heaven, where he quickly found himself dissatisfied with his accommodations. He complained to St. Peter that his room was too small and the view extremely poor. St. Peter told the lawyer that if he was unhappy, he could appeal his room assignment; unfortunately, however, the appeal would probably take three to five years to reach a decision.

"Three years! That's unconscionable!" said the lawyer, but St. Peter just shrugged. The lawyer was then approached by the Devil, who said he could arrange an appeal in a matter of days, if the lawyer would just change the venue to hell.

"How come you can do it so fast down there?" asked the lawyer.

"Because," said Satan, "we've got all the judges."

• 49

Performance of a lifetime.

Brock stood, walked slowly to the podium, smiled. He had no notes, no battered legal pad. Naked. That was the way he liked to do his opening statement. He had prepared, he knew what he was going to say, now he just had to let it flow.

"The first thing you need to know about that man"—here Brock turned and pointed at Jimmy Dale Evans—"is that he will never walk again. Never. His name is Jimmy Dale Evans, and he will *never* walk again. The second thing you need to know, is that however unfortunate or heartrending his medical condition may be, the mere fact of his disability does not mean somebody else should pay for his injuries. To win this case, we have to prove that his injuries were caused by someone else's negligence." He paused, studied the faces of the jury. "Someone else's *shameful* negligence. And we will do that."

Brock unbuttoned his coat, put his hand in his pocket. The adrenaline was flowing as he caught the wave of his own speech. He was standing at the front of courtroom 4-A in Fulton County Superior Court, Judge Wellborn presiding. Because she was a senior judge, they were in one of the large courtrooms, the one with the twenty-foot ceiling and the expansive gallery. Judge Wellborn was a dour woman, her face inordinately wrinkled for her sixty years, and whose white hair was styled in the same absurd flip that she had worn when she passed the bar in 1963. And that gallery contained a pretty good crowd for a civil trial: a couple of newspaper and wire-service people, two of Moncrief's detectives, and film crews from the four local TV stations. A dumb-looking bailiff with a pearl-handled revolver sat near the bench, looking bored and fiddling with his crotch.

At the defendant's table sat B.J. Mills, representing Laughing Dolls. B.J. was a little fat guy with round tortoiseshell glasses that Brock suspected he wore for the sole purpose of making him look smart. With Giddens dead, there was no defendant at the table.

"But I'm not here to instruct you in the law," Brock continued. "Judge Wellborn will do that ably. What I'm here to do is to talk about the facts. And the facts we will introduce are clear. On January 9 of last year Mr. Evans was walking through a bar, a nude dance club called Laughing Dolls. He was not drinking. He was not taking drugs. He was not even ogling the dancers. He was there to perform a professional service. As he was walking through the club an employee of the club slipped off the top of the table on which she was dancing and fell on top of Mr. Evans. It sounds kind of amusing, doesn't it?"

A couple of the jurors smiled obligingly. Brock smiled back, shrugged slightly. "Only it wasn't very funny to Mr. Evans. As he fell under the impact of this dancer's full weight, he went down like a domino." Brock slapped his hand on the podium. "As Mr. Evans fell, his first lumbar vertebra was crushed, severing his spinal column at the thoraco-lumbar junction, causing awful pain and instant paralysis of his legs."

Brock held up his hands as though calming a cheering crowd. All twelve jurors were watching him at least and nobody was asleep. That was something, anyway. "Fine. Fine. These facts are not in dispute. What is most important for this case is that we will introduce evidence demonstrating that Mr. Evans's grievous injuries were caused not just by the actions of a dancer with a bad sense of balance, but by the negligence and reckless conduct of a group of very influential and very well-respected men—the secret owners of Laughing Dolls. It was these men who made it possible for this establishment to be run in a way which the facts will demonstrate was slipshod, careless, and reckless. And that slipshod management resulted in my client's injury.

"Under Georgia law, the results of their cavalier behavior

are compensable. What I mean is that if you, the jury, find that these rich men, these powerful men, employed what the law calls a 'pattern and practice' of management which resulted in my client's terrible injuries, then my client deserves to be paid cash money for their errors.'' Brock slapped the back of one hand into the palm of the other. "Cash money, folks. Cash money.''

Brock went on to explain about the medical basis of the injury, and then laid on the pathos about how poor Mr. Evans would never wiggle his toes inside his shoes, never swim, never dance, never feel the warm caress of a woman's touch on his leg.

When he'd finished that part of the speech, Brock turned and pointed at the defendant's table. "You see before you one man. The record will reflect that this man is a lawyer. He represents Laughing Dolls. But you do not see a single actual defendant. Why? Because—''

B.J. Mills burst out of his seat. "I'm going to have to object. I know where he's going, and the fact that a defendant is not sitting here is just not germane to the case.''

The judge waved wearily at the two men. "Approach the bench, if you would, gentlemen.'' When they reached the front of the courtroom, she said, "Listen up, Mr. Brock. You and I both know what's happened to Mr. Giddens. If I hear you casting aspersions on the defendant because he's been murdered, if I hear you implying that he lived a shady life, if I hear anything like that, counselor, I will give you a very very very hard time. Understood?''

"Yes, your honor,'' Brock said. "But actually that wasn't where I was going.''

B.J. Mills straightened his bogus glasses and looked puzzled.

"Could I be allowed to go on?''

"Go ahead, then.'' Judge Wellborn jiggled her gavel at Brock's face. "But be careful, Mr. Brock. I don't have to tell you Mr. Mills is listening very carefully and would love to force me into calling a mistrial.''

Brock went back to the podium, started up again. "The defendants' table is empty. Ideally it shouldn't be. There should be someone sitting there. But there isn't. Why? Because something over at Laughing Dolls stinks. Something is rotten in Denmark.''

"Your honor!'' B.J. Mills was bounding to his feet again.

"Please!'' Brock said in his most injured voice. "A little latitude, for goodness sake.''

"No, no, no. This direction is entirely impermissible.''

"Okay,'' Brock said. Then he turned to the jury. "Recent information has come to me,'' he said, "indicating the names of some of the men who—in a perfect world—would be seated today at that table.'' Brock paused for a moment. "Mel Prochaska, Lee Darden, Boyd Michaels, Raymond Lata—''

Several people in the gallery gasped, and B.J. Mills erupted from his chair, eyeglasses flashing. "Your honor! My lord! This is outrageous!''

"Is that a motion?'' the judge said.

B.J. Mills's mouth opened and closed a couple of times, and then he said, "Motion for mistrial, your honor.''

"Sidebar,'' Brock said.

The judge rolled her eyes. "This better be good,'' she said.

Brock said, "I just received information late last night which demonstrates conclusively that the financial interests behind Laughing Dolls and a number of related entities were not fully disclosed during the course of this litigation. I have passed these documents on to defense counsel. I realize it sounds improbable that something like this would show up on the eve of trial. Believe me, I *know* how bad it looks.'' Brock tried his best to look sincere. "But I swear to you on my honor, this information reached me late yesterday. Quite frankly, it's not an important part of the case, but it has some relevance with regard to certain insurance issues and therefore needs to be put on the table and into the record as quickly as possible.''

"You have documents?'' the judge said. "Have I seen them?''

"I gave copies to the clerk.''

The judge snapped her fingers at the clerk, who jumped up with a thick file full of documents. She scanned them quickly. "So what is all this mess?'' she said finally.

"A paper trail demonstrating who ultimately controls Laughing Dolls. We were led to believe throughout the entire course of discovery in this case that Mic Giddens was the sole owner of the club. Turns out, he's not. We have been willfully deceived by the defendants and, unfortunately, I don't see any alternative but to use the trial to work through some issues that should have been resolved in discovery."

B.J. Mills said, "Judge, come on. This is outrageous."

"I have to say, Mr. Brock, that this looks awful close to mistrial territory. Not to mention attorney misconduct."

"As to the latter, all I can do is assure you personally it's not," Brock said, trying to strike the right balance between wounded and irate. "In fact, if there was any misconduct, it was on the part of the defense, who owed us a duty to produce true and accurate ownership records in a *much* earlier phase of this litigation. The only way to rectify their—let's be charitable—their oversight, is for me to use this trial to demonstrate who the real owners of the club are. As for the former, why don't you set aside the motion for mistrial until I lay some foundation and go through the documents carefully? If what I claim is not in the ballbark, then I'd welcome a mistrial."

Judge Wellborn looked highly irritated. "You can't introduce new defendants in the middle of trial. You know that. These parties that you're alleging ought to be defendants don't even have representation here."

"Well," Brock said, "my client doesn't seek any additional damages from these gentlemen, nor do we contend that it changes the allocation of damages. Given, quite frankly, the amount of time and effort it's taken to get to this point, we're content to argue that Laughing Dolls and Mic Giddens are the correct plaintiffs for this action. I mean, if we were starting at square one, we'd do it differently; but given the insurance issues, we're okay with things as they stand."

B.J. Mills jumped in. "That's not the point. Just *mentioning* all these murder victims is clearly prejudicial and totally out of line and so we contend that mistrial's the only way to fly here. Or at a minimum, we've got to exclude these documents—which, needless to say, the defendant has had no time to review or to verify for accuracy."

"Mr. Brock?" The judge looked at Brock dubiously. "It's just *coincidence* that all four of these men you claim should have been defendants in this action happen to have been murdered in the past month and a half? I don't buy it.''

"I have no knowledge of any direct connection between those murders and this trial,'' Brock said. A feeling of self-revulsion ran through him. How long could he keep up these lies without cracking? "I agree it's unfortunate the men are dead, and that it gives a rather morbid character to the proceedings. But that's not the point. This material will not go away. We can call a mistrial now, but then I'll push just as vigorously to introduce this material in the subsequent trial. And believe me, when you look at these documents, you'll see that there's no question they should have been produced during discovery. I wouldn't go so far as to say *counsel* was aware of these documents, but I'm quite sure Mr. Giddens was. And you know what? He intentionally deceived the plaintiffs about their existence. I feel extremely confident that even if you call a mistrial now, these documents will still appear in the next trial. Once you look at these documents, you'll see it would be a complete miscarriage of justice if they remain buried. So where does that leave us? A mistrial at this point will end up taking up more of this court's time, further muddy the waters, and ultimately make things worse for the defendant.''

"Oh!" B.J. exclaimed. "So now you're on my side?''

"I'm just arguing for expedient justice.''

"Yeah, yeah, yeah,'' the judge said. "So how long is it going to take, going through all these exhibits?''

"A day. Maybe two.''

"This is the screwiest thing I've ever heard of,'' the judge said, shaking her head. Her white flip bobbed and swayed. She reached tentatively for her bench book, then her thin hand stopped. "Okay, Mr. Brock. Go ahead. Two days. But I want briefs on this mistrial issue by Friday. And if I'm not convinced there's good reason to introduce this evidence, I'm pulling the plug.''

Brock hurried back to the podium before the judge could change her mind, began addressing himself to the jury. "The evidence will show that the defendants, in concert with some very powerful men in this city, caused grievous harm to Mr. Jimmy Dale Evans.'' Brock paused, looked around the courtroom. In the front, a row of reporters were busily scribbling in their notebooks. "All we ask for, folks, is a little justice."

At the other table, B.J. Mills looked up at the judge with pleading eyes. The judge put her hands over her sagging face and shook her wattles hopelessly.

After it was over Brock sat down next to Jimmy Dale. "Well, shithead," he said. "How'd you like my performance?"

Jimmy Dale smiled. "First-rate," he said. "Tip top. Next time I'm in trouble, you're my man."

With as much venom as he could muster, Brock said, "No, Jimmy Dale. There's no next time."

As a somewhat shaken B.J. Mills droned on with his rather predictable opening statement, Brock thought back two days earlier to a long conversation he'd had with Jimmy Dale Evans:

Jimmy Dale was popping wheelies with his wheelchair in Brock's conference room.

"I'll tell you my best lick," Jimmy Dale said, grinning. "The pins. Wasn't that great, sticking the pins in my leg? Wasn't that sweet?"

Brock sat with gritted teeth. His head was pounding from being knocked out with the trophy, and flashes of silver light skittered occasionally across the periphery of his vision. He wanted to stand up and take that trophy and beat Jimmy Dale to death with it. But he couldn't. Because Jimmy Dale had Grace. Somewhere.

Dru sat slumped in a chair next to Brock.

"It's like, 'Hey, look at this poor paralyzed freak; he's sticking pins in his leg and he don't even feel it!' " Jimmy Dale laughed, a booming goofy laugh. "Boy, it hurt like a bitch though. You wouldn't believe."

"Where is Grace?" Dru said for about the fifth time.

"She's safe," Jimmy Dale said. "Trust me."

"Where is she, you bastard?"

Brock put a restraining hand on her arm. "Come on, Dru. That's not helping."

Dru glared at him, pulled her hand away, eyes burning

with anger and frustration. Brock wanted to hold her, to assure her, but he could see it wouldn't help. Right now all she could feel was hatred and recrimination and guilt.

Jimmy Dale popped another wheelie. "Talk all you want, folks. But here's the way it is. I've got your little girl. She's stashed in a house somewhere inside a special room. Soundproofed, hardened, protected by an alarm system. Oh yeah, also booby-trapped. See, the deal is that if you open the door without punching in the right code, the whole house goes up in a big fireball, and it's bye-bye innocent little Grace."

"You bastard," Dru hissed.

"Also—this is a key point, folks, so listen real carefully—every few hours I have to punch in a code on the alarm. Point of that is that if, for example, you call the cops on me or shoot me or something, then at a prearranged time—no code punched into the alarm—hey, the house explodes."

Brock said, "Just tell us what we have to do to get Grace back."

Jimmy Dale looked at Brock with his bright little blue eyes. "You know what I want."

Brock crossed his arms. "Say it."

Jimmy Dale suddenly jumped out of the wheelchair and leaned over the table. "I want you to help me put your father and Reggie Vinyard in jail for murder."

"I don't suppose it bothers you that they didn't kill Raymond Lata or Mel Prochaska or any of those other people?"

"That's exactly the point!" Jimmy Dale said, smiling brightly. "Because, see, I didn't rape that girl back in sixty-three, either. But your Daddy sent me to jail anyway."

It occurred to Brock that if you put aside how sick and crazy the whole thing was, you almost had to admire a guy like Jimmy Dale. Almost, but not quite. Then Brock thought about Grace, sitting alone in some booby-trapped house, and suddenly his mind dipped back into the hate-filled gloom like an airplane lurching into a storm cloud.

"So what am I supposed to do, Jimmy Dale?"

Jimmy Dale explained. It took a while, with plenty of stomping up and down the room, and waving of hands, and then some rolling around and wheelie-pulling in the chair. Jimmy Dale's biscuit-shaped face grew red and seemed to

*expand as he talked—as though he were about to explode
with malignant glee.*

When he was done, Brock sat for a moment in silence. It
was a pretty ingenious plan, he had to admit.

Dru broke the silence. "Don't do it, Brock. You can't."

"Sure you can," Jimmy Dale said. " 'Cause if you don't,
you never see Grace again. Simple equation, y'all."

Dru glared while Brock mulled over what Jimmy Dale had
just told him.

"What I want to know," Brock said finally, "is what the
point of the notes to me were. Why were you trying to scare
me off the case?"

"I wasn't." Jimmy Dale smiled. "See, when I gave you
the case originally, I figured you'd turn up the ownership
records yourself—you know, those documents connecting Vinyard and Cain to Laughing Dolls. But when Giddens withheld
them in discovery, it was obvious I was going to have to
make you realize there was something else going on. Kind of
leading the horse to water type of thing. Reverse psychology,
right?" Jimmy Dale stood up from the wheelchair, stretched
lazily. "See, Brock, I take you to be the stubborn individualist
type. I figured if you got pushed into a corner, it would pretty
much light your ass on fire. So I sent you the card through
Grace. Then I set up Dickie Settles and Gene Meales to get
you chasing after the list. After that, it was all up to you.
The thing I like about sending you the card and all that is
that it insulates me from the whole thing. I mean, why would
I threaten my own lawyer to drop a suit that's liable to put
mucho bucks in my pocket? Nobody'd suspect that in a million years. Neat, huh?"

Brock shook his head in resignation. Janelle Moncrief was
right; he was like a chess player, thinking three moves ahead
of everybody else. He remembered the way he used to feel
when he was in the chess club back in seventh grade, seeing
the endgame coming, feeling trapped and short of breath,
knowing there wasn't a damn thing he could do to stop it.
Only nobody's life had been at stake back then.

"What about the back injury?" Brock said. "How'd you
fake that?"

Jimmy Dale smiled, as though in fond remembrance of
something. "That was tricky. First, I paid this guy at the

hospital, this radiology tech, to switch my X-rays. I'd gotten him to filch a set of scans from some guy that broke his back in a rock-climbing accident. That was the first part. Then I got one of the girls at Laughing Dolls to help me frame my neurologist so he'd give me ongoing reports supporting the diagnosis of paralysis.''

''How'd you do that?''

''I paid her four hundred bucks to kind of seduce him, get him in bed with her. Then I took some real nice video footage, different angles, all kind of athletic moaning and groaning. The guy was married. Once we showed him the video?'' Jimmy Dale slapped his hands together. *''Hotcha! Boy, he just laid right down, put his paws in the air. He was a helpful guy, too. Real . . . willing.''*

''This girl, the one you set the doctor up with. I don't suppose it was—''

''Sure. Caitlin Cobranchy.''

''Why would she do something like that?''

Jimmy Dale looked at Brock coolly. *''Everybody's got their motivations. She's no different from the rest of us.''*

''And the concordance? All those documents?''

''Caitlin ripped those off from Raymond Lata before his untimely demise. She also had a little dalliance going with him. At my behest.''

''Where is she now?''

Jimmy sat back down in the wheelchair. *''Don't worry about that. She'll be there to testify, that's all you need to know.''*

''So this whole thing, from the very beginning, was a setup designed to get back at my Dad—''

''—and Reggie Vinyard and Press Cain.''

''—for what they did to you thirty years ago.''

Jimmy Dale went to the window, looked out at the parking lot below Brock's office window. *''Thirty years,''* he said, his voice falling almost to a whisper. *''Thirty years, I've been planning this thing. Nine years in prison, ten years getting my feet back on the ground, another ten years to set the whole thing up.''*

Brock shook his head, appalled. *''My father claims he has no connection to these strip joints.''*

''True,'' Jimmy Dale said. *''Lata and Vinyard are in on*

it, but Cain and your father had no connections. In fact, until very recently, they didn't know that Lata and Vinyard had invested in the strip club business." Jimmy Dale laughed.

"But I don't understand . . ."

"In the course of our work together I may have, ah, under-represented my involvement in these businesses to you. I was a little bit more than a bookkeeper. Sometimes I helped with some of the deal-making. Only step'n'fetchit kind of stuff—but it was enough that I had access to some of the corporate filings, the bank accounts and so on. So what I did was I made a false paper trail. For instance, I was involved in transferring money from Laughing Dolls to an offshore account—"

"The one in Vanuatu?"

"That's right. But what I did is I set up a bank account owned by a bogus company called GCB, Ltd. I funneled all the money through there and they never even knew it. And guess who's registered as the owner of GCB, Ltd.?"

"I checked it out already. Dad's name's on the account."

"Well, there you go, see? It's easy. Show the bank a fake driver's license, tell them my name is Garrett C. Brock, Jr.—hey, what do they know? Same with the corporate filings with the state. All I had to do was forge an amendment to the bylaws, some kind of bullshit like that, put your Dad's name on it, file it with the secretary of state. Presto, he's an officer in a company he never even heard of."

"But the signatures—they must be forgeries. Somebody will figure it out."

"Sure. But by then it'll be too late, won't it?. They'll be on Hard Copy, Inside Edition, Court TV. Shoooot. They'll never live it down. Hey, it's already too late for my old pal Press Cain." Jimmy Dale cackled. "I just wish I could have seen his face right before he pulled that trigger."

Brock stared malignantly back at him. Jimmy Dale was right. Once his father had been implicated in the murders, an acquittal would be beside the point. His career would be over. "And I guess it was you that killed that guy Dicky Settles?"

"He was an unreliable guy. Weak. And he knew too much." Jimmy Dale shrugged, a half smile on his face. "Hey, sometimes you gotta do what you gotta do."

"And Giddens?"

"You have to admit, Brock, he was a pain in the ass."

"Yeah, but why that particular moment, when I was standing there?"

"Here's what happened. I had intended to race down to the club, get there early and make sure the safe was open—in case Giddens had locked the stuff up in there. Unfortunately I got stuck in traffic and showed up late. So there I was, listening in to your conversation from out in the bar. Well, when Vinyard's investigator fell out of the ceiling and Giddens pulled the gun, I was afraid he was going to blast you. So I had to pop him."

"Then you weren't shooting at me?"

"You?" Jimmy Dale laughed. "Are you kidding? You're my main man!"

Dru, who had been staring blankly at the floor for a long time, suddenly looked up. "How could you do it?" Her voice was choked with rage and horror. "How could you kill all those men, people who had nothing to do with your little problems?"

Jimmy Dale looked away for a minute, an unreadable expression on his face. "Justice," Jimmy Dale muttered. "I just wanted a little justice."

Brock felt a surge of hopelessness. Would they ever get their daughter back from a monster like this? For a moment he felt like he was going to cry. The last time he remembered feeling that way he was a third-grader out on the playground, and a big kid—a fifth-grader—had sat on his chest, pinning his arms with his legs, and shoved moss and pine needles in his mouth. There had been nothing he could do, nothing at all.

"We just want our girl back," Brock said softly. "That's all that matters."

Jimmy Dale spun around in the wheelchair, spoke with a sudden fury. "Do your part, Brock. Just do your part."

"Mr. Brock?" the judge said. "Mr. Brock!"

"I'm sorry, your honor." Brock, noticing that B.J. Mills had finished his opening statement, rose from his chair. "Could you repeat that?"

"Call your first witness."

Brock cleared his throat and said, "The plaintiff calls Mr. Jimmy Dale Evans."

• 50

After they left the courtroom that afternoon, a swarm of news reporters surrounded Brock and Jimmy Dale.

One of the local TV people, the chubby black guy who was covering the Shakespeare story for Channel 5, got off the first question. "Do you have information which might lead to Shakespeare?"

Brock smiled pleasantly at the cameras and said that since he was in the middle of a case he couldn't really comment on any of its particulars. This was sheer bullshit, of course. Jimmy Dale had already tipped several reporters that a big break in the Shakespeare case would be coming during the trial. So all day the newspeople had been sitting there like vultures at the back of the courtroom. But all they had gotten was the one brief mention of Lata, Prochaska, Michaels, and Darden. Now they were starved for blood. They hurled more questions and jabbed Brock with their microphones, eyes frantic for something that might give them the lead piece on the six o'clock news. But Brock had nothing else to say.

Once they were safely inside the BMW, Jimmy Dale said, "Beautiful. It's theater. You lay in the hook, let out the line, and then make them wait for the other shoe to drop."

"You've got a hell of a way with a metaphor," Brock said. Jimmy Dale smiled and patted him on the arm.

"Nice work, Brock. A guy like you could almost bring back my faith in American blind justice."

* * *

When Brock got home he found his father, his grandfather, Reggie Vinyard, and a black man with a patch over one eye sitting around the kitchen table. No one looked happy.

"Well, well, well," Brock said.

Brock's father motioned to him. "Sit down, son. We have to talk."

"Look, it's out of my hands," Brock said. He had already warned his father about what was coming. His father had been characteristically reticent at the time, but now that he had showed up at Brock's house with Reggie, Brock was sure his father was here to lean on him, to try to dissuade him from going through with Jimmy Dale's plan. "Jimmy Dale has Grace and there's nothing I can do but play the role he mapped out for me."

"You mind explaining that role to me?" Reggie said. They still hadn't introduced the guy with the eye patch, a black man in a dark suit and a white shirt with no necktie. There was something familiar about him, but Brock couldn't quite place him.

"Basically I'm going to put you and Dad on the stand and I'm going to hand you documents that link you to Laughing Dolls as well as to Raymond Lata and the other people Jimmy Dale killed. The news media is going to sit there and connect the dots. I suspect that Jimmy Dale may also plant some physical evidence linking you to the crimes."

Reggie grimaced. "Tried in the court of public opinion."

Brock nodded. "Yup."

"That sneaky little piece of shit," Reggie said.

"So how much damage did we take today?" Brock's father said.

"Not much," Brock said. "I sort of made reference to a conspiracy in my opening statement. Just a kind of teaser. Your names weren't mentioned."

"What about Jimmy Dale's testimony?" Reggie said.

"Nothing there. That's the beauty of his plan. Jimmy Dale won't say word one about your connection to the strip clubs or the dead guys. He'll never point a finger, never show malice toward you, nothing. It'll appear that this whole business of scapegoating you guys is a strategy dreamed up by his fiendishly clever lawyer to force a settlement by the insurers."

"The perfect lawyer. Throwing his own Daddy under the bus for the benefit of a client," Reggie said.

"That's the way it's supposed to look."

"What about tomorrow?" Brock's father said. "Any damaging testimony tomorrow?"

Brock shook his head. "No. Jimmy Dale finishes up and then we'll do Caitlin Cobranchy. It'll all be perfectly straight testimony that goes to the substance of our case—the negligence claim against the club."

"And the next day?"

"That's when you go on the stand, Dad."

Reggie and Brock's father looked at each other.

"So we got twenty-four hours," Reggie said.

"For what?" Brock said.

"To get your little girl out of that house."

Brock's eyes hardened. "Bull*shit*. Stop right there. We're not playing games with my daughter's life."

Reggie said, "Let me introduce you to a friend of mine, fine private investigator name of Cleland Davis."

Of course. Now he remembered: the guy who'd been spying on him and Giddens from the air-conditioning duct. He hadn't been wearing the eye patch then.

The one-eyed guy stood and smiled. "How you doing, sir?"

Brock ignored the investigator's outstretched hand. "Look, nothing personal, Mr. Davis," Brock said, "but get the fuck out of my house."

"Brock, Brock, Brock," Reggie said.

"I know what you're doing here," Brock said. "You want to risk my daughter's life to protect your asses. Well, sorry, but I'm not buying it."

Cleland Davis looked at Reggie, then at Brock's father.

"Siddown, Cleland," Reggie said.

The one-eyed investigator sat down gingerly, wincing as he lowered himself the last three inches onto the chair.

"Mr. Davis here followed your client today at lunchtime," Reggie said. "He was led back to a house down in College Park. Show him."

Davis slid several photographs across the table. Brock picked them up. A small one-story house, its clapboard exterior painted a peeling white. In one of the pictures, Jimmy

Dale's green van was parked out front. In another, one of the windows had been circled with a red magic marker.

"I believe that your daughter is being held in this room," the investigator said, tapping at the circled window with his finger. "Hard to tell from this picture, but it's boarded up from the inside."

Brock couldn't tell from the picture. "Is there somebody with her?" Brock said. "Somebody taking care of her?"

The investigator shrugged. "Don't know. Nobody besides Evans came or went during the six hours I was there."

Brock tossed the photographs on the table. "Get out," he said sharply. "Everybody get out. I'm not even considering this."

"Hold on," Brock's father said quietly. "I understand how you feel. But I think there's something else you should know before you make any decisions about this." He picked up a briefcase, opened it, took out an old file folder. "I know you've heard the story about Press Cain and Reggie's sister, about how we framed an innocent man to do the time for Press. But did you ever consider why, out of all the people at that party on that particular night, that we chose Eugene Bailiford?"

"Because he was a dishwasher who'd been in a little trouble before. Because he wasn't some well-connected guy who could buy a good lawyer and fight back."

His father handed him the file. "Read."

Brock opened the file. It was very old and the paper inside was yellowed and crumbling: an ancient rap sheet, typed with a manual typewriter and a faded ribbon. At the top was the name *Eugene Bailiford*. Brock read the rap sheet with a growing sense of horror.

"See?" his father said. "First time he molested a little girl, he was sixteen years old. Did some time in a juvenile home. A year later, another charge, dropped. Two years later he did a stint at Reidsville for sodomizing a minor."

"Jesus Christ," Brock said.

His father looked at him gravely. "The little girl in the case that sent him to Reidsville? She was five years old."

"Now, how much longer you want that sweet child rattling around in an empty house with your client?" Reggie said.

Brock sat down, put his face in his hands. Goddammit,

why did it just keep getting worse and worse? Why? His neck was throbbing and a sick, weak feeling was working its way up out of his legs and into his gut.

"I'm listening," he said finally.

Cleland Davis cleared his throat, touched the patch over his eye with a long finger. "Okay, Brock. Here's what we need you to do . . ."

Grace was sitting in the high chair. It made her mad. Funny told her they didn't have a big people table for her to eat at, so she had to eat in the high chair like a baby. She liked playing with Funny, but Funny didn't make very good food. Funny put yucky mayonnaise on the baloney sandwich, and gave her apple juice instead of grape juice, and everything was wrong. Why didn't Mommy and Daddy come and take her away? Everything was *wrong*.

She was sitting in a high chair like a baby, and the sandwich was on the plate, but the plate didn't have Tweedle-dum and Tweedle-dee on it, it was just a yellow plate with a crack in it, and the room was gloomy and blue and the window painted on the wall wasn't a real window, and she wanted to go outside and play, but Funny wouldn't let her.

Grace picked up her spoon and started singing a song, "Frerr-a Zhocka, Frerr-a Zhocka, dormay voo, dormay voo. Son-a-lamma-tuna, son-a-lamma-tuna, ding dang dong! Ding dang dong!" Pushing her glass of milk with the spoon. Easing it, easing it. "Frerr-a Zhocka, Frerr-a Zhocka . . ." Waggling her head and easing the glass of milk over toward the edge the tray.

Ooops.

The glass of milk fell off the tray—it was a real glass, not a kid's glass—and it smashed on the floor and the milk splattered across the room. Grace started to laugh, and Funny jumped up off the bed and grabbed her arm, and it hurt, and then Grace started to cry.

Funny said: "Are you trying to get yourself in trouble?" Funny had never talked to her like that before.

Why didn't Mommy and Daddy come and take her home? Why didn't they come?

• 52

As they drove down to College Park, a grubby suburb on the south side of Atlanta, Cleland Davis explained to Brock about the transceiver. Cleland was driving, and Brock had the transceiver in his hand. It was about the size of a large button off a woman's suit, painted a flat white. One side of the transceiver was sticky, like tape.

"Alarm systems," Cleland said, grimacing as he shifted his weight on his doughnut pillow. "Here's the theory. Your basic alarm system got three components. A detection loop—that's what triggers the alarm to go off when you open a window or set off a motion detector. An alarm mechanism—that's your bell, your sireen, whatever. Then you gonna have a control mechanism. Most home alarm systems, there's a box on the wall where you punch in the code, turn the thing off or on, set the parameters, whatever. That's your control device."

"So?" Brock said. "Where does that get us?"

"Listen, my friend. Listen." The one-eyed investigator had a soft, gentle voice. "See, ordinarily your weak link in the chain is the detection loop. A window or door contact, if you can reach the wire, you can jump it with a pair of alligator clips. Motion detectors, you can just move real slow. Sounds silly, but it works."

"I still don't—"

"What I just told you, Brock? Listen and learn." It was hard to pick up the expression on the investigator's face since he only had one eye. "Now, let's assume he's got an alarm system. Mostly likely, bought it off the shelf. Way these things work, you punch a code into the keypad, right? Each individual key, when you punch it, it has a unique electronic signature. As you know, all electrical impulses produce a corresponding magnetic field. Now, if you can get close enough, with a magnetic pickup device, you can 'hear' that signature, record it, decode it. Then you know what the code is.''

"I'm still trying to get the relevance. Are you saying he might have wired the room to an alarm and then wired the alarm to this bomb he was telling me about?''

"Very good. He could set it up like a normal alarm, see. All he'd have to do is disconnect the signal to the speaker, run that down to some kind of detonation device.''

Brock held the tiny white disk in his hand. It was so small, it almost weighed nothing at all.

"So what exactly am I supposed to do?''

"Knock on the door, tell him you got to see her right now. Tell him you followed him down here, you been sitting out in the street for two hours, you're in agony over this whole thing, and you just got to see your sweet little girl or you're just gonna flat *die*.'' He looked over at Brock, who was giving him a slightly incredulous stare. "Hell, I don't know, Brock. You the brilliant, fast-talking trial lawyer. Figure something out! Something to get you in the door. Once you're in, you just stick the contact to the alarm controller. It's got a transmitter on it, so we'll be able to pick up the signal with a radio out here in the car.''

"But what if he's got this controller thing hidden?''

"Improvise, man, improvise! I can't tell you every got-damn step.'' He stopped at a red light, turned and spoke in a soft, calm voice. "Look, counselor. When you up there in the courtroom, you an actor. You playing a role. Sometimes you got to act shocked about something that don't shock you at all. Sometimes you got to get irate over nothing. Sometimes you got to act sympathetic to a client you can't stand to hardly even *look* at. It's the same thing right now.''

Brock felt a sick knot in his stomach.

"This thing's not exactly invisible,'' Brock said, looking at the small white button in the palm. "He's going to see it.''

"That's a chance you got to take.''

                    *   *   *

When they reached the house, Brock climbed out of the car, walked up to the door, rang the bell. He had the transceiver tucked against the ham of his hand, one finger resting against it. Trying to keep the shape of his hand natural. He could feel the sweat forming underneath the warm plastic. The peephole darkened, as though someone was looking out. After a moment some hefty-sounding locks clacked and the door opened.

"Well, well, well," Jimmy Dale said through a three-inch crack. "You found me."

Brock's heart was pounding. "I've got to see her."

"This morning I showed you a nice Polaroid of cute little Grace holding up today's copy of the *Atlanta Journal*. Each day I give you a new picture with the latest newspaper. That proves to you she's alive. That's all you get. End of conversation."

"I've got to see her," Brock said. He closed his eyes for a moment, remembering what the investigator had said. He was playing a role. The secret to acting, he supposed, was to believe what you were saying. Then maybe ratchet it up one more notch. That shouldn't be too hard, should it? Thinking: *Go! Just go!*

"Jimmy Dale, I'm—look, I'm wigging out here. Okay? I followed you down here, I've been driving around and around the block, I'm going crazy. Have a little, for chrissake, have a little compassion! I'm trying to be a good boy, huh? I'm trying like hell, okay? Okay?" He let his voice get louder—loud enough the neighbors could hear. If he started making a scene, maybe Jimmy Dale would let him in just to keep him quiet. Besides, now that he'd started thinking about Grace, thinking about how she was probably sitting there, only a few feet away and yet he was helpless to get at her . . . Christ. Feeling like maybe he was going to lose control of the situation. "Jimmy Dale, please! I've got to see my little girl. *This is killing me!*"

Feeling his eyes suddenly choked with tears.

Jimmy Dale's gaze swept up and down the road. He hesitated then flung open the door. "Get inside."

Brock entered a small barren room painted a dull white, water stains yellowing the ceiling. It was empty except for a green folding chair and a card table with a jar of instant coffee, three bars of soap, and a police scanner on it. The police scanner crackled and beeped. An ugly, cramped, depressing place. Brock felt panicky, tired—as though he were moving in slow motion.

Jimmy Dale secured the door with two huge bolts, then pointed to a heavy green door on the other side of the room. "I got her inside a special room," Jimmy Dale said. "There's no way I'm opening that door while you're here. You wearing a wire, Brock? Got the SWAT team waiting for you to say something like, 'Sure is hot in here!' and then they all gonna come busting in the front door?"

Brock surveyed the room. Cleland Davis had been right on the money: there was an alarm controller with a numeric keypad and some winking red lights stuck on the wall next to the heavy door. He felt a momentary elation. This was going to be easy. And there was a peephole in the door.

"Just let me look at her then," he said. "Let me look through the peephole."

"First I frisk you. Turn around."

Brock turned around. He could still feel the warm plastic of the transceiver in his palm.

"Come on. Up against the wall, just like in the movies."

As Brock put his hand against the wall, the transceiver fluttered out of his hand, fell to the floor. His heart jumped, but Jimmy Dale appeared not to notice the small white circle of plastic as it fell to the scarred blue linoleum floor. Jimmy Dale pulled up Brock's shirt, felt around on his chest and back.

"Okay," Jimmy Dale said.

Brock started to kneel as though to tie his shoe, but it didn't seem like a natural motion and Jimmy Dale was staring right at him now. Brock smiled. "Thanks, Jimmy Dale. I know this isn't part of your plan or whatever, but I just kind of panicked. I started imagining all these terrible things."

How the hell was he going to pick up the transceiver?

"Well, Brock, what you waiting for?"

Brock started across the room, feeling a growing sense of gloom and hopelessness with each stride that he took away from the transceiver. What if Jimmy Dale saw it? What if it was broken now? And how could he get back to the front

door, pick it up, cross the room *again* ... and still manage
to stick it to the controller without giving himself away?

He reached the door, looked through the peephole. Grace
was sitting on the bed in a red-striped shirt and underpants,
looking at a picture book. An old Western played silently on
a small black-and-white television sitting on a table behind
her. Tears welled up in his eyes again, and something
clutched at his chest.

"It's past her bedtime," he said softly.

"Yeah, well maybe you interrupted that."

Jimmy Dale may not have meant a double entendre, but
Brock felt a blaze of anger anyway. He turned around and
pointed his finger at Jimmy Dale's face. "Dad showed me
your records. Back when you were Bailiford."

Jimmy Dale's eyes narrowed.

"You touch that little girl," Brock said, "and I will hunt
you to the ends of the earth."

Jimmy Dale sat down at the card table, took a small knife
out of his pocket, and picked up a bar of soap. "That was
all a mistake," Jimmy Dale said mildly. "A little lying kid,
a big misunderstanding."

"Why do I doubt that?" Brock said. He turned and stalked
toward the door.

"Don't you want to talk to her?" Jimmy Dale said.

Brock stopped, halfway across the room. He stood frozen.
Of course I do. But I want the goddamn transceiver, too.
Jimmy Dale's little blue eyes looked up from the bar of soap
he was carving and regarded him suspiciously.

"Alright, alright," Jimmy Dale said. "What are you doing
here? You didn't come to see your damn daughter. I can see
it in your eyes. You scouting the location for the SWAT
team?"

"SWAT team? SWAT team! No, asshole, that's not it. I'm
here to make sure you're not putting your sick, disgusting
hands on my little girl."

Jimmy Dale slammed his soap bar on the table, lunged
forward and grabbed Brock by the shirtfront. He breathed
into Brock's face for a moment, then slung him against the
front door. "Don't you *see?*" he screamed. "I'm not a pervert; I'm not a freak! That's not who I am!" His bright blue
eyes stared into Brock's from a distance of six inches. Brock

could see where Jimmy Dale had cut himself shaving that morning, little brown dots against the mottled red of his jaw. His voice dropped to a whisper. "Don't you see why I want justice, Brock? I just want the world to see me as I really am."

"Which is how?"

Jimmy Dale was trembling, a small white bead of spit perched on his lower lip.

"Pure!" His voice was hoarse, taut. "I am *pure!*"

Out of the corner of his eye, Brock saw the small white disk on the floor. "Get your hands off me," he said. Then he heaved against Jimmy Dale, jerking him off balance and pulling both of their bodies to the right. They fell in a heap on top of the white disk. Where was it? His hand scrabbled across the linoleum but he couldn't feel the transceiver anywhere. Where the hell was it?

Brock's hands searched frantically as the two men slowly got to their feet. It was gone. The transceiver was gone! Brock's heart pounded, and he gasped for breath.

"I'm sorry, Jimmy Dale," Brock said. "I overreacted."

"Get out of here," Jimmy Dale said quietly. He had a red welt on his cheek.

"I'm sorry," Brock said. "I'm sorry. You're right. You got screwed and it's only natural you'd want justice. I mean, you may find this hard to believe, but I actually became a lawyer because the idea of justice appealed to me."

Keep talking. Slow things down.

Jimmy Dale felt his bruised cheek with his hand. Brock was feeling desperate now. He had to stall for more time.

"Let me talk to her," he said. "I meant to. I wanted to. It's just—I'm scared. Okay? I got discombobulated."

Jimmy Dale shrugged. "Go ahead, Brock."

Brock turned toward the green door. Damn it! What had happened to the transceiver? This wasn't working.

"Wait," Jimmy Dale said. "I'm standing right next to you, okay? So, no clever stuff."

Brock nodded. He walked to the door, looked in the peephole, rapped on the unyielding metal with his knuckles. Grace looked up.

"Grace?" Brock called.

His daughter's mouth widened and then her face lit up. She flung the book on the bed. "Daddy?" she cried. "Daddy?"

"Hi, baby," Brock called. "How's my little angel?"

"Daddy!" She ran toward the door, disappearing below the area visible through the peephole. "Where are you, Daddy?"

"I'm outside, honey." Brock felt a lump in his throat. "I can't come in."

"Why not?"

"I just can't." Jesus, how did you explain kidnapping to a four-year-old?

"Can I come out? I want to come out, Daddy." He could hear a tremor in her voice, and her little hands slapped against the door. "Read me a story! Read me *Sam, Bangs and Moonshine.*"

"I can't, honey." Brock pressed his cheek against the cool wood. He could feel the impact of Grace's hands slapping, slapping, slapping against the door.

"Daddy! I want to go home!"

Just one more day, Brock wanted to say. *We'll get you out.* But he couldn't. "Just a little while longer, honey," he said. This time, when the tears came, they coursed down his cheeks. "Just a little while."

"Alright, Brock. That's enough."

Brock wiped his eyes on his sleeve, turned, slumped against the door. Where the hell was the transceiver? It couldn't have just disappeared. He was feeling short of breath, wasted, wrung out, full of despair.

Jimmy Dale started walking toward the door. He was carving on his soap bar again. For a moment Brock thought he saw the transceiver, but then he realized it was just a flake of white soap on the floor. "Let's go," Jimmy Dale said. "Now."

And then he saw it—a small white disk, perfectly round, stuck to the back of Jimmy Dale's shirt. Brock followed Jimmy Dale to the door. Just as he got there Jimmy Dale turned toward him again.

Shit. What now?

Impulsively, Brock grabbed Jimmy Dale and hugged him. "Thank you," Brock said. "Thank you so much." Jimmy Dale's eyes blinking, inches away. His breath smelled of bad

meat. Feeling around on the back of the shirt. Yes! There it
was, the smooth piece of plastic. Brock peeled it off the
fabric. Would it stick to the controller, now that the lint from
Jimmy Dale's shirt had gotten on the adhesive backing?

"Hey," Jimmy Dale said, looking a little surprised. "It's
nothing."

"Oh, wait," Brock said. "I forgot to say good-bye."

Jimmy Dale's eyes narrowed, but he didn't stop Brock as
he marched back across the room. "Honey?" he said.
"Honey, I have to say bye-bye."

"Don't go, Daddy." The little hands slapping on the
door again.

"Bye-bye. I love you."

And then, as he stood by the door, Jimmy Dale turned to
undo the latch and Brock slapped the little disk against the
top lip of the alarm control panel. A wave of relief sluiced
through Brock, as though he'd just been absolved of some
terrible crime.

Out in the car, Cleland Davis said, "Go alright?"

"Jesus, Cleland, I hope I never have to do anything like
that again."

The one-eyed detective adjusted himself on his doughnut
pillow, then put a hand on Brock's shoulder. "You done
good, chief. You done good."

Brock had the urge to weep, but this time he stifled it.
Somehow it didn't feel like the right time, the right place.

• 53

"**I** just feel so dirty," Brock said.

"Dirty?" Dru said.

They were sitting at the kitchen table, holding hands. Brock's grandfather sat on the other side of the table, pretending to read his biography of John C. Calhoun.

"The weird thing about being a trial lawyer," Brock said, "is that sometimes it's like method acting. You know, like you're playing games with your own emotions so that you can impress the jury. It's like part of you feels outrage or sadness or compassion or whatever . . . and then part of you is standing off to the side, watching the performance. Calmly, analytically. It's not that the emotion's not real, it's just that you *use* the emotion in this self-serving way."

Dru squeezed his hand. She had a slightly irritated look on her face. She shrugged. "I guess that's never happened to me."

For a moment Brock envied her. For Dru, things just *were*. She looked at them and she *knew*. For him, on the other hand, the world seemed perpetually obscure, layered with doubt.

"And when I was down there in College Park, I had such a strong feeling about Grace. This terrible feeling of sadness, of hopelessness, of impending loss. And of love. But at the same time I had to manipulate that emotion—*use* it to get Jimmy Dale to do what I wanted. After it was over I felt disgusted with myself, like maybe I was just some kind of fake."

Dru said, "I don't see why you have to make it so complicated."

Even when he'd been talking to Grace through the door, that moment hadn't felt clean; it was weighted down with his own oppressive sense of guilt. *He* had put her there. His own ego and unwillingness to compromise had imprisoned her in that room—just like Jimmy Dale knew it would—and so he could not quite live inside his own grief and joy at that moment. A part of him had somehow stepped aside in his own mind and watched with the cold eyes of an advocate. The only moment in that room that had felt utterly clean, Brock reflected, was when he had grabbed Jimmy Dale by the neck and thrown him on the floor. Rage—it was ugly as hell, but man, was it clean.

Brock's grandfather looked up from his book and leered at Dru, showing off his ancient gray dentures. "You want to know a secret about men, honey?" he told her.

Dru looked at him with flat, intolerant eyes.

"Every man in the world wants a chance like this, a chance to fight for his brood." The Judge laughed. "Life and death, everything's on the line, all faculties at maximum sensitivity."

"Why do you do this?" Dru said. "You're not helping."

The Judge turned his yellowed old eyes toward Brock. "The things that go through your mind in a time like this, they're never pretty. But remember—it's the chance of a lifetime, son. It's what we all dream of, that one brief moment where we get to exercise our mind to its fullest, most ruthless capacity."

"Shut up, shut up, shut up!" Dru said, sticking her fingers in her ears.

The Judge stopped smiling, reached across the table, grabbed Brock's arm with his claw of a hand. "You really want to get that girl back?" His hard old fingers biting into Brock's arm. "To fight evil, sometimes you got to reach down into the ugliest, darkest silt traps of your soul, bring up the demons, the skull tramplers, the Visigoths. To do good, sometimes you got to be bad in the extreme."

Brock looked away. Dru reached over and grabbed his right arm. The old man was clutching at his left.

"You been dreaming about this moment for a long time," the old man said, his voice dropping to a cracked whisper. "The good man pushed to the limit. How's he gonna respond? I know you got the *imagination* to summon up the demons and the skull tramplers. Question is, boy, have you got the guts? Have you got the meanness?''

Then the old man gathered up his book and hobbled toward the back door, his pants sagging off his withered hips.

After a moment the back door banged.

"I *hate* that old man," Dru said, her voice full of a quiet fury.

Brock crossed his arms on the table, laid his head down on them, and closed his eyes. "The problem with that old man," he said softly, "is he's usually right."

The next morning B.J. Mills's cross-examination of Jimmy Dale lasted till lunch.

Brock rolled Jimmy Dale over to Underground Atlanta, a sort of subterranean mall near the courthouse, where they seated themselves in the food court with their messy sandwiches.

"We've got maybe half an hour of redirect, then it's time for Caitlin," Brock said. "Is she going to show this time?"

Jimmy Dale smirked. "I've got to go feed your kid some lunch," he said, backing his wheelchair away from the table. "If I'm late, just tell them I have special physical needs, some kind of bullshit like that. I'll be back."

"Jimmy Dale! Hey! Answer me, you son of a bitch!"

The wheelchair rolled away and was soon lost in the crowd. Brock cursed under his breath. Was he getting ready to spring another surprise?

After Jimmy Dale left, Brock used a pay phone to call Cleland Davis, the investigator, who was staking out the house where Grace was being imprisoned. "Jimmy Dale's on his way."

"Thanks," Davis said. "I'll keep my head down."

One fifteen, Judge Wellborn breezed in with her white flip freshly tended. Jimmy Dale still wasn't there. "Where's your witness?" the judge said.

Brock stood. "He's got special physical needs, your honor. I'm afraid he's going to be a little bit late."

"How come you didn't inform the court about this?" The judge's wattles trembled disapprovingly.

"It's a matter of, ah, I'm not sure how to put this tactfully." Brock gave the judge a wincing, rueful smile. "It's a matter of his bowels, your honor."

The judge drummed her fingers on the bench for a moment. Brock hated this. Not that he might not have trumped up an excuse for a client in any other trial. But for the sham he was perpetrating in this courtroom, every inch he moved toward Jimmy Dale's goal made him feel like a traitor to everything that mattered.

"It's okay," came a voice from the back of the courtroom. "I'm here." And there he was, Jimmy Dale, rolling cheerfully down the aisle.

"Where is she?" Brock whispered when Jimmy Dale reached the plaintiff's table.

Jimmy Dale winked. "Don't worry. She'll be here."

"The last time somebody told me that," Brock said, "I ended up in a world of hurt."

"That was good," Jimmy Dale said. "About the bowels? Very nice touch."

"Fuck you very much," Brock whispered.

When Brock had finished with Jimmy Dale's brief redirect, the judge said, "Call your next witness."

"The plaintiff calls Ms. Caitlin Cobranchy to the stand," Brock said. And then he turned, expecting to see nothing but the courtroom full of bored, pissed-off reporters, tired of sitting around waiting for a story about Shakespeare that didn't seem to be materializing. But there she was, walking up the aisle in a demure blue dress, a strand of seed pearls, and a pair of low blue pumps. Hardly any makeup. Except for her riot of auburn hair, she looked like a young banker on her way to a meeting with an important client.

After Caitlin was sworn in, Brock said, "Ms. Cobranchy, could you tell the court where you were employed on January 9 of last year?"

Caitlin Cobranchy leaned forward slightly. "Laughing Dolls," she said.

"Which is what?"

"It's a strip joint," she said without even a hint of a smile.

Someone in the back of the court tittered. The judge glared at them.

"And what was your position there?"

"I was an exotic dancer." She smiled slightly. "That's a fancy word for a stripper."

"And how long had you been there?"

"About two years."

Brock leaned against the podium. "Let's turn to the night of January 9 of last year. What happened that night?"

"Well, I'd been dancing for about three hours at Laughing Dolls. Several of the dancers had called in sick and so the manager of the club, Mic Giddens, he pressured me into dancing longer shifts than I normally would have. Usually it's like, ten minutes on, ten minutes off, or whatever. But that night, Mr. Giddens made me dance for like an hour at a time. I mean, come on! The tips were good, but I'm standing there on five-inch spike heels, for godsake. Dancing is hard work! Eventually, my calves are seizing up, my shoes are starting to bite, my crotch is getting gummy—" One of the reporters bayed back in the gallery. Judge Wellborn glared. "Hey, I'm just being honest here. So anyway, I'm starting to get pretty tired."

"And what happened then, Miss Cobranchy?"

"I collapsed."

Brock made a face for the benefit of the jury, full of surprise and concern. "Collapsed! How so?"

"I don't mean out of exhaustion; I'm just saying I fell over. Maybe my heel gave out, maybe I got a cramp in my leg, maybe there was a slick spot on the table where I was dancing. I don't know. Whatever it was, I'm dancing, you know, then, bam, I'm falling off the table. There's this guy walking by and he doesn't see me and I just come down right on top of him, and we both fall on the ground. I had the wind knocked out of me, a couple of bruises, but otherwise I was fine. One of the bouncers helped me up, and at that point I recognized the guy I'd fallen on. It was Jimmy Dale Evans. I didn't know his name then, but I knew who he was because he did the books for the club."

Brock nodded.

"So anyway, Jimmy Dale was lying there holding his back and kind of moaning. Maybe screaming was more like it.

You could see he was in a lot of pain. Mic Giddens came over and I said he better call an ambulance for this guy. Well, Mic, he just tells me not to worry about it. He's going, you know, 'Shake it off, Jimmy Dale,' all that kind of thing. But Jimmy Dale didn't get up and so Mic and one of the bouncers hauled Jimmy Dale back to the office. About fifteen or twenty minutes later I asked Mic whether he'd called an ambulance and he said he hadn't, so I went ahead and called 911. The paramedic guys showed up maybe ten minutes later and they took him to the hospital.''

"And that's it?" Brock said.

Caitlin nodded.

Brock asked follow-up questions for about half an hour. As he was about to wrap up his direct, he heard Jimmy Dale clearing his throat behind him. He turned and Jimmy Dale slid a piece of paper across the plaintiff's table.

The paper contained ten questions written in Jimmy Dale's ugly scrawl. Ugly but legible. So old Jimmy Dale had written himself a script. Well, it was hardly surprising.

"Miss Cobranchy, I'd like to return to something we touched on earlier." Brock read the first question: "Did you enjoy being an exotic dancer?"

"No. I hated it," Caitlin said.

"And yet you continued?" Brock again, reading from Jimmy Dale's script.

"Like I said, the money was good. But after a while, you start to get drawn into it, into this whole world. You start to forget what being a normal person is like."

Brock read the next question: "How so?"

"After a while, you stop believing in yourself as a whole person. You start thinking of yourself as tits and ass. You forget you've got anything else going for you."

It was obvious that Jimmy Dale had scripted the final sequence of her testimony just like a play or a movie: Q&A, word for word. For a moment Brock considered balling up the sheet of paper, throwing it away. Scripted testimony was completely prohibited, completely unethical. But then ethics had nothing to do with this trial, anyway. This trial was about survival. No, not even that. This trial was about a four-year-old girl who was trusting in her father to save her life. Nothing more, nothing less. Brock forced himself to keep his mind focused on that. For a moment he could feel, in his memory, the impact of her fists on the door of her prison, the small thuds against his tear-streaked cheek. *Get moving. Get it over with. This is too important to let your emotions drag you down.*

"But surely you didn't *have* to work as a stripper?"

"After you work for a while in one of these places, it's like you've been brainwashed." Caitlin's voice was suddenly full of venom. "These men that owned and operated these places—they don't care about us. All they care about is money. Money, money, money. And if they have to manipulate us and threaten us and beat us and rape us—"

"Objection!" B.J. Mills bounced out of his seat waving his tortoiseshell glasses at the judge.

"I've seen some things there you wouldn't believe. I've seen girls raped, kicked, punched, drugged, screamed at! And not by the customers. I'm talking about the people who *run* the club. I'm talking about the people who *own* it!"

"Miss Cobranchy," the judge cut in. "I'm going to have to ask you to contain yourself."

Caitlin clamped her mouth shut, looked down for a moment. Strong emotions were obviously tearing at her—notwithstanding the fact that this whole thing came off a script. Either she was a hell of an actress or something very bad had happened to her at Laughing Dolls.

Two more questions to go. Brock read from the yellow paper: "Why do you say that, Miss Cobranchy?"

"Listen," Caitlin said, looking up suddenly. "I was an abused child. My father used to rape me." A sudden stir from the back of the courtroom. "My mother knew about it and she did nothing. Respectable family, well-educated, but there you are. I guess I'm just used to being screwed. And the rest of these girls, most of them are from poor families, broken homes, terrible situations. You want to know why Jimmy Dale Evans is sitting there in that wheelchair? These men, they own us as surely as if we were slaves. They push us and push us and push us . . ." Her voice sank and tears started slipping out of her eyes. It was no act. No act at all. Brock looked back at Jimmy Dale. In his protuberant blue eyes, a look of cold satisfaction.

"What men?" Brock read. "Mic Giddens?"

"Not just Mic. He's only a stooge. I'm talking about the people who own Laughing Dolls."

B.J. Mills saw it coming. "Objection!"

But he was too late. Caitlin was up out of her chair, pointing at the defense table. "I'm talking about the men who hide behind their lawyers like children behind their mothers' skirts." Her voice had risen high and shrill and the tears were making small dark stains on her dress.

"Miss Cobranchy!" the judge yelled.

"I'm talking about Mel Prochaska and Lee Darden and Boyd Michaels and Raymond Lata—"

Slamming her gavel. "Miss Cobranchy, sit down!"

"I'm talking about Reggie Vinyard!"

The back of the courtroom was erupting like a pond full of hungry crocodiles. Blood in the water. They'd finally gotten what they were waiting for.

"How long did you prep her?" Brock whispered afterward.

"Oh, we didn't have to spend that long." Jimmy Dale winked. "She's a natural."

"And how much are you paying her?"

Jimmy Dale winked. "Maybe it's better that you didn't know the vulgar details."

• 55

Jimmy Dale Evans sat in the dark listening to Skip Carey announcing the Braves on the radio: Atlanta down 2-3 at the bottom of the seventh, a West Coast game. He'd opened a window to let in some air, but there wasn't much breeze. It was a hot, close darkness, the kind that bred sour memories and unwholesome thoughts.

He wasn't thinking about the game. Wasn't thinking, even, about the courtroom tomorrow, or the fact that the revenge he'd dreamed of for so long was finally beginning to unfold. Dreams had a way of doing that: becoming uninteresting, vaguely depressing even, as soon as they began to take on the clothing of reality. No, he was thinking about the little girl. Brock's little girl.

But it wasn't exactly her either. It was little girls in general. Grace just happened to be the girl closest at hand.

He was thinking back to the evening of June 4, 1962, Reidsville State Penitentiary. Back during his first stint in prison—this was for the molesting beef with the little girls, not the rape thing in '63 with Reggie Vinyard's sister. It had been a few minutes after lockdown, a bare bulb shining dimly into his cell, the screws shuffling around outside, making smart remarks. Somewhere he could hear the sound of a man's heavy nighttime breathing. And he'd had a sort of revelation—*pop!*—just like that, appearing in his brain: "No more."

No more.

That was all there was to it: There would be no more little girls. No more sitting around thinking up ways to use little girls; no more fantasies; no more role-playing with dolls; no more ingratiating himself to children. And certainly no more . . . he had called them "games," the things he'd done to the little girls. No more games with the little girls, not ever.

In that split second he had understood that this was how it would have to be. He would change, would leave that old perverted self behind.

Because Eugene Bailiford—the man who would later became Jimmy Dale Evans—was a man with plans for himself. Plans to own real estate and drive a nice car and have people look at him and say, "There goes *somebody*." Plans, plans— taking correspondence courses in tax preparation and real estate and surveying, trying to make himself better than the skinny old drunk of a father he'd grown up with, living in a shotgun shack with no toilet next to a colored family's tired peanut field in a nowhere little village outside Americus, Georgia. No, sir. Not Eugene Bailiford. Eugene Bailiford was going up to Atlanta, make something of himself.

Which meant (he'd understood this inside of a moment, the distant lightning flash burned on the back of his eyelids, June 4, 1962) that if there was ever to be a Eugene Bailiford of Atlanta, Man of Substance, then there were to be no little girls. Never again.

June 4, 1962. That was the end of Eugene Bailiford, pervert. Dead and buried.

And he'd lived up to his pledge, even after getting rail-roaded for a crime he didn't commit, been steel hard with his self-discipline. Even after nine years in prison (*nine years!*), all his dreams smashed, no skills beyond his prison correspondence courses and some knocking around in the sheet metal shop and the laundry—even after all that, he still hadn't broken his promise to himself. No little girls. No sleeping next to them, feeling the rise and fall of their tiny lungs, seeing their hair splayed out on the pillow, listening to their tiny sighs. Not ever. Not even the occasional fantasy, the occasional dream. And so he'd never driven by the school yards or the kindergartens, never watched them playing, full of life, cheeks freckled, little legs downed with silken hair.

No, none of that. Never, *never* had he broken his promise, *June 4, 1962*.

But here he was, thinking about the little girl (beautiful

child! stunning child!) who lay sleeping on the other side of
that door, and suddenly the old hungers were rushing back
in. Thinking: *If I just* touched *her as she slept, rested my hand
on the small of her back, maybe that would be enough* ...

No. No, goddamn you, no!

But still he got up from the folding chair (*damn you,
Jimmy Dale, damn you to hell!*) and stared through the
peephole anyway. The television flickered morosely in the
dark, giving off just enough flat blue-white light that he
could see her face, eyes squeezed shut, thumb in the mouth.
He imagined the smell of her, the nighttime child-smell of
cotton and spit and clean youthful sweat. He put his hand
on the knob.

"No!"

A voice out of the darkness. A figure hunched in the dim
corner so that it was hard to tell whether it was real or
imagined. "Don't even think about it."

"What?" Jimmy Dale said. "I'm cool." He took his hand
off the knob, sauntered into the kitchen, popped open a Black
Label. When he got back in the room, Belliard had hit a two-
run double. "Four, three Braves," he said to the dark figure
in the corner. "Way to be."

No answer in the silent room. He *was* cool, wasn't he?
Yes, he was. A momentary slip, that's all.

He picked up a small figure off the table, a laughing girl
carved from Ivory soap. He'd sculpted it earlier in the evening. A laughing child wearing only a pair of underpants. He
turned the figure over and over in his hand until his fingers
were slick with lather.

• 56

Brock put in a call to his father first thing in the morning.

"We've hit a snag," his father said.

"What kind of snag? Don't tell me the damn transceiver didn't work."

"Worked fine. Something to do with the decoding. Cleland and his people recorded the signal from the transceiver last night, but they still have to decode it. Problem is, the alarm system was engineered in Taiwan. They managed to get hold of the company in Taipei, but there's only one engineer who knew enough to make sense of the signal. And he was on his day off."

"So we can't go in today?"

"I'm going to have to take the stand, son."

"I was going to put Reggie next."

"No good. Reggie's paper trail is real. Mine was fabricated. Take our time, we can stall until tomorrow. By then we'll have the code and we can go in and get Grace out."

"We? I thought you were going to give the code to the police, let them handle it."

"Damage control, son. Damage control. Got to do it ourselves. We get the police involved, Reggie might as well admit to the investments in open court."

Brock's face was suddenly hot with anger. "I don't give a shit about damage control! *All* that matters is Grace's safety."

"I know. I know. But we will get Grace out. Each day Jimmy Dale has to leave the house, set the alarm, lock her up. We wait until he leaves for trial tomorrow morning, go in, punch in the code, get her out. It's foolproof.''

Brock didn't like it. But he supposed he owed it to his father to play the game that way. After all, what could the police do that he and his father couldn't? "Okay, Dad."

"Meantime, you're just going to have to stall."

"See you in court."

"If I could get you to refer to page . . ." Brock stood at the podium, scratched his head, tried to look puzzled. *Take your time. Take your time. Every second counted.* His father sat in the witness box with a patient, expectant look on his face. "I'm sorry, this would be page, ah, twenty-seven of Plaintiff's Exhibit thirty-five, Bates stamped as number X000274. Are you with me?"

Brock's father, took off his glasses, flipped around in his stack of papers, put on his glasses again. "Hmm . . . Exhibit twenty-seven?" he said. "Page thirty-five? Mine's got a different Bates stamp."

"I'm afraid you got that backward. *Exhibit* thirty-five, *page* twenty-seven."

"Oh!" Brock's father put on his glasses again. "Sorry!"

This was how they had been playing it all morning. The courtroom equivalent of the old four-corners stall in basketball. No shot clock in the American judicial system.

Eleven forty-five. Closing in on lunchtime. The audience had gotten bored, B.J. Mills was getting quick to make objections, and the judge was getting pissed. Worst of all, Brock sensed that Jimmy Dale knew he was stalling. After all, he had managed to go through three hours of his father's testimony without introducing a single piece of the falsified evidence that connected his father to the Laughing Dolls or even to Wentworth.

The judge looked up suddenly, motioned to Brock with her finger. "Before the witness answers, I'd like a moment with counsel." Brock and Mills traipsed dutifully up to the bench. The judge ran her tongue across her spotted lip and then said, "You've been at it for close to three hours and you haven't made a single hit. If I didn't know you better, I'd think you were stalling for time."

Brock raised his eyebrows. "Your honor, I have to admit,

I don't appreciate being put in the position of explaining my trial strategy in front of opposing counsel."

The judge folded her arms and leaned back, stared at him for a few moments. "I don't think that's what I'm doing. I'm asking you if you're stalling."

Brock pretended to be a little put out and said, "I have every confidence we're going to win this case, and every confidence that opposing counsel will appeal it. But there are some complicated collateral insurance issues here, and what I'm doing is laying down a very thorough foundation to cauterize any possible weaknesses in this case as regards, ah, both appellate and insurance matters." Brock rattled off the citations for a couple of vaguely relevant cases. *When in doubt, baffle 'em with bullshit.*

"I better see this leading somewhere pretty soon."

"Naturally, your honor."

Brock walked back to the podium. Could he keep this up for another three and a half hours? He wasn't sure. "Now, Mr. Brock, if I may, please direct your attention to the page we'd referenced before. Could you please read, for the record, the first twelve lines in the second paragraph of that page?"

Brock's father started reading. " 'If the Laughing Dolls (hereinafter referred to as "The Insured") should, upon appropriate 30-day notice, notify The Insurer of its intent . . .' "

In the back of the courtroom, a reporter began to snore.

There was a batting cage with a pitching machine in it down by the food court at Underground Atlanta. Brock put three dollar bills in the machine, grabbed a bat and went inside. Jimmy Dale sat outside the green netting, looking in with a sour face.

"What are you doing in there?" Jimmy Dale said.

Brock popped the first pitch up into the netting. "Trying to improve my swing," he said.

"You know what I'm talking about."

Brock missed the next pitch entirely. "Look, this ain't Perry Mason. The truth is, there's an amazing lack of drama in real courtrooms. I'm doing what we shysters call 'establishing foundation.' See, in a court of law, you have to establish the pedigree of every document. Did the witness ever see the document? Did they prepare it? Did they sign it?"

Brock slammed the next pitch hard. Line drive. It hit the pitching machine with a satisfying clang.

"This is not an ordinary case, Brock. I want names. Over and over and over. I want you to keep repeating the following words. Mel Prochaska. Raymond Lata. Lee Darden—"

"That's what I'm *telling* you, you idiot," Brock said, as he whiffed the next ball. "We're already skating on thin ice with this whole brilliant strategy of yours. If I don't establish a totally bulletproof foundation—who touched which documents and when—then every time I mention Mel Prochaska or Raymond Lata, B.J. Mills is going to coming flying out of his seat with an objection. And each time the judge is going to uphold it. And then pretty soon he's going to say, mention one more dead lawyer and I'm calling a mistrial."

"I think you're trying to let your old man off the hook."

"Shut up and watch," Brock said. The next ball caught him by surprise. He chopped at it and it dribbled down the side of the cage. "I know what I'm doing."

"I'm not so sure," Jimmy Dale said. "Your stance is too open. You need to drive from the hips."

After lunch something went wrong with the air conditioning and the courtroom began getting cold. By three o'clock Brock was starting to shiver. The bailiff with the pearl-handled revolver had slipped out of the courtroom, come back with a brown nylon jacket on. Worse, though, Brock had begun to run out of even vaguely believable foundational questions. Pretty soon he was going to have to move on to the bogus connections between his father and Wentworth. Which was only one step from the strip clubs. And the murders.

By four-thirty Brock's fingertips were turning white. The bailiff had opened the doors in the back of the courtroom, but it was too little, too late. Brock managed to kill fifteen minutes pretending to lose a document, and, on the theory that the whole thing was so boring that everyone surely must have stopped paying attention by now, he asked a series of at least eight or ten questions that he'd already been through word-for-word somewhere in the neighborhood of ten-thirty that morning.

Mills finally started objecting, so Brock had to move on.

At ten minutes till five, the temperature in the room had run down into the high fifties, and Brock had run out of rope. He went back to the table to pick up the exhibit listing his father as general partner in Wentworth, Ltd., brought it back, sat it on the podium. This was it. For the first time he would be introducing something that would mark an unambiguous trail between his father and Laughing Dolls. No matter that it was a forged document filed by Jimmy Dale Evans. Because once the connection was made, it didn't matter whether it was false or not; Brock's father's reputation would be ruined.

"Have I got that exhibit?" The clerk was rubbing her hands.

"It's under seal," Brock said. "Number 32 on our list."

The clerk picked up the court's copy, put her thumb under the seal.

"Hold on," the judge said, looking at the clock. "This is getting ridiculous in here. Let's knock off for the day, see if we can't get those knuckleheads to fix the air conditioning."

Brock couldn't speak. He just nodded and stumbled back to the plaintiff's table.

Afterward Brock rolled Jimmy Dale up the aisle, just as he'd done every day. Once they'd gotten past the cluster of shivering reporters, Jimmy Dale said, "You were stalling, you bastard."

"I *told* you already, I was laying foundation."

Jimmy Dale shook his head. "I guess your little girl's life don't mean that much to you."

Brock felt a needle of dread stab his chest. "I swear to you, Jimmy Dale. I'm trying to make this thing work. You've waited fifteen years, for Christ's sake be patient."

"Huh-uh," Jimmy Dale said. "I don't know why, but you're stalling."

"Jimmy Dale," Brock pleaded, "trust me. I know what I'm doing." The door to the elevator opened.

"Remember who I am." Jimmy Dale's blue eyes bulged malignantly, and a half-smile formed on his face. " 'Cause I got your little girl. And I can do anything I want with her."

The elevator door slid open, and Jimmy Dale rolled inside. Brock sat down on his haunches for a moment, his legs suddenly gone weak and gelid on him. That engineer in Taiwan had better come through with the alarm code. He had to get Grace out of there in the morning.

There was no other way.

• 57

Jimmy Dale pulled into a dark wooded lot a couple of blocks off West Paces Ferry Road. He turned off the lights, climbed out of the van with his reversible gym bag and hiked down the dark, empty street. The large staid houses were unlit, peering darkly out from under lush, ragged trees.

He looked at his watch. One thirty-four in the morning. Right on schedule.

Jimmy Dale walked to the fourth house on the left. Under the scrap of moon, the red brick facade had taken on the greenish cast of deep oceanic water. A large gray Oldsmobile was parked underneath the porte cochere.

Jimmy Dale trotted noiselessly down the long driveway and around to the back of the house. There was a deck off to one side, and an old shed along the back fence. A high, stately oak blanketed the yard in darkness.

Jimmy Dale crouched beside an azalea, letting his eyes adjust, then unzipped the gym bag, took out a trowel and began digging a small hole next to the roots of the azalea. The loam smelled rich with fungus and decaying leaves.

When the hole was a foot and a half deep, he took a knife out of the gym bag, snapped open the blade. A Buck knife with a three-and-a-half-inch blade. In the darkness the stained blade was almost invisible: the blood hid the steel from the night.

Jimmy Dale tossed the knife back in the gym bag, wadded up the bag, and stuffed it in the hole.

When he'd finished burying the bag, he arranged the leaves carefully over the spot. The moon came out, threw a shimmer of pale splotches across the yard. Jimmy Dale looked up at the fine old house and smiled. So much for Brock's old man. Next stop was Reggie Vinyard's place.

Beautiful. Everything going as smooth as glass.

Only as soon as he got out to the street, Jimmy Dale spotted trouble. Down at the end of the road a cop car had pulled into the wooded lot, its headlights shining on Jimmy Dale's van.

Jimmy Dale walked slowly down toward the van, the trowel resting against his leg. When he got closer, he realized it was some kind of private security car, not a city of Atlanta cruiser.

"Hi," Jimmy Dale said to the cop. "Is there a problem?"

"This your vehicle, sir?" A young guy with a bulletproof vest and a crew cut, trying to act like a hard-ass. A bulletproof vest? Jimmy Dale almost laughed. Last time someone had gotten shot in this part of town, Nixon had still been in office.

"Yes, sir, it is," Jimmy Dale said. "I was cutting through to Moore's Mill and all of a sudden I'm out of gas."

"Where've you been, sir?" The guy talking in one of those insinuating cop voices. Probably been trying to get into the Atlanta police department for a couple years, too stupid to pass the police academy entrance exam.

"Getting gas." Jimmy Dale edged closer to the cop, still holding the trowel out of sight.

The rent-a-cop blinked. "Where's your gas can?"

Jimmy Dale shrugged. "Gas station didn't have a can."

The rent-a-cop ran his tongue around his lips, then started copying down the plate number on Jimmy Dale's van. Jimmy Dale tightened his grip on the trowel.

"Afraid I'm gonna have to call this in, sir."

"To who?"

"The police."

Jimmy Dale smiled. "Oh, okay. Think they'd give me a ride?"

As the rent-a-cop reached through the passenger side of his car to get his walkie-talkie off the seat of the car, Jimmy Dale stepped forward and jammed his trowel into the rent-a-cop's neck. The cop grunted, tried to jerk away, but Jimmy Dale forced the trowel deeper, shaking it and driving the cop up off his feet, through the window and into the front seat of the car. Warm blood poured down Jimmy Dale's arms, covered his shirt. *Jesus, this idiot could sure bleed!* The rent-a-cop's legs were kicking over Jimmy Dale's shoulders and his hands thrashed, whacking into the dashboard. When the rent-a-cop stopped twitching, Jimmy Dale shoved his legs through the window into the front seat, then went around to the driver's side and cranked up the car.

Damnation! This was sure going to complicate things.

It was four o'clock in the morning before he got back to the little house in College Park, crawled into his cot and fell into a black, empty sleep.

In the early hours of the morning, Jimmy Dale woke sweating from a dream. He was hard inside his running shorts. He'd been dreaming about the little girl, the one back in 1962. The dream had left him with a feeling of adolescent yearning, a recollection of a time when he was still innocent and young and the world was not quite so hard or ugly.

But there was something wrong. The girl in the dream—he remembered, yes, her little shoulder blades and her moans of fear and the shape of her legs. But she had the wrong face. She was supposed to have brown hair and a scar on her lip. But she didn't. The face in the dream wasn't the girl from 1962. It was the little girl in the other room. Brock's kid. Grace.

Feeling that old urge. Now that his plan was assured, now that all the building blocks were in place, it was as though thirty years of venom had slipped out of him. And what was left? A hungry urge. A hungry, youthful urge to take a little girl in his arms and do what he wanted with her, to make her little body slick with his juices.

And so he decided that maybe after all these years it would be okay if he broke the promise he'd made to himself. Lying there in his hard cot in the dark, empty room. Thinking: he was damn superman now. He could do anything he wanted. He was Jack the Giant Killer. He was endless and boundless and full of power. And besides, he was just about through. Regardless of what happened now—whether Vinyard and Brock finally shrugged off everything that he threw on them, regardless of whether he managed to keep himself clean of the storm that was sure to erupt over the murders and the strip clubs and all that had happened there, it was all beside the point. Because all that was left for Jimmy Dale Evans or Eugene Bailiford or whoever he was, was a few rental properties in slummy parts of town, a few lying, deadbeat tenants, a few struggling laundromats and bars where he could do the books. And that wasn't enough. That wasn't suitable consolation for all that he had lost, all the years and dreams and hopes. That wasn't nearly suitable.

Which left only a few more desperate years before his prostate exploded or his arteries clogged up or his heart quit its incessant beating. A few more desperate years, that was all.

But a tiny soft ghost of a voice added: *and the lovely, sweet purity of little girls.*

So Jimmy Dale got up in the dark, walked through the darkness with an unlit flashlight, punched in the code on the booby-trapped door, opened it quietly, went into the room, turned on his flashlight.

In the bed, the precious little girl slept, head thrown back, arms wide and welcoming, one leg lolling halfway off the mattress. A small brown bear lay facedown at the bottom of the bed. Oh, yes. He'd waited so long. Been through so much, to arrive back here again. Eugene Bailiford felt himself through his pants, hard as a rock, ready to explode.

He smiled in the darkness, felt a hot rush of pleasure and satisfaction and power.

The joke's on you, he thought. *All of you bastards! All of you, all of you, all of you, all of you . . .*

I am Superfuckingman. Feel my revenge.

• 58

Brock woke with a start at 5:45. Sunlight thinly painted against the horizon.

The code. Did they have the code yet? He reached over for the phone, dialed his father's house.

Strangely, there was no answer. His father was supposed to be on the phone to the people in Taiwan. Maybe he'd gone someplace to get a translator. Maybe he was calling from the office.

Brock dialed Reggie Vinyard's home number. No answer there. Were they together, Vinyard and his dad? Brock tried their direct lines at the office. No answer. No answer at Vinyard's car phone number, either. His father, characteristically, did not own a car phone.

Brock began to feel a wisp of panic forming in his chest. He tried one of the two numbers Cleland Davis had given him.

"Davis here." The soft, warm voice of the investigator.

"What's going on?" Brock said. "Is Reggie over there? Or Dad?"

"No," Davis said. "I was hoping *you'd* know where they were. I been trying them for fifteen minutes."

"Shit!" Brock said. "So'd you get the code yet?"

"Your Dad called Taipei late last night. They said the guy would be in later in the day. Meaning early this morning our time. Your Dad's supposed to be getting in touch with him now."

"That's what I thought."

After a moment's pause, Davis said, "Maybe they're on

their way and just forgot to call. Why don't we meet down there at Jimmy Dale's safehouse in College Park.''

Half an hour later Brock and Cleland Davis were sitting in the investigator's blue Ford, parked half a block down the street from the little house. Davis sat gingerly on his doughnut pillow wearing his dark suit and white shirt, no necktie. Today he wasn't wearing his eye patch.

''You sure he's here?'' Brock said. ''I don't see his van.''

''In the carport on the other side of the house,'' Davis said.

Brock picked up the investigator's cel phone, started making calls. Nobody answered at any of the numbers.

''This is starting to make me real nervous,'' Brock said.

Davis didn't say anything, just sat there chewing on a cinnamon biscuit from Hardees.

''You ever wear a necktie?'' Brock said.

The investigator shook his head.

An hour went by and Brock still hadn't reached his father. ''Something bad wrong going on,'' Cleland Davis said. It was the first time he'd spoken in an hour.

Brock had started thinking of worst-case scenarios. What if Jimmy Dale had decided that Brock wasn't going to come through for him in the trial and had attacked Vinyard and his father during the night? What if he'd killed them?

''Where the hell are they?'' Brock said.

Davis shook his head, shifted slowly on his pillow.

After a while Brock started feeling an uncomfortable pressure on his bladder. ''I shouldn't have drunk that coffee.''

The investigator reached into the backseat, handed Brock a plastic jug that looked like it had once carried a quart full of orange juice. ''Surveiller's best friend,'' he said.

''Right here?'' Brock said. ''Right now?''

''Minute Maid,'' Davis said. ''Whizzed in by all the top law enforcement professionals.''

''When you due in court, Brock?''

It was eight-fifteen now. Pretty soon Jimmy Dale ought to be coming out, heading for court. Brock's hands were clammy and his chest was tight. He was surfing a bobbing wave of nausea.

"Nine-thirty," he said.

Davis shook his head dolefully. "He's gonna be leaving any minute."

"What if he goes? Should we follow him?"

"I don't know. Original plan, you and me was going in the house, Reggie and your Dad was gonna follow Jimmy Dale. But now, I don't know. Without the code, I guess we better follow him."

Brock nodded. "The idea of leaving her there alone, though . . ." Brock's voice broke.

"Yeah, but you don't know what Jimmy Dale's up to. What if he's changed plans? I know it's a long shot, but just suppose he freaked last night, whacked Reggie and your Dad? We got to consider that possibility. He might be hitting the road, taking her with him." Cleland Davis rolled his window down, poured the dregs of his coffee on the ground. "How 'bout hand me that Minute Maid jug."

Davis had just gotten his fly unzipped when the cop pulled up next to them, got out with his huge cop flashlight, the kind that was doubled as a truncheon.

"How you fellows doing," the cop said, leaning in the window. He had large, square teeth and a mustache like a British field marshall.

"Fine," Brock said.

The cop had the flashlight resting on his shoulder. His other hand was on his belt, close to his gun. "You gentlemen want to tell me what you're doing here?"

"Surveillance," Brock said.

"Uh-huh." The cop's voice hard, skeptical. "Hands up in plain sight, boys." Brock put his hands on the dash, but Davis was struggling with the jug, trying to keep from pissing on himself.

"I said, hands *UP!*" Evidently Davis wasn't moving fast enough, because all of a sudden the cop's gun came out, and then the cop was calling for back-up on his shoulder mic.

Davis dropped the jug and Brock smelled the reek of urine. "I love this fucking job," the one-eyed investigator mumbled.

"Driver," the cop said. "Out of the car."

Just as Davis started to climb out of the car, the phone rang.

"I need to answer that," Brock said.

"You need to keep your hands on the dash, what you need to do," the cop said, pointing his gun. All Brock could think of was that by now Jimmy Dale Evans—and probably everybody else on the block—was staring out the window at them.

"I don't care if you have to shoot me," Brock said, "but I'm answering that."

"GET OUT OF THE CAR!"

Brock rolled up his window, locked the door. The cop started hammering his flashlight against the window, the gun trained on Brock's head. Brock picked up the receiver anyway.

"Son." Brock's father's voice.

"Jesus Christ, you had us worried." Brock made apologetic motions to the cop. "Where are you?"

"I'm in the Fulton County Jail."

"The *what?*"

"Jail, son. Five counts, murder one. Prochaska, Darden, Lata, the whole nine yards. They even threw in Press Cain."

"How in God's name—"

"Evidently Jimmy Dale planted some evidence around our houses last night. Murder weapons, blank cards, bloodstained clothes, things like that."

Brock slumped down in the seat, feeling sicker and sicker. The stench of urine filling the car didn't help much. Outside Davis was talking furiously to the cop, who still had his gun trained at Brock. Brock's heart was going like crazy.

"Good news, however," Brock's father said, "is that I managed to get through to the guy in Taipei. He even spoke pretty good English. Turned out he was a double-E major at Georgia Tech."

"You got the code?"

"I got the code." There was a sound of muted voices on the other end. "Look, son, I have to go. The number is six four six two."

"Six-four-six-two?" Brock said.

"I've got to go," his father said.

Brock rolled down the window. "I've got the code," he said.

The cop looked at him angrily. "Your friend here explained what y'all are up to," he said. "So I'm gonna let you off easy. But next time I tell you to do something, by God, you better jump to it.''

"Trust me,'' Brock said. "There won't be a next time.''

"What did you tell him?'' Brock said, after the cop car drove away.

"Said we were working for an insurance company investigating a major art theft. Told him our man had two genuine Picassos in there.''

"What'd he say?''

"What's a Pie-casso?'' The investigator smiled for a moment. With the missing eye and the broad white teeth, his smile had a slightly demonic quality. "So who was that on the phone?''

"Dad. We got the code.'' He was about to tell Davis about the arrests, when he noticed a large green van edging slowly out from behind Jimmy Dale's house. "Damn it! There he goes.''

"He must have seen us.''

"We better follow him,'' Davis said. "Just in case.''

"But I've got the code.''

"Won't do no good if the girl's in the car.''

The investigator threw the car in gear, started moving down the street. As they passed the house, the van turned the corner at the end of the road. "Stop!'' Brock said.

"We got to follow him, man.''

"I know, I know. It's just—''

"We can come back!'' Davis's voice was hot with tension.

"No,'' Brock said. "I'm going in.''

Davis shot him a look, then slammed on the brakes, backed up to the house.

Brock jumped out of the car, ran up to the front door of the house. Davis loped after him. Brock tried the handle of the door. Locked.

"Move aside,'' Davis said. He put his foot up, kicked the door three or four times.

"Forget it,'' Brock said. "He's got a huge lock on there.''

Davis picked up a rake that was leaned up against the door, used it to smash the glass out of the front window. He climbed in and Brock followed.

Inside it took a moment for Brock's eyes to adjust. Same bleak room with the cracks in the walls, the same cheap card table, the same police scanner with its blinking red lights. There were also some peculiar little sculptures standing on the table top. They reminded Brock of those tacky Hummel ceramic figurines—except they were made out of some kind of white material. There was something slightly unsettling about the little figures, but Brock didn't have time to decide what it was that caused the feeling.

The door to the room where Grace had been was wide open.

"Oh no," Brock said, racing toward the other room. The bedroom was empty. A large splotch of sticky red liquid stained the middle of the floor. Despair clamped his chest like a vise. Blackness closing in. His legs suddenly went rubbery. "Oh, Christ. Oh, shit."

"This where he was keeping her?"

"She's gone," Brock said, a wave of nausea pouring through him. "You were right. Goddamn it, we should have followed him."

Davis leaned over, touched the liquid with the tip of his finger, sniffed it. "Blood," he said. "Pretty fresh."

Brock ran back out of the room, noticing for the first time that the living room floor, too, was spattered with blood. He threw open the front door. "Come on!" he said. "Maybe we can catch him."

He ran toward the Ford, but when he got there he saw that Davis had not joined him. He was just standing on the front steps shaking his head.

"Come on, goddamn it!" Brock screamed. "He's getting away."

Davis just stood there, shaking his head.

"He's already *got* away," Davis said softly. "Come on. Come on back inside, we better call in the police."

Brock stood rooted to the spot.

"Come on," Davis said. "Maybe we find something."

Brock walked slowly back into the house. All this effort for nothing. What had he done to her? What had the bastard done?

Davis picked up the phone with a handkerchief, started to dial, then set it down. "Better look around first," he said.

Brock sat down in the chair. What was he going to tell Dru? How was he going to explain it? He felt a wave of self-hatred running through his body, a pure physical thing. He could hear the investigator walking around the empty house, his shoes clunking on the bare floor. Opening doors, pulling out drawers. After a moment Brock leaned over and put his face in his hands.

Then, the investigator's voice, full of wonderment: "I think you better come here."

Brock ignored him.

"Brock. Come here!"

Brock stood unsteadily, followed the sound of the voice down to the end of a short hallway. There were smears and splotches of blood on the floor. Bloody footprints going down the hallway. Brock felt a rising sense of horror. What was it? Had he found her back there in the bedroom? Had he found Grace back there? He tried to prepare himself, but it was no good.

For a moment he hesitated at the door, faint with terror, trying to collect himself. The shadow of the investigator fell across the floor. He went in.

The body lay sprawled across the floor.

• 59

Janelle Moncrief stood in the backyard of Reggie Vinyard's home, hands planted on her hips. Three shirtless cops with shovels were working methodically through the bushes at the back of the property, digging holes and then filling them back in. Nothing new had turned up since about five-thirty that morning when they'd found the first bloody clothes buried under a chinaberry tree.

"Lawyers wasting lawyers," a grating voice behind her. "Figures, huh?"

Moncrief turned, saw Detective Dave Bean standing behind her with a shit-eating grin on his face.

"I spose," Moncrief said.

"So how'd this go down?"

"We got an anonymous tip on nine-one-one, three-thirty this morning, said these guys had buried stuff in their backyards. Said it had something to do with Shakespeare."

"Lucky break," Bean said.

Moncrief crossed her arms over her chest. "Hard to say," she said. "Hard to say."

Bean narrowed his eyes. "What do you mean?"

"Seems a little too convenient, you know?"

One of the uniforms took off his blue shirt, started digging in his undershirt.

Bean said, "You aren't telling me you didn't book your perps? What are their names? Vinyard and Brock?"

Moncrief raised her eyebrows imperiously. "I may *look* like one," she said, "but I ain't."

"You booked them."

"I booked them." She slipped her foot out of her shoe, wriggled her toes in the air. "Probably out on bond by now."

Dave Bean shook his head. "Fucking lawyers."

• 60

"This is crazy," Brock said. "I mean, this can't *be!*"

But it was. The pants of the body on the floor had been pulled down and there was a lot of blood where the genitals were supposed to be. There was a lot of blood on the face, too, and the mouth gaped open to reveal a bloody tangle of flesh.

It was Jimmy Dale Evans.

"Just like the others," Davis said. "Cut his wang off, stuck it in his mouth."

"Then who . . ."

"Either you got a hell of a tough little daughter, or we had two perps in the house all along."

Brock stared for a while at the bloody carcass on the floor, not wanting to look but feeling almost hypnotized by the gore—and by a terrible sense of dread. Would it never quit? This thing just kept getting worse and worse. Every time he'd thought he had a handle on the situation, it started spinning out of control again.

So who had killed Jimmy Dale?

Then it dawned on Brock what had been going on. Maybe not the whole thing, but he was sure he knew who else had been in the house, maybe even why they'd killed Jimmy Dale.

"Let's go," Brock said. "I think I know where they're taking Grace."

He left the body bleeding on the stained carpet, started running toward the front door.

* * *

As Brock climbed in the car, the cellular phone rang. Cleland answered, handed the receiver to Brock. "It's for you."

"Brock here."

"How you doing, boy?" Reggie Vinyard's voice. "You find your girl?"

Brock gave Reggie an update.

"You shitting me. Jimmy Dale's dead?"

"Shorn of his manhood."

There was a long silence on the line. "So we probably been wrong all this time about who killed Raymond and everybody. You got any ideas?"

"Somebody with some—how shall we say?—gender identification problems."

"That chick from Laughing Dolls. The bouncer."

"Kit Fulghram," Brock said. "Yeah, that's what I'm thinking."

"Where you suppose she's heading?"

"Laughing Dolls, where else?" Brock paused. "So where are *you* now?"

"Fulton County Court. Being the giants at the bar that we are, me and your daddy managed to get Judge Mitchell out of bed early and have our first appearance, ah, somewhat privately. I'm out on bail, and your Daddy should finish up any minute. How 'bout we meet you down there in, what, fifteen minutes?"

Jimmy Dale Evans's green van was parked outside Laughing Dolls. Brock felt a cooling sense of relief. So Grace was here. Now all he had to do was get her back from this nutcase Kit Fulghram. Cleland Davis pulled up next to the green van. Brock hopped out of his car and checked the doors of Jimmy Dale's vehicle, peered in the windows. The radiator pinged and sighed as it cooled. The van was locked but empty.

"They must have gone into the club," Brock said.

As Davis nodded in agreement, a silver Lincoln Mark VIII pulled into the lot. Reggie Vinyard heaved himself up out of the driver's side. Brock's father got out of the other side, his khakis wrinkled and his hair badly combed. Vinyard, however, looked chipper and fit, ready for a few holes of golf.

"They're inside," Brock said.

"Let's go," Reggie said.

Brock followed Vinyard to the door of the club. "I'd prefer to do this alone," Brock said.

"Now, son—" Reggie Vinyard said, unlocking the door.

But Brock's father cut him off. "If he wants to go in alone, Reggie, then let him go. It's his daughter."

Reggie frowned. "This is *my* club, I'm going in."

"What's that smell?" Cleland Davis said. The three men turned and looked at the investigator, who had stepped away from the others, his one eye half shut, his head lifted. "Smell it?"

"Something's burning," Brock said. Then he saw it, a wisp of black smoke curling lazily over the lip of the roof.

"Son of a *bitch!*" Reggie said. "She's burning it down."

"I'm going in," Brock said.

"Here." Davis thrust a small automatic pistol in Brock's direction. "Just in case."

Brock looked warily at the gun. "No," he said. "I think it's best I stay away from those."

Then he slipped through the door into the darkness. The stink of old beer. And underneath it, the aromatic smell of gasoline.

Brock pushed open the door from the entry room into the main bar. The odor of gasoline had become stronger; it was almost a physical presence in the room. And underneath it, the smell of smoke. Brock touched the glistening surface of a barstool with his finger. It came away moist, oily. He smelled his finger. Yes, it was gasoline. She must have splashed the stuff all over the room.

But where was the fire? There were no flames in the room at all. He'd better find it quickly, because once it spread, the whole place would go up fast. Where was Grace? Where *was* she? He ran across the room to the door of the office. "Grace? Grace?" No answer. *Where was she, damn it?*

Through the crack under the door Brock noticed a rippling orange-white light. The glow of fire. What if Grace was in there? He tried the handle, but it was locked. The metal was so hot he almost couldn't hold onto it.

"No!"

Brock turned to look for the source of the scream. A delicate blue haze had begun to drift across the ceiling, filtering down through the air in the bar. Across the room: a doorway; a female figure silhouetted against the light.

The woman's voice again. "No! Don't open the door!" Was it Kit?

Brock's only thought was that Grace must be inside. Why else would she care if he opened the door? Fear and dread coursed through him. Not fear for himself, but for Grace. He rammed his shoulder against the door, the concussion jarring through his chest. A second time, harder. Still the door wouldn't yield.

A third time.

As the door frame gave way, it occurred to him that maybe she had a different reason for not wanting the door opened. But by then the door had swung open, accompanied by a glottal sucking sound. The heat slammed against Brock's face. Inside the room was completely ablaze, flames skittering up the wall, chasing foul black smoke across the ceiling. There was something monstrous about the fire, as though it had will, volition, deadly purpose. The flames raced across the floor toward him, fueled by the sudden new supply of oxygen.

Brock backed away, slammed the door shut against the monster. But because he'd demolished the lock, he had to hold it shut with his hand. And the knob was growing hotter. The door trembled in his hand, tugged by the fire's greed for air. Finally he had to let go of the blazing knob. The door opened like a mouth and now the room was a blazing furnace.

Brock noticed for the first time that he was standing in a puddle of gasoline.

"Over here," the woman screamed. It was definitely Kit Fulghram. He tried moving toward her, but the fire was already tumbling out the door, racing across the dull brown carpet like a tiny mob of demons. Where was Grace? Maybe Kit still had her. But the flames were cutting off his access to the far door where he'd seen her. He backed toward the bathrooms. It ought to be safe there. Just as he reached the women's bathroom, he heard a great huffing noise, saw a ball of flame racing toward him. It was as though all the air in the room had just caught fire.

Brock stumbled through the door and the shock wave hammered him, knocking him into the bathroom. The heavy door of the bathroom slammed shut and Brock struggled to his knees. Where was Grace? Where was she? His terror at the sight of that wall of fire rushing toward him competed for a moment with his need to find the girl. His mouth was dry and he was panting uncontrollably. Was there any way out?

Not in here. They'd bricked up the windows. No way out. Brock was on the verge of panic. He ran over to the sink, sloshed water all over his body, soaking his clothes. Maybe that would keep him safe from the flames for a few seconds. Didn't most people die of smoke inhalation, not from the flames themselves? He grabbed a handful of paper towels, wet them and pressed them against his face. Through the vent in the bottom of the door, he could see the malignant, shifting light of the fire.

He pushed the door open a few inches. Outside the air had turned a roiling black. But the fire, oddly, was not that strong. Not enough oxygen, Brock supposed. Which meant there wasn't enough to breathe, either. His lungs struggled against the hot, denatured air as he lurched out into the bar again. Everything was on fire, but the flames were low, tired, struggling. The monster was weak.

But Brock could feel himself growing weaker, too, his lungs straining for air. Did he have time to find her before he went down from the fumes?

He ran across the room, dodging the flames. He could feel his eyebrows singeing. Everywhere the bitter smell of destruction. Where was the door he'd seen Kit Fulghram standing in?

There! Across the room, a black metal door. Stumbling toward it.

He burst through the door into a small mechanical room. A hotwater heater in one corner, an ice machine in the other. Kit Fulghram stood against one wall, her broad back to the door, struggling with something.

"Where's Grace?" Brock croaked.

"Help me," she said. "Goddammit I need some help." She wore a T-shirt and her shoulder muscles were bunched and writhing as she strained.

"Where's Grace?"

"Come on!" she said. "We don't have any more time. Some asshole turned off the main valve to the sprinkler system. Now it's stuck. Help me."

"Tell me where she is!" Brock could feel his voice going high and shrill.

"What good will that do you if we can't get out of here?"

Where could she have put Grace? Brock opened the door to look out. A blast of furnace heat and choking air hit him. It had gotten worse out there. She was right. They had to put out the fire or it wouldn't matter anyway.

"What do you need me to do?"

"I think I just stripped it." The valve she was pointing to was connected to a large red pipe extending into the ceiling. A handle hung limply from the valve. Brock reached over, turned the handle. It had obviously lost its purchase on the threads.

"We need a wrench," Brock said.

Outside he could hear small explosions. Liquor bottles? Gas cans? Across the room, Brock saw a small toolbox. He upended the box, scattering screwdrivers and socket sets across the floor. A pipe wrench? No, that would strip it worse. Finally he found a pair of vise grips. That would do it.

"Out of the way," he said. He twisted the adjustment screw in the bottom of the pliers, locked them to the valve shaft, yanked hard. Pain lanced down his neck and into his back, but the valve didn't budge. "This thing's stuck, dammit."

"That's what I *said,*" Kit retorted. "Here. Together."

They heaved once. No good.

"Why did you do it?" Brock said.

"Again."

Brock leaned against Kit, feeling her hard muscles against his shoulder. They heaved again. The vise grips lost their purchase. Brock unclipped them, adjusted the jaws tighter, squeezed them shut. "On three," he said. "One, two . . ."

They pulled together and the vise grips spun the valve on its axle and a shower of brown water came spraying out of the ceiling.

Brock grabbed Kit by the neck and jerked her against the wall. The room was filled with a roaring noise as the sprinkler system filled the rest of the club with steam. "Where is she?" he yelled.

Kit flung him away, ran for the door. When she opened it, a cloud of steam poured into the room and Kit screamed.

It didn't stop her though. She pounded through the scalding mist, heading for the front door. Brock covered his face with a towel to protect it from the steam and the heat of the fire—which had not yet burned out, despite the water cascading from the sprinkler system. He followed Kit toward the front door, the awful smoke and the hot steam tearing at his lungs. As he neared the front door, he felt himself growing weaker, his mind more and more remote from the white rectangle in the wall. Smoke. A smell of rusty pipes and burned plastic in the air.

The rectangle of light wobbling toward him.

And then suddenly he was outside, and the clear air was flooding into his lungs. It felt like somebody was shoving forks down his bronchia. The world was too bright, the colors sizzling in his eyes. Reggie and his father were looking at him with odd expressions on their faces.

"Good lord, Brock," his father said. "Good lord."

"You don't look so good, boy," Reggie added.

Kit was slumped on the ground.

"Where is she?" Brock gasped. "Where's Grace?"

Kit looked up at him blankly.

"Who?"

"Grace. My daughter."

Kit blinked, lizardlike. "Your *daughter?* I thought you were looking for Caitlin Cobranchy."

"Why would I be looking for her?"

"*She* set the fire." Brock stared at her for a moment. Kit said: "If anybody's got your little girl, it must be Caitlin."

Brock looked over at the green van. Taking a while to process everything. The van looked very green now, the green color boiling and popping in his eyes. His head was pounding, and a ribbon of pain lay across his neck and shoulders.

"She set the place on fire," Kit said, "and then she drove off."

"Then why's her car here?" Brock pointed at the van. He noticed vaguely that his hands were red and hairless.

"That's not her car. That's Jimmy Dale's. After she set the fire she drove off in *her* car. It's a little white Mazda."

Of course. She must have had her car parked here. She drove up in Jimmy Dale's van, then switched cars. Had it been Caitlin who'd been killing the lawyers all along? It didn't make sense.

He stumbled toward Cleland Davis's car. "Let's go!" he said.

Cleland Davis piled in, started the car. "Where to?" the investigator said.

"I'm thinking," Brock said. "I'm thinking." Then the cel phone rang.

Brock picked up the phone.

It was his secretary, sounding panicked. "She's here!" his secretary said. "She's here!"

"Who?" Brock said.

• 61

Funny was holding Grace's hand. Funny was acting strange,
like she was ascared of something. They were in an elevator
now. The elevator had a bunch of buttons with numbers on
them. 1. 5. 3. 9. 2. And some buttons had two numbers. 29.
15. 47. 34. 21. There were a lot of buttons.

They had gotten off the elevator a few minutes earlier and
asked a lady if her Daddy was there, but the lady said he
wasn't in the office today, and then the lady and Funny had
an argument and then Funny took out a gun and the lady got
real quiet. Then Funny had taken Grace back in the elevator.

Funny was carrying a radio, the kind Daddy called a
boom box.

Funny was looking at a lit-up number that kept changing.
The little room was swaying and then the doors slid open
and they went outside again. Funny was holding Grace's hand
very hard. It hurt. Grace said, "You're hurting me," but
Funny didn't seem to notice. Funny was talking about stuff,
but she didn't seem to care if Grace was listening or not.

They walked up some cement steps and there was light at
the top and the sound of their footsteps was all wavy. *Poing,
poing, poing.* You could hear the sounds for a long time after
you made it, dying away. Grace slapped her feet on the stairs,
trying to stretch out the wavy sound. Where were they
going? Up.

Poing. Poing. Poing. Feet slapping on the cement stairs.
Sky.

They came out a door and they were on top of a building
and there was a lot of wind, making *ruffle ruffle ruffle* noises,

and everything was far away, and they were walking toward the edge of the building and it was very high and everything was very far away. Trees the size of marbles. Or peas. They got right to the edge and Grace was ascared and Funny was squeezing her hand. Too hard. Too hard, Funny. Funny was lifting her head and looking up at the sky.

There was a railing between the edge and the rest of the roof. On the other side of the railing was a small strip of roof. And then the edge.

Funny climbed over the railing, then picked up Grace and lifted her over too. They were too close to the edge and Grace clung to the railing.

"I'm ascared," Grace said. Funny looked down suddenly, picked Grace up, lifted her into her arms.

"Then let's dance," Funny said. Funny set down the boom box and turned it on and they started to dance with the wind going *ruffle ruffle ruffle* and the trees as small as marbles.

At the top of the stairs to the roof of Brock's office building there was a large blue metal door. When Brock and Davis had arrived at the office, Brock's secretary told him that Caitlin had taken the key to the roof, and then headed toward the elevator.

Brock stopped with his hand on the knob of the blue door and turned to Cleland Davis. "Let me do this alone," he told the investigator. "I don't want to scare her."

Davis looked down at the stairs. "Don't you think I better call the police?"

"Not yet," Brock said. "I don't want her getting freaked out by the cops and doing something that gets Grace hurt."

The investigator nodded.

"Go," Davis said. "Go get your girl."

At first Brock didn't see them. There were several clusters of heating and air-conditioning vents on the roof and so he didn't have a good view. The roof was enclosed by a low steel railing, outside of which was a strip of tar and gravel about six feet wide.

He could hear music, though—the tinny sound coming and going as the wind shifted. As he circled the top of the building, the music got louder. He was holding on to the railing, walking slowly. It made Brock nervous; he wasn't good with heights.

He turned the corner and there they were, dancing.

Brock recognized the song, "I Can See Clearly Now" by somebody from back in the seventies, playing out of a boom box resting next to the railing. Only this wasn't the version Brock knew; it was a kind of white boy R&B version. A nice song.

Caitlin and Grace were on the other side of the railing. Grace was safely close to the railing, but Caitlin was perilously near the edge, dancing gently with her eyes closed, hands stretched over her head. She seemed to have abandoned herself completely to the music. Grace had her back to him.

Brock moved toward them slowly, trying not to make any sound with his feet. Maybe if he could get there before Caitlin saw him, he could grab Grace and get her out of harm's way before Caitlin wigged out on him.

When he was about ten feet from Grace, Caitlin's eyes opened. She saw him and smiled. It was a sweet girlish smile, stripped of any reserve or remorse.

"I figured you'd come," she said.

Brock froze. Grace turned to see who Caitlin was talking to.

"Daddy!" she screamed. She started to run toward him, but Caitlin leaned forward and grabbed her arm. "Come dance with us, Daddy!"

"No, honey. It's time to go."

Grace looked at him solemnly. "Why are you crying, Daddy?"

"Because I'm happy to see you." He took a couple of steps toward the pair.

Caitlin said, "You sure you don't want to dance? It's Doyle Bramhall, isn't he great? He used to be in a band with Stevie Ray Vaughan, before Stevie Ray got famous."

Brock edged closer, and Caitlin stepped back a pace or two, pulling Grace with her.

Brock stopped. Grace was so far away still. Ten feet from his outstretched hand. Five feet from the edge. Caitlin backed up another step. The heights were making Brock feel lightheaded.

"What are you doing, Caitlin?" Brock said.

Caitlin brushed back a lock of her wild red hair, looked down off the building. She was still smiling, but the smile had nothing in it anymore.

"Caitlin! Talk to me."

"I'd rather dance."

Brock shook his head. "Now's not the time, Caitlin."

She shrugged. "When's it ever the time?"

She closed her eyes again, started swaying softly to the music, her limbs loose and relaxed. Brock motioned to Grace to come toward him. She ran along the strip of roof until she reached Brock, her hands reaching through the railing. Brock pulled her over the metal bars and hugged her, smothering her in his arms.

"Oh Daddy," she murmured. "Oh, Daddy you don't smell so nice."

Brock felt himself racked by sobs. Feeling her soft face on his cheek, her little hands clutching him—Brock didn't think he had ever felt anything so strongly in his life.

"Don't cry, Daddy," Grace said.

And then Brock wasn't crying. His eyes were open and he saw that Caitlin was still dancing. But now she was only a foot or two from the edge, as though she were flirting with the plunge. It was then that Brock understood. She'd come up here to kill herself, and now she was just working up the nerve.

Brock called Cleland Davis's name loudly, and after a few seconds the investigator appeared.

"Grace," Brock said. "I want you to go with this man. I'll be with you in just a second."

"I wanna stay with you," Grace whined.

"It's just for a minute," Brock said, kissing her on the cheek. Then he stood and whispered to Davis. "I think Caitlin's going to jump. I don't want Grace to see that. Take her over to the stairwell, and I'll see what I can do about getting Caitlin back on this side of the railing."

Davis nodded, then crouched down and whispered something to her. Grace looked up at Brock.

"It's okay," Brock said. "I'll be down in a second, honey."

After they'd gone, Brock turned to Caitlin. "So what happened?" he said.

Caitlin did a little spin, teetered on the edge for a moment, then danced away again. She sang the chorus of the song with the boom box. She still had the odd half-smile on her lips.

"You might as well get it off your chest, Caitlin."

"Off my *chest?*" Her green eyes widened and suddenly

she wasn't smiling at all. "I don't have anything on my chest."

Brock hesitated. It had occurred to him that other than the simple human reasons for wanting to keep Caitlin from plunging to her death, there were some selfish ones as well. Like, for instance, it would sure be handy if she were still alive to testify before the disciplinary board made a final decision about his case. But what would be the next best thing?

Brock had a pocket dictaphone in the pocket of his coat. He always carried one so he could dictate in the car. He reached inside his jacket and turned the recorder on.

"So it wasn't you that knifed Jimmy Dale, Caitlin?"

"Of course I did. It's just I don't feel bad about it."

"Oh?"

"Do you have no paternal feeling, Brock?" She had an appalled look on her face. "He was going to molest your daughter for godsake. Something had to be done!"

Brock didn't say anything. He looked off the edge of the building and for a moment felt a little woozy. The wind snatched at his necktie. It occurred to him that he was supposed to be in court in about half an hour. Well, at this point, it hardly mattered.

"How could you tell?" Brock said.

The song had finished. Caitlin went over and restarted the track on her CD player. "I sure as hell like this song," she said.

"Me too," Brock said.

She started dancing again, hips and arms undulating gently, red hair tossing in the wind. She was a seductive dancer. But it was not the bald seductiveness of the strip club; her dance was sexy—but there was also something frighteningly innocent and naive about it. Frightening because it was not a man that she was flirting with but the precipice, the void.

"Jimmy Dale hired me," she said. "A long time ago. He hired me to have an affair with Ray Lata, to filch some things from his office."

"The concordance?"

Caitlin nodded. "Yeah."

"And you did it? Just for *money?*"

Caitlin tossed her hair in the wind. "I've done a lot of

stupid, degrading shit for money. Raymond was a nice enough guy. I didn't mind being with him."

"What else?"

"Then he paid me to make friends with Grace. Jimmy Dale got me a job with this maid service, Maid Rite. The idea was that I'd go to Grace's day-care center, pretend I was cleaning up, and then make friends with Grace. Once we'd made friends, I started sneaking into your house."

"Why?"

"It was all part of his plan to scare you, to make you dig deeper into the financial stuff behind Laughing Dolls. Then after he kidnapped Grace, he paid me to take care of her while he was in court. Feed her, play with her, whatever." She shook her hair. "By then I was in too deep to say no. And it was a good thing I was there." Her eyes took on a distant look.

"What do you mean?"

" 'Cause, man, I could see the signs. The way he looked at her. Touched her. I could see he wanted her."

"You mean you didn't know about his conviction?"

"What conviction?"

"For child molesting, back in the sixties."

"No. It figures, though." Caitlin shook her head. "But once we were in the house I could see it in his eyes. I could see the signs." She paused. "Like I said in the trial, my father molested me. I knew the signs. I knew the goddamn signs." Spitting out the words.

"But what about the killings? Prochaska, Darden, Raymond Lata—all those people."

Caitlin started dancing vigorously, angrily, throwing her hips around. She didn't say anything.

"Was it you?"

But Caitlin just kept dancing. After a while the song was over. Caitlin went over and turned off the CD player, then walked out to the edge of the roof.

"Come on," Brock said. "Do you have to stand so close to the damn edge? It's making me queasy."

Caitlin didn't move. The wind tugged at her hair. Finally she spoke. "The son of a bitch. The son of a bitch tried to rape me."

"Who?"

"Mel. Mel Prochaska." She reached up, wiped something out of her eye. "He thought because he was a part owner in the club, you know, that he could just do anything in there. And one time he tried to rape me. He slapped me and I struggled and then he got hit in the head. He got hit in the head and then it all came back, all the things my Dad used to do to me." She paused. "He was a doctor. You know, a *respectable* man." Her lips curled scornfully. "He used to burn me with cigarettes, put things inside me. Knife handles, chair legs . . ."

Brock stood beside the railing, frozen. He wanted to go to her, to help her somehow, but was too frightened by the height to climb over the railing. His neck was rigid and hot with pain.

"Anyway, I guess I hit Mel in the head. He was saying all these mean things, and grabbing me and hurting me. And . . . I just hit him. With a beer bottle. He fell on the floor and he was twitching around for a minute and then he raised up on one elbow and he goes, 'You little bitch'—that was what my Dad used to whisper in my ear when he was doing things to me." Caitlin shuddered. "I don't remember the rest too clearly. I must have hit him again with the bottle. It didn't break or anything. Then I took this knife." She stared off at the horizon. "I took a knife and I cut him and he was screaming and screaming and my hands were all bloody and I just wanted him to shut up."

Brock didn't know what to say.

"Next thing I know, there's Jimmy Dale sitting there looking at me. Grinning at me." Caitlin turned and looked at Brock. "That must have been when he got the idea."

"What idea?"

"I don't know what Jimmy Dale's original plan was. As far as I know, it was just a financial scheme. He was going to frame your Dad and Reggie for money laundering or something. But when he saw Mel Prochaska lying there on the floor, that's when he thought up the idea of Shakespeare."

Brock nodded.

"Anyway, he helped me clean up. Acts all understanding and everything. Then he takes the body away and that's the last I see of Mel Prochaska. He goes, 'No problem, you just made a little mistake.' Says he'd fix everything." She shook her head.

"Of course then two weeks later it was Lee Darden. Then two weeks after that it was Boyd Michaels." She put her face in her hands. "I knew it was Jimmy Dale that was killing them."

"So it wasn't you?"

"Nah. Just Prochaska. That was the only one." Caitlin frowned. "And Jimmy Dale of course. I didn't know he was a perv until I saw him around your daughter. Soon as I saw him with her, though—saw the way he was looking at her, that wistful hungry evil look in his eyes? Like he wanted to suck her soul out? Man, I knew. And I knew I'd have to kill him, too."

Caitlin turned and stepped right up to the lip of the roof, her toes half an inch over the edge. She didn't look down, just stared off at the horizon. High above them, a jet left a brilliant white contrail in the blue sky.

"Come on," Brock said gently. "Time to get off the roof."

But Caitlin just stood there swaying slightly in the wind, her arms hanging limp at her sides. After a moment she looked over her shoulder and smiled regretfully at Brock.

"I'm sorry," she said.

And then she lifted her arms a foot or so away from her body and stepped off the side, like someone jumping into a wading pool. Her hair and her plain print skirt billowed upward and then she was gone.

Brock stood for a moment, not breathing. For a moment his mind couldn't make sense of what had just happened. Then he was running back across the roof, yelling, "Cleland, Cleland, Cleland! Call the cops! She just jumped!"

And as he yelled he was thinking, *What good can the cops do now? What good can anyone do?*

He banged through the door and down the stairs.

"Cleland! Cleland!"

He reached the bottom of the stairs, but no one was there. "Cleland?" His voice echoing down concrete corridor.

Brock heard something that sounded like a groan. He ran to the end of the hallway—no one at the elevator—then ran back to the stairs leading to the roof.

He saw Cleland Davis then, his head sticking out from under the stairs. His arms and legs were bound with duct tape and the patch had come off his eye. The scar tissue puckered and winked as he struggled with the tape that bound him.

"What happened?" Brock said. "Where's Grace?"

The investigator looked up with his one yellow eye. "He's got her again."

Brock stared at him. "I don't understand."

"It's Jimmy Dale," Cleland said. "He's alive."

• 63

Pain. Jimmy Dale had never felt pain like this before. He was clutching onto the girl, trying to keep himself from fainting.

Watching the numbers on the elevator.

He had to keep his mind on one thing. Had to put the pain away and think about revenge. Two of them left: Reggie Vinyard and Brock's old man.

Concentrate. Destroy them. Concentrate.

An hour earlier when he'd regained consciousness in the empty house, he'd been disoriented, almost blinded with the pain. He'd coughed the bloody thing out his mouth, stared at it uncomprehendingly for a moment before he finally understood what had happened.

It was that lunatic, Caitlin. He'd gone in the bedroom to look at Grace—just to look, for godsake—and she must have come up behind him and hit him over the head with something. And then she'd cut him, taken his dick off and stuck it in his mouth. The insane bitch. All he was going to do was look!

Jimmy Dale had dragged himself up off the floor and gone into the other room. The door was open, the girl was gone, Caitlin was gone. His throat was sour with blood.

Then he had fainted again. Lying there on the floor in shock, his blood pressure had probably gone down to nothing, and so the bleeding must have stopped after a while. But now that he had stood up, the wound was leaking blood all down his legs. Had to do something. Had to do something fast or he'd bleed to death. Think!

Black again.

He awoke on the floor of the kitchen, staggered to his feet, rifled through the kitchen drawers. There: an old flat-head screwdriver, that would do it. He turned on the front burner of the stove, stuck the screwdriver in the blue flame. After a minute the screwdriver started to glow. He took it off the burner, stuck it between his legs to cauterize the wound.

There was a noise of frying meat, a wisp of smoke, a smell like burned hamburger. And an excruciating pain. There: that would stop the bleeding for a while.

Where would Caitlin have gone? Brock's office? Yes, that had to be it. Jimmy Dale had struggled to his feet, hobbled toward the door.

As he had stumbled through the door, Brock's secretary's face had gone pale. It must have been the blood all over him.

"Where's Brock?" he had croaked.

"My gosh, what happened to you?"

"Where the hell's Brock?"

"You want me to call an ambulance?"

Jimmy Dale had picked up a letter opener off the desk and put it against the secretary's throat. "Where is he?"

The secretary's eyes widened. She hesitated. "He's in court."

Jimmy Dale studied her face. He didn't believe her, so he stabbed the letter opener into her hand, pinning it to the desk. The secretary had shrieked, clawed at the piece of brass protruding from the back of her hand. "Omygod! Omygod!"

"Where's Brock?"

"On the roof!" she had squealed. "On the roof!"

When the elevator doors opened, Jimmy Dale pulled the little girl through the doors and stumbled into the lobby. Outside in the street everyone was staring at a car with its roof crushed in. Jimmy Dale saw a wisp of red hair hanging off the side of the car. He pushed through the crowd and into the street where he flagged down a cab. The cab driver, a Nigerian, got a nervous look on his face when he saw the blood on Jimmy Dale's hands and his pants.

Grace started crying.

"What you doing to that girl, mon?" the cabdriver said.

Jimmy Dale slipped his gun from his pocket, put it up near the cabdriver's big eyes. "Downtown," he gasped. "Fulton County courthouse."

The cabdriver said something Jimmy Dale couldn't understand, then he put the car in gear.

• 64

The SWAT team was waiting in the corridor when Brock reached the fourth floor of the Fulton County courthouse. The hallway swarmed with law enforcement people—sheriff's deputies, regular uniform cops, a couple of hard-asses from the Red Dog unit showing off their bloused pants, their combat boots, their knotty forearms.

Less than ten minutes earlier Brock had received a call from the police telling him that Jimmy Dale was holed up in Judge Wellborn's courtroom, that he was demanding Brock come to the room. Jimmy Dale had told the cops that if Brock didn't show up, he'd start killing everybody in the courtroom. Starting with Grace.

The head of the SWAT team said, "You don't have to go in there. I'm just telling you what he's demanding."

"Let me make a phone call and then I'm going in," Brock said.

"You got any idea what he wants?"

"Justice," Brock said.

The cop gave him a funny look.

Brock stepped over to a pay phone, called his grandfather's number.

"I think you were right, Judge," Brock said when his grandfather came on the phone.

"How's that?"

Brock explained that he needed his grandfather to do him a favor.

"You sure about this?" the Judge said.

"Just do it. Please."

Brock's grandfather laughed. "We shall trample out the vintage where the grapes of wrath are stored," he said. And then he hung up the phone.

Jimmy Dale was seated up front in the chair where the court clerk usually sat. In his lap was a terrified Grace, a small automatic pistol pointed at her head. Brock took a deep breath. Would this never end? He was nearing the last of his reserves of self-control, and needles of pain were shooting from his neck down his spine into the backs of his legs.

Behind Jimmy Dale, Judge Wellborn sat at her bench. At the defendant's table sat B.J. Mills—along with Reggie Vinyard and Brock's father. A court reporter perched, birdlike and tentative, at her machine, and the clerk sat over at a computer to the left of the bench. Everyone was wooden with fright, eyes staring out of motionless faces.

"Marvelous," Jimmy Dale said. "Everybody's here."

"I thought you were dead," Brock said.

"I almost was." Jimmy Dale's face was haggard, blanched. His hands were covered with dried blood. For a moment he seemed close to unconsciousness, but then he rallied and pushed himself unsteadily to his feet.

"Daddy . . ." Grace extended her hand hesitantly toward Brock.

"Everything's going to be okay, honey," Brock said, coming down the aisle.

Jimmy Dale pointed at the plaintiff's table. "Sit down, Brock," he said. When Brock had settled into the chair, Jimmy Dale continued, now in a louder voice. "Well, folks, looks like we got a little change of plan. In the interest of judicial expedience we're gonna fold up the case of *Jimmy Dale Evans vs. Laughing Dolls et al.* and we're gonna take up another matter."

The old judge narrowed her eyes. "Sir, this is *my* courtroom."

Jimmy Dale pointed his gun at the judge. "Shut up till I tell you to talk, your honor."

The judge leaned back, eyes widening truculently. It struck Brock that there was almost nothing a judge hated worse than losing control of their courtroom. He just prayed she didn't let her judicial vanity stand in the way of getting everybody out of the room alive.

"Bailiff," Jimmy Dale said, "you want to do the honors?"

The bailiff, a skinny sheriff's deputy with a hairlip scar under one nostril, looked up sheepishly. The bailiff mumbled, "All rise. Fulton County Superior Court now in session, Judge Eunice Wellborn presiding."

Everyone in the room looked around uneasily.

"He said, all *rise,* goddammit!" Jimmy Dale pointed the gun around the room. Everyone stood. Jimmy Dale nodded at the judge.

"Ah, be seated," the judge said, her voice high and thready, one finger stroking the wattles under her chin.

Jimmy Dale stared furiously at the court reporter, who was sitting frozen in front of her steno machine. "Court's in session, you cretin. Start typing."

The stenographer looked at the judge, who nodded curtly. She touched the keys of her machine a few times.

"Go ahead, Brock," Jimmy Dale said. "Dismiss the case."

Brock looked at him questioningly.

"I said dismiss the case."

Brock stood. "If it please the court, my client has indicated he wishes to, um, dismiss without prejudice the case of Jimmy Dale Evans versus Laughing Dolls."

The judge squinted, calculating how best to maintain some semblance of control in her court. "Any objections, Mr. Mills?" she said finally.

B.J. Mills rose to a sort of half squat. "No, your honor."

"Case number K-2273 is hereby dismissed," the judge said. "The clerk will please enter an order."

The court clerk started scribbling furiously, obviously glad to have something to do.

"Now we're gonna move on to some old business," Jimmy Dale said. "An old case. State of Georgia versus Eugene Bailiford."

The judge narrowed her eyes. "I'm afraid I fail to understand what you're trying to accomplish."

Jimmy Dale's features were pale and loose, but his eyes were still bright and intent. "*State of Georgia versus Eugene*

Bailiford. It was a case tried in the old courthouse over there about thirty years ago. Now we're gonna try it again.''

"Sir," Judge Wellborn said, "I'm not empowered to do such a thing."

"Is that right?"

"Yes, sir."

"Well, as it happens, I *am* so empowered."

"By what authority?"

"By the same authority that empowers all our fine legal institutions." Jimmy Dale smiled sarcastically, held up his gun. "This."

The judge licked her lips, looked at Brock, then over at Reggie Vinyard and Brock's father.

Jimmy Dale handed her a piece of paper. "Read it, Judge."

The judge looked at the paper, eyes narrowed. "I hate to burst your bubble, Mr. Evans, but this proceeding will have no force of law. You understand that, don't you?" Her tone of voice suggesting she was talking to a fourth-grade moron.

Brock clenched his jaw and a sheet of pain cascaded down his neck. Why didn't the pompous idiot just play along? If the judge didn't get her act together, Grace was liable to end up dead. Jimmy Dale's fingers were laced through Grace's hair. She was wriggling under his hands, but she couldn't get away.

"Just *read* it, Eunice," Brock said through his teeth.

The judge raised her eyebrows. "This is still my courtroom, Mr. Brock, and you will address me as 'your honor.'" Then she turned to Jimmy Dale. "As for you, Mr. Evans, I don't care what crazy notion is running through your mind, I will not have *my* courtroom used for some bogus, asinine drumhead trial."

Jimmy Dale looked at the judge for a moment. "Fair enough . . . your honor," he said.

Then he shot her in the face.

Judge Wellborn stood up as though someone had stuck a pin in her, looked momentarily bewildered, then collapsed forward onto the bench, blood pouring from a hole beneath her left eye. A high keening came out of Grace's mouth for a moment, then stopped.

"Well, folks . . ." Jimmy Dale said, smiling blithely,

"Now we got that straight, let the record reflect that *I'm* the judge. Everybody comfortable with that?"

There was no sound in the courtroom.

"Then let's get started." Jimmy Dale stood unsteadily. "Ladies and gentlemen, I now call case number B-3888, State of Georgia versus Eugene Bailiford. The clerk will please read the indictment."

The clerk, a thin black woman in a purple suit, looked at Jimmy Dale hesitantly.

"It's up there on the judge's desk," Jimmy Dale said, sitting back down.

The clerk reached over, picked up the crumbling old paper off the bench. It had a runnel of the dead judge's blood on one side, which she brushed away unconsciously with the palm of her hand. She read in a singsong voice: "The Grand Jury selected, chosen and sworn in the County of Fulton, in the name and on behalf of the citizens of Georgia, charge and accuse Eugene V. Bailiford of Atlanta, Georgia, with the offense of rape, OCGA 16-6-1; for that the said Eugene V. Bailiford did undertake the rape of Jacqueline Canty on October 13, 1963, contrary to the laws of said state, the good order and dignity thereof." Then she sat down.

"I hereby plead not guilty," Jimmy Dale said. "Now, in the interest of getting the show on the road, I'm gonna waive opening statements. Mr. Brock, seeing as you're a little more knowledgeable about the case before this court, you get to represent the state."

"Sorry?" Brock said.

"You're the prosecutor, Mr. Brock. Call your first witness."

Brock looked around the room, hoping to see his grandfather. No such luck. The old man hadn't gotten here yet. "I guess I'd want to call Jacqueline Canty first, Jimmy Dale."

"Well, you don't have that luxury." Jimmy Dale's eyes squeezed closed for a moment. He was in obvious pain. Brock was hoping that pretty soon the adrenaline would wear off and he'd collapse. But how long would that take? Suddenly Jimmy Dale's eyes snapped open and he pointed the gun at Brock. "And like the lady said, from here on out, you'll refer to this court as Your Honor."

"Okay."

"Now, get a move on."

"Before we get started," Brock said, "the judge was right. What are you trying to accomplish here . . . your honor?"

Jimmy Dale leaned forward in his chair. Grace reached out her hand and Brock took it in his. She had a bruise on her lip, and her eyes were full of confusion and weariness. Jimmy Dale still had his blood-encrusted fingers tangled in her fine blond hair.

"We've reached the end of the tether, Brock," Jimmy Dale said, his voice barely more than a whisper. "All the stuff I planned has come unglued. But I still got the girl. So I want to hear it from their mouths. I got a right to justice. It's all up to you. You're the last advocate here, the last advocate of the truth. You're all that's left."

"Yeah, but what do you *want?*" Brock said.

"I want to hear it from their lips. I want it right there." Jimmy Dale waved his gun at the court reporter. "The truth, goddammit, Brock. Unvarnished and duly transcribed."

"Fair enough," Brock said.

He went back to the podium and said, "The state calls Mr. Reggie Vinyard to the stand."

"Like hell," Reggie Vinyard said.

Jimmy Dale raised the pistol.

Shit, Brock was thinking. *Here we go again.*

65

Judge Garrett Brock, Sr., parked his 1967 Lincoln Continental in front of a fire hydrant next to the courthouse and got slowly out of the car. Hell, these days he had to do everything slow. Couldn't even take a whiz quickly anymore.

Even though it was a fine spring day, he was wearing a knee-length raincoat. Lying on the seat was the item his grandson had asked him to bring, a long heavy package wrapped in brown paper. He pulled the package off the seat, slipped it under his coat and then slammed the door.

Inside the courthouse there were cops everywhere. They'd run a cordon across the metal detectors and they weren't letting anybody in or out. The Judge hobbled slowly toward the metal detectors.

When one of the cops challenged him, a kid that looked about like a sophomore in high school, the old man said, "I'm Judge Garrett Brock, young man. My son and grandson and great-granddaughter are up there being held hostage. They need me."

"I'm sorry, sir." The kid touched the old man's elbow.

"Don't be putting your hand on me, boy!"

"Sir, I'm gonna have to ask you—"

"You ain't asking me shit." With that, the old man started trudging toward the metal detector. One of the sheriff's deputies, the guys that ran the metal detectors, started hustling over. "My kids are up there," the old man snapped. "Judge Wellborn personally requested me, matter of judicial courtesy, that I come up there and help out."

The bewildered deputy went to get somebody and so Garrett Brock, Sr., trudged right through the metal detector, which began beeping loudly.

"Sir! Sir! I'm afraid we're going to have to—"

"It's my goddamn replacement hip, set the thing off," the old man said.

In the confusion, nobody got around to running the portable metal detector over him and nobody stopped him as he shuffled toward the elevator bank.

When he got to the fourth floor, there seemed to be even more confusion. So nobody noticed when he snuck around to the conference room on the left side of the courtroom, and nobody noticed when he slipped in through the side door of the court.

Nobody even noticed as he started tearing the brown paper off the package he'd smuggled in under his coat.

66

Jimmy Dale pointed the gun at Vinyard, but he didn't fire.

Grace was paying no attention to Jimmy Dale now. Only to her father.

"It's okay, hon," Brock said. He leaned forward and stroked her cheek. He felt the softness of her skin with a tactile intensity he'd never experienced before: a strange pressure running through his fingers and up his arm.

Vinyard turned and looked at Brock. "You want to call a real witness, call your father. I wasn't there. I didn't see a damn thing."

Brock looked at Vinyard, then at his father. His father was staring straight ahead.

"He's right," Jimmy Dale said. "Do it."

Brock stretched his aching neck. "The state calls Garrett Brock, Junior."

Brock's father stood, buttoned his suit coat, and walked to the witness stand with a slow, dignified gait. His face was calm and open.

"Hang on, sweetheart," Brock said, still touching Grace's cheek. "Just hang on."

As Brock returned to the podium to begin his examination, he noticed his grandfather sitting in the back of the courtroom. Good. Now he just had to arrange everything properly. That was going to be a trick. His heart began to pound. One mistake and Grace would die. The old man winked, a minuscule twitch of one withered cheek.

Brock took a deep breath, turned back to his father and

said, "Tell me about the events on the night of May 12, 1963."

His father touched the bridge of his nose for a moment, then looked solemnly at Jimmy Dale. "Hasn't this gone on long enough?"

Jimmy Dale looked back, his eyes feverish. "Answer the question."

Brock's father looked down at his hands, started shaking his head slowly, regretfully. "What I did was wrong," he said. "It wasn't Reggie's fault. It wasn't Press's fault. It was wrong and I'm responsible." And then there was a note of pleading in his voice, a tone that startled Brock because he'd never heard it from his father before. "But Jimmy Dale, you have to understand—he was my best friend."

Jimmy Dale said, "The prosecutor has asked you a question."

"He was my friend! I'm sorry, Jimmy Dale, but he was my friend."

Jimmy Dale waved his pistol at Brock's father. "The court is instructing you to answer the prosecutor's question, sir."

Brock's father wiped one eye with the tip of his thumb. "It wasn't you, Jimmy Dale. Okay?" he said. "Is that good enough?" He stood up and looked out at the court. "Jimmy Dale Evans or Eugene Bailiford or whoever he is—it wasn't him that raped Jacqueline Canty."

Jimmy Dale's eyes burned. He was finally having his moment, but it wasn't giving him satisfaction. "That's not good enough! Tell it all. You're in the witness-box and you're in *my* courtroom. The state's attorney has asked you a question, now I expect you to give a full and accurate answer. Is that clear?"

Brock's father sat slowly, and a curtain of composure descended over his face. "Yes, your honor."

"Then do it."

Brock's father closed his eyes for a moment, winced as though stung by some terrible recollection, and then began. "I was at a party, a fund-raiser for Piedmont Hospital, with my oldest and best friend, Preston Cain. We mingled, went our separate ways. Later I entered a room and found him in what appeared to be a compromising position with another man."

His eyebrows rose slightly.

"My oldest and best friend! Imagine that. Well, perhaps *you* can, but at that time I could not. In those days one didn't even mention homosexuality in a voice louder than a whisper. It was literally an unspeakable thing. So I could only assume that my friend Press was not doing what he seemed to be doing. It must have been . . . well, a sort of *trompe l'oeil*. A trick of the eye.

"At this point two other people came into the room. One was a fellow who was a resident at the hospital, and the other was a young black girl whose name I did not know at the time. It came out in conversation that she was a student at Spelman who was serving drinks at the party. I later found out her name was Jacqueline Canty. You have to understand, this was a terribly odd situation. It really broke the etiquette of the time for a black person even to sit in a room with three men and have a conversation. In fact, back then it would have been a little odd even for a white woman to have been in that room by herself. Not a breach of etiquette, per se— just a little unusual.

"At any rate I had started ribbing Press Cain about this 'compromising situation' we found him in. The other fellow joined in. I guess I didn't notice how angry it made Press. Then we moved on to other topics of conversation and the young doctor, who was quite drunk, started flirting with Jacqueline Canty. The whole situation was quite uncomfortable. It was 1963, you see. Blacks and whites weren't supposed to mix. Especially black and white men and women. But we knew that the social mores would be changing soon—it was in the air in those days—and so there was this uncertainty about what was socially permissible. And not just permissible!" There was sudden wonderment in his voice. "We were no longer sure what was *right!*

"Well, presently the other fellow in the room, the young doctor, he started mixing his flirtation with Jacqueline Canty with more jokes about Press Cain's manhood—or lack thereof."

Suddenly Brock's father's shoulders sagged and he shook his head. "You know, I have trouble re-creating the next moment. I have—there's a sort of disjunction here, because to this day what happened next fails to make sense." He stopped and looked off in the distance. "The next thing I knew, Press had jumped on Jacqueline and was ripping her dress off. It was such a shock that for a while none of us tried to stop him—not even Jacqueline Canty. Then he raped her."

The courtroom was dead silent for a long time. Brock noticed suddenly that the court reporter was looking expectantly at him, her hands poised over the keys of her machine.

Brock spoke: "In the weeks that followed, Press Cain was charged with the rape, correct?"

"Strictly speaking, he was never charged. Miss Canty made a statement to the police, and the police stalled. The SCLC then picketed, claiming a cover-up. Assuming the civil rights groups had kept up the pressure, charges would have been imminent."

"So, did you do anything to keep those charges from being filed?"

"Yes. I approached Reggie Vinyard, who was not only the NAACP's point man on the case but was also Jacqueline Canty's half-brother, and I made him an offer."

"Which was . . ."

"Access. I told him that if he got his sister to change her story, I'd give him access to the power structure of Atlanta in a way that no black man had ever had in the whole history of the city. I said all Reggie had to do was convince his sister to change her story, drop her charges, and I'd give him the keys to the city.

"Imagine what you could do for your movement, for your people, I said, if only you could sit down with the right men, work things out face-to-face with the men in this town who make things happen. I painted him a pretty picture: racial harmony, a new South rising from the ashes of our racist past, the whole bit. And then I made him a solemn promise: I told him I was leaving the district attorney's office, that I had a partnership offer from the most powerful firm in town, and that as soon as I'd consolidated my position, I'd make sure he was offered a partnership there, too."

So that was what it had all been about. Reggie's grand ambitions. So now the mystery was solved. "A bribe, in other words," Brock said. "And he said yes?"

His father shook his head. "No. He laughed at me. So I sweetened the pot. I offered him the Big Win. I told him about Eugene Bailiford, about his sex crime record. I said that if Reggie could get his sister to change her charge, to point her finger at Bailiford, say it was *him* that had raped her and not Press Bain, then I would make sure the district attorney's office—of which I was a member—would put Bailiford away to great fanfare. First white man convicted of raping a black woman since Reconstruction. A huge, huge public relations coup for Reggie's client. And more importantly, from a legal standpoint, I said that the DA's office would not oppose certain changes in jury-selection procedures which the NAACP was extremely eager to effect."

"And so you made a deal?"

His father nodded gravely.

"Why do you suppose he went along with you?"

"He's a lawyer." Brock's father smiled without humor. "No, it's not that simple. I gave him the Big Win. A man like Reggie couldn't say no to the Big Win. See, he knew he couldn't have beaten Press Cain. Press had too much going for him—connections, money, privilege, manners, poise. And that would have hurt Reggie's chances with the jury-selection issues. Back then, blacks were rare as hen's teeth on juries in this state. With one fell swoop we offered to give black folks a fair shake in court in the state of Georgia. It was quite a thing that Reggie accomplished."

Brock could hear the soft clack of the court reporter's stenotype, taking down every word. Brock couldn't think of anything more to say, and yet there was something hanging in the back of his mind, something that wouldn't quite resolve itself that he needed to ask.

And suddenly the question burst on him: "*Why?*" Brock shouted. "Why, Dad? All the things you taught me about honesty and integrity and honor—was that all just a bunch of shit?"

"No, son, it was not." His voice was firm, but he wouldn't meet Brock's eye. "What we did to Eugene Bailiford was unconscionable." He smiled suddenly, a sad boyish smile. "You ask me why? I did it because Press Cain was my friend. For that one thing, I am not sorry. I did it out of loyalty and out of compassion."

Brock cocked his head. "Compassion?" he said. As best he could recall it was a word he'd never heard his father utter before. Honesty, integrity, probity—all those hard and unbending virtues, yes. But . . . *compassion?*

"My best friend, Press Cain, was a queer. A fag. A fruit. I use those ugly words because that's how we felt back then. Today we've begun to say, 'Well, it's just the way some people are.' But back then it was the worst thing you could possibly say about a man. You see, I realized the moment that he jumped on top of the Canty girl that what we'd been saying was true, all those jokes we'd been making about him. He *was* a queer, a fruit, a fag. Nothing else but the fear of that knowledge could have driven him to the terrible act he committed against that poor girl."

He paused for a moment, and the barest hint of a smile touched the corners of his mouth. "I suppose most men back then would have felt betrayed by him. But I didn't. I just felt sad for him, infinitely sad, because I knew that some essential part of him would have to remain forever hidden or he could not get on as a man in this town." Brock's father still had the melancholy smile on his face. "So I protected him."

"And all the high-minded reasons you gave to Reggie?" Brock said. "Harmony of the races? Judicial reform? Black men in the top law firms? New rules for jury selection? That was all bullshit."

Brock's father's eyes snapped towards him. "Not to Reggie Vinyard."

Brock studied his father's sober face. He felt oddly closer to the man than he ever had in his life. In that moment his father seemed more human, more tangible than ever before. Brock had an urge to go up and throw his arms around him.

But in that very moment he realized what he needed to do next, and so he turned his back on his father.

"Your honor, I'd like to ask Mr. Garrett Brock, Sr., to come up front." Brock pointed to his grandfather in the back of the courtroom. "I believe he has an exhibit which the plaintiff, excuse me, which the state would like to proffer to the court."

The room was silent as the old man stood and walked toward the front of the court. He wore a long seedy-looking raincoat and his gait was slow and hobbling. Everyone watched impatiently as he neared the rail separating the gallery from the front of the court.

Brock turned to look at Jimmy Dale. Jimmy Dale leaned back slowly in his chair. Tilting back and back until he stopped with a thump as the chair hit the bench behind him. A small, bitter smile appeared on his lips.

When he reached the railing, the old man leaned forward. "You ready for this, Brock?" he whispered.

Brock looked at the floor for a moment. "Yes," he said finally.

"Sure?"

"Just give it to me."

The old man pulled back his coat, revealing the old Marlin duck gun, hidden under his coat.

Brock snatched the gun, turned, pointed it at Jimmy Dale. "Let her go, Jimmy Dale," Brock said, walking swiftly toward him.

Jimmy Dale raised his gun to Grace's head. But his hand moved slowly, almost as though he were under water. He said nothing, just stared at Brock. Brock could hardly breathe.

"Come on, Grace," Brock said. "Come to Daddy."

Jimmy Dale kept staring, his eyes full of hatred. Grace struggled but couldn't free her hair from Jimmy Dale's grip.

"Look at yourself!" Brock said. "It's gone far enough."

Jimmy Dale's eyes were still pinned on him. But then something in them melted, as though all his hatred and anguish had suddenly disappeared. And what was left in them? Brock wasn't sure. Resignation? Sadness? Regret? It just wasn't clear. Contrary to what they say, the eyes are no kind of window to the soul, not when it really counts. The heart doesn't yield up its secrets that easily.

Jimmy Dale's hand relaxed a little, and his gun dropped slowly until it was pointing at the ground.

"Kill him!" It was Reggie Vinyard. "Kill his ass, Brock!"

But Brock wasn't listening. "Come to me, sweetheart," he told his daughter. And she did. Jimmy Dale's hand slipped from her hair, and she dashed around the clerk's desk toward him.

Vinyard again: "Kill the son of a bitch!"

Jimmy Dale still stared at him, his eyes empty and bland.

Brock tried to bring himself to pull the trigger, but he had no stomach for it. There'd been too much death already. All he could feel was his daughter's arms as she flung herself against him, encircling his legs, burying her head in his crotch.

"Kill him, Brock!"

Jimmy Dale's vapid eyes stared and stared.

His grandfather's ragged voice cut in. "No need, Reggie. He's dead."

Brock felt the old man's gnarled hands pulling the gun away from him.

Once he had the gun in his hands, Brock's grandfather added: "On the other hand, better safe than sorry."

There was a deafening blast from the duck gun. Jimmy Dale's lifeless blue eyes didn't even blink as his chest erupted and he slid over sideways, disappearing behind the court clerk's blood-spattered desk.

Grace started crying then, her body wracked with sobs. After a moment Brock was weeping, too. For the first time in so many years he could hardly remember it, he was filled with a pure and wholesome joy, a feeling so sharp and strong it threatened to overwhelm him. He dropped to his knees.

And so Brock did not hear Judge Reggie B. Vinyard approach the court reporter and demand that she give him the paper tape from her dictating machine, nor did he notice as Reggie Vinyard took out his slim gold cigar lighter, nor did he notice as Reggie Vinyard set fire to the steno tape, burning it until it was reduced entirely to ash.

For there was nothing that Brock heard or saw or felt in that room, or indeed in all the world, but those grasping arms and the solemn and holy bond of man and child.

"Hey there, little girl," Brock whispered. "Hey there."

CLOSING
ARGUMENTS

●

A young lawyer was attending the funeral of a former senior partner of his firm. Another mourner arrived late and asked the lawyer where they were in the service. The attorney gestured at the minister and replied, "You didn't miss anything. He's just opening for the defense."

67

Judge Reggie B. Vinyard was an unusually persuasive witness. With just the right mixture of arrogance and folksiness, he explained to the review panel of the disciplinary board that Caitlin Cobranchy had approached him on the twenty-first of March for the purpose of producing an affidavit detailing what she had heard in a conversation between one Mr. Mic Giddens and one Garrett C. Brock, III, Esquire, attorney-at-law. He explained, further, that in view of the uncommonness of the request (he was, after all, a corporate attorney and rarely dealt with matters of this sort), he had required her to go over the events in some detail. Further, Judge Vinyard said, if he had not felt *entirely assured* of her veracity when she stated that Mr. Brock did not extend any offer to exchange money or other consideration in return for perjured testimony in the Jimmy Dale Evans matter, then rest assured, he would never in a million years have consented to sign the document. Never in a million years, people.

When one member of the review panel asked how the affidavit had gotten into the hands of Mr. Richard Settles, deceased, the gentleman who had been murdered in a nude dance establishment called the Painted Lady, Reggie Vinyard shook his large head and expressed some puzzlement on the subject.

Another member of the panel, a female attorney from Savannah, wondered whether—in view of the recent information regarding the affiant's suicidal state as well as her role in several recent homicides—the affiant was able to distinguish truth from fiction.

Judge Vinyard smiled. "In view of her evident, ah, distaste for lawyers, I'd say the fact she came forward with this affidavit makes it all the more likely that she was speaking the truth."

The review panel excused Judge Vinyard, at which time there was a motion from the floor to overturn the recommendation of the investigatory panel on the matter, and herewith dismiss all disciplinary charges against Mr. Garrett C. Brock, III. The motion was seconded, a vote held, and a note was made by the secretary that Mr. Brock's file was to be returned to the investigatory panel along with a draft letter of dismissal.

After Reggie Vinyard left the room where the review panel was meeting, he saw Brock in the hallway and shook his hand warmly. "Everything gonna work out fine, Brock," he said.

"I appreciate your doing this," Brock said. "But . . . why did you lie to me the first time? Why did you tell that your signature on Caitlin's affidavit was a forgery?"

"It *was* a forgery." Vinyard smiled. "Hell, I wouldn't have known Caitlin Cobranchy if she'd hit me in the head."

"Then why did you just tell the review panel you signed it?"

The judge clapped him on the shoulder. " 'Cause I like you, boy."

Brock watched the judge turn on his heel and disappear around the corner, his big shoulders quaking with laughter.

68

The announcement for Press Cain's funeral had come on a four-by-five-inch card, cream colored, bearing the name of the firm Clay, Brock, Vinyard & Cain.

Brock sat between Dru and Grace on the third row of the First United Methodist Church, down on Peachtree. There were plenty of lawyers there, but also a lot of the gay friends that Press had managed to keep quietly separate from everyone in his professional life. It seemed sad and pathetic to Brock that Cain had lived his entire life this way, the two parts of his soul walled off from each other. A tragic, deadening waste.

After the minister had wound up his brief, dull oration, Brock's father walked up to the podium and said, "In the end, prose fails us. In the end, the law fails us. In the end, our bodies fail us. In the end, in the end, in the last cold remove, perhaps even God may fail us." He paused and looked out at the church full of prosperous people—a tall man with a long face and a rigid posture. "But friendship—" He stopped again, his voice quaking slightly. "But friendship, love—the love of two men for each other, the love of a woman for a man, the love of a father for his children—this alone endures."

For a long time he just stood there, gripping the podium with both hands, his head averted from the crowd as though anticipating a slap in the face. Finally he spoke again: "So I can say nothing more than this. Press Cain was my friend."

After he sat down, a song started playing over the sound system, a song Brock had chosen.

After Caitlin Cobranchy had jumped from the top of the SouthBank Building, Brock had taken it on himself to clean out her apartment, to handle the funeral and the dealings with the police. He had felt responsible, he supposed.

Among the belongings that had been returned to him by the police was the boom box she'd had up at the top of the SouthBank Building, the one with the song she'd danced to before she threw herself off the roof. The police had put it in a plastic bag with some kind of code scribbled on it.

It was during her sparsely attended funeral at the Unitarian Church that Brock had realized he should have brought the disc along, played ''I Can See Clearly Now'' in her memory. When he got home, he took out the CD that was sitting in his disc player—it was that silly heavy metal song ''Scream!'' by One Eighty-Seven—and put in Caitlin's disc.

It was just a schmaltzy old tune, full of hope and promise, and at that moment Brock had decided that since it was too late to play it at Caitlin's funeral, he'd see if he could wangle his father into playing it at Press Cain's.

So there, as he sat in the pew at the First United Methodist Church, the song came booming out of the speakers, with the nice shuffling Texas guitar and this Doyle Bramhall guy's smooth voice.

Brock closed his eyes, letting the wonderful, foolish song wash through him. And, without planning it or turning it over in his mind, he got slowly to his feet and began to dance. People turned and stared at him and for a moment he felt like a fool. But then Grace jumped up on the pew and began to dance with the joyous abandon that only a four-year-old can feel or act upon. A few seconds later Dru, laughing, tears running down her face, got to her feet, too.

Two rows down Merlee Pentecost stood up in her mac-rame dress, walked over to the aisle, and began doing some goofy dance from the sixties—the mashed potato or the herky-jerky or something like that. And then two men got up and began to dance with each other. And then two more and two more.

And soon the whole church was up, and people were dancing and laughing and crying in the aisles.

Then Brock took his dancing wife and his dancing daughter

in his arms and said, "I love you both so much that my heart can hardly stand it."

"We know that," Dru whispered. "We know."

And over his wife's shoulder Brock saw his father standing straight and still beside the front pew, looking off into the remorseless distance. *Dad!* Brock thought. *Oh, Dad.*